SAVING ELLIE

SAVING ELLIE

WHITNEY R.B.

❀ Created with Vellum

FOREWORD

Books aren't required to have content warnings or disclaimers, but I like to warn my readers of any potential triggers. If you don't need a content warning, feel free to skip the next couple paragraphs, but for those that need them, I list the possible triggers in this book below.

This book touches on: dark themes, violence, graphic scenes, suggestive themes, mild language, parental death, past abuse, eating disorders, depression, confinement, and discussion of suicide.

While some of these may only appear in one chapter, I would never want to risk someone's personal health while reading my book.

For those who read the first *Saving Ellie*, thank you from the bottom of my heart for reading it and now giving this new edition a chance. I hope you love this one even more.

While you read you may notice similarities. This is because I used the first edition of *Saving Ellie* as a stepping-stone to this one. With that said, I did completely rewrite this book, so while a scene may seem similar, it's still different from before. There's also a lot of new content. With all of that said, I hope you enjoy this new edition of *Saving Ellie*.

For the ones that didn't give up.

Ash

Stars invade my vision with the force of the blow. No matter how many times I get punched in the face, the effect is the same. A touch of pain, flashes of light, and a side of dizziness.

"Fight back, Ash." Zac bares his teeth in frustration.

I bite back a groan while the white spots fade. I wipe the blood from my mouth, grimacing at my split lip. "You know I won't."

"Why?" He runs a hand through his dirty-blond hair. He seems more on edge than usual today. He also threw more power into that punch than I'm used to from him.

"I already told you why." I sigh as I roll my neck, trying to relieve the tension. "I won't fight my—"

"I know that," he says. "But why? I just want—" He stills, his blue eyes are wild, jumping around our surroundings.

From what I can see, there's nothing in the pines around us. Then again, my senses are off right now. But it's always been just me and him, has been for years now. He finds me while I'm on patrol and attacks, trying to incite a challenge. I always expect it, yet I never do anything about it.

A breeze ruffles our clothes. There's a chill in the air promising snow and a hint of something else. My eyes narrow across the field. Maybe I spoke too soon. It seems we do have company today.

"What do we have here?" Zac's beta Austin walks out into the open not even a minute later. His red hair is a striking contrast against the green of the trees and the blue sky. He's flanked by Zac's other beta, Eryn, and delta, Rick. Austin looks back at his companions. "I told you they would be here."

Zac growls. "What are you doing here?"

I spit blood on the ground near them as they grow closer. I've never liked the lycans he chose to stand behind him. They only want power and have no respect for anyone, including their alpha.

Eryn grimaces but still flashes me a flirty smile when she catches me watching. She takes a step back in surprise when my lips curl in disgust. I'm sick of her advances. Going for any male lycan with two legs, her loyalty sways as swift as the wind. She's been persistent in her pursuits of not only getting into mine but my best friends' pants, as well. She quickly rebounds, shooting me a glare as she flips her blonde hair over her left shoulder.

"I'm tired of this going nowhere," Austin says. "How long has this been going on? Years? I think you need help in teaching Ash his place."

A rumble starts in the back of my throat.

"I'm perfectly capable without you," Zac says with a bite. "Don't undermine me."

My gaze snaps to him in shock. I don't think I've ever heard him stand against them before.

"Word's getting out that you shouldn't be alpha, Zac." Rick wraps an arm around Eryn's shoulders. "Maybe it's time for Eryn and I to take over as alpha couple."

Growls erupt through Zac and I. Zac jolts, turning toward me with wide eyes.

"What? We may not get along, but better you than them."

He frowns as he turns back to them, giving me a side-eye before directing his attention to them.

"See what I mean?" Rick laughs.

I take a step forward without thinking, but Zac's arm juts out, stopping me. "Don't encourage them," he says in a hushed tone, which confuses me. Is he trying to protect me? Isn't fighting what he wants? He's been wanting me to challenge him for years, to prove that he's the rightful alpha, but I won't, no matter how many punches he throws my way.

"Growing soft, Zac?" Austin grins, wetting his lips.

"No," Zac says through clenched teeth, dropping his arm.

"Then you won't mind if I take a turn." Rick pushes past Zac to throw a punch, but I easily block it and retaliate with a breaking punch to his nose.

Rick curses, holding his bleeding extremity, his eyes tearing up. "I thought he wouldn't fight back." He throws an accusatory glare at Zac.

"I never said I wouldn't fight you." I shake out my fist. It's been awhile since I last threw a punch. It felt great.

Rick's eyes narrow, then jerks his head to Austin.

I step back as Austin stalks toward me.

The only warning I get is a scent of magic in the air before two other lycans grab me from behind. I should've smelled them before they even got close, but it seems like they had help from a witch to block my senses.

"How?" I grind out, straining against the lycans hold.

"Potions." Austin smirks as he advances with Rick.

Even as a pureblood, my odds look grim at four against one.

I grunt as Austin and Rick take turns pummeling me in the ribs, stomach, and face. I kick out, catching Rick in the balls.

He goes down like a rock. I partial-shift my hands and dig my claws into the lycans that hold me.

They curse and let go. I pivot around, whipping them both in the neck with the edge of my hands, knocking them out.

I sweep my legs under Austin as he comes up from behind. He stumbles but regains balance quickly. I grab one of his legs and twist it into an odd angle. He screams in pain and crumbles to the ground.

Rick recovers from the groin shot and catches me in the calf with his pointy shoes. I swear he wore them with the sole purpose of inflicting more pain because they're ugly as hell. I block a punch to the face and knee him in the stomach.

I see Eryn advancing in my peripheral vision as I'm focused on Rick, but I fail to dodge as her claws slash across my face.

A roar tears from my throat as I reach for her, but she slips away.

"I wish you didn't heal so fast. I was hoping for a nice scar." She lunges again, this time aiming for my stomach. I take a step back to avoid the attack, but Rick is there, holding me in place just as her nails slice across my abdomen.

Rick throws me onto the ground as I grip my stomach. I need to heal it, but it's deep, too deep to expend the energy right now. I look down at the blood on my hands and curse myself for being out of shape. I need to start training with Russell again.

I stumble to my feet and shift into my wolf form. I push through the pain as I kick my hind legs out into Rick, then headbutt Eryn's side, sending her flying into a tree.

I turn and lunge at Rick, who's halfway through his shift. I lock my jaw around his arm, piercing his flesh with my canines.

He shouts and digs a partial-shifted hand into my wounded stomach. I release him and stagger back as a wave of dizziness hits me. He finishes shifting and bites into my neck before I can refocus.

"Enough," Zac roars, freezing us both. "I never said I wanted him dead. If this continues, that's what will happen."

Rick growls around my neck, reluctant to free his prey.

"Let go." Zac's voice rumbles with the power of an alpha, forcing Rick to remove his teeth. Austin gives me a death glare as Eryn helps him up. He slings an arm over her to use her as a crutch while he limps away.

"Grab your friends." Zac fixates on Rick.

Rick growls with irritation but nudges his bleary-eyed accomplices on the ground until they stand up.

Zac is last to leave. He glances back with a frown, then turns away completely.

My shoulders slump once I'm alone, but I'm unable to relax. I need to make it to my safehouse before I faint from the blood loss. But my body is too weak to shift back into its human form. I'm fighting the urge to give in, to collapse onto the ground. My progress is painfully slow as I stumble through the pines. I force my eyes to focus as the sun sets and snow begins to fall.

I might not make it in time.

Ellie

gaze up at the shadowy inn, shivering as the chilled breeze seeps through the gaps of my coat. I should've made sure the zipper worked before I bought it, but that's what I get for purchasing it from a second-hand clothing store. Gripping the ends tighter together with one hand, I walk up the steps until I reach the front door. Like I feared, the handle is locked when I try twisting it. I figured this might be the case when I saw the neglected yard and boarded windows of the decrepit building.

This place has been abandoned.

Gripping the straps of my backpack, I lean over to peer between the wooden slats, but can't make anything out. I walk around the wrap-around porch. All the windows are the same, and the back door is locked.

I sigh, using my numb fingers to pull out my new burner phone and map. Shining the screen light on the paper, I find where the bus driver circled. After I arrived by plane, I had to wait an additional two hours before I could board a bus that would take me near this small town. If you can even call it that. It's literally a two-street town, one leading to the residential homes, the other to this inn.

Had I accidentally picked a ghost town?

Technically, it would be Jane's fault since she suggested this spot, but I should've done more research.

I bite my lip as I look around. There's no other building besides a small barn off on the side, surrounded by pine trees, but it appears to be in better shape than the inn.

I glance down at my phone to find no signal and the clock blinking 6:30 p.m. When I examined the buses schedules earlier, I saw that only one bus takes this route once a week. Meaning I need to find different transportation and a different place to sleep.

How long would it take to walk to the residential area? What would I do when I got there? Start knocking on doors to see who's willing to take in a stray?

I glance down the paved road, dread sinking into my stomach as snow drifts down, small patches of white already forming on the ground.

Whatever I decide, I need to do it soon.

Clutching my coat, my chest tightens. My stomach churns at the thought of trusting strangers with my safety.

Stuffing my phone and map back in my pocket, I try the handle again. Surprise, surprise, it's still locked. Now would be a good time to pick a lock—if I knew how.

I tug on wooden slats while walking around the inn, trying each window, but none give an inch. I bite back a growl of frustration. Why the heck is this locked up like a fortress? This isn't my first time squatting, but it's the first time I haven't been able to get inside a place.

My eyes travel back to the barn. It's the last place I can try before I head to the residential area. I'm not sure I'd even make it with how the weather is turning. The snow's coming down hard as I run to the barn doors, but they don't even rattle from my efforts.

7

"What the heck?"

There are only a few windows, but each one is locked. At least they aren't barred—that gives me hope. If I can't find a way in, maybe I could break one of the windows. Before trying to find a rock, I walk around to the back and find a door.

Do barns usually have back doors?

When I try the handle, my mouth parts in surprise as it turns.

I can't help glancing around, guilt eating at me about breaking in. Technically I'm not breaking in since the door's unlocked, and it's just a barn. Who would be upset with someone squatting with some hay and dirt?

Will I even be able to stay warm in a barn during a blizzard? Horses do, right?

My rambling thoughts are cut off when I finish opening the door.

Instead of finding stalls and hay, I find a studio apartment. My hand fumbles along the wall until I find a light switch, illuminating the kitchen and dining area I just walked into. There's a rectangular table with four chairs to the side of a small but fancy kitchen. Diagonally across is a cozy living room with two couches facing each other, a rug and coffee table separating them. An upholstered queen bed with two nightstands sit on a plush rug beside it to my left.

This is definitely not a barn. How can I stay in here knowing this is someone's home? I turn to leave but hesitate before I step back into the snow. Where will I go instead? And why was this place even unlocked?

I peer back at the bed that looks so soft. I swear it's calling my name. I survey the place, then glance back outside.

The night is overtaking the sky now, and the snow hasn't died down.

I sigh and close the door. Just for tonight. Tomorrow I'll find reception and rent a taxi if I have to, even if it costs a good chunk of Jane's money.

I set my backpack on the table, then rummage through it. Frowning at the food I have left, I grab my water bottle and a granola bar. I was betting on ordering a meal at the inn, so I didn't replenish my supplies as much as I usually do. I could rummage around the kitchen, but stealing food is something I can't bring myself to do.

After unraveling the granola bar and taking a bite, I grab a pair of pajamas from my backpack. As I change into the old, large t-shirt and shorts, a sigh of relief escapes me. It's good to be in comfortable clothes again. Once I chug the water down, I stuff my worn clothes in my bag, along with my trash.

As I search for the bathroom, I find the thermostat on the wall behind the kitchen next to two closed doors. It's set to sixty degrees Fahrenheit. It must cost a small fortune to heat this place during the winter. I open the first door and peek inside, finding the bathroom. Stepping inside, I flip the light on and brush my teeth. Afterward, I hold my bottle under the tap and gaze up into my reflection.

What would my parents think if they could see me now? Dirty and homeless. Illegally staying the night in someone else's home.

The shock of cold water against my skin jerks me out of my thoughts as the bottle overflows. I quickly turn the faucet off and recap the bottle.

My bare feet patter against the cold wood flooring as I turn off all the lights. I walk over to the bed but pause before getting in. I let my toes curl in the soft fibers of the rug as I graze my hand across the comforter.

This is crazy. I feel like Goldilocks. I glance out the window at the relentless snowfall. But I don't really have much of a choice right now.

Letting out a pent-up breath, I rearrange and fluff the pillows. The lingering dust kicks up, tickling my nose. I rub it while turning down the comforter. As I slide into the bed, goosebumps erupt across my skin from the cool sheets against my bare legs.

I turn onto my side and stare at the moonlight cast across the living room. The heat kicks on just as my eyes snag on the dull light of the thermostat.

My eyes adjust to the darkened room, taking in the minimal

decorations. What kind of person remodels a barn in the middle of nowhere?

It sounds like something I would do. Build a safe haven to escape. Far away from everyone else. I wish I could stay longer than one night, but I know how unrealistic that is. This isn't my home. The owner could come back at any moment.

Besides, I can't stay here for long. In three months, I'll be moving on to the next place.

Turning over, I place a spare pillow on my legs—needing the weight to comfort me—then resettle to look out the window. Despite the nice bed and how exhausted my body is, my mind won't shut off.

A chill runs through me and I curl up into a ball. On cold nights like tonight, I used to sneak into my parents' bed and listen to them tell stories. One of my favorites was the one where people could change into animals. A large dog snuggling up against me sounds really nice right now.

But I'm alone.

I squeeze my eyes shut as my chest gets tight and clutch the comforter to my chest. Why did they have to leave that night? Why did they leave me all alone? Their happy smiles and the love that poured out of their eyes as they said goodbye is burned into my mind. I wish I'd known that was the last time I'd see them. I would've begged them to stay.

A cold breeze drifts across my exposed face and arm, jerking me awake. I can't remember falling asleep, I'm not even sure how long I was asleep for, but something seems off...

The door is open.

But I can't see anything else. It's too dark.

Dark. It's too dark. There's no light.

Visions of the basement resurface.

Jolting up, I lean over and switch the lamp light on.

I freeze at the sight.

Instead of Goldilocks getting caught by the three bears, I've been caught by one giant wolf.

3

Ellie

My pulse races as the wolf and I have a staring contest. My mind has to be broken because there's no way there's actually a wolf in the middle of the room. A huge wolf to be exact, with fur as dark as night. *Are wolves normally this large?* This isn't what I pictured when others spoke of wolves. I pictured them smaller for one, but also wild and menacing. But as I stare at this beast in front of me, the words that come to mind are elegant and beautiful.

And intimidating.

Confusion swirls in its intense glacier-blue eyes as they bore into mine. The wolf takes a step forward and my mind goes blank as I'm filled with utter terror.

What are you supposed to do when you encounter a wolf? I faintly recall seeing on the internet how to react when it's a bear, but

I'm not completely positive I remember it correctly. It doesn't really matter though, since this is clearly not a bear.

The wolf loses its balance as it takes another step, swaying on its feet. Its eyes glaze over before it collapses on the ground.

I hold my breath as I stare at its limp form, daring it to move. My eyes flicker over the wolf and the open door, my gaze snagging on bloody tracks before snapping back to the wolf.

Is it injured?

My mind screams at me to not move as I place my feet on the ground. Slowly, I tiptoe closer to the wolf.

As I draw near, bile rises in my throat. Large gashes across its stomach ooze blood onto the rug. I should not be seeing this much exposed flesh on a live animal.

Fear grips me and I stumble back. My eyes go back to the open door. If something could injure a beast this size, what else could be out there?

Taking another step back, I draw in a deep breath to try to calm my nerves. I have two options right now: grab my things and trek through the snow or stay here with a wounded animal that could very well be bleeding out.

How long would it take for it to bleed out completely? Could I stay here and watch an animal die right in front of me?

The open door is not only letting freezing cold air in, but snow as well.

Leaving isn't an option.

My decision made, I quickly get up and close the door, then comb through my backpack. If I'm going to stay here, I might as well try to save it, even if I get my head bit off for trying.

I find what I was searching for and walk toward the wolf.

One thing I always make sure to do is overstock my first aid kit. It has come in handy more times than not in the past three years. Not just for myself, but for the people I meet when squatting. I can't look away when others are hurt. Apparently, that also applies to animals now.

There's just something that pulls me to it. Deep down I know it's because when I was injured and alone, I'd wished there was someone there to help me.

I shake my head to refocus. Despite not wanting to rummage through the kitchen, I end up going through all the cabinets until I find a bowl and a few small towels. I fill the bowl with warm water, then set up near the wolf. I eye it constantly, but the only movement I notice is its labored breathing.

Kneeling down about a foot away on the soft rug, I open my kit. With nothing left to set up, I glance at the wolf, my bottom lip between my teeth. How different is sewing up an animal from a human? I swallow a lump. I'm really going to do this, aren't I?

I hesitate, then scoot closer. As gently as I can, I wipe the blood around the gaping wounds with a wet towel. The wolf tenses and I freeze. There's no other sign of it waking. My heart races as I examine the wolf closer and there's blood near his head and legs.

To get a better look at the wounds, I'm going to have to touch the wolf with my hands.

Alright, Ellie, you can do this.

The wolf is unconscious, so there's nothing to worry about.

Yeah, right. It could wake up and rip my head off, for starters. Taking a deep breath to refocus, I set my shoulders. I'm just delaying the inevitable and if I keep procrastinating, it *will* die.

Reaching out, I lightly stroke its fur with my fingertips. I'm surprised at how soft it is. I press deeper into the fur until I connect with its warm skin. A zap goes through my hand and I bite back a yelp, jerking my hand away. My whole body tingles with the aftershocks.

What the heck was that? Static electricity?

I glare at the wolf, but all it does is nuzzle its head into the rug with a groan. I find it oddly cute.

I run a shaking hand down my face with a sigh. This is taking way too long.

"Come on, Ellie," I grumble, frustrated. "You've been through worse."

I try again and this time no strange zapping happens, only little tingles. Deciding they're probably just an aftereffect of the first zap, I ignore them.

Gently probing through the rest of its fur, I find multiple wounds, but minor compared to its abdomen. I also find out the wolf is actually a he. So there's that.

Now for the hardest part. I gnaw on my bottom lip as I pick up my needle. I wish I had something to numb the pain for animals, but at least he's unconscious. Letting out a heavy breath, I focus on his torso.

Time to put on my big girl pants.

I try to be quick and precise as I stitch the skin together. I push the needle through the skin at an angle until it pokes through the other side. Then I pull the needle all the way out and form a simple overhead knot with two loops, creating a suture. I cut the remaining thread and begin again, just below my first stitch. Sewing skin stopped bothering me a long time ago. It's the cries that pain me more as I try to help, but this wolf doesn't make a peep.

Once done with the abdomen, I pull away fur around his neck that's matted with dried blood. My hands shake when I find deep teeth marks on his neck. An animal did this. I exhale slowly as I wring out another towel. Thankfully, it appears to have stopped bleeding. I clean up the dried blood as best as I can and place a bandage over it.

Leaning back, I examine my handy work. There's no doubt that this is a fierce beast, but it has a beauty to it that I wouldn't expect. As I clean up, my gaze is drawn to it. No, *him*. Shaking my head, I focus on scrubbing my hands and arms. My eyelids grow heavy, reminding me how fatigued I am. I quickly dry my hands and slip back into bed. I wrap myself in a cocoon trying to keep the chill out, but I toss and turn in spite of my exhaustion, visions of my past haunting me. Knowing there's a large wolf just a few feet away doesn't help, but I eventually drift off into a restless sleep.

Ash

She whimpers in her sleep. The same little human who stitched me up. Me, a monstrous-looking wolf.

And the little noises she makes call to me. Strange as it sounds, I want to comfort her. I want to know what troubles someone so brave. A woman I don't know is rousing something inside of me that I thought had died years ago.

When our eyes had first connected, even when I was delirious with pain, something stirred inside me. There was fear in her hazel eyes, but also an inner strength. It drew me in.

Another whimper escapes from her. I lift my head to get a better look at her in the bed, but the movement stretches my wounds and forces me to rest once more. My stomach and neck throb under the bandages she carefully placed, but my skin is already slowly knitting back together. She cared for me.

What's haunting you, little human?

I want to shift back, to ask her all my burning questions.

Why she's here—specifically in my bed, in my barn—and what's troubling her. Why did she tend to me? And why does she know how to stitch someone up?

But even on the mend, I shouldn't shift for another few days. Even then I won't.

Because the same feeling that is drawing me to her is also warning me to be cautious. That having a giant wolf shift into a large man would freak her out. Like it would anyone.

So, I can't shift when she's trapped in this place with me. I don't want to scare her more. Or change her reality. Because once you know that magic and shifters exist, there's no going back. Your mind won't let you.

It's better if she only thinks of me as a wolf.

Once I'm healed enough, I'll leave. I won't terrify her longer than I have to.

5

Ellie

he warmth and brightness of sunbeams on my skin wakes me up from my fitful slumber. I slowly get up, my body still aching from yesterday's journey. I glance at the wolf, my breath hitching as we make eye contact. He watches me with curious eyes and a tilt of the head.

With the wolf awake, I'm even more hesitant to go near it. So I don't. Instead, I pull my legs back onto the bed and stare at him, but it isn't long before my bladder calls for my attention. I crawl over the bed to have a straight shot to the bathroom. I slowly place my feet on the ground, then shoot across the floor and slam the door shut behind me.

I let out a heavy breath as I lean against it. I catch my reflection in the mirror, all wild eyes and bedhead. Bursting out laughing, I try to contain it with a hand over my mouth.

This is ridiculous. Never in my life did I think I would squat with a wolf.

Shaking my head, I step away from the door, relieve myself, and wash up. I place my hands on the counter and look at the door. I need to get out of here, but I need to pass the wolf to do that.

Or I can take a shower and delay seeing the wolf.

I remove my clothes and wait for the water to heat up.

Am I really going to take a shower while there's a wolf lurking in the next room?

Yes, yes I am.

I step into the shower and let the warm water run over me. It slowly chips away the stress that has been building up. I reach for shampoo but pause when I realize I don't have any of my hygiene supplies.

"Seriously, Ellie?" There's a bar of soap and a men's two-in-one bottle. So this *is* a man's place. With the minimalistic style I thought it could be, but I wasn't entirely sure. I guess I could've gone into the closet that's next to the bathroom, but I don't really want to snoop. Grabbing the soap, I wash my body as I debate on what to do.

I could use the men's two-in-one for my hair, but I hate trying to detangle without *real* conditioner. I lightly knock my head against the shower wall as another realization hits me—I forgot my clothes. That doesn't leave me much of a choice. I rinse off the suds and get out. Leaving the shower on, I'm relieved to find a towel in a cabinet. I wrap it around myself then go to the door, but my hand hovers over the handle.

I just won't look at the wolf. I'll walk right past him as if he's not even there and then go back to my shower as if nothing happened.

Nodding once in determination, I open the door.

Despite my pep talk about acting normal, I rush out toward my bag. I hold the towel in place with one hand while frantically searching my bag with the other. Once I find my conditioner and a set of clean clothes, I clutch them to my chest. I turn around and bite back a scream.

The wolf has moved.

Not only has it moved, but he's standing right in front of me.

The wolf is a lot bigger than I remember, his head almost level with my chest. How was he able to move with all his injuries? He was bleeding out just last night.

His eyes darken.

I gulp.

He's probably hungry, right?

Unable to conceal his injuries completely, the wolf limps closer. I'm frozen in place until he's a breath away.

What does he want?

It's getting harder to breathe, air saws in and out of my lungs. I'm not ready to be wolf chow. He huffs, limps to my side, then nudges my back, pushing me. I stumble a bit, then look over my shoulder at him. I can't tell if I'm shaking from the cooling water on my skin or, I suppose, the enormous beast inches behind me.

The wolf nudges me again, toward the shower where I can still hear the water running. When I start moving, making my way back to the bathroom, he slowly follows. Once at the door, I spin around to give him a bewildered look.

He tilts his head.

"You're not going to eat me?"

He huffs again, and I *swear* he rolls his eyes.

"Are you wanting to join?"

His eyes spark, but he lies down.

"So, no."

He huffs again.

I swallow. "Okay, then…" I slowly walk backward into the bathroom and slam the door. I clutch my towel and things to my chest.

What just happened?

I OPEN the door to find the wolf asleep. The only movement is the slow rise and fall of his chest. Carefully stepping around him in my set of clean clothes, I make my way back to my bag. I get my bag ready, stuff my arms into the sleeves of my broken-zipper coat, grab the bag, and cram my feet into my boots. I can't chance staying here longer with a wolf. It may seem civilized and housebroken, but it's also *a wolf.*

Opening the front door, my eyes widen as I'm greeted with at least three feet of snow, chunks breaking off and falling inside.

No.

This isn't normal for late September, right? This has to be some fluke and the weather will go back to normal tomorrow.

But what am I going to do now? I'm snowed in. I've never been snowed in in my entire life. How am I supposed to get out? I start to hyperventilate. I can't be stuck here. I need to be able to leave. The walls are closing in. *I can't breathe.* Clawing at my throat, my vision blurs with visions of dark cement walls and damp floors.

Soft fur brushes against my arm, jerking me out of my memories. The wolf is in front of me with his paw up, looking at me with big, concerned eyes. He whines in the back of his throat as he nuzzles against my stomach.

My chin wobbles. Why doesn't he attack? Why is an animal kinder than most of the human population? My hand hovers over the wolf before I let my fingers run through the fur on his head, relishing in the softness. My throat is still tight, and my hands shake as I touch this large animal, but there's a calmness that comes with it as well. There's enough peace in his touch to want to push those anxious feelings away.

Why do I feel safe with him?

I sniffle and wipe my nose with my sleeve. "Thank you," I whisper.

He nudges me back before closing the door with a strangely dexterous combination of his body and head.

I set my things back down to remove my coat and boots. My stomach growls, and I make eye contact with the wolf before his eyes drop to my stomach.

"You hungry, too?" I kneel to unzip my backpack. "I'll give you food as long as you don't eat me," I say as I rummage through my bag. I know I have some beef jerky I could give him. Would dried meat even satisfy a wolf?

Shaking my head, I grab it anyway. It's all I have to give. I tear it open, throw it on the ground near him, and fill a bowl with water. I place it near him before grabbing myself another granola bar. I bite into it as I watch him chew. He could probably inhale it in one bite, but he's taking the time to savor it.

Thunder booms, startling me into a near granola-induced choking attack. Firmly gripping the granola bar, I walk over to the window. My chest tightens as I find another storm brewing. The tree line slowly fades from view with fog and snow taking its place. It's odd how quickly the storm turned. My hands shake as granola pieces crumble onto the floor.

How long will I be stuck here?

My heart stutters as the lights flicker. In the uncertain light, I catch sight of the wolf. His glacier-eyes bright against his dark fur as he stares back at me.

The lights shut off.

The silence is deafening as I desperately try to get my eyes to adjust, but it's so dark. I drop the rest of the granola bar onto the floor. I stumble toward where I hope the bed is. My leg slams against the bed frame and I fumble to get under the covers.

My whole body shakes as memories flood back.

I curl up into a ball.

Please, no. I can't have a panic attack right now. Not when a wolf lurks near.

I squeeze my eyes shut as tears break through. The scars on my back start to ache. The metallic smell of blood burns my nose; I don't think the scent ever left. I can almost hear his footsteps, the crack of the whip, whimpers that don't sound like me but are.

This place is the opposite of that room, but one little trigger and I'm gone. I cry and curl into myself as much as possible as my senses are overwhelmed. The memories won't stop until I'm unconscious. Just like *he* never stopped until I was.

6

Ellie

"*H*appy birthday, Eleanor." *Marcus' heavy footsteps are like thunder in my mind as he walks down the steps to the basement.*

I never told him my preferred name. He would ruin that, just like how he ruined my birthday.

When he reaches the basement landing, his large frame dwarfs the space. "You must be what—sixteen now?" He grins, but it isn't a kind smile. He glances behind me and frowns. "What are you doing here?"

Will stands behind me. He came down to wish me a happy birthday, even though I told him it wasn't a good idea. He isn't supposed to talk to me, let alone see me.

Will grabs my hand, and I turn to him. "Leave," I whisper.

He looks hurt, but what is he going to do against Marcus? He's the same age as me. Marcus is so much stronger and larger.

"Well?" His tone is sharp. Our foster father is losing his patience.

"*Please,*" I beg Will. Tears building up, I don't want him witnessing this. He suffers enough abuse as it is, even if it's more subtle than mine.

Instead of leaving, he shows a rare act of bravery that makes me sick to my stomach. Those never turn out well with Marcus.

The will to fight, to live, to defend is something we both have in common, but I hide mine better so that I don't get punished for it.

Despite his hands shaking, Will's voice comes out strong. "Leave her alone."

"What was that, little twerp?"

He swallows but doesn't back down. "I said, leave her alone."

Anger rises in Marcus' eyes. He clenches his jaw as fists form at his side. His nostrils flare and a growl sounds in the back of his throat.

"Will, I'll be okay," I say frantically, but it's too late.

Marcus grabs Will's arm and throws him on the ground. There's a crack when Will's head hits. Marcus' boot-clad feet hit Will's stomach over and over. A scream leaves my mouth as I watch blood seep out from his head.

"Get off him!" I grab Marcus' arm, trying to make him stop, but he shakes me off and pushes me down instead.

Blinking away black dots, I get back up on shaking legs and wrap my arms around Marcus' waist, trying to pry him away. My scrawny arms shake from the strain. My dirty, chipped nails dig into him.

"Stop!" I scream. Tears stream down my face as he kicks Will again.

"Get off me, girl." Marcus pries me off him, throws me on the ground, and begins to take his anger out on me. I rather it be me than Will.

Staring at Will through blurry eyes, I pray that he'll get up and leave, that he'll make it out of here safe and sound, but more blood leaves his body. I stare and stare and stare some more, hoping he'll open his eyes and move, but his blood continues to flow. Soon his chest stops moving and I know, I know he won't ever open those golden-brown eyes again. Sobs rack through me at the realization while Marcus continues his onslaught.

After what seems like forever, Marcus stops and nudges me onto my stomach.

"Now, time for your present."

I tremble at the crack of the whip —

. . .

THE BED SHIFTS, waking me up. I'm shivering and covered in sweat. I look to my side to find the wolf staring at me.

In the bed.

Yelping in surprise, I try to untangle myself from the sheets and almost fall off the bed in the process.

He presses a paw to my shoulder.

My eyes widen as they meet his glowing, glacier-blue ones.

The wolf presses harder until I lie back down. He snuggles against my side.

I'm frozen in place as he nuzzles my neck, and I catch his scent of fresh snow and pine. He smells like a sunny winter day back in Philly and snow days with my parents. Without even realizing it, I relax and stroke his ebony fur. The anxiety is no longer at the forefront of my mind. I used to dream of touching the clouds. I think if I could, this would be what it felt like. My hand digs deeper until I touch the warmth of his skin and begin tracing circles absent-mindedly.

My fingers freeze as a deep rumble in his chest begins. But just as fast it stops. He huffs, and I start back up and so does the growly rumble. A grin crosses my face. It's not really a purr, but more like a happy hum.

After a few minutes, I remove my hand and he lets out a small growl. I bite my lip to hold back a giggle as I continue once more. It's strange—and enticing—that such a large beast would snuggle against me, let alone demand my touch.

My eyes grow heavy as I listen to the rumble while stroking his fur. His warmth envelopes me, and it's not long before I drift off to sleep, forgetting the horrors of the past, at least for tonight.

Ash

I couldn't leave her. We've been stuck in the barn for a week, but here I remain, completely entranced with this little human.

Even though the snow is too deep for humans, it doesn't bother me in this form. *So why am I still here?* Is it simply because I'm curious about her? Has she questioned why a wolf is hanging around?

She's been mostly quiet, keeping to herself, but she's still intriguing. Everything I'd expect her to do, she does the opposite: to offer me food and water, allow me outside to relieve myself, but instead of locking me out, she keeps the door open. And I keep coming back.

She digs into her large hiker backpack until she pulls out a small sketchbook, a charcoal pencil, and an eraser, then moves over to the table and sits down.

"Alright, I'm going to need you to hold still." She points at me with her pencil. "Or else I won't be able to draw you adequately."

I huff in response, because I have no idea how else to communicate with her in this form, before obliging.

"Huh, you really can understand me, can't you?"

I barely refrain from grinning.

Her gaze travels to me on and off as her hand moves the pencil across the paper. It's only been a few minutes when words trickle past her lips. "You know, I didn't always draw." She bites her lip as she grabs her eraser. "I picked up drawing when I went into the foster care system. It was something that helped me escape my new life." She shrugs, lightly brushing the paper with the eraser, then sighs. "After my parents died, I was thrust from home to home for the first two years. Just after I turned thirteen, I was placed with Marcus and his wife." A frown forms as she goes back to the pencil.

I already have a bad feeling about where she's going with this.

"I remember being so excited to be in a home where I could get all the attention. Which did happen. But not in the way I'd hoped." She laughs bitterly, and I bite back a growl. "No, definitely not how I'd hoped."

I can't hold back a growl any longer.

She jolts and looks at me. She blinks, shakes her head, and looks back down at her paper. "Anyway, I drew a lot, and the more I drew the better I got and the more I liked it. Even when I didn't have paper. I would draw in the dust and dirt on the ground. It was the only escape I had."

I can't sit anymore. Not when she's talking about this and looking like that—broken, lost, and lonely. Is this what is haunting her?

When she looks back up, her eyes widen when she finds me in front of her. She flinches as I lightly nudge her arm.

"You weren't supposed to move," she whispers.

My heart breaks as tears leave her eyes.

She tentatively reaches up with one hand and touches her face, her lips parting in surprise when she finds her tears. She drops her pencil and furiously wipes her eyes and cheeks.

"I'm sorry, I didn't even know I was crying."

A whine escapes from the back of my throat as I nuzzle her stomach. She's so soft and small. She's been through so much, but she's still so strong. I wish there was more I could do to comfort her. I wish I could give her a hug.

Her hands drop to my head and neck. "Thank you."

I lift my head then place my paws on the seat cushion to lean in. I bend my front legs as I cover her with my body, but I make sure to be careful not to place too much pressure on her. I tuck my head near her neck, trying my best to give her a hug in this form.

My efforts are rewarded when her arms go around me, and her head buries into my neck. Her soft cries turn into sobs, and my soul aches with each little heartbreaking noise she makes.

"Thank you," she whimpers into my neck, and all I can do is offer this small comfort.

I JUMP onto the bed to join the little human as she settles in to read her book, *The Princess Bride*. She's been quiet since she cried on my shoulder yesterday. I'm not sure if that's a good or bad thing. It's hard to get a read on her sometimes. I know with Russell it wouldn't mean anything dire, just that he might need some time alone to think things over, while with Foster it would mean something else entirely. I'd need to force whatever is bothering him out to help him. Is she like either of them? Or maybe she's somewhere in the middle?

She opens the book to her bookmark, and I watch her enchanting eyes, gold with green specks, follow the words on the page as her full, pink lips silently move. I don't think she has any other books because she's grabbed the same one each day. Even started it over when she first finished it.

I can't deny anymore that it isn't just curiosity that has kept me here. I've grown to care for her, at least a bit. Doesn't help that she's also beautiful. Her hazel eyes are lined with long lashes and her curly hair a dirty blonde. A dust of freckles is splayed across her fair-skinned nose.

What would she think of me if she saw me as a man?

She jolts when she finds me watching her like some creep. "Jeez, you scared me." She places a hand to her chest. "Why are you staring at me, boy?"

My eyes narrow. She's called me that a few times before, and I hate it more every time I hear it.

"Right. You don't like that nickname." She rests her head back against the bed frame. "Well, I don't know what else to call you," she says through a yawn. Her gaze goes skyward and a frown works its way on her face. Is she thinking about her past right now? Or her future? Where does she plan to go after this?

I lightly bump her arm with my snout then point to her book.

Her brows scrunch together. "Do you want me to read to you?"

I nudge her arm, which I hope she takes to mean yes. A giggle pushes past her lips when I lightly nudge her again. "Alright, sorry." She readjusts by sitting up some more. "I hope you know I'm not going to start over just for you."

I rest my head beside her as she reads out loud again. The sound of her voice soothes my troubled thoughts. She also smells amazing, like fall and spring combined—roses, vanilla, fresh air. I would bathe in her scent if I could. But instead, I'll simply enjoy the sound of her voice and scent before I no longer can.

Ellie

It took two weeks for the snow to clear enough for me to leave. I ran out of food after a week of rationing and had to rummage through the renovated barn for more. Thankfully, there were cans of beans, fruit, and veggies, and a can opener. I should've looked sooner, but it's so hard for me to steal other people's things.

I turn off the lights and wait for the wolf to step outside before shutting the door. Turning around, I find him sitting, waiting patiently for me. The wolf healed after just a few days. I'm not sure if that's strange or normal for animals. I also don't know why he waited to leave until now, with me, rather than sooner. I let him out a few times a day to allow him to do his business, but he always came back.

And I'm happy that he did. I'm not sure if I could've stayed sane, stuck there all alone. Whenever a storm rolled through, something would trigger me, and I'd be a mess even with him by my side. Who knows how much worse I'd get if he wasn't there. It's such a simple thing, but having the wolf around made a huge difference. I have Jane, but having someone physically around, even if it's a wolf, knowing a little about my past, makes me feel less alone.

But now, even in such a short amount of time, I've grown attached. And I never get attached anymore, not since Will died. Everything I end up caring about gets destroyed. Maybe since he's an animal it won't be the case this time.

I sigh. Who am I kidding? Do I need to keep reminding myself that I can't keep a wolf as a pet? How would I even take care of him? I glance down at him to find his eyes already on mine. It's crazy that his eyes speak more to me than any other person I've ever met. They're so expressive. So warm.

"I guess this is goodbye." I give him a wobbly smile. What's wrong with me? Why is this harder than saying goodbye to the few friends I made over the years?

He nudges my leg before his gaze connects with mine.

"Why can't you be my pet?" I blurt out.

He blinks, then I swear he laughs at me. If wolves could laugh, his huffing and puffing would be it.

I can't help pouting. "It isn't that ridiculous of a thought," I mumble.

He gets up and nuzzles his head against my leg, longer this time.

"Apology accepted." I pet his head.

Sighing, I look toward the road then squat down to get on his level, but when I do, he ends up being taller.

He gently nuzzles my cheek.

There's only a slight hesitation before I wrap my arms around him. Touch is still hard, but it helps that he's only an animal. "Goodbye, my friend." I only allow myself to hug him for a minute longer before standing up and tugging my coat down. I give him a curt nod and turn toward the road. My feet slightly sink with each step, a bit of snow seeping into my boots, making my toes cold. No one has plowed the road since the storms, but thankfully trees line the path on each side.

Hearing light crunching behind me, I peer over my shoulder. He's following me. He's not even trying to be sneaky about it.

I whirl around with my hands on my hips. "What do you think you're doing? Go on back into the forest, you can't follow me into town."

He rolls his eyes at me somehow before stepping closer and nudging me to move.

My eyes narrow, but I survey my surroundings. I guess it wouldn't hurt if we walked together since no one is around.

I sigh in resignation. "Alright, but only until we get to the fork in the road."

After a few minutes of walking, with the wolf beside me, I pull out my phone and check for a signal. Nothing yet. Every couple of minutes I check again. There was no reception the entire time I was at the barn. Jane must be freaking out.

Just as we draw closer to the fork in the road one bar pops up, along with Jane's number. It ends before I can answer. I quickly redial and she answers after the first ring.

"Ellie?"

"Yes, it's me."

"Are you okay? Where the hell have you been? I've been trying to call you for two weeks now, but it always went straight to voicemail."

"Yeah, I'm so sorry." I glance down at the wolf. "The inn you sent me to is no longer running."

"What? I could've sworn it was. I've stayed there before."

I pause mid-stride. "What do you mean you've stayed there before?"

"I...that isn't important, it was years ago. The better question is where did you stay if the inn was closed?"

"I squatted at a barn nearby."

"For two weeks?"

"There was a storm." I forego mentioning the state of said barn and glance again at the wolf. I stop at the intersection, the wolf still by my side.

"Ellie."

"I know, but I really didn't have a choice."

"Where are you now?"

"Well, I actually need you to look up some nearby hotels or a number for a taxi around here."

"I told you we should've gotten you a smartphone."

"It's too expensive and you know it." I change phones every move, there's no way we could afford it. And by we, I mean her. The money I make is small and sometimes illegal. These simple flip phones work just fine for what I need.

She grumbles under her breath. Her end goes quiet. I remove my ear from the phone and look down, afraid it had died, but it still says the call is running. "Jane?"

"I'm still here," she responds. "I know you don't like staying with strangers, but..."

"What is it?"

"My sister lives in that town."

"Jane." Having me near someone she knows is just asking for trouble, even worse that it's a relative. We can't have Marcus link us. He could be watching Jane for all we know.

"I know, but hear me out. You're on the other side of the country from me. To give me a peace of mind, I needed someone I could trust near you. I can't get to you fast enough if you need help. So, I don't regret my choice."

I close my eyes and hold my breath. I understand where she's coming from, but it's risky. "You won't give me the number for a taxi, will you?"

"Nope."

I let out a heavy breath. "Fine."

"Fine?"

"I'll stay with her, but just for the night. How do I find her?"

RED DOOR. Blue house.

That's the description Jane gave me of her sister's house. It's the only house like that. You won't miss it, she said. I'll call to tell her you're coming.

The wolf followed me all the way to the house. I walk up the porch steps, eyeing the porch swing on the right. When I get to the door, I turn around, but he's gone. I scan the area, my heart rate picking up, but the wolf is nowhere to be found. I fight the sadness that rears up, but I can't help feeling lost now. Like I shouldn't be here.

I spin around at the sound of the door creaking open.

"Ellie?"

"Hi, yes, I'm Ellie." I fidget, pulling my coat tighter around myself. Despite her being Jane's sister, I'm not good with strangers. Or any human beings, really.

I meet her eyes and come face-to-face with a slightly older version of Jane, maybe late thirties, but with darker brown skin and hair and matching eyes full of warmth.

"Come on in. I'm Emma. Jane has told me so much about you."

Biting my lip, I scrape the snow and mud off my boots outside before entering.

As I remove my shoes, I glance around her home. Right off the entrance is a set of stairs leading up. On the left is a cozy looking living area with a fireplace, mounted flat screen, and two leather couches. I can see part of a dining table next to it.

"Are you hungry? Would you like some hot chocolate?" Emma asks.

At the mention of food, my stomach growls and my cheeks heat up. "That sounds nice."

"I just ate breakfast, but I have some eggs left and I can make some toast," she says as she leads me down a hallway off to the right of the stairs. We pass three closed doors before reaching an archway that leads into a kitchen with a small, round table. Her cabinets are mahogany with dark green granite countertops.

She walks around the island in her kitchen and opens the stainless-steel fridge—next to the backdoor—and grabs a carton of milk. My eyes track her as she grabs a plate, piles some eggs on it, and nukes it. She puts two pieces of bread in the toaster and pours some milk in a pot on the stove.

Emma glances over her shoulder. "Go ahead and sit. Get comfortable. I'm not going to bite you."

I set my backpack against the wall then remove my coat and sit down. "Is there anything I can help you with?"

"I'm okay, hun." The microwave beeps, and she takes out the eggs. "My sister said you got caught up in the storm and had to stay in a barn." She raises a brow as she turns and places the plate with a fork in front of me, full of eggs and two pieces of toast.

"Uh...yeah."

"The owner of that barn is actually a friend of mine."

My eyes widen. *Busted.* My heart races. "I-I...I'm sorry?"

She *tsks*, then chuckles. "No worries. As long as you didn't steal anything, I won't say a thing."

I quickly shake my head. "I didn't."

She nods, eyeing my bag. "With only having that bag on you, I assumed so or else I wouldn't have let you in." My cheeks heat again as she turns back to the stove, stirring the milk. "Also helps that Jane vouched for you." She takes out two mugs from a cabinet and sets them near the stove. "She mentioned you need a place to stay for a few months."

I nod, but then realize she can't see me. "Yes, ma'am."

"No need to call me that, sweetie, Emma is just fine." She turns around with steaming mugs in her hands and places one in front of me. "Go ahead and eat before it gets cold."

I pick up my fork and shovel the food down, but try to still be polite. I'm used to not eating much, but it's been too long since I had a home cooked meal, even if it is just reheated eggs.

Once I finish, she leads me back down the hallway to a door nearest the front of the house and opens it. "You're welcome to stay here as long as you want, even the full three months."

"I don't have a way to pay you." Besides Jane's money, but I don't mention it.

"I didn't expect you to."

"It doesn't feel right," I say, shifting my weight. Squatting in abandoned lots is one thing, but to mooch off someone who I barely know is another. I already do that with Jane. Although, I have gotten to know her better over the phone for the past three years.

She looks at me for a moment. "Well, if that's what you're worried about, I could actually use some help. I review and test products before they go on the market for a living, and it gets busier the closer it gets to Christmas. I end up having to turn down almost half because of the workload. But if I had you to help, I wouldn't need to and that could be how you earn your keep."

I bite my lip. I want to say yes, but since she's Jane's sister it also complicates things. What if Marcus found me? I'd be putting one of Jane's loved ones in danger.

"I'll have to think about it."

"Well, this guest room is yours until you decide otherwise." She gestures to it and I enter. The guest room has a queen bed with light-blue sheets and a brown fuzzy blanket folded at the end. Night-stands flank each side with a lamp placed on the left. Above the bed is a large canvas print that simply reads *Be My Guest*. A dresser is on the opposite side in the center of the wall, along with a window and curtains showing the side yard and trees.

"I hope this will be okay?"

"It's perfect."

Ellie

"*I* have a few friends coming over for dinner tonight," Emma says the next day with her hands loaded with groceries.

"Here, let me help." I grab a few bags from her then set them on the table. I take the cans out of the bags and place them on the counter, which she then puts away in their designated area. I watch her to memorize where she puts what.

"What are we having tonight?" I ask.

"Roast, potatoes, and veggies with a salad. Are you allergic to anything?"

I shake my head.

"Great."

After we put everything away, we fill a crock pot with the meat and veggies. She places the lid on top of the pot and sets the timer. "I'm going to roast the potatoes now, but we'll wait to make the

36

salad." She wipes her hands on her apron and glances at the clock. "We have a little over four hours until they get here. Why don't you relax in the bath before getting ready and once you're done you can help me with the rest?" She shoos me away before I can say a thing.

And taking a bath is exactly what I do. I soak in the tub, letting the warm water soothe my worries, even if it's only for a moment.

My mind wanders to the wolf. His vibrant eyes, his soft ebony fur. His nuzzles and cuddles. The warmth that seeped into me whenever he was near. If he were a pet, I'd keep him, but I know that's ridiculous. Besides, he seemed more intelligent than a normal animal. I mean, I truly felt like he understood me and was interested in me.

I mentally shake myself. Have I finally gone crazy? I must have if I'm having these thoughts about a wolf.

Once the water grows cold, I drain the tub and head to my room in a towel.

I go through my bag, but I only have three outfits and one of them is my pajama set. I hold up my black V-neck that looks the cleanest and my pair of darker jeans with rips at the knees. I pull them on then head back to the bathroom to borrow Emma's blow dryer and style my hair.

When there isn't anything else I can do to pass the time, I head to the kitchen. Emma turns to me when I enter, her light-blue dress contrasting beautifully against her dark features. The yellow and white apron over it adds a lovely pop of color.

I shuffle my weight from foot to foot as I tug on my shirt. "I don't have anything else."

She gives me a reassuring smile. "You look nice, but I have a dress that should fit you, if you'd like."

I nod with downcast eyes, tugging on my dirty and plain clothes.

She gestures for me to follow her upstairs. Pictures line the walls of a younger her and an equally young man arm in arm or on vacation. When we make it to the landing, I follow her down a hall. Her house is larger than I expected. There are at least three rooms upstairs, not including the bathroom and laundry room. Does she pay for all of this just by reviewing products?

"I keep it in my closet even though I know it won't fit me anymore," she says as she opens a door at the end. Once we enter her room, she ducks into another that turns out to be a walk-in closet. Her room is large, with a king-size bed, a dresser, and two nightstands.

Instead of following her, I pause at the dresser and look at an image of her and Jane as teens in front of a tent. I spot another photo of Emma, a bit older, in the arms of a man. Now that I have time to look, I take in his features. His beaming smile and the joy in his eyes really catch my attention. He looks at Emma so lovingly. The next photo I stop on is of them in wedding attire. She is in a beautiful mermaid style wedding gown and he's in a black tuxedo. You can tell he's a man in love. Emma comes out with an olive-green dress on a hanger.

"My late husband." She nods at the photo I'm standing in front of. "He passed away from cancer."

The pain is heavy in her voice.

"How long ago?" I ask softly as I turn my gaze back to the photo. I can't imagine losing a spouse.

"Three years last month."

"I'm sorry."

A faint smile appears on her face. "Some days it comes in waves where I don't think I can even get out of bed and I'm just barely hanging on by a thread from the grief...but other days I see the sunshine. He'd want me to be happy and know that it's okay to have a good day without him. I don't think I'll ever be able to not miss him, but every day the pain gets a bit easier to handle. I know I'll never forget his love."

I blink back tears. That's how I feel about my parents.

She hands me the hanger. "You can go in my bathroom and try it on. I think it'll look great on you and bring out the green in your eyes."

I heed her directions and head into the master suite to change

38

into the dress. When I look in the mirror, my reflection stuns me. I haven't worn a dress in a long time. The last time was when I was fifteen. It was one of those rare times that a social worker actually visited. When Will was introduced to the "family". The first kid to be fostered there since I moved in.

The dress is a bit big, but Emma's right, it makes the green in my eyes pop. Despite feeling beautiful for the first time in a long time, it's obvious that I'm too skinny. The sweetheart neckline exposes my collarbone, which sticks out too far. The dress tapers at my waist, though it's still loose, then flares out and ends at my knobby knees. I've gotten so used to eating almost nothing for years that the habit stuck even after I left Marcus. I've been slowly working on increasing my food intake, but it's not always easy when I'm on the run. I also hate using Jane's money more than I have to.

But maybe if I stay with Emma, food won't be a problem anymore.

Emma knocks. "Almost done?"

I open the door and she beams. "You look beautiful. You'll have to keep it."

"What? Oh, no. I couldn't."

"Nonsense. Now let's go finish dinner before they get here." I follow her back to the kitchen and we both have a slight pep in our steps.

She hands me a bag of premade salad and a bowl. I grab a pair of scissors and open the package, dumping in the lettuce and all the other little parts of the salad. The doorbell rings.

Emma turns away from the oven, her brown eyes bright. "That must be them. Go ahead and finish real quick. I'll get the door." She wipes her hands on her apron before taking it off and placing it on its hook. Finishing up the salad, I listen to her soft footsteps before the door creaks open.

"Mr. Elric. Ash. Thank you for coming," she says.

Carrying the salad in one hand, I grab the plates she has sitting out and make my way to the dining room, trying to keep my hands busy. It's been hard enough adjusting to talking to one person, what am I going to do with more in the room? Hopefully they are able to keep the conversation going between the three of them.

I set the salad down, but before placing the plates, I glance toward the door and almost drop them. I never understood why girls swooned over the "tall, dark, and handsome" guys, but now I do.

He shrugs off a black leather jacket, revealing a white shirt that contrasts lovely with his light-brown skin. I swallow, unable to tear my eyes away as he hangs his jacket, his shirt slightly stretching against muscular arms and chest that tapers into a lean waist and dark jeans.

"Hello, Emma." His voice is smooth and deep. He runs a hand through his ebony locks, lifting it off his forehead. His eyes meet mine, and I can't help the little gasp that escapes as vibrant glacier-blue eyes meet mine and widen slightly as he takes me in. A corner of his mouth turns up into a half-smile, which I quickly look away from. Finishing up, I set the plates in their spots and pat my hair. I haven't had the chance to look in the mirror since helping Emma with dinner. Do I still look decent?

I mentally scold myself. I should *not* be thinking about this man. Yes, he's attractive, but I don't know him. Nor should I drag anyone else into my mess—worrying Jane is enough. Besides, I'm only in this area for a few months.

"This is Ellie, she's staying with me right now." I turn around at Emma's words. "This is Mr. Elric." She gestures to a man who's only slightly taller than Emma. He appears to be in his early forties with light skin and salt-and-pepper hair.

Mr. Elric frowns. "Emma, please call me Tom. I'm not that much older than you." Emma's cheeks darken as he holds out a hand. "Pleasure to meet you, Ellie."

I shake his hand quickly, not wanting anyone to notice it trembling.

"And this is Ash," Emma says, gesturing to tall, dark, and handsome. He must be over six feet. He's taller than all of us, but not in an abnormal way.

"Hello, Ellie." He offers his hand.

"Hi." I quickly take it and have every intention of letting go just as fast, but a jolt spikes up my arm, starting from our joined hands, leaving a tingling sensation throughout my body. His grip tightens on mine, keeping my hand prisoner, and his eyes seem to glow brighter. My anxiety spikes through the roof. What the heck?

"Go ahead and take a seat while I get the main course," Emma says, snapping us out of whatever trance we were in.

When I give a little tug, he quickly releases his hold, and Tom offers to help Emma.

"Sorry about that," Ash mutters, pulling out a chair at one of the heads and gestures for me to sit. He takes the seat to my right. "So, Ellie. Are you from around here?"

"No, this is my first time here."

"Oh? I hope it hasn't been too bad. We don't normally have this many storms this early."

The barn instantly comes to mind. Despite the triggers, it could've been a lot worse. Sometimes it was even enjoyable in the wolf's company.

"No, it wasn't completely horrible," I say.

A small smile appears on his face, making him even more attractive, and I can't help staring. I'm tempted to start loading up on salad just to distract myself from his good looks.

"That's good." He places his elbows on the table, his hands overlapping under his chin. "So, where are you from?" he asks with a tilt of his head.

What a loaded question. I never know how to answer it when someone asks. Do they want to know where I just moved from or where I was born and lived most of my life?

I fidget with the fabric of my dress, keeping my eyes lowered. "Most recently, New Mexico."

"Long way from home."

I shrug. "It wasn't really home to me."

Glancing up, I find his eyes still locked on me. "Where is home then?"

Is it me, or is it getting harder to breathe in here? I wipe my sweaty hands on my dress. "I..." I don't finish my sentence because Emma and Tom walk in. I let out a heavy breath. I wouldn't know how to answer, anyway. Nowhere feels like home, to be honest.

Ash removes his arms from the table as Tom places the roast and veggies in the middle of the table and Emma carries in the potatoes. While both of Emma's tables only hold four, this table is slightly larger than her kitchen one. Tom insists she sits at the head and holds out her chair before taking the spot next to her.

I move to reach for the tongs for the salad, but freeze when Emma says, "Time to say grace." The three of them join hands while Ash holds his out to me.

I glance up at him, and he gives me a small encouraging smile.

Taking a deep breath, I prepare myself. I can do this. It's just for a prayer. Once Emma's done saying grace, I'll get my hand back. He's not going to keep it forever.

I set my hand in his as shaky nerves flood through me. His hand is warm and tingles go up my arm at the contact. My hand seems so small in his. I find that I don't mind it. This isn't as bad as I thought. Looking up, I notice Ash's brows drawn together as he stares at my hand.

Tom offers his hand, and I need to give myself another pep-talk. I try not to cringe when I place mine in his.

Emma says grace, and I quickly avert my gaze to my plate. After grace, we each begin piling food on our plates.

"Would you like some vegetables?" Ash asks as it comes around.

"Yes, please."

"This much okay?" He holds up a spoon full of cooked veggies covered in butter and salt.

"Sure," I answer as he places some on my plate.

"So, Ash, did you just arrive in town today?"

Ash glances over at me before turning back to Emma and answering, "I did. I was thinking of staying at the barn more often."

My eyes widen as my fork clatters against the plate, but I quickly pick it back up, my face flushing. Is this Emma's friend that owns the barn? It can't be the same barn, right?

I can sense Ash's gaze, but I refuse to look up. Emma, not missing a beat, perks up. "Does that mean we get to see this barn you redid?"

My heart races as I watch Ash from the corner of my eye. He sucks in a lip between his teeth then glances at me again.

Why does he keep looking at me?

"I don't know. You and Tom, and now Ellie"—he nods at me— "are the only ones that know about it. I would like to keep it that way."

This *has* to be the owner of the barn where I squatted. My gaze jumps to Emma, but she's not making any indication that she'll spill my secret.

"You'll have to come by here then," Emma says as she spears a potato.

"I'd love that." Ash's gaze lands on me. "How long do you plan on staying here?"

My lips part but I swiftly press them together again and give a shrug. Another loaded question. Does he mean here at Emma's or Alaska in general?

"I told her she could stay here as long as she wants," Emma says.

"Yes, well, I don't want to be a burden," I say. Nor do I want to put her in danger.

"You wouldn't be. I have this huge house all to myself, I'd rather you stay and keep me company."

I bite my lip. "I'm considering it."

She grins as if she's already won and goes back to eating. Tom touches her arm, engaging her in a private conversation.

"Where would you go if you didn't stay with Emma?" Ash asks.

Lifting a shoulder in a half-shrug, I stab a piece of lettuce. "Not far, but I only plan on staying here for a few months."

"Where do you plan on going after?"

I put food in my mouth to stall my answer. I don't actually know where I'll go after. I usually figure it out the first week I move, but

I'd been trapped with a wolf in a barn. Maybe *Ash's* barn. "Maybe Canada. I've always wanted to see Niagara Falls."

"It's quite beautiful."

"Yeah? You've seen it?"

He nods. "A few times. It can get crowded, though."

"I love waterfalls. They are so powerful, yet beautiful."

His head tilts slightly as he rubs the dark stubble on his chin. "I never thought of them that way before. Have you seen a lot of waterfalls?"

"A few."

"Do you travel often?" he asks.

I hesitate. "I guess you could say I do." If moving equals traveling.

"Do you enjoy it?"

My eyes fall to my plate, suddenly not very hungry anymore. I place my fork down and push the plate slightly away. What's with the twenty questions? "I don't mind it, I guess." It's a lie. I hate moving so often. Maybe if I traveled for fun it wouldn't be so bad. But I can't wait for the day Marcus gives up, and I can settle somewhere nice and peaceful. I shrink into myself under his intriguing gaze. "What about you?" I try not to squirm in my seat. He's watching me too intently.

"I enjoy it every once in a while, but it's always nice to be home."

"Did you grow up here?" I ask.

His eyes warm as he looks over at Emma and Tom. "For most of my life. There are a lot of people here I consider family."

"Does your family still live here as well?" Wouldn't it be nice to live in the same town as your parents? To be able to hug them and see them or ask for help whenever. But Philadelphia is too painful for me now without them. I don't ever want to go back.

His smile dims. "No, my parents have passed."

My heart sinks. I know what that's like all too well.

"I'm sorry. Mine have, too." I surprise myself by sharing.

His eyes jump to mine, and we share a look that only two people

44

who lost their parents could share. A familiarity grows inside of me. As if my soul knows his.

"Have I met you before?" I ask. I doubt I could forget a face like his, but it feels like I know him.

He averts his eyes. "No, I don't believe so."

I go back to eating, resigned. "Maybe you just have one of those faces," I mutter.

A corner of his mouth quirks up. "Maybe."

Spending time with Emma, Tom, and Ash was nice, but now that I'm alone in bed, I oddly miss my wolf.

My wolf? When did I start thinking he was mine?

Sighing, I rub my eyes. It's not like I should be lonely since I now have Emma to stay with. But I am. The only time I forgot about the wolf was tonight when Ash and Mr. Elric came over. But Ash's insanely good looks and smooth voice might have been more of a distraction than Mr. Elric.

As I get into bed, my phone buzzes with a call from Jane.

"Hey," I answer.

"So you made it to my sister's safely?"

"I did." I pause. "You didn't tell her about what happened to me, right?"

"Of course not, Ellie. It isn't my story to tell."

I let out a breath of relief. "Thank you."

"On another note, I heard my sister offered to let you stay with her long term."

I guess Emma mentioned it to her. "Yeah, but don't worry, I don't think I'm going to."

"Why not?"

"What do you mean, why not? I thought that's why you were calling—to make sure I didn't."

"Of course not. I want you to stay with her."

"Jane. I don't want to put her in danger."

"Ellie, it isn't likely that he'll find you there, and it would put me at ease to know you have a roof over your head and warm food in your belly. Besides, you're always complaining that you have to use my money for everything. Now you won't have to, you'll be earning your own keep."

I sigh. I guess Emma also told her about the job offer. "Well, if you're sure. But if there's any sign of trouble, I'm gone."

"Of course. But you'll be fine, and so will my sister."

After we hang up, I get up and go to the window, pushing the curtains aside. I pull the blinds up and look up at the sky. It's a full moon tonight, lighting the landscape in front of me.

My eyes drag down as I notice movements in the woods near the house. Fear strikes me. Are there bears here? I wish I knew more about Alaska. Apparently, I need to be educated on the wildlife here since I came across an abnormally large wolf and don't know if bears are even native here.

I place my hand on the cold glass and try to get a better look. The longer I stare at the large creature, the less scared I am and the more I realize how sleek it looks—almost familiar.

Could it be?

But just as quick, it's gone. I close the curtains and get ready for bed.

10

Ellie

I toss and turn all night. It's only the second night without my wolf and already the nightmares are back in full force. I miss him. I didn't realize how much comfort he brought me until now. And I don't know what to do about it. Trying to find him isn't really an option.

I walk into the kitchen and find Emma in front of the stove. "Morning," I say. "Would you like some help?"

She looks over her shoulder and smiles. "Good morning. I'm fine, but I hope you don't mind having eggs and toast again."

I sit down at the table. "I don't. I'm happy with whatever."

Emma dishes out two plates, then places mine in front of me before sitting down. She takes a bite of her eggs. "What did you think of Tom and Ash?"

"They're nice," I say before biting into my toast.

"You and Ash seemed to have gotten along well. He's a nice guy."

I nod, trying to keep my emotions down. I don't want her to get her hopes up. We simply had a nice conversation where I didn't feel too socially awkward for once. "You and Tom seem close."

Her cheeks darken. "We've known each other for a long time."

I pause and stare at her. She likes him. I didn't ring check him last night to see if he is married or not. "Are you two together?"

Her fork clatters on her plate. She fumbles with it as she picks it back up. "We're not."

"Is he seeing anyone?"

Her eyes jump to mine. "Are you interested?"

A laugh bursts out of me. "No. Geez, he's like twice my age, Emma."

"Right. I don't know what I was thinking."

"So…?"

"He's single, I believe."

"And?"

"And what? You're quite nosy all of a sudden."

I frown. I am, aren't I? "I'm sorry. I didn't mean to pry."

She sighs, waving a hand dismissively. "It's fine. I do like him, but it could never happen."

"Why is that?"

"He's not interested. He thinks of me only as a friend."

My brows jump at that. He didn't seem like he only liked her as a friend at dinner last night. Friends don't normally touch their friends as often as he touched her. Although, who am I to say? I haven't ever had a boyfriend, and my closest friend is Jane—who I've only seen in person once—which was only for a few months right after I escaped.

I mean…there was Will…but nothing ever happened.

"Anyway, have you thought about my offer to stay?" she asks.

I nod. "I talked to Jane last night." I give her a pointed look to which she grins. "She convinced me to stay."

As if it was possible, her face lights up more. "I'm so glad."

"Is the offer to work for you still good?" I don't want to live here without earning it.

"Of course. We can start today if you'd like."

I nod. "I'd like that a lot."

I'M JUST FINISHING PUTTING my now-clean clothes away when there's a knock on my open door. "You ready?" Emma asks.

"Yep." I close the dresser and follow her down the hall.

We enter a study that's just off the kitchen. Inside, there's a bunch of boxes that dot the ground leading to a desk with a computer in the corner. One of the walls of the office is floor-to-ceiling shelves full of books.

"Go ahead and sit." She gestures to a blue loveseat that sits beside the desk and against the wall under the only window. She hands me an already open box. "Go ahead and take out whatever is in there. We'll test and review this product first."

"Alright." I open the flaps and pull out another box with a picture of over-the-ear headphones. I find a note with it asking for us to test the sound in both ears and how well they cancel outside noise. I hand them both to Emma.

She explains how it works. We each will test products then review them, but for today we'll do them together so I can get the hang of it.

After we finish testing them for what they ask, Emma opens a document on her computer and starts typing.

"Now I'll write our review in this document and rate it compared to others in the market, then we get to keep the product. Do you have a laptop?"

I shake my head.

"We'll have to take turns then, once we each have our own products. I only have one computer."

I place the headphones back into the box and set it on the

49

ground. Emma is silent as she types. I think back on what I saw last night outside my window. It couldn't have been my wolf. It had to be a bear. Right?

"Emma, are there bears here?" I ask.

Emma pauses her typing and looks up from her computer. "Yes, but they're probably hibernating by now."

"So, it isn't likely to see one nearby?"

"No, at least not this year with the snowfall having started early. Other years, if it's still warm in October, they could be hanging around. Why?"

"I was just wondering." I know without a doubt now that it wasn't a bear I saw last night, but my wolf. And the thought sends a little thrill inside of me.

11

Ellie

t's been a week since I told Emma I'd stay. I haven't seen my wolf or Ash again, but Tom has stopped by at least twice to see Emma. My nightmares have refused to leave, which means more sleepless nights.

I sip my hot chocolate. Chatting over hot chocolate has become our daily thing after we work.

Emma clears her throat and sets her mug down on the table. My brows knit together; she seems nervous. She blushes while looking into her drink. "I'm going to be going out tonight."

I tilt my head, waiting for her to finish.

"Mr. Elric asked me on a date."

I smile. "That's great." I thought I saw something going on between them at dinner last week. I pause. "Shouldn't you be calling him by his first name?"

"Uh, yes." She lightly laughs. "Tom asked me on a date." She glances up.

I grin. "What are the plans?" I take a few sips of my delicious drink.

I watch Emma follow the rim of the mug with her finger. She deserves to be with someone and not alone in an empty house. They both do.

"We're going to the next town over for dinner and bowling."

"That sounds fun."

She nods with a smile and clears her throat. "I haven't been on a date in a long time." She pauses. "But you're young and have probably been on plenty of dates. So, I was wondering if you could help me pick out an outfit. It's all I have left."

I drink the remainder of my hot chocolate, and I look at her. I did notice earlier that her hair and makeup were more done up than usual. "I'm not sure how much help I'll be, but I'll try."

I'm not going to admit to her that I'm twenty and have never been on a date.

She beams. "Thank you." She stands, and I follow her up the stairs. I trail my hand along the wooden banister as I note the pictures of her and her late husband placed on her beige walls. Does she feel strange going on a date with someone that isn't her husband even though he's gone?

We walk through her master bedroom and into her walk-in closet.

"So, bowling," I say. "You'll probably want to wear something cute and comfy."

She nods in agreement, and we browse through her closet together. I find an emerald green, long-sleeve blouse that matches the dark-washed skinny jeans she picked out.

"I'll just wait in your room while you try them on."

I walk out of her closet, closing the door behind me. I plop myself at the end of her bed, my feet dangling off.

A smile grows on my face. I'm helping a friend pick out clothes for a date. It feels good to be normal for once.

She walks out in the outfit, holding a pair of black knee-high boots. "Would these boots work well?"

I nod. "You look great."

She smiles shyly. "Thanks." She perks up when we hear the doorbell. "That must be him." She quickly puts on her boots before we head downstairs. I peer over her shoulder as she answers the door, but it's not just Tom who is at the door, but also Ash. "Ash, I wasn't expecting you."

"Tom told me he had a date with you. I thought I'd come and keep Ellie company while you're away. I hope that's all right."

A sly grin appears on Emma's face and a mischievous gleam enters her eyes as she looks back at me. "I'm sure she'd just *love* your company, Ash. Come on in." I hope my blush isn't noticeable.

Ash comes in holding a pizza box in one hand and a grocery bag in the other.

"Well, you two kids behave while the adults go out." She winks. I don't even get a glimpse of Tom before she closes the door.

Ash holds up the pizza box. "I'll take this to the kitchen." I follow him down the hall and into the kitchen. He sets down the pizza on the counter. "I brought a few movies and some snacks." He offers me the bag. I open it and peer inside.

I hold my breath as giddiness bubbles up. Setting the bag down on the counter, I dig through it. I see every kind of candy you could think of: sour candies, a mix of chocolates, sweet and savory ones. There's even more that I don't recognize. My mouth waters. I haven't had treats in so long, never willing to spend Jane's money on something that wasn't needed.

Looking up at Ash, I find him wearing a shy smile with a hand on the back of his neck. "I may have gone overboard," he says. "I just wasn't sure what you liked."

I grab one of the candy bags that I didn't recognize. "What's this?"

"Oh." His smile grows as he takes a step toward me. "I threw in some of my Filipino candies."

"You've been to the Philippines recently?"

"No, but I do from time to time. I'm half-Filipino." He meets my gaze, and his light-brown skin darkens. "I keep a stash of candy from there."

I grin. "That's so cool. I've never had candy from there before. Do you have family still there?"

He shakes his head, and his eyes grow solemn. "No, I…I don't. I go to remember my roots."

My heart breaks a little inside for him. "I'm sorry."

"It's alright, Ellie darling." He lightly chucks me under the chin. His touch is brief but warm and makes my stomach flutter, this time not from anxiety.

"Darling?" My voice comes out softer than I mean it to.

He cocks a brow. "Yes?"

I bite back a laugh. "I meant, you called me darling?" Do people still call each other darling? I don't want to admit it, but I kind of love the endearing nickname.

He grins as he turns to open the pizza box. "Ah, yes. Ellie darling. It just seemed to fit."

I try to hide my smile as I place the candy back in the bag.

"So…do you mind me asking what's your other half?" I ask, glancing at Ash beside me on the couch. Is it rude to ask that kind of question?

"Other half?"

I'm grateful for the dim lights as my cheeks heat. "You said you were half-Filipino."

"Ah, right." Ash leans back, the light from the television lighting up his front as he casually throws an arm behind me on the couch. I try not to shiver as his fingers lightly play with the ends of my hair. "You're probably wondering about my eyes."

I hesitate but give a reluctant nod.

He chuckles. "I don't mind answering. My mother was British.

My father was Filipino. They met at a...convention, fell in love, got mat—married, then had me."

The way he fumbles is odd, but I decide to ignore it. "What kind of convention did they meet at?"

He glances at me and lightly tugs a strand of hair. "A work one."

"Very descriptive."

He laughs. "Aren't we supposed to be watching?"

I bite my lip and face the TV. Ash brought five different movies but made me choose. I picked the superhero one because it was the only one I recognized. You would think my eyes would be glued to the screen since I rarely watch movies, but I'm more intrigued with the man beside me. And the dark-blue t-shirt he's wearing shouldn't look so good on him. My nerves spike in awareness just at the thought.

His arm brushes against me as he reaches for the bag of candy on the coffee table and plops it on my lap. "Indulge, Ellie darling." His deep voice sends a shiver through me.

I open it and give him a side-eye. "You sure you know what you're asking? I'm not sure I'm willing to share."

His smile grows. "Not even one?"

"Hmm." I tilt my head back and forth in mock thought. "Maybe just one."

"Such a sacrifice you'll be making."

"I may share more...but only because I don't want a stomachache."

He throws his head back with a laugh, and I can't hold back my smile any longer. "Noted," he says, leaning closer to me, lightly pressing his body against mine, his heat seeping into me. "I want you to try this one." He reaches into the bag and grabs one of the Filipino candies. He removes his other hand from behind me and rips the wrapper off. "Open your mouth," he says softly. My heart skips a beat when he holds it close to my lips.

Trying not to squirm, I open my mouth, and he plops it in. He brushes his fingertips against my lips as he pulls his hand away, sending a little thrill through me.

I swirl the hard candy around with my tongue. It reminds me of strawberries and cream. Sweet enough that it makes me squirm in my seat as giddiness bubbles up.

"What?" He chuckles.

"Candy makes me a bit giddy."

Mirth twinkles in his eyes as his smile grows. "So you like candy."

I shrug and grab another, but before I can place it in my mouth, Ash blocks it with his hand.

I meet his eyes with raised brows.

"I better help you space these out—to save you from that stomachache, of course."

A grin forms as I ask, "And you're choosing this to be your one?"

He shrugs, dropping his hand. "If I only get one, I want it to be this one."

"Alright." I hold it up, but instead of taking it he parts his lips. Not thinking much of it, I slip the hard candy inside, feeling his warm breath and smooth lips against my fingers. Soft. Hot. My mind seems to short circuit when his tongue flickers out and licks my fingertips.

My eyes flash to his, finding his heated gaze already on me. I realize my hand is still touching his lips when he flicks his tongue out again. I snatch it back and stare at him with wide eyes.

He gives me a wink, then leans back against the couch to watch the movie again. A grin plays across his lips when he notices my mouth gaping open and chucks my chin to close it. "Get comfortable, Ellie, this is only the first movie."

"Ellie darling," whispers a soft but distinguishably male voice. There's a light probing on my head.

"Hmm?" I turn on my back. The probing actually feels really nice, more like a massage. I could stay like this for a while.

"It sounds like Emma is home."

My eyes pop open, and the first thing I see is the blue of Ash's eyes as he looks down on me with a soft smile. He has one hand in my hair, lightly massaging my scalp. And it's heavenly.

I jerk up.

I fell asleep on his lap.

Hastily, I wipe my mouth, praying I didn't drool, and glance at his jeans, sighing in relief when I don't see any wet spots.

I turn an ear toward the door when I remember what he said. But I don't hear anything.

"You sure?"

He nods. "They'll be in soon."

I turn and look at the movie, but nothing is playing anymore. "How long was I out?"

"About forty-five minutes."

My eyes widen in horror as I meet his gaze. I can't believe I fell asleep on him. "I'm so sorry."

"Why are you sorry?" he asks.

"For falling asleep on you."

"Oh, I didn't mind. I'm glad you felt comfortable enough to fall asleep, but I should be the one to say sorry."

"Why?"

He chuckles. "Well, for one, I didn't mean to bore you."

"What? You didn't bore me," I say. "I just haven't been sleeping well."

"I didn't realize..." His eyes soften. "I shouldn't have woken you, yet another reason I need to apologize."

"Ash."

His lips curl into a slow, sensual smile. "I like the sound of my name on your lips."

My breath hitches just as I hear the door open, then close. Emma walks in, beaming, and sits on the other couch with a content sigh.

A corner of Ash's mouth twitches. "Seems someone had a good night."

Emma grins. "We made it official."

"You're a couple now?" I ask as a slow grin takes over.

She nods enthusiastically.

"Good." Ash squeezes my shoulder before getting up. "Walk me out?" He offers me his hand up.

"What about all your food and movies?"

"Keep them. I bought them for you."

"You're just trying to sweeten her up," Emma says.

Ash grins. "Is it working?" He meets my gaze.

When we pause at the door, Emma shouts from the other room, "You're supposed to walk him all the way out."

My face heats as I follow him out, closing the door behind me. "I guess I'll walk you to your car."

He chuckles and stops near the steps. "That's not necessary, the porch is fine."

"Oh. Well—" I wrap my arms around myself, trying to fight the chill in the air. "Thank you for coming over and keeping me company."

Ash takes a step closer, my eyes level with his chest, his body heat radiating. "Are you single, Ellie?"

My lips part in shock. "W-what?" My eyes jump to his.

"Is there someone waiting for you back on the mainland?"

"Mainland?" *Brain, work.*

His proximity is making my hormones go haywire.

He smiles. "That's what we call the rest of the states."

"Oh, no."

He arches a brow. "No, as in you aren't single, or no, as in you don't have someone waiting for you?"

"Yes—I mean, no, I don't have someone waiting for me."

"So, you're single."

"Yes."

He grins. "Good," he says softly as he draws nearer. "Can I?" he asks, his lips hover close to my cheek. I give a small nod before his lips just barely brush my cheek, and he pulls away. "Thank you for tonight." He caresses my cheek as he pushes a strand of hair behind my ear. "I hope to see you again soon."

"Me too," I say, my voice coming out in a whisper.

His lips curve up. "Goodnight, Ellie." He drops his hand and walks down the steps.

My eyes scan the area. "Wait, where's your car?"

He slightly turns his body toward me. "I planned on walking home."

"But it's so far." And cold. He doesn't even have a jacket on.

My entire body stiffens as I realize my mistake. But instead of questioning how I know where his place is, he shrugs. "I'll be fine. I've done it before."

I bite my lip.

He walks back up the steps to me, then lightly grabs my chin, smoothing his thumb over my bottom lip until I release it from my teeth. "Really, I'll be fine. I'm just going to run home. The cold doesn't bother me much."

I sigh, letting the tension leave from my body, then nod. He removes his hand from my chin.

"Okay. I'm just worried."

"Well," he says. "I could text you once I make it home safe."

I perk up. "Yeah?"

He nods as he pulls out his phone and offers it to me. "Could I get your number?" he asks, palming the back of his neck with one hand.

"Sure." I pray my shaking hands don't give me away as I take his phone. I swipe it open, finding no password blocking me. I open the contact app, but then I get stuck. How do I add a new one? I've never had a smartphone before.

"What's wrong?"

Gnawing on my lip, I glance up at him through my lashes. "I don't know how to add my number."

My eyes zero in on his lips as his mouth slightly parts. "Right."

He draws closer, his side brushing up against mine. I get a whiff of his cologne—or is that just his natural scent?—with pine undertones. No one should be allowed to smell this good. "Alright, now you can add your info."

I blink. He opened a new contact without me realizing it. I add my number and name, then hand it back to him. He smiles down at it before tucking it back in his pocket.

He reaches out, hesitates, then drops his arms. "Is it okay if I gave you a hug?"

My mouth parts in shock. "Uh, y-yes. Thank you for asking."

He smiles shyly as he steps toward me again. I'm stiff as he leans down, enveloping me in a hug. I try to calm my racing heart and relax against him. *Why can't I just be normal?* Why does every touch send me close to the edge? I let out a pent-up breath and wrap my arms around him. The longer he holds me, the calmer I feel. My knotted stomach slowly ebbs away, and I relish in the contrast of my soft body to his hard. This isn't so bad. This…this actually feels good. When was the last time I hugged someone? I grip the back of his shirt and take everything in. The warmth and happiness that comes as all my senses are consumed by him.

I pause.

"Are you sniffing me?" I ask.

His chest rumbles through me as he chuckles. "I am, but you're doing the same."

I squirm against him in embarrassment, but he doesn't let me loose. "Just a little longer," he says softly into my hair as he grips me tighter, but not painfully.

Placing my head on his chest, I relax against him. "Why did you ask permission to hug me, just to refuse to let go when I want?" My thoughts spill from my mouth without thinking and I instantly regret it when he tenses and moves to release me. I grip him tighter, refusing to let go.

"I'm sorry," he mumbles. "You can let me go."

"I don't want to." And when I don't let go, his arms wrap around me once more.

"Why did you ask permission?" I ask, closing my eyes. He's done it twice now.

"I could tell you have a hard time touching people." His voice vibrates through me and it's oddly soothing. Something about not seeing him but touching and smelling him makes this more intimate, and my defenses slip.

Actually, if I'm being honest, *he* makes me lower my defenses.

"It's different with you," I whisper, but I know he hears me when his body forms even more with mine. And it is different. Yes, the anxiety and the stress are still there, but it's easier to get past it with him.

One of his hands slowly slides up my back before tangling in my hair. He squeezes me lightly, then releases me. "I'll text you once I make it back. Goodnight, Ellie." He gives me a smile and trots down the stairs.

He jogs down the street but looks over his shoulder and waves before he gets too far. I watch him until he's no longer in sight, and even then, I stand there watching as snow drifts down. I hope it doesn't get worse before he makes it home.

The snow reminds me of the wolf and I look to the woods, but unlike last time, it's empty. I check every night out my window. I saw him one more time after the first initial one, but that's it.

Realizing I don't actually have my phone on me, I head back inside. Emma isn't downstairs any longer, so I assume she's in bed. I lock the door, then head to my bedroom. I grab my phone off the nightstand to find a text from an unknown number.

Hey, it's Ash. I made it home safely. Thank you for hanging out with me tonight. Sweet dreams, Ellie darling.

A smile spreads across my face as I read his message. He got home faster than I thought he would.

I'm a bit slow to respond since I rarely text. Jane and I usually just call each other. I keep messing up. Maybe I should get a smartphone just so texting gets easier.

Thank you for texting me. I'm glad you're home safe. Goodnight, Ash.

Ellie

*H*alloween is just over two weeks away and Emma has somehow convinced me to go to the store with her. I try to keep out of sight as much as possible on the off chance someone will recognize me. I was in the paper for weeks in Pennsylvania. It was strange seeing my own face as a missing person. It even said my foster family missed me.

What a joke.

"Any ideas on what you want to be for Halloween?" Emma asks. Picking a costume was probably what swayed me to come. I'm oddly excited to dress up for Halloween. The last time I got to really celebrate was when I was ten. My parents died just before Halloween when I was eleven, so that year involved staying inside a temporary home until they found a foster family to take me in. Little did I know that I would stop being able to dress up once I entered the foster system. No one was as bad as Marcus, but the others didn't want to spend money for costumes for all their foster kids.

"No, I figured I'd see my options first before deciding what to be. Do you have a costume already?"

Her eyes stay on the road as she nods. "Yes, I was planning on wearing the costume I wore last year."

"That's lame. You should pick out a costume with me."

She thinks for a moment, tapping her fingers on the back of the steering wheel. "I don't know." She pauses. "What would I be?"

"What's Tom being?"

She gives me a pointed look.

I grin. "Come on, you two are a couple now. Don't couples, you know, dress up as other couples?"

She laughs. "Yes, I suppose so."

"So talk to Tom and match."

"Okay. Yeah. I like that idea." She smiles as she pulls into a parking space. The sign above the building says Wade's Grocery. "First, we shop for food. Then, we'll buy some decorations and a costume at the holiday store."

"Holiday store?" I ask, following her out of the car and into the store.

"We don't have a store just for Halloween decorations. Instead, there's a store that rotates items for each holiday. It's how it stays in business all year round."

"Wouldn't that make it more expensive for them to have to buy every holiday decor?"

She grabs a cart and goes down an aisle. "Yes and no. Whatever is left each year is recycled for the next. They only receive new things if they have space. So the decorations may be outdated for some holidays, but no one really minds."

We're already near the back of the store when Emma stops. "Oh, crap." She looks back the way we came. "I forgot to grab some bread. Do you mind going back and getting some? It's down the first aisle."

"Sure."

"Thank you. I'm going to grab some milk and eggs."

"Okay." I turn around and head back to the bread aisle.

Turning the corner to the aisle, I run into a solid chest.

The man's hands reach out and grab my shoulders to keep me from falling.

Nausea rolls through me. "Sorry," I say, shrugging off his touch and stepping away.

"It's fine."

I look up, meeting blue eyes. He's attractive, but I'm not drawn to him like I am to Ash. He looks down on me with a crease between his dirty-blond brows and matching blond hair that's slightly spiked in the front. His features are almost pretty.

Ducking my head, I step farther back. "Sorry again," I mutter before rushing past him. I scan the aisle for the bread I know Emma likes. I just want to grab it and go.

I shouldn't have come. Being in public gives me too much anxiety; my hands are already shaking and it's hard to focus on the labels in front of me. Gripping my jacket, I tug it tighter around myself and take the deep breaths that Jane taught me to do when I feel a panic attack coming on.

Finally finding the bread, I snatch one up and look behind me. The guy is still there, but he's looking at the tortilla section. His head turns toward me with a look of intrigue and confusion plastered on his face.

I pivot and walk as fast as I can without raising too much attention. I make it to the back of the store and see Emma placing two gallons of milk in her cart. She looks up and gives me a smile.

"Hey, thanks." She takes the loaf of bread from me and places it on the carton of eggs.

Giving her a quick nod, I stick my hands in my coat pocket to keep them from shaking. The incident still affecting me more than I'd like to admit. Too much unknown could happen in a grocery store. What if Marcus ends up finding me here?

I know I'm being paranoid. I know it's not healthy to want to be a hermit, but I also know it's not normal to be locked up and abused in a basement for years. I glance behind me and freeze.

The man's in the orange juice section, right next to the milk. He catches my eye and gives me a small smile.

It's fake.

I don't know how I know, but I do.

"Looks like someone is interested in you."

Turning my attention back to Emma, I notice she's looking at the guy too, but unlike me, she thinks his smile is genuine. Or maybe I'm just reading too much into this. Maybe Marcus has scarred me so badly that I think every man has evil intentions for me.

Ash's face pops into my head.

Maybe not all.

And if I think more about it, I feel fine around Tom as well.

"He's just being friendly," I say. "What else is on your list?"

She pulls it out of her pocket and begins rattling off all the items she needs.

I don't split off from her again as we make our way through the store, but I sense eyes on me the entire time. Every once in a while, I'll look back and catch sight of the guy or a glimpse of his black leather jacket.

As we go into the check out, he's in the one next to us.

"Am I crazy to think he's following us?" I say quickly to Emma.

She turns away from the belt and follows my gaze. She gives him a polite smile and then me a pointed look.

"He's just shopping, but maybe he'd like to ask you on a date." She winks.

I sigh and help her load the rest of the food on the belt.

After paying, we head out to her car and begin pulling the bags into her trunk.

"Want me to take that?"

I look up and see the guy again. I recoil away from him.

He gestures to our now empty cart.

"Oh, yes. Thank you," Emma says.

"Happy to help." He grabs it from Emma, and I watch him as he pushes it into a spot.

"Do you know him?" I ask.

Emma closes the trunk. "I've seen him around sometimes when I come here. I believe he lives in a different town, though."

"Is he always this...friendly?"

She looks over at him. "Not usually. But I've never had a young, pretty girl with me before."

I frown. I have serious doubts that's the reason he's following us.

We get back in her car and drive to the holiday store, which is only about five minutes away. The inside reminds me of a dollar store, but instead of a variety of things, everything is themed for Halloween.

Emma grabs a basket and I follow her to the decoration aisle. We go through them slowly and Emma picks out a few items. One is a snow globe with a haunted house inside and gravestones. Afterwards we walk over to the other side of the store where there are rows and rows of costumes.

"How about we split up? Divide and conquer," she says.

"Sounds good to me."

She walks over to the next aisle as I begin browsing. I find a fairy costume in my size that's pretty cute and not too revealing. The less skin I show, the more comfortable I'll be. I see a pirate costume that I like even more, so I look through them to find my size.

"Funny seeing you here."

I jump and find the guy from the grocery store standing close— too close. I take a step away from him. He may be attractive, but I'm getting serious creeper vibes from him. Did he follow us here? Why is he here? It's one thing to need a costume, but he's in the women's section.

"Yeah, funny." I take another step back.

He grabs my arms, inhibiting my departure.

I recoil from his touch but can't pry my arm out of my hands.

"Let go," I cry.

"Why do you smell like Ash?" he says in an even tone.

My body stiffens. "Wha—"

"Hey, Ellie, I found—what's going on here?" Emma comes down the aisle.

The guy eases his grip and I snatch my arm back.

"Just having a friendly discussion. Ellie asked for my help in picking out a costume."

"No, I—" My words die out of my mouth at the look he gives me. It has a warning in them. But I don't think he'd hurt me, despite his rough grip and strange, stalking behaviors.

"How nice of you." Emma side-eyes him. She looks at the pirate costumes we're in front of. "That would be cute on you, Ellie. Let's take that one. I forgot I have a few guests coming tonight, so we need to go." She grabs one in my size and we book it to the cash register.

"Are you okay?" she asks quietly.

I nod, but my hands are shaking, and I can't get them to stop. "Are we really having guests tonight?"

"No," she says as she gives me a cheeky grin. "It was just an excuse to get away."

I sigh. "Thanks."

She glances behind us, but the man isn't there anymore.

"He knows Ash," I say.

Her brows go up as her gaze meets mine. "Huh, not that surprising since he's lived here for a long time."

"I guess you're right." But something tells me that this is more important than I realize.

13

Ellie

I'm crazy. Absolutely crazy. I miss my wolf. I miss the comfort he brought me. I haven't been able to sleep, and since the incident in town, I can't function during the day. I need him. But I should *not* be back at this barn. I also definitely shouldn't be crouched down behind some bushes *watching* the barn, as if the wolf will just happen to walk out the door. I roll my eyes at myself. I seriously doubt the wolf is actually inside or anywhere near this place anymore, but since this is where I met him—inside the barn, to be exact—here I am, *watching the barn.*

I gnaw on my bottom lip, thinking of who else could walk out of the barn. Ash. Maybe that's the real reason I'm here. I haven't seen him since our movie night.

But what if Ash is home and he sees me loitering around his property?

I shift my weight to my other leg, continuing my watch of the barn.

Why am I even scouting the barn? Shouldn't I be looking for the wolf in the forest?

"What are you doing here?"

I jump up and spin around, coming face-to-face with Ash. He's leaning against a tree with his arms crossed and a brow quirked.

"I, uh." I glance at the bush I was hiding behind. "I lost something." I cringe.

Great lie, Ellie.

Mirth dances in his gaze. "Is that so? And what, pray tell, did you lose?"

"My earring." My hands jump to my ears, making sure I don't actually have any in.

"Both of them?"

"Yes," I answer since both holes are empty.

"Mmhmm. So, *earrings*." He smirks. "Would you like some help?"

"No! I mean, no, I'm okay."

He rolls his lips in as he tries to hold back a laugh. I don't know why he lets me go on when he knows I'm lying. But he continues to lean against the tree, so I crouch back down and pretend to search for my non-existent earrings.

"You know what—" I stand back up and put my hands on my hips. "What are you doing here?"

"This is my place."

"This is the forest."

He chuckles with a shake of his head. "The barn, Ellie."

My cheeks heat. "Right."

He laughs. "Come on." He straightens and gestures with his head to the barn then walks past me, and because I'm curious, I follow him.

"Why did you renovate a barn?"

He slightly tilts his head as he glances at me. "How did you know I renovated it?"

"I-uh—it was brought up at dinner."

I catch a small smile on his face before he turns away and opens the door. "Right. I almost forgot. I just needed a place to escape." I sigh in relief.

We walk in and I find that it's the same as how I left it, except there's a loaf of bread on the table and shoes by the door.

"To escape? From what?" It seems we're more alike than I thought. When I squatted here, I had wished this was my safe haven.

"Just from...problems," he says as he closes the door behind us. "Take a seat. Do you want some hot chocolate?"

What is up with everyone drinking hot chocolate here? Not that I particularly mind. "Sure." He walks over to the kitchen as I shrug off my coat before sitting at the table.

"When did you move here?" I ask, watching Ash take out a pot and pour milk into it.

"I bought and renovated this place a few years ago, but I just recently started using it more."

"Oh, why is that?"

He glances at me. "I like it better here."

"Does that mean you have another house somewhere?"

"Yes. About an hour's drive away." He pauses, his body tensing. "I actually was planning on stopping by Emma's later today."

"Oh? Why?"

He turns to me. "I have to leave for a couple of weeks."

"What?" I blink, trying to stifle the disappointment that sinks my stomach.

He averts his gaze. "I have some things I need to take care of."

"Will you...will you be around for Halloween?" Seriously, *Halloween* is what you care about, Ellie?

His brows pull in as he looks at me. "I'll try...but I can't make any promises."

My gaze drops to my lap. "Okay. I understand," I say, but I really don't. I want to ask him what he needs to take care of, but I'm not sure I can.

"Why don't you come over and help me?"

"Huh?" I ask. Help him with what?

He smiles. "The hot chocolate."

"Right. Okay." I stand and walk over.

Ash trails a hand down my arm, and I try not to flinch. But instead of anxiety rolling through me, it soothes and excites me. Why is that?

"Have you ever made homemade hot chocolate before?" he asks.

I shake my head. "Emma uses the packets."

"I figured." His hand caresses my inner wrist before twinning his fingers with mine. "Ellie darling."

I try to keep my body still while my insides swirl in a jumbled mess of emotions. Desire, disappointment, fear, hope. "Hmm?"

He chuckles lightly. "Look at me."

His eyes bore in mine as I met his gaze. "I'll be back." He tucks an errant strand of hair behind my ear. "I can't stay away from you for long."

My breath hitches. "You barely know me."

He leans closer, his breath a whisper away. "But I want to. I want to know everything about you."

Ash tugs me by our joined hands as he walks over to a cabinet. He grabs a handful of chocolate bars and places them on a cutting board that's already on his small island.

There's tangible loss when he lets go of my hand to unravel one of the bars and grab a knife. With a tilt of his head, he gestures for me to get closer. He takes my right hand and gently places the knife's handle into my palm.

He lightly grips my hips and adjusts me in front of the cutting board, but stays behind me, his heat seeping into mine. He leans his head down above my shoulder, his warm breath on my ear. "All you have to do is cut the bars into small pieces."

"Okay." My voice comes out breathy.

I chop the chocolate, not paying a whole lot of attention to how I'm cutting it because of the distraction at my back.

Ash chuckles softly and places his hand on mine, stilling my motions. "Like this." He takes hold of my hand, and in smoother motions helps me cut the bar into smaller pieces. "Good." He takes a deep breath, then moves away from me.

Did he just smell me?

I glance over my shoulder, but his back is already turned to me as he heats the milk on the stove.

"Now what?" I ask once finished.

He glances at me as he reaches over to remove a bowl from a cabinet. He slides the cut chocolate into the bowl and places it in the microwave.

"Now we melt it before adding it into the milk."

In intervals, he heats it and stirs until he deems it just right.

"The mugs are in the cabinet on the right of the microwave, mind grabbing two?" he asks as he mixes the chocolate into the milk.

"Sure." I open the cabinet, but realize they're on the top shelf, out of reach.

Without turning, I feel a presence at my back. Ash reaches over me, his body lightly pressing into me. He grabs two mugs with one hand, clinking them together. "Sorry, I didn't realize they were up that high."

He closes the cabinet then places his hand on my lower back. "Would you like anything to eat?" He's so close, my senses are overloading.

"I'm okay," I answer softly.

Humming in thought, his hand slides around my waist. His fingers gently grip my hip. "I'll lay something out just in case."

I swallow and give a small nod.

His hand trails my back as he moves away. "Marshmallows?"

A puff of air rushes out as I turn to face him, letting my lower back dig into the counter. "Sure." Is it just me, or has he gotten more touchy?

He plops some marshmallows in both mugs before handing me one. "Let's sit on the couch." He motions for us to move, and I follow him. Once I sit down, he grabs a blanket and offers it to me, then relaxes next to me. I pull my legs up onto the couch.

"So, where did you grow up?" he asks.

I blow on my cup. "Philadelphia."

His eyes narrow as he takes a sip of his hot chocolate. I look down at the steam billowing from his mug.

"I've been there a few times. It's pretty. Weather's nice."

"Yeah, it is." I nod. "Is your mouth okay?"

His brows furrow as he licks his bottom lip, my eyes tracking the movement. "Yes, why?"

"It's just...the drink. Isn't it hot?"

"Oh, uh, yes. It's hot." He glances down at his mug as if it offended him. "I just have a high tolerance to the heat and the cold."

"That must be nice." Not being able to feel the cold? I could've really used that special ability recently. Or better yet, when I lived with Marcus.

He shrugs. "I don't know any different."

I turn more toward him, holding my mug in between us.

"Do you plan on moving back?" he asks.

"No," I answer a little too quickly and clear my throat. "I don't plan on moving back."

"Why not?"

"There's nothing left for me there."

His eyes are full of understanding. "Do you want to talk about it?"

Contrasting emotions, dread and anticipation build up. Just the thought of thinking of everything that happened in Philly makes me sick to my stomach. I've only spoken about it once before and that was to Jane, but even she doesn't know everything. So why do I find that I want to share everything with him?

"I think...I think I would like to. With you. But maybe not right now." I need to work up to it. Prepare myself to relive it again, even though I do almost every night.

"You said you grew up here?" I ask before drinking. "Oh my gosh." I wiggle. "This is delicious."

He grins. "Way better than powder."

"Definitely. This can't just be melted chocolate."

He chuckles. "It isn't, I added a secret ingredient." He winks. "But, yes. I grew up here since I was about twelve."

"Where were you before?"

"London. It's where I was born."

"You don't have an accent."

"I don't." He pushes his ebony hair off his forehead as he shifts in his seat. "My accent gradually disappeared the longer I lived here. My friend, on the other hand, has a thick British accent. He spends most of his time there when he isn't traveling."

I nod, taking another sip. "You said you don't mind it. Have you traveled a lot?"

"In the past." He moves an arm to rest on the couch behind me. "It's how I met Russell."

"Russell?" I ask and take another long drink.

"Russell and Foster are like brothers to me. Foster is the one from London. Russell is from Ireland."

"Is that where you met?"

He looks at his mug. "It is. But Russell is here. Maybe you could meet him sometime."

Meeting a friend. That's big, right? "I'd love to."

"So." He takes my empty mug from me and places them both on the coffee table. "What about you?"

"Friends-wise?" He nods. "Only one." I avoid his eyes. "I don't see her much." Would Jane be considered a friend or a guardian? Both?

"What about siblings?" he asks.

I shake my head. "Only child." I wrap my arms around my legs, still sitting sideways on the couch.

"I see." Does he, though? Does he realize how lonely I've been since my parents died? I tug the blanket tighter around myself.

"What about you?" I ask.

He stiffens. "I have one sibling." Alright, touchy subject for him, too.

Ash stands, taking our mugs with him, and places them in the sink. He opens the fridge and grabs a small platter of fruit and veggies. "So, are you going to tell me the real reason you were snooping near my place?"

My eyes widen as I watch him stride over, placing the tray onto the coffee table. "I-I, I wasn't."

He arches a brow as he pops a tomato in his mouth. He lounges next to me again, closer than before as he places an arm on top of the couch behind me. I have trouble focusing as my legs press against his.

His eyes flicker to my chest. Can he tell how fast my heart is beating? "You're not a very good liar, Ellie."

I sigh. I'm really not. "I wasn't snooping. Not really."

"Then what were you doing?"

"You'll think I'm crazy."

He grins as he leans closer. "Maybe I like crazy."

I narrow my eyes at him. "Ash."

He pulls away. "Just tell me."

Fine. If he thinks I'm crazy, that's the end of it. Besides, I feel crazy. "I was looking for a wolf."

"Now, was that so hard?"

I eye him. "You don't seem surprised."

He shrugs. "There are lots of wolves in these parts."

"But you don't find it strange that I was looking for one?"

"Do you want me to?"

"No," I say a little too fast.

He quirks a brow. "Then don't worry about it."

I bite my lip and look away. "Maybe you're the strange one."

He laughs. "Maybe I am." He checks his watch, then curses under his breath. "Daylight is almost gone—how about I walk you back?"

"Oh." I cringe at how sad my voice sounds. "It's fine, I can go back on my own."

"I insist." He stands and offers me a hand up.

I take off the blanket and place my hand in his—calloused but soft.

His hands linger on mine before I turn and pick up my coat.

Turning back around, I see Ash staring at me with his brows scrunched together.

"What's wrong?" I ask.

"Is this your coat?"

Looking down at my second-hand coat with a broken zipper, I shift my weight in embarrassment.

Taking my silence as a yes, he scowls with a growl. Then walks away to the closet next to the bathroom.

Did he really just growl at me? "What are you doing?" I call after him.

Instead of answering, he walks back out with a black coat. He strides over to me, takes my coat, and stuffs the new one in my hands. "This is yours now."

"What?" I shove it back into his hands. "I can't take this."

He shoves it back, but gentler than I did. "Yes, you can. I have no need for it."

I hold it up. "It's too big."

"Just take this until I can buy you one that fits."

"Ash."

"Ellie."

"You're not going to buy me a new coat."

"I will, and I'll buy you five if you don't take this one."

"Seriously?"

His lips curl. "Do you want to chance it?"

"Fine." I send him a glare. "I'll accept this only if you don't buy me another one."

"Fine. Now put it on."

I sigh and stuff my arms in the sleeves and zip it up. It's huge, but I kind of love it. I discreetly hold the collar to my nose. I hold back a moan at how good it smells—pine and musk.

My cheeks warm when I catch the grin on his face as he turns and opens the door for me.

14

Ellie

*T*ime has seemed to slow down since Ash left, making these past two weeks full of loneliness. I stare at my phone on the table as I tap my fingers against the wood. I let out a groan when I check the time and see I've been just sitting here for half an hour, waiting for a response. Ash and I have been texting on and off, but his responses always take a while to come back.

When did I become so desperate for attention? I've been fine for years without it. I'll be okay without Ash's.

So why can't I stop thinking about him?

Every time I pick up my pencil, I draw him, and whenever I pick up my book, I compare Ash to Wesley. It's ridiculous. I can't even read my favorite book.

One thing that's helped keep my mind off him is seeing my wolf. I've caught glimpses of him three different nights since Ash left. Not sure if seeing him makes me feel more or less crazy, though.

The doorbell rings and I jump up. I watch from the archway as Emma walks down the stairs in a long black dress, her naturally curly hair straightened. She gives me a soft smile before answering the door. She's dressed up as Morticia from *The Addams Family*.

I tug on my vest and wipe my sweaty palms on my black skirt. I have fishnet tights underneath with black boots. Emma helped me to do my makeup and create messy curls to tie it all together. It's more of a sexy pirate costume rather than a realistic one.

My phone buzzes and I'm hit with disappointment before Emma even opens the door.

Ash: I'm sorry, I can't make it tonight. I hope you have fun. Happy Halloween!

Emma ushers Tom in, who enters holding a cane, and wearing a black-and-white striped tux. His salt-and-pepper hair is slicked back. The only thing missing is a mustache.

"Where's Ash?" Emma asks, grabbing her coat, and Tom helps her put it on.

Tom's looks over her shoulder at me, guilt written all over his face. "He called me and told me he couldn't make it. He sends his regards."

I nod. "I just got a text from him."

"Oh." Emma looks at me. "Well, we'll just have fun without him."

"I don't know if—"

"Don't finish that sentence." Emma points at me as Tom grabs my coat. "You look awesome and should show off."

I bite my lip.

"I'm not taking no for an answer."

I laugh halfheartedly. "Alright. Let's go," I say as I take my coat from Tom and follow them out the door.

THE NEIGHBOR'S party was more stressful than I thought it would be. I thought, since I was used to having Emma and Tom as company, I'd be fine with a group of strangers. Yeah, definitely not. My anxiety was through the roof the entire time as I tried to avoid bumping into anyone. The party wasn't like what you see in the movies, everyone was older than me and just enjoying each other's company, but people were still drinking. As the night drew on, bottles were emptied, and boundary lines were blurred. Thankfully, Tom stayed sober and Emma only drank two cups, which made her a little tipsy but not drunk.

"Night, Ellie. I hope your head stops hurting."

"Thanks, Tom. I think I just need sleep." I wave goodbye to them as they drive off to Tom's for the night.

I trudge up the porch stairs. It's a full moon tonight, illuminating the woods around Emma's house. The light bounces off the snow from recent storms, but the trees are merely immobile shadows. My heart skips a beat as something moves between them. I squint and can just barely make out a large animal hovering beside a tree, almost as if a random boulder was placed there.

Could it be?

It moves again. Slick and sleek. Dangerous, yet elegant.

It's my wolf. I know it is. Without thinking, I'm down the steps and across Emma's yard. Snow seeps into my shoes, and the air continues to nip at my exposed skin, but I don't care. I halt at the edge of the forest.

This is crazy. What the heck am I doing?

I study the trees in front of me, wind whipping my hair to the side.

This isn't a good idea.

But then I see him.

My wolf.

His glacier-blue eyes pierce through the darkness, and I take a step forward. Then another—until I'm practically running.

I collapse against the wolf, melting into him as I wrap my arms around him. My fingers dig into his soft ebony fur as I breathe in deeply. His scent is refreshing, mixing in with the wind. He smells just like I remembered: the woods, pines, and fresh snow, but better.

"I missed you," I whisper. This animal was the first one to bring me peace and calmness at night. I've been craving it. All my emotions tumble out. Just when I thought life was looking up, Ash disappeared. The one connection I felt could go somewhere. He must've been able to sense I was too much trouble. Too closed-off. I made him run for the hills. It became obvious tonight with him not showing up and his lack of communication. What was I even thinking?

Tears spill as I hold the wolf tighter. He is exactly what I need right now. His calm, playful personality always makes me forget my troubles.

I indulge in the softness of his fur as I run my hands through it, trying to memorize it in every way.

"I thought I'd never see you again."

He hunches down and nuzzles my neck.

Pulling back, I look into the wolf's eyes. I'm hit with a sense of familiarity. I blink and it's gone.

I sit back on my leg and really look at him. He sits and stares back with a tilt of his head that's super cute. Reminding me of what puppies do when they're confused. He doesn't act like a normal wolf—not that I've had much experience with wolves prior to him. But there's just something different about him.

I run my hand down his neck. "It's good to see you."

He stands and nudges me up. He tilts his head, as if he's asking me to follow him.

I look back through the trees at Emma's house. Is it smart to follow a wolf through the woods? Probably not, but oddly, I trust him.

As we walk, the only sounds are the soft rustle of leaves as the chilly breeze brushes through them, the crickets, the snaps of twigs, and the crunch of snow under my feet.

We walk until we come up on a small opening in the trees, full of forget-me-nots and patches of snow. How is that possible? Don't flowers bloom in the spring?

As we wander through them, I'm hit with their fragrance. I take a deep breath through my nose and smile. "I don't think I've ever smelled forget-me-nots before."

The wolf nudges my hand, regaining my attention, before walking ahead of me. He stops where the flowers are sparse and only grass remains. He lays down and meets my gaze, beckoning me to join him with his eyes. I sit next to him in a dry spot, but shiver at the cold ground beneath me. Noticing, he shifts closer, nudging me to lay down then snuggling with me. He covers my exposed legs with his tail.

I take comfort in the warmth of his body against mine. As I cuddle against him, I look up at the sky. My breath hitches. Pale green and pink stripes cover the night sky, stars shining through them. It's almost as if it's alive, the foggy colors slowly moving above us in waves. Something so beautiful, but simple. The aurora borealis.

Sniffing with a quivering lip, I'm hit with a wave of emotion. This touches me deeper than I expected it could. It's so magical. Makes me feel like anything is possible.

I rub my eyes. I've cried more times in the past two months than I have in years. I close my eyes to try to gain composure. Why did the wolf bring me here? Did he know I needed to see this?

He nuzzles my hair. I smile and bury my head into his fur. I think I'll just stay like this for a while.

15

Ellie

*B*irds tweeting is the first thing I hear, followed by the soft breathing of my wolf. My brows scrunch together, my eyes still closed. His breathing seems different. Also instead of fur, I feel warm, smooth skin.

My eyes pop open, and I'm met with a sleeping man beside me. His features shadowed from the rising sun.

I jolt up, jostling the arm that was around me, and scurry away.

The man is naked except for black boxer briefs. I blink. *Where's my wolf?* I quickly look around, but he's nowhere to be found. I focus back on the man and it clicks. This isn't just any man. The smooth light-brown skin, the chiseled jaw with scruff and ebony hair.

Ash.

I gasp and quickly cover my mouth as he stirs. His hand searching the area where I had been sleeping beside him. His brows furrow, then his whole body stiffens.

He opens his eyes, and they instantly connect with mine, panic swirling in his gaze. "I can explain," he says, his voice thick from sleep. I remain frozen as he sits up. He grimaces, and I realize he's injured. The side he was sleeping on is covered in an ugly purplish-blue bruise.

He doesn't move closer once he's in a sitting position, instead he runs a hand down his face and mutters a few swear words. "This was not how I wanted you to find out."

My eyes strain as I stare at him, my hands shaking over my mouth.

He peeks at me through his fingers and lets out a pent-up breath as he removes his hand. Looking resigned, he says, "I know you have questions. You can ask me."

It takes me a moment to drop my hands, but even then, my mouth can't seem to form words. I hold myself as I try to process what has happened. And Ash doesn't rush me.

Finally, I come up with a coherent thought. "How?"

He nods slowly. "How?"

I wave my hand, gesturing to him and his practically naked body.

"How did I get here? Or how did I shift from a wolf to a man?"

I shake my head. He can't possibly mean that he and the wolf are one and the same.

Ash lounges back on his hands, tipping his head back to look up at the sky. The bruising along his side is even more noticeable in this position. He has to have at least one broken rib. What happened to him?

When I don't say anything else, he says, "I've been trying to figure out a way to tell you. To tell you who I really am. That I am both the wolf and the man. That you can let your guard down with me. But I couldn't just spit out that I'm a wolf. How crazy would that sound?"

My hands keep a tight grip on my coat as a chilled breeze seeps through.

His eyes travel to me once more. "You look beautiful, by the way. I really like the sexy pirate look."

I scowl, narrowing my eyes at him. "No."

"No?"

"Don't try to change the subject."

The corners of his lips twitch. "It was worth a shot." He sighs, leaning forward while holding his side. "Well, do you believe me?"

"That you're a wolf?"

He nods, resting his arms on his knees. "Not just any wolf though, but the wolf you've been spending time with."

That can't be possible. "How?" I ask again.

His brows scrunch together. "I've already—"

"How is this possible?"

"That's kind of a long story."

I give him a look, and he lets out a breath. "I'll give you the short version for now. I don't want to overwhelm you."

I bark out a humorless laugh. "Like this isn't already over-whelming?"

He closes his eyes. "You're right, I'm sorry." He takes a deep breath, but cringes and touches his side.

"How did you get that?" I ask.

His glacier-blue eyes connect with mine, and my heart speeds up. I frown at my reaction and glare at him.

"Just someone in the pack."

"Pack?"

He grunts in frustration, running a hand down his face again. "I've never had to explain this to anyone before. I'm not sure how to do this right." He sighs. "Let me backtrack to your first question, and then I can explain everything else." I nod, my palms sweating. He can't really be a wolf, right? That just doesn't make sense. My gaze trails the smooth expansive of skin he's showing. He's defi-nitely a man. How can he also be a wolf?

He straightens slightly. "I'm a lycan, better known as a wolf-shifter, werewolf, whatever."

My brain short circuits as I shake my head. Nope, can't process this. It's just not possible. "And how is that possible?"

"I was born this way. There's magic that runs through my body that allows me to shift."

"And are there more of you? More lycans?"

"Yes, there's a lot of us throughout the world. My parents were both lycans, and I was born one."

My mind is running a million miles a minute trying to piece this together. "Have lycans always existed?"

"No, but I don't think you're ready to hear how my kind came to be."

I fold my arms, fighting the urge to stand and stomp my foot. "I beg to differ."

"Have you accepted that I'm a wolf in the past five minutes?" My shoulders slump, and he continues, "I thought so."

I glare at him.

"Sorry," he says, then curses. "I'm doing a terrible job at explaining this. Let's just...let's just take this one step at a time."

"Fine. So you were born a wolf-shifter, a lycan. Have you always been able to shift into a wolf?"

"Yes, well, since puberty."

"Prove it."

"Now?"

"No, tomorrow," I deadpan.

With a sigh, he eases onto his hands and knees.

My heart seems to stop beating as I hold my breath, watching his body transform. His shift is quick as his body enlarges and morphs. His face changes before my eyes and fur erupts...everywhere.

He...he changed.

Into a wolf.

My wolf.

I jump up. "This can't be possible." I pace and eye him. His eyes glow in his wolf form, but they're still the same glacier blue. His fur is the same ebony as his hair. How is this even real? How did I not make the connection?

Because you didn't think werewolves existed before this, Ellie.

I freeze in place as he walks toward me. He stops in front of me and sits. I reach out but hesitate. Meeting his eyes in question, he nods then lowers his head. My heart skips a beat as I brush my fingers against the fur—*his* fur—and find it's just as soft as last night. *Would Ash's hair feel this soft as well?*

He huffs before his body shifts back into a man. Into Ash. Still naked except for his black boxers.

My brows scrunch together. "How?"

His arms flex as he pushes off the ground to stand. He's so close it's hard not to ogle his toned pecs and abs. Even his thighs and calves are attractive.

I bite my lip, turning my gaze away. Now is *not* the time.

"How?" His voice is just a breath away, sending a shiver down my spine.

I vaguely gesture to his underwear, keeping my eyes averted.

"Ah. All my boxers are made with magic-infused fibers."

Magic-infused fibers? "Why not clothes as well?" I glance at him.

"There's only a handful of witches that can make them. And it's time consuming to create them so they only offer underwear and some jewelry at a higher cost."

So witches also exist? I mentally shake my head. Right now is not the best time to contemplate other supernatural beings' existence. I can't even wrap my mind around him being my wolf—no, not mine, *a* wolf. I meet his eyes. "So, you're a werewolf."

He nods. "A lycan."

"Right." I take a step back but realize that just gives me a better view. I clear my throat. "How did this happen?" He tilts his head and I clear my throat. "You—shifting." I fidget with my zipper on the coat he gave me. "You've never done this around me before. And you seemed surprised that you did."

"You're right, I didn't mean to shift this time. But I don't regret it happening. I'm glad you know now." He takes a step closer, but I take another step backward. Hurt flashes in his eyes, and I try not to feel guilty.

"If you didn't mean for this to happen, how did it?" I ask.

He blinks, then straightens, clenching and unclenching his hands. "Shifts can be triggered by emotions. When emotions are high, the shift is close to the surface just waiting to be tapped into, sometimes it happens without even tapping into it, which is called a forced shift."

"You mean, shifting into your wolf."

"Yes."

"But this was the opposite."

He nods. "And like the opposite of heightened emotions, when we're calm or relaxed, our bodies will shift back into our natural form, retract if you will. When we're awake, it's easy to control, but that's not the case when we're asleep."

"Okay." I take that information in. Emotions and stress can trigger shifts. I guess that makes sense. "So, is there, like, a wolf inside of you?" I've read some wolf-shifter stories before, usually they have a wolf or something inside of them.

"No." His lips curl into a small smile. "It's not like the books. The wolf part of me is just that. A part of me. Just like my heart and lungs are. It makes me who I am, what I am. But I'm still me in that form."

"But the sniffing, cuddling…" I blush.

He bites his lip. "It's part magic, part me. I like the way you smell. Also helps that I have a better sense of smell than humans. The cuddling? I *may* have taken advantage because that's all you thought I was. I wanted to comfort you, but that doesn't excuse my behavior." His chest puffs out as he takes a deep breath in, before letting it out in a gush. "And I'm sorry for that. It was wrong."

I nod. I know I should be angry, but I'm not. He *did* comfort me. But I'm still grateful he realizes the deception was wrong. "Thank you for apologizing." More questions form in my mind. "Okay, two things."

"Hit me." He pauses. "Physically or metaphorically. I know I deserve it." He gives me a sad smile.

I shake my head. "I'm not going to hit you. But I do have questions. You mentioned magic?"

"How else would you explain this?" He gestures to himself. My eyes linger on all his naked skin before I can force my gaze away, again.

"That still doesn't explain magic."

"Can you really explain magic?" he asks.

"I don't know. I didn't believe in magic two minutes ago. How did this magic appear? How—"

Ash lightly touches my biceps, grounding me. "Ellie," he says my name like a prayer. "I know you have a million questions—and I promise to answer them all in time—but let's not dig too deep about this yet. You're already having a hard time believing this. And I'm not even sure where magic comes from. I know our origin story, but it doesn't explain the magic." He gives me an encouraging smile.

I swallow and nod.

"What's your second thing?"

I blink. "Oh, right. You said you involuntarily shifted back this time because you were relaxed."

"Yes." His hands move down my arms until he reaches mine.

"B-but—" I try to keep my thought process. I was around him when he was a wolf for two whole weeks and multiple times when he was...not. I remember thinking his eyes seemed familiar when I met him at Emma's all those weeks ago. "What about all the other times you slept next to me?"

He lightly squeezes my hands. "The first two nights I was unable to shift because of how severe my injuries were."

"So, you can't shift when you're injured?"

He tilts his head side-to-side. "I mean, I could, but it would've injured me more. I may have even passed out in the middle of it."

"Okay." Well, that makes sense. "And after you got better?"

"I didn't sleep long enough to shift back."

"So you did it on purpose."

"I did. I know not shifting and revealing myself was wrong, but did you really want me to shift back then?"

"Yes." I turn around, yanking my hands out of his. "I don't know. Maybe not." I spin back to face him. "Why didn't you?"

"I thought it would be a bad idea for me to show myself as a man while you were trapped in the barn with me. Especially after your nightmares. I didn't want to make it worse for you. You were already struggling."

"I...I was." Maybe it was good that he didn't. "But we met after the barn. Why didn't you tell me then?" It's as if a light bulb goes off inside my head. "You weren't ever going to tell me, were you? That's why you left and barely talked to me. You were cutting me off."

"No." He moves quickly toward me, flinching from the jerky movement, and grabs my hands. His face falls even more when I remove them from his. "I-I'm sorry," he says, his hands forming fists at his side. "But no, that's not why I left or was distant. The distance wasn't on purpose. I was—" He looks away and closes his eyes with a sigh before reopening them, reconnecting with my gaze. "There's some other lycans that don't particularly like me. I left to keep you safe, to not let them realize how much you mean to me."

"But you're here anyway?" A realization hit me. "You've been checking on me."

He nods, a wave of relief crossing his face. "Only when I know no one has followed me. I come to make sure you're still safe."

I wrap my arms around myself. "Why? Why do you care so much about me? We barely know each other."

"I may not know all the details of your life, Ellie, but I know you. I know your soul and I know that you know mine. Can't you feel that pull?"

"I..." I do. I feel the pull, it's always been there. This tug and desire to be with him, even when he was a wolf.

"The more I'm with you and the more I care about you, the stronger it gets," he says. "I'm—" He cuts himself off and shakes his head.

That tug—it must be the reason why I miss him and want to be with him. Even now it's urging me to be closer, to connect deeper.

Was it actually my own desire? Or has my desire to be with him all stemmed from this tug?

"I don't understand," I say.

"I can only describe it as a mate link, but since you're only human, that can't be possible."

"Mate link?" I shake my head.

"It's...a mate link is between two destined mates. I'll explain more another time. But do you believe me? That I really wasn't leaving you? At least not for good. I always planned on coming back and telling you about myself. I just...when you came out and saw me, when I saw your tears and how much you were hurting. From *me*. I couldn't walk away, and with the combination of being sleep deprived...I went into a deep sleep."

Nodding, I stare at his clenched fists. Ash...Ash is a wolf. Well, I guess he's still a man, but a man that can shift into a wolf. "This is kind of confusing."

"I know." Ash reaches up with one hand and lightly caresses my cheek. "It's why I only wanted to explain one thing at a time."

"What you explained, though...it doesn't actually explain *why* you care. Is this link forcing you?" *Is it forcing me?*

His hand drops. "No. Of course not." He clenches his jaw as he looks up at the sky before his gaze drops back down to mine. "I'm not even sure what it is, but it's not forcing anything. It didn't even initiate it. Being trapped with you in my barn did." He chuckles lightly. "It just encourages me to act on the things I'm already feeling."

"Which is?" I whisper, too afraid to speak any louder in case this reality shatters, and I wake up back in the basement. I'm not even too concerned with him being a wolf or that magic exists. But having someone care for me deeply? That will change my life more than magic ever could.

"Feelings that are definitely more than friendship. I want you, Ellie, your heart, soul, and body. Every piece of you. I want to know it all."

My bottom lip wobbles. Knowing that his feelings for me are

real, that it's more than some force or link, means everything. He wants me for me. Even though I'm damaged. Which means this can't be real. *He* can't be real. He's too good to be true, but my truth spills out anyway. "I want you, too."

He straightens, his gaze earnest. "Really?"

"Yes, but I still have questions, and I am mad that you didn't tell me sooner."

He nods slowly. "Completely understandable. I'm sorry that I didn't."

I bite my lip. "But were you really always planning on telling me, even though you knew I would be leaving soon?"

"I was..." He tilts his head down, ashamed. "I was hoping you'd change your mind. That you'd stay here with me. You seemed happy living with Emma and I thought maybe you'd want to stay longer and see how it goes, for us. And now that I know you care..."

I take a step back and shake my head. "I—I can't stay. I'm still leaving." What am I doing? I'm being stupid. How could I allow myself to dwell on these thoughts? I know better. Me and him—we can never be.

Ash's eyes widen with swirls of emotion: shock, panic, anguish. "I don't understand." He takes a step forward, his hands outstretched to hold me, but I move farther away.

"There's a reason I can't stay here long, Ash. After Christmas, I'm leaving."

"Then let me come with you. I want to be wherever you are."

My heart skips a beat. Come with me? Would he really want to live a life with me on the run? No, I can't do that to him. He barely knows me and I can't let another suffer this kind of life. It isn't living. *Golden hair stained in red flashes through my mind. Brown eyes staring at me, devoid of life.*

"I need...I need some time to think." I walk backward, shaking my head, trying to dislodge the image. "I need to go." I whirl around and run away. He yells my name, but I'm grateful when there's no sounds of pursuit.

16

Ellie

It's been a week since I found out about Ash, and my head and heart are still at war with each other. My head tells me I need to forget about him and run to the next place, but my heart is yearning for him. If I were being honest, my body does as well. It remembers how it felt sleeping in his arms.

I miss him when I know I shouldn't.

And I know he's still out in the forest watching over me, which just makes it so much worse.

But maybe if I stay here, Ash could protect me. I quickly push that wayward thought away. Look what happened to Will when he tried to protect me. Ash may be a lycan, but Marcus is a monster.

I walk into the kitchen for lunch to find a note from Emma on the fridge.

Went to get groceries.

I'll be back before dinner.

Love, Emma

Emma doesn't know what happened last week. When I got home, she still was at Tom's. I grab a granola bar and a banana and head back to my room to read. That's all I've been doing lately. I can't pick up *Princess Bride* without thinking of Ash, but I can read other—non-romance—books just fine. Thank goodness for Emma's love of nonfiction.

I'm just finishing my light lunch when the doorbell rings. I ignore it, continuing to read. Whoever it is will get the hint that no one is home.

After a minute it rings again but doesn't stop.

"Seriously?" I mutter under my breath.

I place a bookmark inside the book and put it on the nightstand then walk into the foyer. I look through the peephole just as the ringing stops. There's a man, but he's turned away from the door. All I can see is his green shirt. Maybe it's the postman? Sometimes he needs a signature, but he doesn't normally ring the doorbell like a madman.

Keeping the top latch hooked, I open the door, allowing only a small amount of the door to open.

"Hello, can I help you?" I ask.

The guy turns around, and I freeze in shock. It's the guy from the grocery store. He glances to the side then hunches down, his blue eyes meeting mine. "Ellie." Warning bells sound off in my head.

"Who are you?" I demand.

"Zac."

"What do you want?"

He closes his eyes. "May I come in?"

"Why? If you're looking for Emma, she isn't here."

His eyes flash open, and it almost seems like regret.

I realize my mistake.

I did the worst thing I could possibly do besides answering the door. I just admitted I was home alone.

Zac is pushed aside and my body locks up in terror as Marcus looms on the other side of the door. No. This...this isn't real. I go to slam the door shut, but he slips his hand in, blocking it. Instead of his hand getting smashed, the door frame dents.

"What the—" Is his hand made out of steel or something?

"Eleanor." His voice sends my nerves into overdrive. My entire body shivers.

"N-no. No." This can't be real. Tears blur my vision as I try slamming the door on his hand again, but it disappears.

"You know, that's not very nice."

The chain busts as the door flies open and bounces off the wall, creating a dent. And in strolls my living nightmare. The one who tormented me. The one I ran away from.

Marcus.

His skin is more tanned and his body bulkier than I remember, but his menacing brown eyes and slicked back dark brown hair are the same.

His hand—his hand is no longer human. At least not entirely. His nails have grown and darkened into fine points, his hair thicker than I remember on his hands and exposed arms, almost like fur.

Marcus reaches out quicker than I can react and swipes his claws across my face. I scream and stagger back, my cheek stinging. I touch my face with a shaky hand and it comes back bloody.

My gaze snaps back to him as he prowls toward me.

I find my footing and race toward the back door, his heavy footsteps following. He's fast, faster than anyone I've seen and makes it to the back door before me. Changing tactics, I make a dash into the kitchen and yank two knives from their holders.

My hands shake as I hold them up. Gritting my teeth, I force them to still. I'm no longer the helpless young girl I once was. I'm not going down without a fight this time.

Marcus cackles. "Look at you. All grown up."

I'm pretty sure he's enjoying this. This must be some sick game to him.

He strides to me, but all I can do is back away with the knives up. The shaking is getting worse.

"Don't come near me."

"Or what? You'll poke me?" he taunts with an unkind grin.

"What do you want?" I scream, my terror getting the best of me. Why is he so intent on me even after all these years? Why does he want me so badly?

"Oh, so many things." He laughs. "And to get those things I need your blood."

My entire body freezes. My blood? The reason I left begins to resurface. Blood on his fingertips. Manic laughing. Whispers of excitement through the phone.

I shake my head, my chest tight as I back away, stumbling over my own feet until my back hits the counter.

"Stay away." My voice is weaker than I'd like as I wave the knives in the air, warding him away.

Marcus moves forward within arms reach. I try to swipe him with my knife, but he easily dodges and lands a punch in my side.

Gasping, I bend over. With only one punch, he cracked a rib. Ignoring the pain, I move around the kitchen island to put distance between us. Although, who am I kidding? I can't win this fight. I know he's just toying with me. If he wanted to, he could end this right now. He has a sick grin on his face; he likes the chase. Marcus' canines elongate and his brown eyes darken and start to glow.

What the heck is going on? Is he a lycan, too? Is it even possible for them to partial-shift? There's so much I still need to learn. I regret leaving Ash even more now.

Noticing movement to the side, Zac hovers in the archway to the kitchen with fists clenched at his sides. What does he have to do with all of this? Did he lead Marcus to me?

Marcus takes a step closer, close enough for me to reach. I shake off my inner shock. There's no time to ponder what's happening or how he found me. I take advantage of the moment and slice him across his forearm, creating a deep gash. *Thank goodness Emma has sharp knives.* Marcus roars in anger.

95

"You'll pay for that," he says, grinding his teeth.

He charges, and in the blink of an eye, he has both of my wrists in his hands. He grips my tendons so tight—I scream. I'm forced to drop the knives, letting them clank onto the floor.

I kick at him, trying to break free, but he's unfazed. If anything, I'm just irritating him more.

He throws me on the ground, my head hitting the hard tile, scrambling my thoughts. I groan as he kicks me in the stomach, then the ribs. I curl up trying to protect myself, but it's getting hard to breathe.

"Don't ever touch me," he says, snarling.

He grabs a fist full of hair and pulls my head up, his other fist connecting with my face. A metallic taste enters the back of my throat. I cough, blood spraying his chest. He growls, but my vision is blurry. I only see stars. I feel warm blood ease its way between my lips and drip onto my chin.

He drops me down on my stomach. Glancing around, I see a knife not too far away. I try to scramble to it, but my body feels heavy.

Marcus growls and steps on my back, forcing me back down. "Don't even think about it."

"Marcus, you're taking this too far." Zac's voice is close. I search the room and find him just a few feet away. He looks sick to his stomach.

"Shut up, pup. I know what I'm doing."

"She's supposed to be brought in alive."

"What—" I start, but Marcus stomps on me, cutting me off and splaying me across the floor.

I can't catch my breath.

Sharp white pain erupts across my back, claws tearing through my flesh. He doesn't stop, and I scream until my voice is hoarse and my vision darkens. I thought I'd be numb to the pain like I used to be, but I'm not.

My back burns and throbs, even the air against my wounds sends my nervous system into shock. I'm unable to move, but I fight

SAVING ELLIE

to stay awake as my consciousness fades in and out. I need to get out of here if I have any chance of surviving.

"Zac, you fool," Marcus bellows from across the room.

I hadn't even realized Marcus had stopped raking me with his claws. Turning my head, I press my cheek against the cold ground, and find Zac holding a red-faced Marcus against the table.

"You're going to kill her. This isn't what was supposed to happen," Zac yells, holding Marcus down.

"You know nothing," Marcus spits.

"And you say I'm the pup? Look at you. You can't even control your anger."

Marcus looks feral as he growls. Blood drips down Zac's arms as Marcus digs his claws into his biceps. How is Zac able to hold him down?

Zac looks over at me, disgust covering his face, before turning back to Marcus. I'm not sure if that was disgust for me, Marcus, or himself. "Remember who wants her. He won't be happy when we bring her in looking like this. I don't know if she'll even make it."

"She'll be fine. She'll heal."

"She hasn't turned yet. Can you not tell? Aren't you an alpha?"

There's silence before Marcus speaks again. "I did wonder why she never shifted…"

"Probably from all the abuse you put her through."

Marcus' growl is cut off as the back door bursts open, banging against the wall, and I force my eyes to focus.

There's a man standing in the doorway.

I blink rapidly. It's not just any man. It's Ash.

Ash scans the room until they land on me. His face is laced with confusion but quickly contorts into fury.

He takes a step and suddenly he isn't there anymore. My brain is slowly processing where he went.

Looking around, I find Ash holding Zac by his throat.

Marcus begins to change, his body morphing. His bones shift, fur bursts from his arms, his body enlarging onto all fours until there's only a large, dark brown wolf. He's in an aggressive stance, snarls erupting from him with his fur and ears up.

He leaps at Ash, but Ash side-steps and throws Zac at the wolf. They collide and crash into the cabinets, completely busting them.

My eyes grow heavy but I force them open as I watch. They stand back up and Zac is the next one to morph. My eyes trail back to Ash, whose body is completely tense.

Ash glances down at me, with fury and pain, before turning his attention back to Zac—who is now a golden-haired wolf. Marcus and Zac are wolves. My brain hasn't quite caught up to processing what is happening.

Ash takes a step forward in front of me, blocking me from them. My breath leaves me as his body shifts as well, but much faster than the other two. His shirt and pants rip off of him as he changes into a wolf.

Zac's wolf form dashes out of the barely-hanging-on-its-hinges back door. Marcus and Ash follow close behind.

Going in and out of consciousness, I hear snarling and growling, and even some whimpering. After what seems like forever, it grows silent.

I try to move again, but it's pointless. My mind is reeling despite the shape my body is in. *How did Marcus find me?* Am I going to die on Emma's kitchen floor? Did I really run for the past three years just for this? Is this really how my life comes to an end? Tears roll down my face as sobs rack through my body, causing my body to flare up in pain. *I don't want to die.*

Sensing a presence, I glance up. I see a black shape in the doorway. I blink a few times until it comes into focus. My wolf, no, Ash in his wolf form, is standing at the threshold. I extend my arm toward him and open my mouth, but no words come out. Tears are pooling and running down my face. I want to tell him I'm sorry for running away from him. To tell him everything I've been hiding.

He slowly walks to me with sorrowful wolf eyes. I watch his fur ripple and his body shift. In the blink of an eye, he is no longer a wolf, but Ash in nothing but boxers.

Ash falls to his knees beside me, his own tears streaming down his face.

"Ellie." His voice is deep and thick with emotions; it's a balm for my aching heart and body. I watch a muscle twitch in his jaw. "I'm sorry I wasn't here sooner. But I'm here now. Everything will be okay."

He sets into motion. I cry out when he grabs under my arms and lifts me up. He holds me flush with his body and puts my arms around his neck, stretching my wounds. I sob from the pain.

"Hold on, Ellie. I know it hurts," he says, his voice strained, "but just...hold on." He urges my legs to wrap around him, his hands span the back of my thighs to hold me up.

Blackness seeps into my consciousness. I don't have any energy left to hold on. My breaths are shallow and the pain is slipping away. Death is slowly approaching. Losing my grip, I start slipping downward.

He quickly adjusts his grip. One large arm supporting my butt, the other across my shoulders touching parts of my wounds, but I can't feel them anymore. Everything is starting to seem so peaceful. Why did I fear death? All my worries seem to fade away.

He dashes out of the house and into the forest.

"Please hold on, my little human."

"HOW IS SHE? Will she make it?" a deep voice asks, lined with worry.

"It'll be touch and go," a woman's voice says. "She's extremely injured. We put her on a ventilator because one of her lungs collapsed. Her organs are bruised, and she lost almost forty percent of her blood. She has a few broken ribs and a concussion... I'm surprised she wasn't dead when you brought her in. She's one tough human."

Is she talking about me?

"Yes...she is," the man murmurs. At first, I think he's answering me, but soon realize he's agreeing with the woman in the room.

I try to open my eyes, but they're too heavy. I try to speak, but there's something in my throat.

"I think she's waking up," the man says with a touch of panic.

"What? She shouldn't be waking up yet," she says. "I'll give her more of the sedative."

He hums in response. There's warmth and a slight pressure in my limp hand. The warmth spreads and becomes tingles throughout my whole body. "You'll be okay, Ellie, just hold on for me," the man says softly. My hand is lightly squeezed.

Ah. My hand is being held, that makes sense. Who's holding it though? He seems so familiar. Blackness ebbs its way into my mind as the drugs take effect.

Ash

I'm a fool, an utterly stupid fool. Somehow Zac found out about the time I've spent with Ellie. That's the only explanation I can come up with for why he would target her.

I left to go back to the pack, to show my face, to take suspicion off of my whereabouts. But even after having been gone for weeks in the past, I found Zac and his betas sniffing around, asking others where I was. I even caught a few of his pals following me around. On Halloween they got sick of asking where I hide, and instead decided to get rough with me. Usually they leave me to heal somewhere alone, but that night they must have followed me.

I curse at myself.

I should've been more careful, should've stayed away.

But I couldn't.

I had to see her, had to check up on her. Even if it was in the shadows as a wolf.

But then she saw me. She *ran* to me.

And when she fell asleep snuggled up against me, on top of forget-me-nots and snow...I knew I would never be able to stay away.

I've never felt such a deep connection with anyone else before. She's special, I know that. When it came time for her to leave the barn, I couldn't walk away then, just like I couldn't walk away now. I had to get to know her. And I wanted her to know me as a man.

She may be human and I lycan, but I want her. As we laid under the aurora borealis, I realized that I didn't want to give her up. Didn't want to let her go. Didn't want to be just a wolf to her anymore. I wanted my arms wrapped around her, holding her tight. But I didn't know how to tell her the truth. Because what would she say, what would she do, if I told her?

I swear under my breath and look at our joined hands. That doesn't matter anymore though. She knows, and now she's hurt.

Bringing her hand to my lips, I kiss it. I notice bruising on her wrist and clench my jaw, anger boiling up.

How could I have let this happen?

Zac and the other lycan got away; one of his buddies, I'm sure. But I'll remember his scent—rotten and metallic.

Zac has to come back anyway and face the challenge I issued. But I'll find the other. I'll make them both pay for what they did to her.

They almost killed her. So if making them pay means killing them, even Zac, then so be it. If I had arrived just a little later, she would've been gone.

My mind continues to rage as Ellie's body finally relaxes from the sedative Kathy gave her. I gaze upon her face. A bandage covers one cheek where angry claw marks reside. The rest of her face is swollen and covered with bruises. Her body is in much worse shape with broken ribs, shredded skin, and torn muscle. I thought my heart had stopped when I saw her beaten and bleeding on the kitchen floor. Seeing her so pale, and her heartbeat so weak, nearly killed me.

I grip her hand in mine, the warmth of her skin reminding me she's alive. Hearing her heartbeat with my own ears and watching her chest rise and fall with my own eyes are the only things that keep me calm.

"Ash, you should go clean yourself up," Kathy, the pack doctor, says, standing at the end of Ellie's bed. "She's out of the woods now."

I look down at myself and see red. My anger simmers under the surface. Ready to burst and attack anyone in my path.

Wearing only a pair of boxers, Ellie's blood coats my bare chest. I've never been more grateful for my speed. If I was just a little slower, I'm not sure I would've made it in time.

They almost killed her.

Why was Zac there? Who was that other lycan? Why did they attack her? Zac has never attacked anyone else before because of me. Why now?

Another thought pops in my head, connecting dots.

Ellie first came here a month and a half ago, but living here was only ever short-term for her. She never planned on staying. She said as much. Is this why? Is Zac somehow connected to her past? Has she been running from something? Someone?

Maybe I'm wrong in assuming this has anything to do with me. So that leaves the question, who was the lycan with Zac?

"Ash," Kathy repeats, interrupting my thoughts.

Gritting my teeth, I nod and let go of Ellie's hand. "Could you?" I ask.

"Of course." Kathy takes my seat once I stand. I won't be able to do anything if someone's not there watching over her.

I thank Kathy and head into the room's connecting bathroom.

When I walk in, there's already a pile of clothes laid out for me.

Every year, members of the pack donate clothes to the hospital, since lycans tend to go through them faster than normal. But I'll need to make a call to Russell to bring over my things. I'm not ready to leave Ellie today. Or tomorrow.

I keep one ear tuned to her heartbeat in the other room while turning on the shower.

The hospital dialed Emma and Russell while I watched Kathy and a few nurses work on Ellie. They first called Russell to get the blood cleaned up and have his construction company begin repairs to her kitchen and doors. Next they warned Emma about her place. She wanted details, and when they asked me, I had none to give. I had time to figure out a logical explanation, but my mind has been completely consumed by Ellie.

I place my hands on the counter and look in the mirror. My shift is still close to the surface. My eyes glow and my canines ache to be released. Veins bulge up my forearms as I strain to contain myself. I can't shift here. Not when Ellie needs me. Not when I need to be near her.

When steam billows from the shower, I remove my boxers and throw them away. Even if I could save them, they're covered in Ellie's blood. A reminder that she almost died today. I fist the wall next to me and mutter a curse when it goes through the drywall. I'm going to need to fix that before she wakes up.

I throw the shower curtain aside and step in. Letting the boiling water run down me in ribbons of red. I close my eyes. *So much blood.* How did she survive losing so much blood?

Tears mix in with the water before I can stop them.

I almost lost her today.

If I was just a little later, she would've died.

My parents' cold, lifeless bodies laying on the floor pops into my head. I push the images out of my mind.

But she didn't die. Not like them. I made it in time.

I should've been there sooner. I should've known something was wrong.

Another curse passes my lips as I yank the handle down, turning off the water.

Stepping out of the shower, I grab a towel and start drying off.

I need to find out more about what really happened and why. But first, I need to make sure she stays alive. That she's taken care of.

Because she's *my* little human.

Whether she realizes it or not.

18

Ellie

"*Mom, do you and dad really have to go tonight?*" *I ask, watching my mom put on some light makeup while I sit on the closed toilet seat in their master bathroom. Her golden curls match mine. Dad and her have an emergency meeting tonight for some group they are a part of.*

My mom pauses and glances at me through the mirror before turning around. She places a hand on my knee. "I know you were looking forward to our family movie night, but we'll do it tomorrow night instead. Okay?"

I nod but can't hide my disappointment. "Okay."

"Now, go get ready for bed. I'll be in soon to tuck you in. The babysitter will be here after you fall asleep."

"Fine," I say with a huff. I jump off the toilet seat and walk to my room.

After changing into my pajamas and brushing my teeth, I head to my parents' room, but stop outside their door when I hear them talking.

"We need to tell her, Gabriel. She just turned eleven. Most children know by now."

Are they talking about me? What don't I know? I look through the crack of the open door to my parents' room. They are standing at the end of their bed; my dad's putting on a tie.

He sighs. "Addison, I don't think she's ready. She's not like the other kids. Besides, no one even knows she exists."

"She has the right to know who she really is."

Who I really am? No one knows I exist?

"It doesn't matter," my father says. "It's still years before anything happens. We have time."

My mom walks to him and takes the tie into her own hands, helping him. "I know we do, but it's better to prepare her in advance. I don't want her in the dark about what she'll have to go through." She pulls the tie taut and pats his chest, giving him a pointed look.

He sighs, but the corners of his mouth tug upward into a smile. "I can never say no to you. We'll tell her tomorrow."

"That's what I love about you—you can't resist me." She stands up on her toes and gives him a light peck. "Let's go say goodnight to her."

I quickly turn away and dash back into my room. I make it back into my bed and throw the covers over myself just as they walk in.

"Sweetheart?"

I hum in response as I try to settle my rapid breathing.

"We just wanted to come in and say goodnight before you fell asleep."

I turn over and look at them. She turned the hall light on, so all I can see is their silhouettes.

She walks over to my bed and sits down, the light shines on her face. She's so young compared to my other friends' moms.

"I also wanted to say I love you."

I sit up and give her a hug. "I love you too, Mom."

My dad walks over and sits down beside me and places a kiss on my forehead. He wraps an arm around me. "Sorry we have to reschedule. But we'll have fun tomorrow."

"I know, Daddy, and I'm going to hold you to it."

He chuckles and ruffles my hair. "I look forward to it." He squeezes me once more before standing and waiting for Mom.

She urges me to lay back down and tucks me in and plants a kiss on my cheek. "Love you, sweetheart. We'll see you in the morning."

I nod and give them a small smile. I watch as they walk out of my room, wondering what she and Dad were talking about. She closes the door, engulfing the room in darkness.

I WAKE UP CHOKING—SOMETHING is lodged in my throat. Bringing my hands up to my mouth, I try to remove whatever it is.

My hands are pushed down, and I open my eyes, panic swelling in my chest, and find myself surrounded by strangers. Who are these people? Where am I?

My heart pounds as I try freeing my arms, but they tighten their grips. Tears well up in my eyes as my chest tightens. My fight and flight instincts are trying to take over. I want to scream, but I can't. I can't breathe.

I gag around the object still in my throat. *I need to get out of here.*

"Ellie darling, it's okay. They are trying to help you," a deep, soothing male says. I freeze. My gaze rises to Ash hovering above me.

He saved me.

A plastic tube is removed from my mouth. The nurses check my vitals before looking at Ash, who nods to them and they leave the room.

"Ash?" I croak, my voice sounding strange to my own ears.

"I'm here," Ash says and helps me sit up. He hands me a glass of water.

My arm shakes as I try to hold it, but I'm so weak that it starts to slip through my fingers.

Ash's reflexes move like lightning, his hand closes around mine to keep the cup from falling.

Tingles travel up from my hand and through my arm—it's a shock to my system. I've felt them before, but my senses seem heightened. Ash's eyes connect with mine, seeming to pierce them with his intensity.

I avert my gaze and let go, allowing him to hold the glass. He gently leads it to my lips and helps me drink.

"Where am I?" I ask once my thirst is quenched.

I notice the room I'm in. I've never actually been in a hospital before, but I've seen enough shows and movies to tell that I'm probably in one. Sterile with little to no decorations. There's a chair on my right next to a door that the nurses left through and a couch on my left near an open door that appears to be a bathroom.

"A hospital," he says, as he sets my now empty glass down.

"How long have I been here?"

"Five days."

"What?" I frown. I've been here for *five days*?

"Do you remember what happened?"

Memories start flooding back. I look down at myself, patting my ribs.

I'm wearing a hospital gown, but I can feel bandages against my skin under it. "I'm alive," I say. My hands go to my face next. It's tender, and I have a bandage covering my left cheek.

My eyes widen as I peer up at him. It wasn't a dream. The memories are jumbled, but it's slowly coming together. One thing I remember clearly is Ash bursting in. "You saved me."

"I did." He pulls the chair closer to the bed and sits. "Why do you sound surprised?"

"I...I left you."

A scowl forms on his face. "And you think because you were angry with me that I'd suddenly stop caring? That I wouldn't try to keep you safe?"

"No. I just..."

His eyes blaze as he continues, "Especially when I know you're running from something, other than me."

My mouth gapes open. "How?"

"I put it together." He leans closer, his eyes searching mine. "What are you running from, Ellie? Or yet, *who* are you running from?"

My mouth snaps shut, and I avert my gaze. "It doesn't concern you."

His hands form fists. "I think it does," he says through a clenched jaw. He sweeps an arm out, gesturing to me. "Look at you, you're in a *hospital*. If I wasn't there, you'd be *dead*."

I school my face. "It just means I need to move on to the next place sooner than I planned."

"And if they follow you?" he asks, his tone hard.

I straighten my spine despite the pain. "I'll just keep going. It wouldn't be the first time. Even if it's staying at rundown places with druggies or homeless people, I've always found a place."

His nostrils flare. "And you say that with pride? Those aren't places you want to stay, Ellie."

"What choice do I have? The only option is *to keep moving*."

"You plan on running for the rest of your life?" He gives me an exasperated look. "How long *have* you been running?"

How old am I? "About three years."

Ash clenches his jaw. "Three years too long."

"What? And staying with him was the better option?" I ask, folding my arms over my chest. But I quickly uncross them as it stretches the wounds on my back.

A growl rips from his throat, but I don't feel threatened or scared. "*Him* is the other male. The dark-haired one that hurt you, right? What's his name?"

"How do you know it wasn't the other man?"

His gaze burns as he stares at my injured cheek. "I know the other. I'll deal with him later."

"He didn't hurt me."

Ash's eyes snap to mine. "He didn't?" Then they narrow. "But he was there and didn't stop it."

"He tried," I say. Not until it was practically too late, but still...he tried.

"Not hard enough." He growls out the words, sending a shiver through me, but not from fear. His eyes soften as he notices. "I'm sorry. How are you feeling?"

It's hard to swallow as tears burn my eyes. How can he go from angry to sweet so fast? "Could be better." I meet his gaze. "Thank you, for saving me."

His face falls as he stiffens. "I shouldn't have been saving you. I should've been protecting you. You shouldn't have gotten hurt at all."

"How could you have known?" I ask. "I'm just lucky you got there when you did."

"I'm still sorry."

"You're apologizing for not saving me fast enough?" I shake my head, but cut it short when a headache flares up. "Don't be so hard on yourself. You did everything right."

A corner of his mouth curls. "You're too good to me."

I sigh and readjust how I'm laying, my body becoming more aware of just how injured I am. "So, you know Zac?" I ask, trying to distract myself.

His head jerks back. "*You* know Zac?"

The lights seem to grow brighter. I close my eyes against the glare as the headache worsens. "Not really." My voice comes out soft. "I ran into him at a grocery store a couple weeks ago." Literally.

"That's how he..."

I peek an eye open. "How he what?"

His brows are scrunched together. "Knew about you. It's why I left. Other lycans had started to scout near the area, I just thought it was because I was careless."

"Why would it matter?"

"Apparently it does. Since Zac led..." He trails off, waiting for a name.

Reclosing my eyes, I let out a sigh. The pounding in my head won't stop. "Marcus."

"Right. Since he led Marcus to you."

And now I need to move.

But I'm tired of running.

Moving four times a year for the past three years has been exhausting to say the least, and honestly I moved more often than that when I couldn't find a place to stay and just went from abandoned lot to abandoned lot.

Emma. I sit up, my eyes popping open. Bile rises to the surface. I clamp a hand over my mouth to keep it in while holding my stomach with the other.

Ash touches my arm. "Ellie? Are you alright?"

I shake my head, but that just makes everything worse. I feel disoriented. The dizziness is getting worse with each passing second, but I need to know. Uncovering my mouth, I force out, "Emma."

His hand moves up and down my arm in a soothing manner. "Emma is okay, she's staying with Tom. No one else got hurt. Emma also let her sister know—Jane, I believe she said was her name—that you're okay."

A weight lifts off my shoulders. I can't believe I forgot about her for a moment. Just the thought of her getting hurt makes my stomach twist worse. I groan as another wave of nausea comes. "I feel sick."

Ash's touch leaves my arm. There's the sound of footsteps and the opening of a door. "Kathy."

I flinch at his panic-laced yell and press a palm to my forehead as I lean back into the bed.

Sharp pain erupts along my back. I let out a harsh gasp and slowly move forward off my wounds.

But in this position, each time I breathe, knives stab me from the inside out.

Another wave of dizziness hits and spots dot my vision. I grip onto the railing on the left side of my bed to ground myself. Am I about to pass out?

I don't remember it hurting this bad in the past. I thought I would be used to pain by now, but I was wrong.

Can you ever really get used to pain?

Or do you just become numb and shut your senses off?

Ash is back and grabs my arm to steady me. "What hurts?"

"Everything," I whisper, tears pricking my eyes.

Glancing over at him, through blurry eyes, concern lines his gaze as he looks me over. "You shouldn't be feeling this much pain." His voice is strained.

Noticing me watching him, he cups the back of my head and gently pulls me toward him, allowing me to rest my forehead on his stomach. "Just rest like this until Kathy comes."

Even overwhelmed with pain, it doesn't escape my notice that he's on a first name basis with the doctor.

I take a deep breath through my nose, breathing in his scent, and it calms me, even easing some of the pain. Ash's hand tangles into my hair as his fingers massage my scalp.

How could I doubt Ash's intentions with me? Action speaks louder than words. He's been taking care of me from the beginning. And it's not like he was trying to be purposely deceitful.

But I'm so overwhelmed with everything.

I press a hand to my chest as an ache manifests. The monitor startles me, beeping loudly. Ash allows me to look up when the door opens.

A woman in a white lab coat with long blonde hair slicked back into a sleek ponytail strides in with two nurses in tow. "Hello, Ellie, I'm Dr. Kathy," she says while putting gloves on. "Can you tell me where it hurts?"

"My head and back, and my chest feels tight. I'm also nauseous."

Her eyes narrow on the screen behind me as she takes a step closer, her hands outreached. I involuntarily flinch back. She holds her hands up, palms facing me. "I'm just going to check your heart rate. Can I do that?"

Taking a deep breath, I nod. Ash's hand falls to the back of my neck, lightly squeezing. "I'll be right here with you."

Dr. Kathy uses her stethoscope on my wrist, her mouth silently moving as her gaze unfocuses.

She peers down at me after a moment. "Do you suffer from anxiety, Ellie?"

"I do."

She steps away and removes her gloves. "You'll need more pain meds, but I believe you also suffered a panic attack."

I rub my forehead. "This was different from my past ones."

She nods as if expecting my response. "Panic attacks don't always manifest the same. But the signs this time were your high pulse, the tightening of your chest, and nauseousness." Her gaze moves back to the heart monitor. "It seems you're doing better now. Are you still in any pain?" I nod and she turns to the nurses and rattles off a few instructions to them.

Once they leave, she turns back to Ash and me. "I'm having them bring me some pain meds for you. If these don't work, the best I can do is give you a sedative to sleep through the worst of it."

My eyes widen, I don't want to be sedated. I don't want to miss another five days. I want answers and time to wrap my head around everything.

Ash looks down at me and grabs my hand when he notices my petrified stare. "What is it?"

"I don't want to go under."

He squeezes my hand. "Then I'll make sure it doesn't happen." He lowers himself until we're eye-level. His eyes are so warm, despite the iciness to them. There's a little furrow of worry between his eyes, and I have a strange desire to smooth it out.

"I can hear how fast your heart is racing, Ellie darling. Take a deep breath with me. In...and out." We take a few more deep breaths together until my body relaxes. A relieved smile appears on his face. "That's my girl. You're going to be okay. I'm not going to leave you."

I nod and tighten my grip on his hand. In this cold and sterile room, he's my light and warmth.

His gaze moves to Dr. Kathy behind me.

"Ellie?" Dr. Kathy says. I look over my shoulder at her as one of the nurses begins to add something to my IV. "Do you normally burn through medicine fast?"

"What?"

"I needed to double your sedative and, to err on the side of caution, we doubled your pain meds. But now I'm tripling it."

I glance between her, the nurses, and Ash. "That's not normal, right?"

She shakes her head. "It's not."

"Well, I've never been in a hospital before, so I couldn't tell you."

"Oh." She looks down at her hands. "Take these," she says and hands me two circular pills. "They are for the pain. I can't give you anymore after this until later today."

I turn for my water, but Ash is already there holding it out for me. I reach for it, but he doesn't hand it to me. Side-eyeing him, I place the pills in my mouth as he brings the glass to my lips.

"I would give you anxiety medication if they worked instantly," Dr. Kathy continues as I swallow the pills, "but they can take up to a month to begin working. Even then it might not work, and we'd have to try a different kind. Would you at least like me to prescribe something?"

I shake my head as Ash sets the water back on the table. "No, thank you." I don't plan on being here for a month, let alone two. I can't try new drugs while on the run. Besides, I don't have the money for this. "When can I leave? And how much is this going to cost?"

"I'd advise not leaving here for another week. As for the bills..." Her eyes cut to Ash behind me. "You'd have to talk to Ash about that. He insisted all expenses go through him."

My head snaps to Ash and I grimace at the movement. "Why?"

"I'll let you two discuss that in private," Dr. Kathy says. "If you need anything else, just have Ash come get me or push this button on your bed." She taps the side of the railing that's attached to the bed and leaves, followed by the two nurses.

Ash sits down in the chair beside me again, keeping hold of my hand, slowly rubbing his thumb across the back of it. His gaze is unfocused as he stares at the sheets.

"Ash?"

He blinks and meets my gaze. "Yes?"

"Why are you paying for my stay?"

"Because I want to. It's my fault you're in this mess. Besides, I want to take care of you."

"First of all, it wasn't. Marcus was bound to catch up to me. You can't pay for me. I don't have insurance, and this hospital visit will cost a small fortune."

"Money isn't a problem for me."

"So you're rich?"

He chuckles. "I guess you could say that."

I frown. "I still don't want to take your money."

"And you're going to pay for it?"

My eyes widen. "I, um..." I can't use Jane's money. I know she would insist, but I can't force her to pay for this when she's already paid for so much.

He sighs. "I thought so. You don't have the funds and I need to spend my money somehow, anyway. I have too much of it. Although I'd rather spend it by showering you with gifts than hospital bills, but I'll take what I can get." He gives me a half-smile with eyes full of mirth.

I let go of his hand to slightly smack him on the arm.

His smile grows as he grabs my hand back, placing a kiss on my knuckles. He lets his lips linger on my skin. His warm breath brushes across my knuckles as he asks, "Are you still mad at me?"

My heart aches at his puppy-dog eyes. I shake my head. "No. Just no more hiding things from me, okay?"

"Deal."

There's a light knock on the door, interrupting our conversation. It opens to reveal a petite woman, maybe in her mid-twenties, with pale skin and light-blonde hair styled in a long bob holding a tray.

She sets it down on the table next to me and turns it so it's above my lap. She keeps her eyes downcast as she speaks. "I'm Alice. I'll be handling all your meals while you're here." She takes off the lid of the meal, revealing chicken, mashed potatoes, green beans, and a cup of fruit. How am I supposed to eat all of this? "Would you like water, milk, or juice?"

"Water, please."

Alice nods and accepts my water cup from Ash then leaves the room. When she comes back, she places the full cup next to my meal. She does all of this while avoiding my gaze. "Is there anything else you'd like?"

I shake my head, but realize she still isn't looking at me. "No, I'm okay. Thank you."

She nods again before rushing out the room.

"That was odd," I say.

"She's been conditioned to act a certain way."

"What?" I rub my eyes.

He slumps in the chair, his solemn eyes focused on the closed door. "There's a lot you still don't know about lycans."

My eyelids grow heavy and droop. "I would like to know more." I fight back a yawn.

"You're tired. We can talk more about this tomorrow. You also still need to tell me about Marcus."

"I know."

"Do you want to take a nap now or after you eat?"

"Now," I respond.

Ash stands and moves the table away. I shift onto my side. The pain meds are in full effect. I cover my mouth as a yawn takes over my face. Ash grabs the remote to lower my bed until it's almost completely flat. He steps away, but hesitates, his gaze moving from the bed, to the chair, to the door.

"What is it?" I ask sleepily.

He rubs both hands down his face. It's the first sign he's shown of his exhaustion. I take a closer look at him and notice blue crescents under his eyes, the haggard mess of his hair, and his grown out facial hair.

"I think you need to sleep as well," I say.

He nods, but I can still see the conflict in his eyes.

"What's wrong?" I ask.

His gaze bores into mine. "I don't want to leave you."

I quirk a brow. "I never said you had to."

He frowns. "I don't want to sleep in the chair again."

"Then don't."

"Or the couch."

"Okay."

"I'm not sleeping on the floor, either."

A grin blooms on my face as I hold back a laugh. "Then don't."

His eyes light up and a smirk appears on his face. "Are you saying I can sleep with you?"

Heat creeps up my face. "Well, when you put it that way. No, you can't."

He laughs, but moves closer. "Scoot over, I don't want to hurt your back by sleeping behind you."

I scoot my way back with a smile still in place.

He presses a few buttons on the remote and the lights dim. He climbs into the bed. It's a tight fit, considering how tall he is, but it also feels right being so close to him. He shifts until he's comfortable, one hand on my hip, the other under the pillow. I relish in his warm, solid body against mine, my hands pressed up against his chest.

"This is strange," I murmur.

"How so?" he asks, his voice soft as he already begins to fall asleep.

"I don't feel anxious right now."

He hums. "Probably the pain meds kicking in, helping you relax."

"You've also always been a wolf when we've done this in the past."

His chest rumbles through my hands as he chuckles. "True, but it's always been me."

"It really has, hasn't it?" I snuggle closer against him and it isn't long before both of us are fast asleep.

117

19

Ellie

"Thanks, Alice," Ash whispers, but instead of us being on our sides like when we fell asleep, Ash is on his back, and I'm splayed across half his body. He has one arm wrapped around me, keeping me close, but avoiding my injuries.

I open my eyes to find the room still dark except for the blaring light coming from the slight crack in the open door. I watch Alice's back as she retreats from the room and notice there's a new tray of food on the moving table beside the bed.

"You're awake." Ash's chest rumbles through me.

I nod, my face still pressed against his chest.

"Are you hungry? Do you want food? Water? More medicine?"

I smile at his rapid-fire questions. "Water and medicine," I say, still groggy.

He helps me sit up then reaches over to the table to grab my water. "They brought in more pills earlier, but I didn't want them to wake you. Thought you needed the sleep."

Apparently, he was right since I slept through the night, even though I had already been asleep for five days. "Thank you," I mutter before downing the water and pills, only a slight tremor in my hands.

"How are you feeling?" he asks as we lay back down.

Blinking, I evaluate myself. I'm not in as much pain as I was yesterday. My head seems clearer, and some of the aches are gone. But I'm definitely not one hundred percent yet. "I'm doing okay. I slept better than I have in a long time, despite the tight fit."

His arm around me tightens. "The tight fit was the best part." His voice is rough. "Thank you for letting me sleep with you," he says.

I tilt my head up to gaze at his face. "Thank you for joining me." I reach up to touch his scruff—the hair on his face is surprisingly soft. He closes his eyes and hums.

"That feels good," he says.

I smile. "I'm glad."

I continue to explore the stubble on his face but examine his other features closer. The curve of his lips, the straightness of his nose, his hair against his light-brown skin, his long ebony eyelashes. I feather over his lips and he groans. He parts his lips and his tongue peeks out, licking the tips of my fingers.

My breath hitches as I jerk my hand back and a giggle bubbles up.

He smirks, his eyes still closed.

"You did that when I fed you candy, too."

He chuckles. "I did, didn't I?" He opens his eyes to peer down at me. "Sorry."

I shake my head with a smile. "Why?"

He shrugs, slightly jostling me. "I'm not sure. My bad attempt at flirting?"

In the middle of his sentence, there's a short knock on the door, and Dr. Kathy walks in.

A tint of red underlines Ash's light-brown skin.

I try to hide my grin by covering it with my hand, but he tugs my hand away and matches my smile. He helps me up, but leans close, saying softly in my ear, "Do you take pleasure in my discomfort?"

I shiver as his warm breath caresses over my skin. Even in the morning he smells good. How is that possible? "Maybe a little."

"Good morning," Dr. Kathy says, pulling on a set of gloves as she stands beside the bed. "May I?" She gestures to my back and I nod. I lean into Ash as she parts my gown to reveal my back. She gently removes the bandages before her fingers lightly probe my skin. "Does this hurt?" she asks.

"Not a lot, just a bit uncomfortable. But Ash just gave me some more pain meds."

She's silent for a moment as she continues to examine my back. "Huh."

"What?" I peer over my shoulder at my back then at her.

She glances at me as she grabs new bandages. She puts some kind of ointment on my wounds before covering my back. "You're just healing faster than I expected."

"That's good though, right?" I ask.

"Oh yes, of course. Just surprising." She ties my gown back up and lightly pats my shoulder. "I'm done now." I move over until I'm sitting beside Ash on the bed.

"So, how is she?" Ash asks.

"Everything is looking good. Better than she should, if I'm being honest."

Better than I should? Ash takes my hand and squeezes it.

I lean forward. "Does that mean I can leave sooner?"

She hesitates, looking between the two of us. "I'm not sure yet. Let me keep an eye on your injuries for a few more days before giving you a definite answer."

"Okay," I say. I really don't want to stay here longer than I have to. I don't like being confined.

"Ash, could I speak to you for a moment?"

"Sure."

Dr. Kathy shifts her weight when he doesn't move. She gestures with her head to the door. "Out in the hall, please."

His eyes narrow, but nods after a moment. He squeezes my hand before following Dr. Kathy into the hall. I lay down as a headache forms. Isn't that supposed to be covered with the medicine? Maybe I should ask for more once Ash comes back in.

"I wanted to talk to you about Ellie's injuries," I hear Dr. Kathy's muffled voice. Did they accidentally leave the door cracked?

"You said that she's healing well," Ash says, also muffled.

I turn my head and squint at the door.

"And she is. It's odd how fast she's healing, but that's not what I wanted to talk to you about."

"Then what did you want to talk to me about?" Ash asks.

"I wanted to speak to you about her back," she says. "Because of the amount of built up scar tissue, it reduced the amount of damage she received internally. I'm pretty sure it saved her life."

"And why did you need to discuss that with me without her? It sounds like a good thing."

I sit up and stare at the closed door. *How am I hearing this conversation?*

"Yes and no. Yes, because she would've died without that scar tissue. No, because it made me wonder what caused her to have so much. And I wanted to discuss this without her because of what I think it might mean."

"I see."

I squeeze my eyes shut as my heart pounds.

"Ash, I think she's been tortured." She pauses. "And not just once, but for an extended amount of time. Probably from the very person that recently did this to her. The wounds are similar."

I lay back down deep in thought. Is that what Marcus did? I know it was considered abuse, but torture? It makes it seem what he did was worse than I thought, if that's even possible.

The door flies open, and Ash strides in, a scowl etched onto his face. His eyes are blazing, promising pain, but when they connect with mine, they soften. I audibly swallow as he makes determined steps toward me.

I didn't imagine their conversation.

Ash stops right next to the bed, his entire body tense. "Who hurt you?"

"...Marcus."

"No, I mean before this." He gestures to me, still laying in bed. "Marcus made you run, but was he also the one who hurt you?"

I give a small nod as I clutch the thin hospital blanket to me.

He curses and lays a fist on my table, cracking it in half. He lets more choice words slip at the damage.

My chin wobbles as I try to hold back tears.

Uncontrollable shakes rack through my body as I realize just how close to death I really got. Marcus almost killed me. *He found me.* No matter how far I run, he will find me. He says he cares about my blood, but obviously not enough to keep me alive.

Ash levels with my face, completely different than he was a moment ago. His eyes are full of devotion, and his body is no longer taut with anger. He lightly nudges me to move over before joining me, his touches gentle and loving. He caresses my arms, my face, my neck. He cups the back of my head to pull me closer to him.

"I didn't mean to scare you. I'm sorry," he says into my hair, his voice rough with sorrow and self-loathing.

I press on his chest to lean away and look at him. "I'm not afraid of you," I say softly.

"I won't let him hurt you ever again. I'll protect you."

I sniffle. "I believe you."

He pulls me close once more. "Sleep. I'll hold and watch over you."

IT'S the sound of Alice entering with my lunch that wakes me this time. She's as quiet as a mouse, but I'm still able to hear her quiet shuffling of the trays before she leaves. I also feel the light touches from Ash, as he—almost absentmindedly—massages my scalp. He seems to do that a lot, not that I mind.

A buzzing sound goes off, and it sounds like it's coming from the bed.

Ash shifts his body while keeping me steady. He digs into his pocket and pulls out his phone. The screen lights his face as he reads whatever popped up. He stuffs it back in his pocket. His eyes connect with mine. "I have an errand I need to run." My body tenses. He must notice because he adds, "But you'll be safe here."

"Hospitals have visiting hours, right? What if Marcus gets in? What if—"

"Ellie, he won't be able to."

My chest is tight as my mind swirls with questions and possibilities. "How do you know? You won't be here, and he could pose as a visitor and—"

He pushes a finger against my lips. "And he still won't be able to. This is a pack hospital. Even though he's a lycan, he won't be able to come in."

"But what if Zac lets him in?"

He nods. "Zac may be alpha, but he isn't the head of the hospital. He has no say."

"Alpha? Who's the head?"

Ash grins. "Kathy. She doesn't normally let humans stay, but considering who attacked you and her love of my parents, she allowed it."

I gnaw on my lip. "So, this hospital has lycans who won't let him through?"

He nods. "You'll be safe. They won't even let Zac in if he tries. But neither have tried in the week you've been here."

"Okay, and this is a pack hospital."

"Yes," he says, and his smile grows. "And pack means the same as what you'd read from your fantasy novels."

"A group of wolf-shifters living together and there's some order to it?"

He laughs. "Yep, that about sums it up."

"And Zac is the alpha. What does that mean? Same as the books, too?"

"Yeah, but it's a bit different." His hand tangles into my hair and he begins to massage my scalp lightly. "Alpha or alpha couple are the head of the pack. They have two betas—a right- and left-hand man or woman—and a delta right under them that help run the pack. The delta is in charge of choosing a head warrior, head healer, and head hunter. All of them together make up the council of the pack."

"Alpha couple? Warrior, healer, hunter?"

"Right, sorry." He trails his other hand down my arm. "Alpha couple is what it sounds like. For example, Zac is the alpha, but say he mated—him and his mate would be the alpha couple together. Warriors, healers, and hunters are after the delta. They are all ranked the same, but the delta—with the help of the alphas and betas—chooses one from each group to be the head, usually the most skilled and trustworthy, and so on."

"And how do you know a warrior from a hunter? How do those three work?"

"The size of your wolf helps determine where you're placed. It's a good indicator of how much magic is in you. But it's also determined by skills, and what comes more naturally to you. Warriors are physical. Healers are spiritual. Hunters, or trackers as some call them, are the brains."

"Okay...and you are?"

A slow grin takes form on his face. "I'm smart and athletic, so it was close between warrior and hunter, but hunter won in the end."

I smile, smoothing my hand over his shirt. I can't see him being fully one or the other, so knowing it was tied seems right. It fits him.

"When do they determine where you're placed?" I ask.

"Usually sometime in your late twenties."

"And this is a pack hospital?" I repeat.

"Yes, Kathy is the head healer and runs the hospital, but it's for more than just our pack. Surrounding packs use this hospital as well."

"Do all healers work here?" I ask. "I can't really see Dr. Kathy being spiritual."

A rumble runs through me at his chuckle. "She's not, in the religious sense. It more relates to the spiritual aspects of healing your soul and body, whether that be through science or religion. Kathy is probably a bit of a hunter, too, now that I'm thinking about it." He lightly tugs one of my curls. "Anyway, not all healers work here. Some are therapists, while some work in spas or treatment centers. Usually anywhere that can be used for healing, whether that be emotionally, mentally, spiritually, magically, or physically."

"Magically? Like if something is wrong with the magic in your body?"

"Yep."

"Will you explain to me about magic now?" I ask, peering up at him.

"Nope," he says, popping the 'p' while bopping my nose. "That's a much longer explanation that I'll tell you at a different time. Right now, I need to head out." He helps me sit up before getting out of the bed. Grabbing his keys and a wallet off the table, he tips his head toward my lunch. "Eat. I'll be back tonight." He kisses me on the forehead then walks out the door.

Ash

*N*ight has fallen, but I'm back earlier than I expected. I'm almost to Ellie's room with a book and a bag in hand when Alice stops me. She wrings her hands together, keeping her blue eyes downcast. "Can I talk to you for a moment, Ash?"

"Of course. What's wrong?"

"I just came from Ellie's room," she s ays softly with a shaky voice. "And at first, I thought it was because she needed sleep, but now…"

"But now?" I say, trying to keep my voice as non-threatening as possible.

Her throat slightly bobs as she swallows. "But now, after today, I believe something is wrong."

"What do you mean? What happened?" I ask, panic beginning to rise.

Alice wraps her arms around herself. "She's barely touched any of the meals I've brought her. I thought maybe she didn't like the food, but when I asked, she said it was fine." Alice's spine straightens, despite her gaze leveled to my chest. "She barely eats, and I thought it best to speak to you about my concerns."

Why isn't she eating? Foolish little human. Don't you know how fragile you are?

"Thank you, Alice. I agree. I'm glad you brought it to my attention."

Her eyes widen as they lift to my chin, but her gaze doesn't pass any further. She tucks a strand of her hair behind her ears. She gives me a small nod. "Thank you for listening."

"Alice, you know I will always listen. Foster and Russell would too," I add for good measure.

Her mouth parts. "I know. Do you..." She bites her lip. "Do you think Ellie will be okay?"

"Yes, she'll be okay. I'll make sure of it."

Her shoulders slump in relief. "Good. Good." She glances behind her while biting her lower lip. "I need to get back. Thank you again," she says before racing off.

Sighing, I watch her retreating back. Alice has been picked on since she was little, even before she could shift, because her mom was human. Foster, Russell, and I have always tried to make her feel wanted in our pack, but there's only so much we can do. And after my parents were killed and Foster left the pack, she grew even further apart from Russell and me.

I glance at the book in my hand as I turn to Ellie's door.

Walking in, my heart lifts at Ellie's smile, her eyes shine as she watches me stride toward her.

My phone buzzes, and I hold back a sigh as I pull it out. I see Ellie eyeing the book in my hand, but I've already decided she can't have it until she eats. Looking at my screen, I curse under my breath as I see a text message from Russell.

Expect a call from Foster. I told him about your "little challenge".

Just as I finish reading, Foster's name pops up as an incoming call. I quickly decline. I can sense Ellie's curious gaze. Despite her not connecting me and my wolf, she's smart. She's quick to notice things, sometimes what others wouldn't.

A text message pops up, this time from Foster.

If you don't answer, I'll contact Kathy.

Another message pops up underneath it.

Yes, I know where you are.

I swear again and hold back a smile when Ellie giggles.

"What's making you have such a foul mouth?" Ellie asks.

A smirk tugs my lips on one side. "If you knew, you'd be swearing too."

She laughs, and it's a balm to my aching soul. Ever since I failed to protect her, I haven't been able to rest well unless she's in sight.

"I doubt it," she says.

The phone rings again. Foster's name pops up, but this time I answer instead of declining. I sit down in my designated chair beside Ellie's bed, placing the bag on the ground.

"Hey," I answer.

"Don't 'hey' me." My smile grows at the angry British accent on the other line.

"What exactly did Russell tell you?" I ask.

"Did you really challenge Zac?"

I sigh, so everything. "Yes, I did."

"And the human is okay," he says.

One of my brows rises in surprise. "That wasn't a question."

"Alice told me."

"You two still talk?" I ask. "She's always been more open with you."

"Because you and Russell are too intimidating, but we don't chat as much as I'd like," he says.

I scowl. "I'm not intimidating."

Ellie smiles and mouths, *you are.*

She chuckles as I let out a mock growl. "I'm not as intimidating as Russell."

"You're with her right now, aren't you?" he asks.

"I am."

"Put me on speaker, mate."

"No." There's no way I'm letting charming Foster talk to her. "You'll meet her, eventually."

"So, you're serious about her then."

I gaze at Ellie, taking in her, lounging in the uncomfortable bed as she channel surfs. Her hair is messy from sleep, and she's still wearing the horribly ugly hospital gown that still seems to entice me. Her eyes aren't on me now, but whenever she blesses me with her gaze, her vibrant green-brown eyes radiate with kindness and strength. "I am."

"I'm glad you found her. Does she know about you?"

I let out a small laugh. "I guess you didn't get the full story from Russell. She's known for about two weeks now."

"And she's okay with it?" he asks.

Ellie tucks a strand of hair behind her ear as takes a sip of her water.

"I have no idea," I say.

"Do you think she'll stay with you?"

"I hope so. She'll have to stay with me until I know she'll be safe." Her gaze snaps to me. *Ah, caught the little eavesdropper.* I grin as her eyes narrow. She had no idea what I was planning.

He sighs through the phone. "Good, and Zac?"

My grin drops. "It'll happen in three weeks." I don't want to think too much about the challenge. I don't want to think about the outcome even more.

"Excellent, I'll be back in time."

I straighten. "Foster, you don't—"

"I do. It's time I come back anyway. You know Russell and I will always have your back."

I relax against the chair. I would never ask them to go against an alpha, but knowing they'll stand behind me without having to ask is a weight lifted off my shoulders. And if I win, I'd have to pick new betas and a delta. Russell and Foster are my first two picks. Maybe Sophie as my delta, if she and Russell can get along.

"I appreciate it," I say, but I don't elaborate.

"What about that other lycan?" Foster asks.

My entire body tenses. "Marcus," I growl softly into the phone, trying not to alert Ellie, but her hands grip the blanket tighter.

"And you've never seen him before," he states rather than asks.

"No," I say through clenched teeth. "I haven't, but Ellie knows him."

"That's…not good. You need help protecting your girl?"

I smile. *My girl*, I like that.

"Probably. I'm going to have shifts around my home with only lycans I can trust. But I'm going to have to let you go. I'll see you soon."

"Talk soon."

I click off then turn my phone off. It's time to get answers from Ellie, but first, to put some much-needed food in her belly.

21

Ellie

Once Ash hangs up, I turn off the television. I'm buzzing with the need to see what book he brought. It's been calling to me as it rests on his lap—face down—the entire time he's been on the phone. I find it highly unfair that he didn't just give it to me while he was talking. Instead, I had to eavesdrop while he was chatting with Foster, pretending to search for something to watch.

And I have some concerns.

Like me staying with him.

I may have forgiven him and believe his whole wolf-shifter thing, but once I get discharged, I'm running far and fast.

"Are you hungry?"

I blink. *What?* Out of everything he could've said, that was last on the list. "Not particularly. Why?"

"Alice told me about your eating habits."

"My eating habits?"

He nods and leans back with his arms crossed, suddenly all business-like. "You can't get this book until I see you eat. Everything."

"What, am I five suddenly?"

His eyes narrow. "Your eating is worse than a five-year-old."

"No one can eat all their food all the time, Ash."

"But you barely touch yours—ever."

I sigh. "Alright, you might have a point. But I know I have this problem, so it's fine."

He gives me an exasperated look. "That doesn't make it 'fine', Ellie. What makes it fine is if you're going to do something to fix it. So, are you?"

"Fix it?" I bite my lip. He nods, and I let out a pent-up breath. "I was starting to do better until I got hospitalized. I didn't eat for five days before I woke up. Marcus entered my life again, and I'm itching all the time with a headache that won't seem to go away."

He grows still.

His eyes catch on all the red marks on my body from scratching. "I'm sorry I didn't notice sooner," he says, leaning closer, scooting to the edge of his chair. "I'll talk to Kathy about your headaches and itching. But with the other thing, let me help you." His eyes are earnest as he looks at me.

"It won't be easy for me to change."

"I don't expect it to be."

"It's been going on since I was thirteen."

"And you're twenty now, right?" he asks.

I nod. "Seven years."

The corners of his mouth turn down. "That's a long time, and it'll take a while to help you, but"—he gestures to my food—"we'll start now and slowly increase your intake. We can talk to Kathy tomorrow about everything and get her opinion to see if we need to be referred to anyone."

I sniffle and rub my eyes as tears threaten to spill. Why does his concern and kindness affect me so deeply? "And the book?" I eye it.

He chuckles. "Still can't have it until you eat, but I won't force you to eat everything. I didn't realize how big of an issue this was for you."

I wring my blanket. "Yeah," I say softly.

"Ellie," Ash says quietly as he takes my hands. "It's nothing to be ashamed of or embarrassed about. It's a disorder, and we'll get through it together."

"A forced disorder."

He blinks, rubbing just above one eyebrow. "What?"

I bite my lip, considering telling him. Letting out a pent-up breath, I say, "Marcus...barely gave me enough food to survive when I was under his 'care'." My gaze drops to our joined hands. His grip tightens, but it's not painful. "Even after, while on the run, I didn't carry much food with me. Took up too much space."

"Who is Marcus to you?" Ash asks so quietly I almost don't catch his question.

My hands tremble as memories flood in. "He...he was my foster father. I went to him and his wife when I was thirteen."

"Why is he chasing you?"

I shrug, keeping my gaze on our hands. "He apparently wants my blood."

His brows rise. "That's...concerning and not what I was expecting you to say."

"I escaped three years ago and have been running ever since. It's why I can't stay here."

"I'll come with you then. I already told you that I want to be wherever you are."

I remove my hands. "It's not that simple, Ash."

He takes my hands back. "But it is."

"He won't give up. Marcus is relentless and angry. You saw what he did when he finally found me. You could die."

"And what about you?" His words come out low with anger. "Do you even realize how close to death you got?" He clenches his jaw. "I almost lost you."

I flinch. "What does that have to do with anything?"

He gives me an incredulous look. "You almost dying has every-

133

thing to do with it." He takes a fortifying breath, trying to contain his anger. "I know I failed in protecting you, but I promise I won't again. There are so many things I wish I could've changed, but I'm going to make it right. I care about you and want you safe."

I blink away tears. "You didn't fail, Ash," I whisper. "You've been doing everything right. I just—I can't chance you getting hurt because I care about you too."

He pauses before a slow smile grows. "You care about me?"

Swallowing, I give him a nod.

"So, you understand how I feel about you getting hurt and why I can't just let you leave without me."

I bite my lip. "I understand, but it's still not happening."

He closes his eyes and inhales through his nose. "You're going to be the death of me."

"Actually." I tilt my head. "I'm doing this to keep you alive—you really should be thanking me."

He shakes his head and lets out a sigh. "Tell me more about Marcus."

"Are you sure you want to know?"

He closes his eyes as he inhales deeply through his nose. His eyes pierce mine when he opens them. "Yes. I need to know."

"Okay."

"While you eat."

I glare at him but remove the lid of the meal, revealing a loaded sandwich cut in half and a side salad. I grimace at the amount of food that's been stuffed between the slices of bread. "I would also like to call Jane."

He nods, with his arms resting on his knees. "Emma told me she's kept her updated on you. But you can call after you eat and tell me about Marcus."

"And see the book."

His grin is fast. "And *keep* the book."

My brows rise as I grab one of the halves. "I would very much like that. I've been dying to read something."

His eyes flash with distress. "Poor choice of words, Ellie darling."

"Ah, sorry." I take a bite, hearing the crunch of the lettuce as my teeth sink in. I cover my mouth before speaking. "Tell me more about lycans while I eat then I'll talk after." Talking while eating is not the best look, I'm sure. But I'm also in a butt ugly gown and deeply in need of a shower, so I can't really look worse right now.

He leans back in the chair, his eyes tracking my movements. "I'm not really sure where to start." He stops to collect his thoughts.

"Packs?" I offer with food still in my mouth.

He nods. "Packs are like you mentioned, a group of lycans, but there are hundreds of them throughout the world. Each pack is run by either an alpha or an alpha couple."

Swallowing, I hold up a finger. "Why have a couple when there's already an alpha?" I hold up a second finger. "And mated?" I squeak and take a sip of my water. Isn't that when two animals come together and make babies? I choke on water at the thought.

Concern is etched on his face. "You alright?"

I nod and gesture for him to proceed.

He eyes me before sitting back again. "We encourage mating and having a family, and having a partner is a family. From there you can build upon it if you want. Someone to guide and love your family with you. It's the same with a pack. Two leaders are better than one, right?"

"I like that," I say, taking another bite.

He matches my smile. "Me too. My parents were the alpha couple before they…died." He clears his throat. "I got to watch how they work firsthand. And mated is like marriage in human terms, but on a deeper level."

I let out a breath. Not as bad as I thought. They aren't animals. "And destined mates?" I mumble around my food, remembering him mentioning it when I first found out about him being a wolf.

"There are two different types of mates. Chosen and destined. We believe we have destined mates from the magic that we were created from."

"Destined mates are kind of like soulmates?" I ask, but he gestures to my food, so I take another bite.

"Yes, but they are rare to find."

"So, that's why there's a thing called chosen mate," I say between bites.

"Exactly. It means they chose their mate without fate intervening."

"So, if you meet your destined mate, you won't have a choice whether you want them or not? You'll just be mates? How do you even know it's your mate when you meet?" The questions tumble out of my mouth. I know Ash said the connection he feels between us makes him think of the mate bond. But that's not possible, right? And what would happen if he actually found his mate? Would that change how he feels about me?

He tilts his head. "For a human, you're thinking a lot about this."

"I...I guess you're right, but I'm curious. I want to know how your world works."

And if your feelings will change if your destined mate suddenly shows up.

"I'm glad." He smiles. "But no, when you meet your destined mate, you will have a choice. People do reject the mate link if they've already chosen a mate or already love someone else." He glances at my plate, my sandwich now gone. "You don't have to eat the salad. Would you like to change clothes, though?"

"I don't have any other clothes."

He picks up a bag that I forgot he brought in. "I got some for you." He moves the table away and sets the bag on the bed beside me.

I start sorting through it. "None of these are mine."

"They are now. Emma complained to me that you don't have many, so she gave me your sizes, and I bought some for you." He palms the back of his neck. "I hope I didn't overstep."

I shake my head as my face heats up. There's not only shirts and pants, but also underwear and bras. "She told you my bra size, too?"

He coughs, growing red under his light-brown skin. "Uh, yeah. Do you need help up?" He quickly stands, offering his hand.

I move the bag then take his hand, keeping my gaze low. "I would like to shower first."

"I'll help you with that."

My leg muscles and feet ache from their lack of use as Ash gently guides me to the bathroom.

He has me sit on a stool in the bathroom before turning on the water. He places a towel and new clothes out for me.

"Oh," he mutters then leaves the room. He comes back with two bottles, one shampoo the other conditioner, and a little bag of other hygiene supplies.

My heart swells. "You really thought of everything."

"I just want to make sure you're getting taken care of." He tests the water with a few fingers. "This shouldn't be too warm." His eyes travel the length of my body, his Adam's apple bobs as he swallows. A shiver runs through me. Why is he looking at me like that? I look disgusting.

"Do you need any more help?" he asks, his voice thick.

I shake my head. "I can do the rest. Thank you."

He glances at the door. "Okay, I'll be just outside the door. Just say call out if you need anything."

"Will do."

He nods and walks out, closing the door behind him.

22

Ellie

*A*fter my shower, I change into a pair of sweats and a loose t-shirt, but I forgo the bra due to the injuries that still line my back. I come out of the bathroom with a brush in hand and find Ash waiting where he said he would.

He's by my side as I walk back to the bed, hovers next to me while I sit, and watches as I run the brush through my hair.

"May I?" he asks, holding out a hand.

I pause and stare at it with a slight tilt of my head. "Brush my hair?"

He nods.

"Uh." I look down at the brush. "Sure."

He takes it from me before climbing onto the bed, lightly nudging me so he can get behind me.

His fingers graze the back of my neck as he gathers my hair. He holds it tight as he brushes the ends first, getting the tangles out. But he's gentle, only small tugs that are oddly pleasant.

"It seems like you've done this before," I say.

"Yes, I've lived long enough to learn how to brush a woman's hair."

I frown. I don't like that answer. Whose hair has he been brushing?

When I don't say anything he says, "When my mother was alive, I would brush her hair whenever my father was dealing with the pack."

"Oh." Now I feel petty. I was jealous of his mother. Wait—is that what I was feeling? "Did he leave a lot?"

"Not a lot, but at least once a month for a few days. They were the alpha couple, like I mentioned earlier, but my father would leave to visit other packs for either meetings, settling disputes, trade, etcetera. My mother would leave at times too, but she liked staying home with me more. They would always discuss what would be best for the pack together before he left. They led together as one."

"I like that."

"Me too." I hear the smile in his voice. "When I was young, before my father would leave, he would always tell me that I needed to make sure my mother wasn't lonely—that I should take care of her. I tried my best. I remember hearing her once tell my father how much she loved having her hair done at salons. I couldn't do her hair like a stylist, but I decided that I could comb it and do a simple braid. The first time I braided her hair was a mess, but not from a lack of effort." He chuckles. "My mother took one look in the mirror and said she loved it. She even kept it in when she went into town later that day. Because of how proud she was of me and how much she said she loved it, I continued to brush and braid her hair even as I grew older."

"She sounds amazing." I smile at his story. "I never brushed my mother's hair, but I would always watch her get ready before she would brush mine." I frown. I think she was the last one to brush my hair. I blink as tears threaten to spill. I don't want to think about that right now. "How old are you?" I turn around to look at him.

He sits back. "One hundred and fifteen."

"One hundred and fifteen as in?"

"One hundred and fifteen years."

My mouth gapes. "So old."

He cringes and averts his gaze. "Is that a turn off?" He looks at me through his lashes.

I look at him closer, his smooth, light-brown skin. His lush ebony hair that's almost in his glacier-blue eyes. He could easily pass as someone in their mid to late twenties. And strangely, I don't feel put off that he's so much older than me. But why is that? Why does he look so young when he's over a hundred years old? Is it because he's a lycan?

"Not really, actually," I say.

He chuckles with relief. "Thank heavens. I'm not sure what I would've done if you said yes. I almost came out and said I was joking."

I laugh. "I don't know why, but I don't mind. Maybe if you looked that old I would, but it doesn't bug me, probably because you look close to my age." Pausing, I tilt my head. "Why do you exactly—look my age? Do lycans age differently?"

He nods. "Once a lycan hits their early twenties, time seems to slow. Which makes age gaps common among us, so I wasn't too concerned about your age."

I bite my lip. "You don't think I'm too young?"

He grins with adoration in his eyes. "Definitely not too young. In lycan terms, I'm considered young."

"What's considered old?"

"High hundreds—thousands."

"There are lycans that old?" I ask. It's strange thinking that there are others that have been around that long. What do they do with all that time? My life is just a blip to theirs, and I already don't know what I'd do if I was no longer worried about Marcus.

Actually, that's a lie. I'd find a place to settle down and go from there.

"Only a few," he says, urging me to turn back around.

He continues to brush my hair. The bristles press lightly into my scalp before moving down, sending thrills of pleasure down my spine. After each stroke, he runs his fingers through the strands. I bask in the light touches of his fingertips along my neck as he talks and continues to brush my hair even though it's no longer tangled.

"Can you tell me more about mates?" I ask. I may just be romanticizing them, but they sound wonderful.

"It's said that when you meet your mate, you're drawn to them, deeper than anyone else. That you'll sense a strong connection to them, and I've heard when you touch, it's like you've been electrified."

"You've heard? So...you haven't met your mate yet?" *Is that hope bubbling up inside?*

"I haven't and may never. It's uncommon to find your mate."

He's said that before. "Why?"

"Because we're spread out all over the world and don't socialize with many packs outside our own."

"But you've traveled to different parts of the world."

"Yes, but that's not very common. Especially until recently when the only options of transportation were either horse and buggy or ships."

"Wait, you don't have some magical way to travel?"

He chuckles. "Maybe witches do, but we don't really socialize with them."

I straighten before fully facing him. "What else is real? Fairies? Elves? Vampires?"

"No, no, and kind of."

I gape at him. "Kind of vampires?"

"The myth of vampires originated from them, but they're actually called stryxes. They aren't undead and don't need blood to survive, but they drink it anyway." He gently turns me back around.

Vampires, or I guess stryxes, and witches are real. Now that I know lycans exist and allow myself to believe it, it's not so difficult to believe that stryxes and witches exist, too. Even if it's hard to wrap my brain around all of it. But I've gotten off topic.

A sigh escapes as he continues to brush my hair. A thrill runs through me. I don't know what it is about someone else touching my hair, but it brings a different kind of pleasure.

"So, it's hard to find your mate," I say.

"Yes. Many choose each other. My parents were one of them, making them the alpha couple and chosen mates."

I look over my shoulder at him. "Why aren't you an alpha?"

His eyes widen in alarm. "I was supposed to be."

"Because your parents were?"

"Yes and no. I was the only pureblood in the pack once my parents were killed. It just made sense for me to become alpha."

"Pureblood? Is that similar to being an alpha?"

"No, pureblood isn't a ranking. It's just something you're born with, like race, or being human."

"What does it mean?"

He sighs. "A lot would explain it by saying my blood isn't 'tainted' by human ancestors."

I frown. "I don't like the sound of that."

"I don't either. I wish I could change it, but the more human ancestors you have, the weaker the magic is in your blood. You'll have even less magic if one parent is a human. Purebloods are the opposite. They don't have any human ancestors. They're powerful with enhanced abilities that are even greater than normal lycans. Add special abilities on top of that... Purebloods are nearly impossible to beat unless by another pureblood."

"Special abilities?" I ask as his fingers slip into my hair. He begins to massage my head, distracting me from my never-ending questions. His fingers work in little circles along my scalp. I close my eyes as a small moan slips past my lips. It's like my brain has turned to mush from the bliss his fingers bring.

"I'm fast," he says. "While lycans are faster than humans, I'm even faster than other purebloods."

So, Ash is extremely fast, and other purebloods can have similar enhancements. Are Zac or Marcus purebloods, too? Do they have special abilities I need to be wary of?

Ash's fingers move skillfully from my scalp to my neck where he lightly squeezes. He stops then pulls my hair to the side and over one shoulder. He caresses the sliver of skin that's exposed below my neck.

I track the warmth of his other hand to my shoulder. He places them both on my shoulders and massages them; the tension slips away with his touch. I pull my legs up and hold on to them as he kneads all the aches and pains away.

My mind and body go into a daze. I rest my head on my knees and slightly nod off as I focus on the touch of his hands.

When he stops, it's almost as if I'm jerked out of a dream.

I quickly wipe away the bit of drool that has escaped, hoping he didn't notice.

"Is a braid okay?" he asks, already expertly weaving my strands into one. He finishes it off with a hair tie I didn't realize he had.

"Is Alice a healer lycan?" I ask as another question pops in my head. I turn to him as he leans back into the bed. He moves over so I can settle beside him. The bed is small enough that our sides are pressed up against each other.

"Uh, no." His eyes dull. "She's an omega."

"What's that?" He hasn't mentioned this ranking yet.

He runs a hand down his face with a sigh. "Omegas are ranked last. They are the ones with the least amount of magic in their blood."

"And Alice is one."

"She is. Although her father is the head warrior, her mother was a human. She got most of her traits from her as well. She probably has the least magic in the entire pack. Enough to transform into a small wolf and to live longer. But her senses are barely above a human."

A light bulb goes off in my head. "Is that why she doesn't look us in the eyes?"

He peers down at me. "You noticed that too, huh? Yes. She has been bullied despite her powerful family and friends. It's hard to change people's opinions and actions when they don't want to change."

"It's a losing battle only if you give up. What do omegas do? Everyone else seems to have a role or job."

He sags deeper in the bed. "Clean, cook, take care of children, things like that."

I frown. That's nothing like the others. "Does she want to do those things? Does she get a choice in what she does? Do any omegas?"

He runs a hand down his face. "Not really. No one really does."

"That's horrible. She must hate being an omega."

"I believe she does. She doesn't talk to me much. Foster, Russell, and I try to get her involved with us, but she never agrees unless her father joins. Foster says it's because it makes the bullying worse. People don't realize how much we need omegas. They keep us tied together, filling in the cracks. Without them, our pack wouldn't run as smoothly, but I wish they had a choice in what they want to do and pursue." He leans his head back against the bed frame with a sigh. "My world isn't perfect. Far from it."

"Neither is mine, though. Humans are just as corrupt and mean."

He chuckles without humor. "Yeah, everyone is pretty messed up."

I tilt my head as I survey him. "Not everyone. I've met a lot of good people while moving around. And..." I bite my lip.

He side-eyes me. "And?"

"And well...you. You're included, next to Jane and Emma, of course."

A grin breaks across his face as he chuckles. "Of course," he says with a hint of a laugh. He sits up and leans in, his lips brush the shell of my ear. "Thank you. You're pretty amazing yourself."

I clench the hospital blanket as a thrill shoots through me.

"Now, let me give you your gift." He leans away and grabs the book. He sets it on my lap, face down. It's larger than any other hardcovers I've seen. I flip it to the front and a gasp escapes me.

"Is this...?"

Glancing at Ash, I find him nervously biting his lip. "Do you like it?" he asks.

Looking back down, I skim my fingers over the gold foil title, *The Princess Bride*. My favorite book. My copy was old and a paperback. Not that I didn't love and cherish it, but this? This is a deluxe edition in hardcover. Turning the cover, I find a colored map printed on the end pages. "It's beautiful."

"Is that a yes?"

My smile grows as tears blur my vision. "Yes. Thank you so much." I look up and my next breath leaves me.

He beams.

I don't think I've seen him smile this big before. He's breathtaking. His whole face lights up. The warmth that hides in his eyes explodes out and transforms his already handsome face.

"Go ahead and go through it." He nods toward the book.

With shaky hands, I turn a page, then quickly the next. There's art *inside* the book. I could go through this all night just staring at the pictures.

I'll have to call Jane tomorrow.

23

Ellie

$\mathcal{A}$sh and I are laying in the hospital bed, as per usual, as we wait for Dr. Kathy to come do a final check so we can leave. I've been in the hospital exactly two weeks today. Dr. Kathy is allowing me to be discharged earlier than planned, but only in the care of Ash. Although only minor injuries remain—scabbing on my cheek and back—I still have a slight concussion.

But that means I'll have to figure out a different way to leave without him knowing. Otherwise he'll stop me.

Ash gets out of the bed when there's a short knock on the door.

Dr. Kathy enters, pausing mid-step. She straightens and tugs down on her lab coat. "Ready?"

I nod and swing my legs over the side of the bed.

"Okay, I just need you to sign these papers." Ash grabs the offered papers for me. After I sign, Ash hands me a gray sweatshirt. I tilt my head in question.

He smiles. "It's cold outside."

I pull the sweatshirt over my head while taking a deep breath of his scent—pine, fresh snow, and a hint of musk. I bite my lip as swirls of desire stir in my stomach.

Dr. Kathy briefly leaves to bring in a nurse who rolls a wheelchair into the room.

I eye it. "I can walk."

She stops next to the bed. "It's policy. Everyone is wheeled out." She gestures for me to sit.

I sit down in the chair while Ash grabs my bag, throwing it over a shoulder.

I glance up at him as the nurse wheels me out the door and into the hall. "Are you taking me back to Emma's?"

"No, it isn't safe there for anyone."

"Then where? A hotel?" I have some money that could tide me over in a hotel for a few days. From what Dr. Kathy said, I have a week or two left until I'm completely better. I'm healing a lot faster than she expected.

I've traveled in worse conditions than how I am now, but my head has been aching so much that I end up sleeping most of the day away. I need to rest until it becomes manageable. I also need to get my stuff back from Emma.

Ash glances down at me as he walks beside my wheelchair. "Something like that."

My brows knit together. What does that even mean?

When we reach outside, a blast of frigid air hits us. Even with Ash's sweatshirt on, the cold seeps in. The sidewalk and road have been plowed, and piles of snow are lined on each side of the street. Everything else is coated with white. Ash stops beside the curb in front of a navy Ford truck. He opens the passenger side then walks back to me. He hesitates for a moment before leaning down and picking me up.

I squeal, looking at him with wide eyes. "W-why?" I ask, my arms tucked to my chest, trying to hide the pleasure that flushes through me from the heat of his body near mine.

He smirks. "I figured this would be easier," he says, setting me down in the seat. He leans over, pressing his body against mine, sending a buzz through me and lighting up my nerves. I hold my breath, trying not to inhale him as he buckles me.

He closes the door and walks around to his seat. He gets in and starts the car.

"You know, I can walk."

He shifts the gear to drive then pulls out of the hospital parking lot. "Yep," he says, popping the P.

I cross my arms. "I can also buckle myself."

He hums with a smirk.

"You're insufferable."

He glances at me with a twinkle in his eye. "Just looking out for you."

Exhaling slowly, I look out the window, surveying our surroundings. We're driving through a town I've never seen before. The buildings are old but look sturdy. It has a small-town vibe to it. We pass by mom-and-pop shops and a small grocery store. The lights along main street flicker on one by one as the sun sets.

"Where are we?"

"It's a lycan town."

I blink and glance over at him. "What? Those exist?"

He chuckles. "Just like I exist."

"What is it called?" I ask, peering back out the window. We pass by a small hotel. My brows knit together. Isn't he going to stop?

"Northdrift."

I turn to him. "What?"

"That's the town's name."

"Oh, thanks," I say softly, looking back outside. We're passing the town limits of Northdrift and heading into the surrounding thick forests.

"Aren't you going to take me to a hotel?" I ask, starting to panic.

He glances at me. "You're not staying at a hotel."

I pause. He's joking, right? "Yes, I am."

"Did you see me stop anywhere?"

"Well, no."

His grip tightens on the steering wheel. "Northdrift is a lycan town, and you're a human," he says. "You're not even supposed to know about it. That's one reason why you're not staying here. The second is because I want to be close by to make sure nothing happens to you. I can't do that if you're in a hotel hours away from me."

My eyes widen. "Hours? Where are we going?"

"My place." He glances at me, his face completely blank.

"Why are we going to your house?"

"Because it's the easiest place to protect you. I'm not letting you out of my sight after what happened to you." He side-eyes me. "But you should get some rest. It'll take a while to get there. We'll talk more once we do. The roads are dangerous this time of year, especially at night."

"Okay." I lean back and gaze out the window. We pass clusters of pine trees that are covered in a blanket of snow. Past the trees is a river that weaves in and out of mountain ranges. In the distance, those same mountains stand tall with white peaks, but in the light of the moon and the fading sun, the color changes to a soft blue. The stars twinkle into existence behind the mountains as the night takes over. I watch stars appear gradually in the sky until my eyes droop.

Maybe I will take a nap. My head is killing me anyway.

24

Ellie

I'm lightly nudged awake. "Ellie darling, we're here," Ash softly says.

I rub my eyes then look out the front windshield. We're stopped in front of a cabin encompassed by pines. It's easily larger than Emma's home.

Ash gets out, taking my bag with him. It hangs off one shoulder as he makes his way to my side. I open the door before he gets to me. I start to climb out, but suddenly he's beside me, tucking one arm behind the knee and the other around my back. He lifts me, cradling me into his chest.

"Ash," I say, my voice breathy. I take a deep breath to get more voice and less air into my next words. "I can walk."

"I know."

I bite my lip to hide my smile. I shouldn't be enjoying this.

"You're being ridiculous. I walked around the hospital for the past week. Why won't you let me walk?"

He glances down at me. "It's icy, and since you still have a slight concussion, I'm not taking any chances."

My heart warms.

Ash leans against the doorframe of the front entrance and sets my butt down on his lifted knee. "Hold onto my neck for a second," he says.

I obey, bringing us closer, and enjoy how my arms feel around his neck. He drops one arm around me, fetches his keys out of his back pocket, and opens the door, making it seem so easy while holding me. His arm is around my back again, grazing my ribs as he steps inside.

"It wasn't icy there. You could've set me down—actually, you can still set me down. We're inside."

"I don't want to."

"Oh." I'm taken back by his honesty. I'm not quite sure how to respond, but a warmth creeps up my face.

Glancing down, his eyes twinkle as he carries me through the threshold. He kicks the door shut behind us. There's a hallway just past the entryway on our right that he takes.

He stops right in front of the farthest room on the left and sets me down in front of a closed door. Turning the handle, he then pushes the door open with one arm, holding it open for me. Looking down at me he tilts his head to the door, indicating he wants me to go in first.

My hands fidget with the bottom of his sweatshirt, suddenly nervous. I look straight ahead into the room. The light from the hallway rests on a window across the room with blush curtains framing it. A skewed reflection of us appears in it. My breath catches as I notice Ash looking at me, waiting patiently. He doesn't move, doesn't rush me, just waits. I take a deep breath and enter the room, flipping the switch on the wall.

A gasp escapes as the room lights up. To my right sits a queen-size bed with a beautiful cream comforter full of ruffles, with matching cream and blush pillows. My gaze then locks onto a tall walnut bookcase brimming with books. I can't wait to browse through his collection.

Next my eyes snag on a vase of white roses on the nightstand. The walls are my favorite color, a dark forest-green like the evergreen trees near my parents' home. I'm speechless. It's beautiful.

I look over at Ash who's hovering at the door. His head is slightly tilted down with his hand on the back of his neck. He looks up at me through his dark lashes. "Do you like it?" he asks.

I have so many questions, but the only one that comes out is, "How?"

With brows drawing together, he drops his hand. "How?"

"How did you do this? How'd you know what I like?" I wave my hand around the room. "I love it, every single piece of it."

"I may not have noticed your eating habits, but I watched and listened more than you realize. Even when I was a wolf. I know you, Ellie. I may not have known you long, but it feels like I've known you my whole life." A corner of his mouth tips up. "Also helps you're not very good at hiding your emotions."

I roll my eyes, but a smile seems to be permanently etched on my face.

"I have more clothes for you in the dresser behind you. Your duffle bag I placed under the bed." He swallows as his eyes stay focused on said dresser. He walks over to it and pulls one of the drawers open.

He takes out a pair of light gray pajamas that have white polka dots on them. They're soft and look warm. They're quite cute, too. Then I watch him open another drawer and pull out a pair of pink panties.

"Ash." My face burns as if it's on fire as I snatch the underwear from him. "Did you really just pull out panties for me? Please tell me those aren't used."

"What? No." He chuckles with a shake of his head. "Why would I get you used underwear? I only bought new"—he coughs, trying not to laugh—"panties, as you call them." He hands me the pajamas.

I clutch them to my chest, hiding the panties between me and the clothes. "This room doesn't have a closet," he says, "but it's the only room next to mine, so I hope the dresser will be enough for you."

"Yes, thank you. The dresser is plenty. This whole room is more than enough, as well as the clothes."

He clears his throat and rubs the back of his neck. "Well, I'll let you get settled in and go to bed."

"Ash?" I stop him before he leaves. "I can't stay here. I can't put you or anyone else in danger by staying here. He'll just keep coming for me."

He straightens. "Ellie, you'll be safe with me, I promise. Please don't run."

And with the way he looks at me, I know he means it. My cheeks burn, but I ignore it. I'm not used to getting so much attention. "I need to. I can't stay here long. You didn't have to do all of this because once my concussion is gone, I need to leave. I *will* leave."

He hums. "We'll see."

My eyes narrow. "Ash."

He gives me a small smile. "I'll let you get ready for bed now." He closes the door behind him.

With a sigh I peer around the room once more. I remove my worn clothes and put on new ones. I kind of love that he chose what I'm wearing, even though I'm beyond embarrassed he now knows what underwear I'll have on.

I smile at the softness of the pajamas against my skin. Ash keeps showering me with gifts and all I've managed to give him is...well, nothing.

Moving to the door, I open it a crack. Will Ash sleep with me again tonight? Shaking my head at my thoughts, I close the door. He wants to sleep in his own bed, I'm sure. He's already said as much.

So why do I feel like I should wait for him?

I stride over to the bookcase. There's no point waiting for him. Nor should I. I need to detach myself from him. I'll just read a book tonight to help me fall asleep. Browsing through the selection on display, I find a few romance novels. There's also poetry, science fiction, mystery, history—human and lycan—and even some fantasy. I smile at the last. Who knew he liked to read about fantasy characters and creatures? I pause. Well, I guess they aren't all make believe.

I want to read about the history of lycans, but my head is throbbing again. I pick a romance instead. Although, maybe I should pick something I don't like to read if I want to fall asleep. It's cold under the sheets as I climb into bed without Ash. I didn't realize how much he radiated heat. It must be a lycan thing.

Letting out a pent-up breath, I settle in the bed. I'm exhausted even with the four-hour nap in the car, but my mind won't shut off. Opening the book, I begin to read. I only make it through a few pages when my head begins to pound. Rubbing at my temples, I try to ease the pain, but it's not working. Maybe I should just try to sleep.

I set the book down on the nightstand and turn off the lights. I sink back into the sheets, the dark helping my head, but Ash's missing presence is more noticeable. I take comfort in knowing that his room is beside mine. We literally share a wall.

Sighing, I roll over, wrapping the sheets around myself. Even though I'm in his house, the bed doesn't smell like him.

I'm being ridiculous. Why do I need to keep reminding myself that I'm leaving soon? I need to get used to sleeping alone again. Closing my eyes, I try to will myself to sleep, but I toss and turn more than not before sleep eventually overpowers me.

Terror fills me as I recognize the four windowless, cinder block walls. No, I can't be back here. I escaped from this place.

"You thought you could get away?" I spin around at Marcus' laugh, his canines long and dripping blood. His eyes darken and glow as his hands change into claws. My gaze drops, finding Ash lying on the ground between us, lifeless. His normally light-brown skin, pale and sickly. His eyes, glazed over and empty.

No, this isn't right.

"I told you I had plans for you, and no one gets in my way when I want something."

This isn't real. It can't be. Ash isn't supposed to die. It's me who is. It's the whole reason I planned on leaving.

I didn't leave fast enough.

Why didn't I leave sooner? There were opportunities, but I ignored them. I enjoyed being with Ash too much. And now it has cost him his life.

I fall to my knees, pain erupting in my chest. "Ash," *I whimper.*

On my hands and knees, I crawl to him, not having the strength to stand and walk, as my heart breaks.

Marcus steps over him, leaning down in front of me. He grips my throat, his nails digging into my neck as he holds me in the air, blood trickling down. I claw at his monstrous hands, not caring if I die. I just want to be with Ash. He's alive, he has to be. He can't be dead.

"Ash." Tears stream down my face and fall into my mouth.

Marcus laughs maniacally. "Don't worry, Eleanor, you'll see him in the next life."

"ELLIE."

I gasp, jerking awake, and squirm up the bed. Hot tears stream down my face as I claw at my neck, Marcus' phantom fingers still gripping my throat.

Ash climbs onto the bed and pulls me to him, cradling me against his chest. "Are you okay?" There's a hint of panic in his voice. When I look at him, his eyes are ablaze with fear.

I take a few shaky deep breaths before nodding, but the terror still lingers. Ash's arms bulge around me as he lays us down, keeping me flush against him as he holds me tight. My face, arms, and hands tingle with the contact of his bare skin.

"That was worse than the others. I need—do you mind if I stay?" Ash asks.

Shaking my head, I wrap my arms around him. I know why it was worse. It wasn't me who I was desperate to save, it was Ash.

I sniffle and press myself against him. He caresses my bare arm. My entire body shudders not just from the reminder of my dream, but from being in close contact with a shirtless Ash.

"Ash," I whisper.

"Shh." He rolls onto his back, bringing me with him, and pulls the covers over us. "Sleep, my little human, I'll watch over you." He nuzzles his head into my hair, his large hand gently palming my back. I lay on his chest, listening to the steady rhythm of his heartbeat, proof that he's still alive, that he didn't die. That my dream wasn't real.

25

Ellie

a slight vibration wakes me the next morning. Ash's fingers feather up and down my exposed arm as he holds me in his warm embrace. We didn't move an inch from our position last night.

His hand stills as well as the vibrations. *Was he humming?* "Good morning," he says, his voice rough from sleep.

I peer up at him, his lips thin as he gazes down at me.

"Ash?" What could he be upset about this early?

He sighs, his hand caresses my arm once more. He looks straight ahead, not meeting my gaze as he says, "I didn't want to ask or bring it up again. I wanted you to tell me on your own, but"—his gaze meets mine once more—"I can't ignore what happened last night." His other hand comes up and moves strands of hair out of my face. "That was the worst dream I've seen you have. I need to know, Ellie. I need to know what haunts you even in your sleep. I know it's Marcus. But I can't ignore just how badly he affects you."

Forcing my gaze away from his, I grip the covers and pull them closer to my chest. I knew he would want to know. I know I need to tell him, but speaking about it means reliving it.

Ash's arm tenses as he pulls me flush against him. "But I don't want to force you. If you truly can't speak to me about it, I understand and won't bring it up again."

That's the odd thing, I do want to talk to him about it. For the first time ever, I want to talk to someone, share what happened. But not just share with anyone, I want to confide in *him*. "I want to tell you." My voice is quiet as I speak. "It's hard, but I'm going to. Just be patient with me."

"Of course, whenever you're ready." His voice is soft as he caresses my arm. "We can stay in bed all day today."

I tilt my head to gaze up at him, concern and devotion shine in his eyes. The question, "why me?" pops into my head. Why did he choose me to look at in that way?

I glance away before speaking and focus on a random spot on the wall. "I was eleven when my parents died," I begin. "Without any other family members to take me in, I was sent to foster care." Taking a deep breath, I let it out slowly through my nose. "But when I was thirteen, they placed me with Marcus and his wife. I heard you and Dr. Kathy talking about my back." His hand stills. "It was him. It was Marcus. He...he was the one who hurt me to the point where I wish death would come, just so I could escape."

Ash has grown tense, but now that I've started, I can't stop. It's freeing to speak about it, even if my entire body is shaking. "I slowly stopped caring about living, I didn't want to survive after his beatings, but he somehow knew the fine line to keep me from dying. After two years of being under his thumb, he allowed me out of the basement. I was able to take a shower and eat a normal sized meal. I thought maybe I was getting placed somewhere else." A rough laugh pushes past my lip as the pressure of tears burn. I remember trying to contain my excitement that I'd get to leave. "Instead, he was getting another kid. Will." I sniffle and rub my nose. "He was a few months older than me, and because he was a male, he was treated slightly better than me. He got a room above ground and was fed more often than I was. He was abused as well, just not as bad."

"Ellie." Ash says my name like a prayer. He turns onto his side, tugging me closer, wrapping me in his full embrace.

Shaking my head, I press my fingers into Ash's bare skin to keep my hands from shaking. "Will would sneak down whenever they were gone, giving me food and keeping me company. I should've told him to stop. I knew he'd get caught." My voice catches.

I press my face into Ash's chest, breathing him in, allowing his scent to calm me. "It was my birthday, and Will thought maybe Marcus would be lenient if he were caught. He'd never been around for my last two birthdays before, so he didn't know how much worse those days actually were."

I swallow, my throat tightening at the memory of what happened next. I snuggle closer. "He...he tried to defend me. Tried to stand up for me. Marcus killed him." At that last part, a sob breaks through. Will was the first person to care about me since my parents died. It was nice to be wanted and cared for, but I learned the hard way that everyone I love will die. My parents. Will.

I can't let that happen to Ash.

Ash lightly squeezes me to him. "Oh, Ellie darling." He doesn't say anything else, but he doesn't need to. Just holding me and being here for me is enough.

I wait until I calm down enough before telling him the rest. "That was a wakeup call for me. I realized I didn't want to die, but that would be the only ending if I stayed."

"You escaped," he says, his hand moving up and down my back.

I nod, my forehead rubbing against his warm, smooth skin. "When I decided I wanted to live, I had no idea how I would escape. I tried to focus on his habits, his moods, and how often he came down. I wanted to be able to read his thoughts through his actions. But it didn't matter as long as I was locked in the basement."

Ash pulls me up, shocking me out of my thoughts. He cups my face with one hand, brushing a thumb against my cheek. I hadn't realized I started to cry. His eyes bore into mine, giving me the courage to continue.

I focus on the scruff along Ash's jaw, his gaze too intense. "It was pure luck that I was able to get out." My brows scrunch together. "My memory is a bit hazy, but he was excited about something after getting off the phone. I know it had to do with me." A chill slices through my body, and I shiver.

Ash runs his fingers through my hair as I continue, "In his excitement he forgot to lock the door. I waited for what felt like hours before sneaking up the stairs. I was badly injured, but I was numb to the pain. When I finally found the courage to open the door, I found him passed out on the couch surrounded with beer bottles and no signs of Beatrice. Somehow, I was able to pass him and reach the yard. They had shrubs instead of walls, which was fortunate for me. I had forgotten I was even injured, because of the adrenaline, until I collapsed in Jane's yard, about five houses down from his.

"When I came to, I was in a bed on my stomach. Jane was hovering over me, tending to my back. She knew I was Marcus' foster kid and wanted me to testify against him, but I couldn't. She's a lawyer, but I didn't think we could win. He's too powerful. So instead she created a second bank account for me, but under her name. No one ever checks your ID anymore as long as you know the pin or have the same signature. Once I was healed enough, she set up a rental place in California, also under her name, and bought the first set of bus passes. I've been using her name and money ever since. I would move every couple of months to remain hidden. But it seems like I stayed here too long."

The room is so quiet now that I've stopped talking. The only sound is our breathing as he holds me in a tight embrace. Ash presses his face against mine—there's wetness and the whiskers from his beard prickle my skin.

He's crying.

For me.

He caresses my hair and I take comfort in his touch, in his presence, my nightmares being replaced by his familiar scent and strong, warm arms.

"I'll never let him, or anyone else, hurt you again," he says softly into my hair. "I'm so sorry, Ellie."

"It's okay," I say back.

His determined gaze meets mine, his long, dark lashes framing his beautiful, glacier-blue eyes. "It's not, and I'm going to find him. You should never have to be afraid of him hurting you again."

My heart swells as I look at him. How did I get so lucky? How did someone like him come to care so fiercely for someone like me?

I blink as tears threaten to spill. "Ash, I can't risk you. You survived against him last time, but you might not be so fortunate the next time."

He shrugs. "He's a weak lycan, only attacking those who are weaker than him. If he fights fair, it would be an easy win."

"You know he won't."

His chin dips slightly. There's dark circles under his eyes. Did he not sleep last night? Was his voice rough just from non-use? "I do. We'll figure something out, but you'll be safe with me."

Not wanting to argue about it anymore, I move away from the subject. "You look tired."

He quirks a brow but doesn't miss a beat. "Isn't that another way of saying I look like crap?"

"You could never look like crap."

He takes a piece of my hair and twirls it around his finger. "Does that mean you find me attractive?"

My cheeks heat. "Yes."

A slow grin takes over his face. "I find you attractive as well."

My face grows hotter.

He tugs the piece of hair as he changes the topic. "Thanksgiving is in three days."

I blink. Time seems to have slipped away from me. I've already been in Alaska for two months.

"I have some people who want to come spend it here with us and meet you. Just four people, Alice being one of them."

"Okay..."

"Is that okay?" he asks.

My brows scrunch together. "Why are you asking me? This is your house."

"Yes, but you matter to me. If meeting new people is too much for you, I'll tell them no."

My eyes lower to his naked chest that's lightly dusted with black curls. I shake my head, trying to refocus.

Thanksgiving. Four people. Can I handle that?

"No, they can come. But we can stay in bed today though, right?" Despite being stuck in a hospital for two weeks, I have no desire to move after the emotional output I just did.

"Of course," he says as his fingers trail over my cheek. "Today we'll relax. Maybe even tomorrow. There's no rush, Ellie darling."

26

Ellie

wo days pass by quicker than I'd like. Ash and I watched movies, read books, napped, ate—it was exactly what I needed to start feeling better. My head still aches on and off, but I know I'm getting closer to being able to leave.

I raise my arms to stretch in bed. My shirt slightly rises but pulls against a weight around my waist. There's a chuckle, and my eyes pop open. Ash is on his side facing me, his body just an inch away from mine. It's the weight of his arm that's around my waist.

"Good morning," he says, his eyes hooded. I catch his gaze lingering on my lips. Warmth spreads across my chest and face as my body reacts to his voice and nearness.

"Morning," I squeak.

A lazy smile appears on his face as he moves closer, his body pressing up against mine. He throws a heavy leg over me, trapping me in place. He nuzzles his head in my hair and breathes deeply. "You smell so good."

"What are you doing?" I ask.

"You're the one who cuddled with me all last night, little human, more than usual."

"I-um, I'm sorry?"

He chuckles. "Don't be." His hand moves to my bare hip. My breath hitches. Goosebumps erupt as he rubs circles along my skin with his thumb. Turning his mouth to my ear, he says, "I didn't mind." His warm breath sends shivers down my spine.

My heart rate spikes when he places a warm, lingering kiss below my ear. I hold my breath as he moves lower, dotting more along my jaw and moving down my neck. "So, I cuddled with you. And now?" I say against his onslaught of kisses.

A small giggle escapes me as his scruff tickles my neck.

I feel his smirk against my skin as he tugs me closer. "Now it's my turn."

My cheeks heat.

He snuggles closer with his head resting on my shoulder. After a moment, I relax against him and close my eyes. We lay together in silence, and I'm almost asleep again when he murmurs, "You're so beautiful." He kisses my forehead then rolls out of bed.

Sitting up, my eyes linger on him as he stands in the soft moonlight. It's morning, but the moon slowly monopolizes the sky here in Alaska as winter progresses.

Ash is beautiful, inside and out, but his body is a masterpiece. His muscles bunch and move as he stretches. His smooth, light-brown skin showcases his defined back muscles and the dimples at the base of his back. His pants hang almost a little too low. I swallow.

I drop my gaze when he turns back to me, not wanting to be caught ogling him.

Looking through my lashes, I take a chance and find him smirking. I draw the covers higher to hide under, but not before I catch a glimpse of his toned chest and abs. My body warms thinking about him. I take a deep breath, trying to calm my racing heart. Even though I was pressed up against him for most of the night, seeing what I was pressed up against is completely different.

"No hiding." Ash gently pulls the covers away from my face with a grin. He sits down on the bed. "Do you think you're up for a few visitors today? They'll only stay for the evening."

I gnaw on my lip. "I guess."

He tugs my bottom tip away from my teeth. "It's okay to say no."

Looking down, I fidget with one of the ruffles. "No—I mean, yes I'm up for a few visitors."

He eyes me, but he must not be too concerned because he doesn't ask me about it again. "Okay, well, I'm going to make us some breakfast. Do you like pancakes?"

"Who doesn't?"

He smiles. "Touché. I'm going to go to my room and grab a shirt first. I'll meet you in the kitchen."

I watch him leave then get up and make myself decent. I use the half-bath in the hallway before making my way to the kitchen.

My heart skips a beat when I see Ash in front of the stainless-steel stove, barefoot, wearing a white t-shirt and baggy sweats while flipping pancakes. What would it be like to see this every morning?

There's an island that separates the kitchen and the table. Ash's table is rectangular and larger than Emma's. The back door lies just beyond the table. The cabinets are a dark walnut and countertops a black quartz, giving the kitchen a rustic and modern vibe.

My hands cover my stomach as it rumbles.

Ash chuckles, turning his head toward me. "Glad to see you're hungry for a change."

I smile shyly and take a seat at the table as he brings two plates over. My eyes bug out at the large stack he places in front of me. "I can't eat this much." My appetite may be getting better, but not by this much.

"I don't expect you to. Just eat what you can." He hands me the syrup and places a fork near my plate.

A sigh escapes me as I rub my temple, a headache already forming.

He eyes me. "You've been doing that a lot lately. How are you feeling?"

I shrug and lather my meal with syrup. "I've been getting headaches on and off, but I figure that's from my concussion."

His eyes narrow on my food as he nods. "Let me know if it gets worse or if anything else starts to hurt. I'm afraid I may have brought you home too soon," he says, taking the syrup I offer back.

"Will do," I say and take a bite. Although if that means going back to the hospital, I'm not sure I will. I'm just glad the itching stopped.

After ten minutes, the mountain of pancakes is practically gone.

He laughs at my surprised face. "This is a good thing, Ellie."

I shake my head in disbelief. It seems too sudden to be able to eat that much. It's barely been a week since we started.

Ash stands and starts clearing the table.

I jump up. "Let me."

He saved me—the least I can do is wash the dishes.

I try to take them out of his hands, but he raises them and maneuvers away. He places the dishes in the stainless sink that lays below a window.

I huff. "I can do it. Please let me do something for you." Nudging him away, I plant myself in between him and the sink. I turn the faucet on.

"You don't need to do anything for me. Besides, you're still not one hundred percent yet." Ash grips the edge of the sink on each side of me, trapping me.

My heart rate spikes at his proximity. "Yes, I do. You've done so much for me." I grab a scrubber and run a plate under the water, trying to ignore the large male behind me.

My breath catches as he leans in closer, towering behind me, pressing his body against mine. "You being alive is enough for me," he says softly in my ear.

Goosebumps erupt across my skin as a shiver runs down my

neck and through my spine. He gently takes my hands with his. I close my eyes as tingles and sparks intertwine through my blood-stream. His arms press against my sides and in one swift motion he pries the scrubber from my hands, shifts me over, and moves into the spot I just occupied.

His eyes twinkle with mirth as he gives me a cheeky grin.

My cheeks heat up. How did that not affect him?

Biting my bottom lip, I step closer, my side brushing against him, my fingers dusting over his arm. His breath hitches, and I roll my lips inward to fight a smile. I guess I'm not the only one affected.

I take the clean plate out of his hands and start drying it with a towel.

He eyes me, and there's a look in his eyes I can't place.

My brows knit together. "Yes?" I ask, setting the plate aside.

He turns away, continuing on to the next dish. "Nothing."

Once we finish, he turns to me. "I have a surprise for you."

I tilt my head. "A surprise?"

"I'll be right back." And with that, he swiftly walks out of the kitchen.

Uh, okay then.

I clasp my hands together to keep them from fidgeting. What could the surprise be? I look at the table. Should I sit while I wait? How long will he take? Would it be strange to just keep standing here?

Before I can decide what to do, he walks in holding a blue paper bag with glittery tissue paper popping out of it. He offers it to me while his other hand rubs his neck. "This is for you."

I shake my head in bewilderment. Another gift? When did he even have the time to get me something? He's almost always with me.

I hesitantly take the present from him, and it's heavier than I expected. I set it down on the island and start removing the tissue paper. Looking inside, I gasp. There's a full charcoal drawing kit, a calligraphy pen, a sketchbook, and multiple small canvases. Anything I could possibly need to draw.

"You...you didn't have to get me this."

"You don't have much to call your own, and I wanted you to feel more at home here. I want you to be comfortable, and I know how much you enjoy drawing."

I rub my eyes as pressure builds behind them. "You don't know how much this means to me." I swallow the lump in my throat. This is better quality than my own things. This must have cost him a small fortune. "Thank you so much, Ash."

His eyes darken as he swallows. "I'm glad you like it."

I beam. "I love it."

He stills, but then a slow smile appears on his face. "Why don't you go put it in your room? We can talk after you take a shower."

"Okay." I quickly put my new gifts back into the bag. I start heading out of the kitchen but pause mid-step and quickly turn around. I fidget with the bottom of my shirt. "Is there a bathroom I can use?" I've been using the one upstairs, but yesterday only a small trickle came out of the shower.

He rubs the back of his neck. "Right. I guess you would need to use mine."

Heat rises to my cheeks. "Oh."

"Until I can get the plumbing looked at upstairs, it's the only one with a working shower." A sly grin forms on his face. "But don't worry, I promise to stay away so you can shower in peace."

"If I knew you were a man then I wouldn't have done that." I give him a pointed look.

His face drops. "I'm sorry about that. I should've left you rather than stay in wolf form."

My heart races. "I'm glad you didn't." I bite my lip. "What you said in the field, did you mean it?"

He straightens. "Which part?"

"I..." I force my hands to remain still as the desire to fidget rears its head.

Ash takes a step forward, drawing nearer. "The part where I apologized? Because, yes, I'm still sorry." Another step. "Or the part where I said I'll go wherever you are?" Another step. "Or maybe it was where I said I wanted you." His voice grows soft as he stops only a hair's breadth away. His body radiates heat.

"Do you still feel that way?" I ask, my heart beating fast.

His breath caresses over my skin as he speaks near my ear, sending shivers down my spine. "Yes, I do. And I meant all of it. The real question is, how do *you* feel?" My gaze travels to his face when I realize I've been staring at his chest. His eyes search mine.

"How do *I* feel?"

He pulls away. "How do you feel about me, Ellie? Do you want me as much as I want you? Do you want to be together? You said you wanted me, but do you still feel that way?"

"I...I've never been in a relationship before."

He blinks. "I don't care."

"I've never kissed anyone before."

His gaze flickers to my lips and a corner of his mouth turns up. "I find I like that answer a little too much."

"I'm human."

His eyes flash to mine, color draining from his face. "You are." He takes a step back, the space around me now cold and empty. His mouth thins. "I should've considered you wouldn't want to be with someone like me. You'd want to be with someone more...human."

My breath grows shallow. "No, that's not what I meant."

His face has grown cold as the color of his eyes. "Then what did you mean?"

"I meant..." My hands go to my hair, lightly tugging the strands. "I don't know anything about your world. How am I supposed to fit in? How are people supposed to accept us when I'm not like you or them?"

He clears the distance between us in one stride and takes my face in his hands. "It doesn't matter what anyone else thinks. It only matters what you and I want. I want you. All of you. Everything you're willing to give." I try to blink away tears that build up, but they flow down anyways. I've never had someone fight for me this much before. Desire me.

"I'm scared," I say.

I *need* to leave, but I *want* to stay with him. I want to see where this could go. Because what if he really can protect me and this works out? But could I chance him getting injured because I stayed?

His thumbs slide across my cheeks, wiping away my tears. "It's okay to be scared. I'm here. You can lean on me. I'll teach you all you need to know about my world, and we can go slow. I don't want to push you into doing anything you don't want to do."

Taking a deep breath, I look into his soulful eyes. "I want you, Ash, but I don't even know your last name."

He stares for a moment before his head tips back and laughs. "Oh, Ellie darling. I plan on us getting to know each other real well. But if you must know, my last name is Sylvester."

I smile. "Ash Sylvester."

He swallows. "Yes," he says, his voice husky. He clears his throat. "And yours?"

"Eleanor Hollenberg."

His brows scrunch together.

"What's wrong?" Does my name sound funny?

"Your last name sounds familiar to me, but I can't place it." He shakes his head. "But Eleanor...that's beautiful. I didn't realize Ellie was just a nickname."

Butterflies flutter in my stomach when he says my name.

"Why don't you go by Eleanor?"

I shrug. "My parents always called me Ellie, so it stuck."

"What would you like to be called?" he asks.

"I'm happy with Ellie."

He smiles. "Then Ellie darling it is. Now—" He takes hold of my shoulders and turns me toward the entrance of the hall. "It's time for you to get ready while I finish cleaning up. I'll teach you about lycans later."

Ellie

fter placing the gift on my dresser and grabbing some clothes, I head over to his room. I pause at the door, my hand hovering over the doorknob. Isn't there a saying that a room says a lot about a person?

What if I find out he's been hiding some deep, dark secret besides being a lycan? I scoff at myself. *Way to be morbid, Ellie.* Besides, I seriously doubt he'd hide something in his bedroom then let me casually walk in it.

And there's the fact that I trust him and really care about him. I mean, I did admit to him that I want him as more than a friend. My gut tells me he's a good guy, and it's never let me down before.

"Are you going in?"

I jump, turning to find Ash. I press my hand on my heart. "You almost gave me a heart attack."

His lips roll in, trying to keep himself from laughing, but he fails to keep a grin hidden. "Sorry, that wasn't my intention."

We stare at one another for a moment.

"So...are you?" he asks.

"Am I what?"

He chuckles. "Going to go in."

"Oh. Yes. Uh..." I turn back around and quickly enter to hide my rapidly heating face.

I pause. His room is exactly how I imagined. It fits him.

My eyes automatically land on the multiple bookcases filled with hundreds of books. He has a desk snug in between them with a lamp and laptop laying on top. I make my way through the room, passing by his king-size bed. The espresso bed frame and black duvet and navy pillows contrast with his soft gray walls.

"Do you need me to show you how to use the shower?" Ash asks.

I turn my head toward him. "I should be okay."

He nods then leaves the room, closing the door behind him. Taking a deep breath, I look around again, finding the entrance of the bathroom. I walk over and my eyes widen. It has no door!

But his room does. I quickly walk back to the door and lock it. He's not the type of person to walk in on me, but I'm paranoid. I walk back to the bathroom, remove my clothes, and fold them on the counter. I walk over to the shower with glass walls. It's so large it could easily fit five people. There are shower heads in every direction, even one overhead. One wall has three knobs in a vertical line and a few buttons next to them. No screen or anything to help indicate what each does.

What the actual heck is this?

I guess I did need his help. I look down at my bare skin—a bit too late for that.

Reaching in, I mess with the knobs, but when nothing happens I move in more to press one of the buttons. A burst of scalding hot water hits me on the back. I jump back with a scream. Fumbling to get out of the shower, I step on a slippery spot. My foot sliding under me, I start to fall, but strong lean arms catch me.

Squealing, I look up. Ash's intense, glacier-blue eyes meet mine. The hot water spraying him in the back. He gently carries me out of the shower, making sure none of the water hits me again.

"Are you okay?" His voice is strained and deeper than usual.

I nod.

He closes his eyes as his fingers twitch just under my breasts. Remembering I'm naked, I squirm to get out of his arms, but his grip tightens around me, his whole body tensing.

"You might want to stop moving," he says through tight lips.

I freeze, holding my breath, highly aware of his hands and arms on my bare legs and waist. My body tingles from the tips of my toes to the top of my head. His hands are hot on my skin.

He inhales deeply, his nose flaring, and opens his eyes again. His gaze burns into mine. "Is it okay to put you down?"

I nod.

He exhales slowly as he gently sets me down, making sure I don't slip. He puts an arm in the shower, not looking at me as I quickly cover myself with a towel. He touches the water and adjusts the knobs.

"H-how did you get in?" I ask.

His eyes flicker to mine, his gaze never leaving my face. "I broke the door."

I blink. *What?*

He *broke* the door? Just how strong is he?

"May I look at your back?"

My brows scrunch together.

"The hot water," he reminds me. "I want to make sure you aren't burned. My shower is programmed to be hotter because lycans' body temperatures run warmer."

My brows shoot up and I nod again. It stings a bit, but I've felt a lot worse.

He tilts his head to the ceiling, closing his eyes. His hands clench and unclench at his sides before he lets out a heavy breath. He walks around me to my back. A shiver runs down my spine as his hands lightly graze the sliver of skin above the towel. I slowly ease my hold on the towel as he nudges it down until it reveals my entire back. His hands stall close to my waist. My eyebrows furrow, then my body stiffens.

He can see all my scars.

I can't believe I forgot about them, considering I *never* forget about them. Some of them ache just shifting a certain way, but whenever I'm with Ash, my past, my scars all seem to fade away.

I move to turn around, but he places a hand on my shoulder, keeping me in place. He brushes my hair away, his breath against the nape of my neck. "You're beautiful, Ellie. The scars are a part of you. Be proud of them, it means you survived." My breath catches as his lips briefly graze the top of my shoulder.

He steps away, his fingers lingering a bit longer. I quickly turn to him, clenching the towel around my body. His eyes meet mine. "I'm going to go now, be careful." He pauses then smirks. "Not that I really mind if you slip. I'll just catch you again."

My face burns. "And I thought you promised you'd stay away?"

He laughs. "I did, but that's only if you stay upright." He winks then leaves.

28

Ellie

$\mathcal{I}$ pull my bag out from under my bed and rummage through it until I find my hair products. It's been so long since I have actually done anything to it, but these visitors must mean something to Ash since they're visiting for Thanksgiving.

My hand shakes as I stand in front of the mirror, wearing a cream-colored sweater and brown skirt. I start fixing my hair, pulling half of it up and applying product to the curls. My heart hammers in my chest.

He's seen my scars. It's one thing to tell someone about what I went through, it's another for them to see it. Especially since they are even uglier after the latest slashing I got from Marcus.

Does Ash really believe what he said? That I shouldn't be ashamed of them? It's easier said than done, though.

Finally ready, I open the door and hear voices coming from the kitchen. Have his guests already arrived?

My steps are padded with socks against the hardwood floor as I walk down the hall. I pause right before entering the kitchen when someone speaks.

"How are you feeling about, you know, the challenge?"

The challenge?

I don't recognize the voice. He has a thick British accent, so my guess would be Foster, but I'm not still not positive.

Another voice I don't recognize says, "Foster." This masculine voice is gruffer, with a hint of an Irish accent. Russell, maybe?

"What? I wanted to ask before Alice and Charlie get here," the first voice, Foster, responds.

"It's Thanksgiving, and you'll ruin the food," Russell says.

"I can't ruin the food by chatting."

"The negative vibes will sink into it."

"That's bloody ridiculous."

There's a sigh before Ash's voice sounds. "It's still a ways out."

"Two weeks," Foster says. "That's not far, and considering..."

"I know."

"Let's talk about this later," Russell says. "Focus on getting the celery done. I need to put the stuffing in before placing it in the oven."

There's some grumbling and a "fine" from Foster. I'm debating when I should walk in when another question spills from Foster's mouth.

"How has it been going with Ellie?" Foster asks.

I hold my breath, clenching my hand to my chest.

"I think it's been going well, but I don't know if I've changed her mind about staying. There's also..."

"There's also...what?"

I'm dying to peek around the corner and see Ash's expression. What else is he worried about?

"I don't know, there's this connection between us that confuses me."

"What do you mean?" Foster asks.

"It's almost as if..."

"As if...?"

"As if we're destined mates—" The doorbell rings, cutting him off.

Mates? Destined mates?

I didn't realize he still thought that. Are we? Even though I'm human? Why hasn't he talked to me about it more?

Leaning against the wall is how Ash finds me as he walks into the hallway.

His eyes widen. "Ellie?" He glances back, biting his lip. "Are you okay?"

I swallow and give a nod.

"Okay..." He eyes me, his gaze softening. "You look beautiful."

My shaky hands go to my skirt, tugging it down. "Thank you." Should I say something?

He smiles. "I'm going to answer the door. Russell and Foster are in the kitchen, would you like to meet them real quick?"

I straighten and wipe my sweaty hands on my skirt. "Sure."

Walking into the kitchen, I'm greeted with the sight of two men. One is bulky with a short beard, and his russet-colored hair is tied up in a messy man-bun. His sleeves are rolled up, showcasing pale skin and tattoos as he hovers over a raw turkey.

The other is the leanest out of the three, but still muscular. His slightly wavy, dark-chestnut hair is coiffed in the front, but unlike his friends, he's clean shaven. He's tanner than the other, but not as dark as Ash. He's also the first to look up, his knife pausing from the celery, and a giant grin takes over his face.

"This is Foster," Ash says, gesturing to him.

"And you must be the famous Ellie," Foster responds, his forest-green eyes twinkling with warmth, his voice heavy with a British accent.

Ash lets out a sigh as my cheeks heat. "Uh, yes, I guess."

"And this is Russell," Ash continues.

Foster elbows Russell when he doesn't look up.

A small growl leaves him, sending a glare at Foster. "What?"

"Don't be a brute, there's a lady present."

Russell's tawny eyes snap to mine as he straightens. A slight blush peeks through his beard. He clears his throat. "My apologies."

Foster sighs. "Don't mind him, when it comes to cooking, nothing can distract him except So—"

"Foster," Russell says with a growl.

I look to Ash to see him smiling and shaking his head. I find myself smiling with him.

"Well, I need to get the door, please behave for the few minutes I'm gone." He peers down at me and briefly touches my lower back before leaving the kitchen.

I turn back to our guests. Russell is already back to his turkey, while Foster is smiling at me.

"It's nice to meet you, Ellie."

I clasp my hands together in front of me. "It's nice to meet you, too."

He turns his body away from the island. "Would you like to help?"

"Uh, I'm not very good at cooking."

His smile grows. "Me either. I leave it to the brooding expert at my side."

I bite my lip and glance at Russell, but he's completely enthralled in whatever he's doing with the turkey.

"Well, okay," I say.

He gestures for me to come closer, and I stop beside him. He moves the cutting board with celery partly sliced in front of me.

Foster moves to the other side of Russell and helps with the stuffing. "So, Ellie. Do you fancy Ash?"

My heart stalls as my knife pauses midair. "W-what?" I glance over at him and see a giant grin on his face.

It's Russell who lets out a sigh. "Foster, stop teasing her. If I don't get this in the oven soon, we'll be eating raw turkey for Thanksgiving."

Foster chuckles as he gets back to work.

I shake my head as I cut the celery, making a small pile on the side.

Ash enters the kitchen near the dining table with Alice and a man following behind him. Alice's straight pale-blonde hair contrasts nicely with her dark, oversized, blue-green sweater, black leggings, and brown boots.

A smile appears on my face when our eyes meet, and she smiles back before she averts her gaze. I look over to the other visitor next when time seems to freeze.

Dirty-blond hair with blue eyes.

No. That can't be right.

Ash wouldn't invite Zac here after everything that happened. Right?

While my mind tries to catch up, the knife in my hand continues.

Russell's hand comes out fast as lightning, catching the knife before it slices through my finger and instead cuts into his hand.

I let go of the knife with a scream and jump away. "Russell, oh my gosh, I'm so sorry."

Ash is by my side in a flash, holding me up, while tears burn my eyes. My hands shake over my mouth, trying to keep a sob in, as Russell removes the knife from his hand. There's a deep slash across his palm, oozing blood. It's deep. He'll definitely need stitches. "Russell, I'm so sorry," I mutter over and over again.

Russell accepts the cloth Foster hands him and presses it on his wound.

"I have a first aid kit in the hallway," Ash says to Foster.

Foster nods and runs out of the kitchen faster than I can blink.

"I'm okay," Russell says, looking at me with a small smile, still pressing the cloth into the gash.

My tears pause at that smile. Is this the first time I've seen it? He didn't even smile when I came in. But now he's smiling to reassure me.

Ash gently squeezes my shoulders.

My eyes remain on Russell. "I...I don't understand. Why did you...?"

His gaze falls to my hands still clenched over my chest.

"You're human. You would've gotten hurt."

My bottom lip wobbles as tears fall once more. Ash picked good friends. People who care for others, even if it ends up harming them. It makes me miss Jane.

Foster walks back in. Both he and Russell move to the sink to stitch and bandage his hand.

"Do you want to go see Kathy?" Foster asks.

Russell shakes his head. "I'm fine. Doesn't even hurt."

A whimper escapes. How could that *not* hurt?

"Ellie," Ash says softly, turning me in his arms and wrapping me in his embrace. "Are you okay?"

I nod against his chest. He shouldn't be asking me this. My gaze snaps to the side as I remember why this happened in the first place. Both the man and Alice have remained on the other side of the kitchen. My eyes narrow. That can't be Zac, right? Ash would've mentioned him coming.

Noticing my turned attention, Ash loosens his arms. "This is Charlie."

I grip Ash's shirt, taking a closer look at the Zac look-alike, and notice the crow's-feet at the corners of his eyes. Eyes that radiate concern and kindness. He's an older version of Zac.

"He's Alice and Zac's father," Ash says.

I blink. My eyes travel to Alice. Did she know it was her brother that was there with Marcus? From the downcast, guilty look on her face, I'd say she did. Why didn't she say anything?

The conversation I had with Ash about omegas pops into my mind.

Alice is an omega. Of course she wouldn't say anything. We've barely spoken before. She might have even thought I'd blame her for her brother's actions.

"I'm sorry I didn't tell you sooner," Ash says. "They are so different in my mind that I forget how alike they look."

"I-It's okay." I release my hold on him as I turn back to Charlie. "I'm sorry." It's not his fault he looks like Zac. I feel horrible for being scared.

"Nothing to be sorry about, sweetie. I know the reputation my son holds. It's only normal to be afraid."

Foster and Russell move back to the island. I move forward and help Foster clean up the blood that was spilled and throw away any celery that can't be saved. Russell works on the turkey with one hand for a few more minutes before asking Ash to place it in the oven.

"Ellie?" Charlie says. He's on the other side of the kitchen now while Alice washes the used dishes. "I wanted to apologize for the role my son played in attacking you. I don't know where I went wrong with raising him, but I hope you know just how sorry I am that he was part of it. I hope you can forgive this father for the actions of his son."

I shake my head. "I don't hold you accountable for his actions. He wasn't the one who hurt me anyway."

He looks surprised at my comment but nods. "Thank you."

29

Ellie

The aroma of turkey and casseroles increases as time passes. Since we finished preparing the food and placed them in the ovens—why Ash needs four, I have no idea—we've moved to the family room where two leather couches and a rocking chair reside. Instead of watching a movie on his flat-screen television, Ash brought out some games. We're currently sitting on the rug in a circle playing Uno.

Foster places a *blue seven* on top of a *green seven* card. He gives Alice a cheeky grin when she shoots a glare his way.

"You're cheating. I swear, you're cheating."

He laughs. "Nah, how can I cheat? I can't read your cards from the other side of the room."

Alice is a lot more competitive than I thought she'd be. Foster seemed to know that from the beginning and has egged on that side of her. She's like a completely different person.

Russell places a card down using his bandaged hand. Guilt eats at me. I can't believe he did that so that I wouldn't hurt myself.

Charlie's next and shakes his head while placing a blue card on top of Russell's. "You're just easy to read, Alice dear."

Alice's brows scrunch together as her eyes narrow on him. "We play this every Sunday together. If I'm so easy to read, why do I win so often?"

A guilty smile appears on Charlie's face.

She gasps. "Dad!"

Foster howls with laughter, throwing his entire body backward.

A small growl passes Alice's lips as she leans forward to pick up a card, the first one being a blue. She sends Foster a smug grin and places the card down.

I send my own glare at Ash when he places a *skip* down, making it Foster's turn again. How many skips does this man have?

Foster places a *draw two* on top of the pile. Russell follows suit with a second one and Charlie places a *red draw two* on top of that.

Alice throws her cards face down, her blue eyes blazing. "This is ridiculous. You're all cheating."

Foster laughs with a grin. "Take the cards, love."

She grumbles as she grabs six cards and adds them to her pile.

When it finally gets to my turn, I'm finally able to use one of my wild cards and change colors.

"Uno." I grin and a groan comes from Ash.

"This is why I was skipping you."

"Have you been looking at my cards?" I accuse.

He shrugs, but a grin forms on his face. "You don't hide them well."

"I'm clamming," Foster says, placing a card down. "Food almost done, mate?" he asks Russell.

Russell straightens and looks over the couch with narrowed eyes. "Ten more minutes."

"Clamming?" I whisper, leaning into Ash on my left.

Ash chuckles. "He means starving."

"Don't be afraid to call him out on his weird phrases," Alice says, looking at her cards with a scowl before placing a *wild draw four* and calling out, "Yellow."

It hasn't escaped my notice that Alice seems more comfortable here with them than she did while I was in the hospital. Is it because no other eyes are on her to judge or bully her?

Ash groans. "I'm not even going to grab the four cards, Ellie wins."

Foster jerks his head up. "What why?"

I grin and place my last card on the pile, a *wild.*

THE BOYS GO into the kitchen to get the food ready while Alice and I set the table. I'm hit with a sense of nostalgia. The last Thanksgiving I had that was actually good was with my parents before they died. I was only ten, but we would always go outside and play in the snow. My parents would bundle me up, and we'd build a snowman if there was enough snow, have snowball fights, and make snow angels.

"How are you feeling? Any better?" Alice asks, following me with silverware while I place the plates down.

"I'm doing okay." I shrug. "Still have a headache on and off, and I'm tired a lot, but other than that I'm fine."

I glance at her to find her nodding. "That's normal with concussions."

Well, that's a relief.

Walking around, I place a plate down at the head of the table. Who's going to sit where? I eye Alice again. Her pale-blonde hair is much lighter than her brother's or Charlie's. She doesn't really look like either. Her eyes are definitely the same blue as Charlie's and Zac's, but that's about it. She must take after her mother.

Which begs the question, where is she?

"Have you worked in the hospital long?" I ask.

She lets out a heavy breath, placing the last set of silverware down. "Yeah. Since I was sixteen."

I bite my lip. I wish that told me more, but since she's a lycan, I really have no idea how long ago that was. She looks to be not much older than me, maybe twenty-two, but so does Ash and he's over a hundred.

I get a flash of her bright blue eyes as they briefly meet mine before falling back to the table. "I'm thirty-three."

I blink. So, she's young. I was expecting her to say she was in her eighties or something. I look over at the guys, my eyes falling on each one of them. Foster and Russell are bickering over food, Ash is smiling and shaking his head at their antics. Charlie interjects, saying something that causes Foster to burst out in laughter.

How old are they? Are they closer to Ash's or Alice's age? It's so hard to tell. I know Charlie has to be older than everyone, but does being a pureblood or an omega change how fast you age?

Alice follows my gaze. "My dad is in his four hundreds. Russell is one hundred and twenty-one. He just had a birthday. Foster is ninety-eight. Sophie, who isn't here, but usually hangs out with them...or at least she used to...is eighty-six. So they all are around the same age." I turn back to her to find her staring at them, wistfully. She looks at me with a small smile. "I've always felt a bit weird being the youngest."

I try to give her a reassuring smile. "Well, we can be youngins together."

I instantly regret it when her eyes light up, and I remember my plan to leave.

"What's it like being human?" she asks.

I jerk back. "What?"

Her hands clench onto the back of one of the chairs, her eyes downcast. "Sorry, that was a strange question."

"Uh, no. It's fine. I just never thought I'd ever be asked that." I laugh lightly.

She nods. "Because you didn't know we existed before."

I tug on the sleeves of my sweater, tucking my hands inside of it. "Yeah."

Her hand shakes as she tucks a strand of hair behind her ear. "My mom was a human. She died when I was really young. But I always wondered…What if I was raised as one? What would it be like?"

I bite my lip. "I…"

She shakes her head. "It's just…sometimes I wish I was one." She glances up at me. "Having a long life isn't all it's cracked up to be. I don't want to work at the hospital my whole life, serving meals, but that's what everyone expects of me as an omega. I want more out of life. I want to travel, and I want…" She averts her gaze.

"You want?" I ask softly.

Her body stiffens. "It's dumb."

"Try me."

She gnaws on her bottom lip as she tenses more. "I want to find my mate." She visibly relaxes once the words come out. Her shoulders sag, as if this desire has been burdening her for a while.

"Why would that be dumb?" I ask.

She lifts one shoulder in a shrug. "Not many find their mate anymore. Not many even want to."

"Because people don't travel?"

"Yeah, I guess. Or they already found someone they want to spend their long life with. Or they don't want to be tied down." She uses air quotes on 'tied down'. "But purebloods travel so it's more likely that they will find their mate."

My heart sinks. I can't help thinking Ash's feelings might change when he finds his mate.

Why am I even getting upset about this? I can't stay.

"Omegas *never* travel. Their place is in the pack. Whatever pack they are born into they remain for the rest of their life."

My brows scrunch together. "Isn't your brother the alpha, though?"

Why wouldn't he let his own sister travel? And why is she an omega while he's an alpha?

She nods. "Yeah, but he's changed a lot since I was younger."

"You ladies ready to eat?" Charlie comes over, holding a casserole dish with mittens.

Alice straightens and smiles at him. "Yep, I'm starving."

THIS HAS to be the *best* meal I've ever had. Not only does everything smell delicious—it *is* delicious. I moan around another spoonful of sweet-potato casserole. How does it keep getting better with each bite? Did they add magic to the dish or something?

I open my eyes to see Ash staring at me, hunger burning in his gaze. He's sitting at one end of the table. I'm on his right with Alice beside me and Foster at the other end. Charlie is across from Alice, and Russell across from me.

Charlie chuckles, diverting my gaze. "Russell is famous for his cooking. It's always a treat whenever we're invited to dinner."

Russell clears his throat, his fork hovering over his food as he stares at his plate.

"Where did you learn?" I ask.

"Me Nana taught me," he responds gruffly with his thick Irish accent then proceeds to eat without saying another word.

Foster starts up the conversation again for the rest of dinner while I catch glimpses of Ash eyeing me every once in a while.

I'm stuffed to the max by the time everyone is done eating. I didn't realize how much guys could eat. Maybe they eat more since they're lycans.

Ash and I walk them out and wave to them as they drive off.

When the last taillights disappear, Ash turns to me. "Was that too much?"

I shake my head. I'm exhausted, there's no denying that, but it was nice to get to know the people closest to Ash. "I like them."

He grins. "Yeah?"

I nod. "Do...do you think they like me?"

Ash's eyes soften, a smile still in place. "Yeah, they do. They're an accepting bunch."

My smile grows as Ash places his hand on the small of my back and leads me inside. I know I'm leaving soon and shouldn't care what they think of me, but I do. I want them to like me. I want to be accepted into this group of friends that's more like a family. Thinking of friends that are like family makes me miss Jane and Emma. I wonder how they're doing. When I contacted Jane and Emma while I was in the hospital, they were so happy to hear from me, but it's not the same as seeing them in person.

"You okay?"

I smile. It's never hard to smile around Ash. "Yeah, just thinking about Jane and Emma."

He nods in understanding. "I'm sure they're missing you. Ready for bed?"

I sigh with relief. "Definitely."

30

Ellie

*I*t's been just over a week since Thanksgiving, but not much has happened. Ash is always around, and I somehow lost my phone charger, so there's no way to contact a taxi to come get me.

A knock on my door sounds as I pull my hair up into a ponytail.

"Come in," I say.

Ash opens the door. "Hey."

"Hi."

"You have some visitors."

"What?" I tighten my hair. "Visitors?" He never mentioned anyone coming over today.

He grins. "Come and find out for yourself." When I don't move, his smile dims. "Unless you'd rather not? I can tell them that you need to rest."

"No, let's go." I shake my head and set my shoulders.

I've never actually had a visitor before, let alone two. It's a strange feeling. I follow him out of the room and into the family room.

I peer around him.

"Emma!" I smile as she stands up from the couch. My eyes catch onto another beside her. "Jane?"

Jane steps toward me with tears in her eyes. She goes in for a hug, but pauses before making contact. She drops her arms and takes a step back. "I'm sorry, I know how much you don't like to be touched."

Shaking my head, I step forward and wrap my arms around her. I still have some anxiety when I touch her, but it's easier when I initiate it. "I've been working on it. Besides, I'd never turn down a hug from you."

Arms wrap around me from behind, I glance back to find Emma joining the hug. I laugh and hold on tighter. It's almost like coming home. My favorite people are all in one room.

Letting go reluctantly, I ask, "What are you two doing here?"

"The better question is, how are you feeling?" Jane asks.

I give her a pointed look.

Her face lights up as she laughs. "Seriously, I'm not spilling until you tell me how you're doing."

I sigh. "I'm on the mend. I've had a headache I can't seem to kick, so not fully healed, but I'm getting there." I leave out that the headaches have been getting worse with each passing day.

She smiles. "I'm so glad. I wish I could've visited you."

"When did you get here?"

"A few days ago." Jane looks at Emma. Seeing them side by side you can tell they're sisters, but I can also notice the differences better. Jane has lighter brown skin and curlier hair while Emma is taller and her hair is darker. Jane's gotten highlights since the last time I saw her. "After I heard from Emma that you got attacked, I knew I needed to come. I'm sorry it took me so long."

"Well, I'm glad to see you. But do you think that was wise?"

Her eyes narrow. "Marcus was the one to hurt you, wasn't he?"

I dip my chin in acknowledgment.

"If he already knows where you are, it doesn't matter anymore," Jane says, and my eyes flash to Emma. "I told Emma when she told me you got hurt, but to not tell others."

They don't know the truth of what actually happened. They don't know lycans exist, or that Marcus is one, which makes it even scarier that they're here. Are they safe? I peer back at Ash, who steps closer to me.

He must see the fear in my eyes because he dips his head to my ear. "I have multiple lycans watching the house."

I sigh and turn back, catching Jane's concerned brown eyes.

"And I didn't tell anyone. But it would've been nice to know the truth," Emma says, pointing a finger at Ash.

Ash ducks his head.

"I told him not to tell you," I say before he can apologize. "I'm sorry."

Emma eyes us both as she puts her hand down.

"Emma actually has something to tell you," Jane says, touching Emma's arm.

The elder sister's entire face lights up as she holds out a hand, palm facing down. She's wearing a simple band with a diamond in the middle on her ring finger.

Jane rolls her eyes, but a grin is splayed across her face. "Yet another reason to come. I needed to meet her new husband."

I blink. "You're married."

Emma grins with stars in her eyes. "I am. Tom and I eloped. I was worried that it was the wrong time since you were healing in the hospital, but at the same time, I just wanted to be married to him already, and he felt the same way. It's our second marriage for both of us, so why drag it out?"

I match her grin. "I'm so happy for you." I hug her again, forcing the uncomfortable feeling down. I pull away, my brows scrunched together, and look around. "Where's Tom?" You could barely separate them when they were dating—I figured it would be worse once married.

"He wanted us to have some girl time."

Jane nods. "He's getting some major brownie points from me."

I smile. "He's a good guy." I glance at Ash, *my* good guy. He's been patiently standing off to the side, listening in as we reunite.

Noticing my attention, he smiles. "I need to start prepping a dish for tonight. I'll let you three catch up."

We head toward the couches in the family room as Ash walks to the kitchen.

"I'm glad to see you're staying with Ash," Jane says with a sigh as she relaxes.

"What do you mean?" I sit with my legs criss-crossed, grab one of the pillows, and grip it in my arms.

She gestures to Emma lazily. "Emma told me you were being taken care of and I didn't need to worry"—she sits up abruptly—"but how could I not?"

A pang of guilt hits. I made them worry. "I'm sorry I didn't call more."

She waves off my apology. "I didn't expect more. You've never been good at communication."

I frown. Doesn't make it right.

Emma speaks up. "We're just glad you're okay, honey."

Jane's eyes travel behind us to Ash in the kitchen. She leans in. "And having that hot guy to look after you? I'm definitely not going to take you away from that."

My face heats. If anyone else said that I'd be jealous or afraid they'd go after him, but since it's Jane, embarrassment is at the forefront. "Jane, you don't even like men."

She shrugs. "Doesn't mean I'm blind."

"He is attractive, even if he is a little young for my tastes," Emma says.

I chuckle. If only she knew. She's closer to his age than me. "He is nice looking."

Jane gasps, holding a hand to her chest in mock-horror. "Just nice? Are you blind?"

I shake my head, smiling at her antics. "Alright, alright." I chuckle. I lean in with a hushed tone. "I find him very attractive. Happy now?" I glance at Ash and freeze. He has a small smile on his face as his eyes flicker to mine.

I forgot he could hear us. Dang lycan hearing.

My face burns as I quickly avert my gaze, fidgeting with a corner of the pillow.

"Much," Jane said. "And you seem healthier...happier. Are you happy, Ellie?"

I pause.

A smile forms on my face. I am happy, aren't I?

When was the last time I was this happy? Before Marcus? Maybe not even then. The last time I felt true happiness was probably when my parents were still alive.

"I am."

Her face lights up. "Yeah? I was hoping so. And maybe with a man in your life, Marcus will back off. Ash told us he's locked up now, but for how long?"

My head jerks back as if I was physically slapped. "What do you mean?" It sounds like Ash lied to them about Marcus, but I would've, too. Anything to keep them feeling safe. But still...they think he can't hurt me right now, can't hurt them.

"Maybe being with Ash will deter Marcus if he gets out," Jane says.

"Or he'll go after Ash, too."

"That is a possibility."

"A possibility I'm not willing to chance." I shake my head. "You're the last person who I thought would suggest relying on a man," I say, then instantly regret it. "I'm sorry. I just wasn't expecting you to say something like that."

Jane usually brags about how much more reliable women are. She became successful all on her own. She's an amazing attorney and was willing to stick her neck out for me to put Marcus behind bars. But I knew—and deep down she did, too—that he would find a way to make sure that didn't happen, probably by killing us. So I refused, and there's not much she can do without me testifying against him.

She sighs. "Just because I'm anti-men for me doesn't mean *you* should be anti-men. Of course, I'm not suggesting relying on a man because you're incapable of being on your own. You *are* strong on your own, but you *do* need help. It's not bad to ask for help and rely on others. And I think you should rely on more than just me. You need help from anywhere you can get it, and there's only so much I can do. Emma tells me Ash is an amazing guy, and not only has he been taking care of you, but he can protect you better than I can."

"That may be true, but what if it ends up being too much for him and he gets hurt?" I ask. "I'd rather leave before anyone gets hurt."

"You mean, besides yourself?"

"Yes."

She shakes her head. "You can't live your life like this anymore, Ellie."

"I don't have a choice."

"Yes, you do. I'm telling you that you do."

"By staying with Ash?" I glance over my shoulder at him and make eye contact with his piercing glacier-blue eyes. He's going to have some words with me later, I can already tell.

"Yes. He probably can protect you better than I can."

From the hurt in her voice, that must have been hard for her to say.

I turn my gaze away from Ash, finding her staring at me in earnest. I grab one of her hands and squeeze. "Jane, you've done more than enough." I sniffle and rub my nose, trying not to break down. She's the only reason I survived. "You gave me a chance to live. I couldn't have made it this long without you."

"Ellie." Her eyes glisten from unshed tears. "I just want you safe. Please consider it."

I close my eyes. "Okay, I'll think about it."

"That's all I ask."

31

Ellie

After dinner, Ash went to his study to work while Emma, Jane, and I watched a movie—though we ended up talking through most of it.

Once the credits rolled, I led Emma and Jane to two of the guest rooms upstairs before stopping in front of Ash's office at the top of the stairs. My knuckles just barely graze the door when his muffled voice tells me to come in.

Pushing the door open, I find him at a traditional desk facing the door. His eyes light up when he sees me. "Take a seat. I'm almost done." His gaze drops back to his computer and clicking starts up as his fingers press against the keys. He told me he had to work, but what does he actually do?

I gaze around the room as I settle onto a couch on one side of the room with shelves bookending it. Comparing this place to his little hideaway barn, Ash's taste is a mix of traditional and minimalistic with a touch of modern. He also loves books. That might have to do with his age, though. He's been around long enough to accumulate this many.

"Why do you have the renovated barn when you have this place?" I ask.

The tapping stops as Ash focuses on me. His gaze pierces mine. "Do you remember how you found me that first time?"

I nod. How could I forget? He was bleeding out—dying—right in front of me.

"I've never actually thanked you for caring for me. Thank you, Ellie. I might've died if you hadn't patched me up. That was extremely brave."

"And stupid." I bite my lip, embarrassed, but before he can speak again, I say, "I didn't feel as scared as I probably should've. I mean, I definitely was scared, but there was always something that pulled me toward you, that made me feel safe, even if I didn't realize it was there in the beginning."

A small smile appears. "You listened to your instincts. When I finally woke, I felt the same as you. It's why I didn't shift and reveal myself. I didn't feel like I should."

"I'd probably have freaked to be honest. And ran again."

His shoulders rise before falling as tension leaves him. "I'm glad I didn't, then."

His piercing eyes see too much, so I peer around the room instead, not really seeing.

He may be glad, but I'm conflicted. If he had revealed himself, Marcus never would have found me here, but then again—I would've never gotten to know him, or even Emma.

"And to answer your question," Ash says. "Do you remember when I mentioned that there were other lycans that don't like me, and I needed to keep my distance from you?" I nod. "Well, I bought that barn and renovated it to escape from them. No one knows about it. No one but you."

"And Emma and Tom."

He chuckles. "Yes, them too, but they are human so I wasn't

worried about them."

"What about your friends?"

He tilts his head. "Foster and Russell?"

I nod.

"Ah, they know about it, but not where it is. It's my escape from the lycan world."

"Huh. Why did you choose the barn?" I stand and make my way across the room when my eyes snag on a shelf of photos.

"The field I led you to, where we watched the aurora borealis, that's where my mother would take me to watch it when I was a child. We stopped when I became an adult, but it has always been one of my favorite places."

I blink at the pictures.

One is of him, Foster, and Russell. They each are smiling, Foster is in the middle with his arms around Ash and Russell's shoulders. Do they worry about Ash and the reason he needs a barn?

"Wait." I spin around. "Your barn was unlocked."

He blinks a few times then nods. "Yes. I usually know when Zac is planning to roughen me up. I unlock the barn a day or two before in case I need to open it in wolf form. I can pull down a handle but not use a key." He shrugs.

"If you know when, why don't you just run away?"

He sighs. "Stupidity?"

He doesn't elaborate, so I turn back to the bookshelf and look at the next picture. It's of a man with ebony hair laughing with a woman with golden locks who is lovingly gazing at him, and a young version of Ash watching them with a huge grin on his face. I'm mesmerized by the joy that encompasses his whole body. I want to see him like that. I want to be the one that causes it.

Picking up the next picture, my brows rise as I find a younger Alice with a shy smile, along with Charlie that has an arm around her shoulders. My hands shake as I set the picture down. There's a younger Zac at the very edge of the picture with a noticeable gap separating him from the other two.

"Were you friends with Zac once?" I ask, peering over at him.

His face shutters with emotions I can't place. "No, but we used to be more civil to one another. It changed when my parents died and he stepped up to be the alpha."

"Oh." I bite my lip, casting my eyes around the room, surveying it in greater depth. I note picture frames of certificates along the wall near the door.

Curious, I make my way toward it. Finding land certificates and ownerships, along with awards, a bachelor's and master's degree in business, and a variety of certificates that all deal with real estate.

"That's what I do."

"What?" I whirl around to find him still sitting at his desk, but he's leaning back in his chair now with his arms folded as he watches me.

"Real estate." He uncrosses an arm to gesture at the wall. "It's how I make my money."

"Right. Because you're rich."

He chuckles. "I guess you could say that."

"Everything you do is legal, right?"

He arches a brow. "Everything I do is legal."

I give a short nod and say, "Good." I make my way back to the couch and sit. "I've heard real estate can be iffy."

He gives me an amused smile. "Ah, but I'm sure they aren't as old as I. My parents bought property and land when they were cheap almost a hundred years ago, and I took over their companies and made my own purchases when I came of age."

"Do you sell the land now?"

"Some of it, but I mostly rent it out, or build then rent those out. I have rentals around the area as well as storefronts that can be rented for businesses. I use Russell's construction company and Foster helps me with investments, which has also helped me make a profit."

"You're really close to them, aren't you?"

He nods. "They are both like brothers to me. I'm sure they'd like to see you again, that is, if you don't plan on skipping out on me."

I purse my lips. "Ash."

Ash sighs as he stands. "We can head to bed now." He rounds the desk before offering a hand to help me up. He doesn't move away though, leaving me no room. My body rubs against his as I stand. He's solid and warm, towering over me, his chest in line with my face. My heart races, and it takes me too long to try to step away from him.

My breath hitches as he grabs my biceps, keeping me in place. "Do you still plan on leaving?"

My gaze jumps to his. "I-I can't stay. You know that." I know I told Jane I'd think about it, and I will, but tonight my mind still hasn't changed.

"You'd be safe with me." His eyes grow so intense that I have to look away.

"No one is safe with me."

"How do you know that for sure?" He nudges my chin up with a finger. "Ellie darling, I can protect you."

"But who would protect you?"

He blanches. "What?"

"I don't want you getting hurt."

His eyes soften as his hand moves from my chin to cup the side of my face. "I'll be okay. I heal fast."

"I don't want you hurt, period." His eyes track my movement as I cover his hand with mine. "Even if you can heal from it."

Gaze locking back on mine, he says, "I won't be."

"That's what I thought about my parents. I thought they'd always come back, no matter where they went or what happened."

I fight the impulse to smooth out the crease between his brows as he frowns. "Do you remember what happened?" he asks.

Blink rapidly, I try to keep the memories at bay, but recite what first comes to mind. "They were in a car accident when I was eleven. Hit by a drunk driver, but I wasn't there. I was too young to see their bodies."

"Who saw their bodies, then?"

Closing my eyes for a moment, I allow my memories to rise. My stomach cramps as feelings and thoughts resurface. The turmoil I felt when I found out I was an orphan overwhelms me. I quickly shut those thoughts down and reopen my eyes. "I...I don't actually know. The cops came that night with a social worker to take me to a temporary home. And when it was time for the funeral, they were in closed caskets."

He pulls me into a hug, trapping my shaking hands between us. "I'm so sorry."

"It's okay. It was a long time ago," I say into his chest.

"Grief and heartache don't stop just because it was a long time ago," he says, holding me close.

I rest my head on his chest as my heart pings, his words ringing true.

"My parents." He goes silent, but I don't push. I know how hard it can be to speak about loved ones that are gone. It helps at times, but only when it's on your own terms. "They were murdered," he says.

A chill runs through me. "W-what?" I clench his shirt between us, his arms the only thing holding me up. "How?" I peer up at him.

His jaw ticks as he stares forward. "I don't know. I found them drained of blood in their room after a run one day."

"Stryx?" My voice shakes.

Just a small shake of his head answers my question as he peers down at me. "From what I could see, there weren't any bite marks. But that doesn't mean they weren't involved."

I lightly push away to examine his face better. "Didn't you just tell me lycans heal fast?"

He gives me a soft smile, but it doesn't reach his eyes. "Stryx bites are the one thing we can't heal quickly from. They can infect us with poison."

My eyes widen. "That's terrifying. Can your bites do that?"

He shakes his head. "No, and stryxes are able to control the poisons."

"How different are these stryxes from the stories of vampires?" I ask.

One of his hands comes up to tuck a hair behind my ear. "A lot about them are different, except that they do drink blood. They don't need to drink blood to survive, but most do anyway. I'm not sure if it's because their bodies have evolved to need it, or because it makes them stronger."

"Stronger?"

He nods. "When a stryx drinks from a lycan or witch, they're also drinking their essence, so while it's in their system, they're stronger."

"And a stryx might've drank your parents' blood."

"It's possible. Only explanation I can think of."

A knot forms in my gut. I'm digging for information when I should be comforting him. He doesn't even have the closure of how they died. "Ash...I'm so sorry. I don't even know what to say."

I've never been good at consoling someone.

He takes a deep breath, his exhale ruffling a few strands of my hair. "You don't need to say anything."

"Do you know who killed them?"

"I don't." My heart sinks as he caresses my back in a soothing manner. "I've had a few leads over the years, but never have had any signs until now."

"Until now?" I ask.

"I think Marcus is connected somehow. His scent. It took me a while to piece it together, but his scent was there when I found my parents."

Fear grips like ice up my spine. "Ash!" I push at his chest. "You could be next."

"Ellie, I'll be okay," he says, pulling me tighter against him once more, one hand cupping the back of my head to his chest. "I don't plan on taking action yet, nor have I actually found him." He smooths the hair on the back of my head. "I need to know where he is and what his plans are. And when I act, it will be after precise planning. I've put some feelers out about Marcus. There haven't been any sightings yet, but we'll be the first to know if there are any."

I squeeze my eyes shut, gripping his shirt. "There's no stopping you."

He pulls away to meet my gaze. "Just like you're determined to leave, I'm determined to protect you. It's not even because he's probably involved with my parents' murder. What he did to you is enough for me to want to kill him ten times over. His motivations may be more complicated than I realized, but mine have remained the same—you. You are my motivation. I'm going to protect you. If you'll let me."

Jane's words come back from earlier. That I need to rely on others more when they offer their help.

She's right. I can't do this on my own. I've never been able to. I was able to escape, but I would've died without Jane's help. I would've again if Ash hadn't been there. Is staying really worth the possibility of him getting hurt, though?

But if he's determined to 'take care' of Marcus whether I'm around or not, maybe it's okay to stay. And besides, I still have headaches that come and go. Am I really able to run when I still need to take naps during the day?

"Okay."

His eyes widen. "Really? You'll stay?"

I nod.

His face lights up and he crushes me to his chest. "Thank you, Ellie. I'll protect you with everything I have."

But that's what I'm afraid of.

If there's any chance of him dying, I'm gone.

But for now, I'll stay.

32

Ellie

Emma and Jane stayed for a few days before heading back to Tom's yesterday.

I briefly glance up from my drawing when I sense a presence near. "Hey." I smile at Ash as he walks into the kitchen. I go back to sketching.

His hand rests on my shoulder in greeting. "Is that me?"

A grin plays across my face. "It is." I lean away and move the paper so he can get a better look.

He sits beside me at the table, hovering over the page, his fingers lightly touching the edge. "I look…" His brows furrow.

"What?" I bite my lip. Does he hate it?

"Intense." He glances at me before his gaze returns to the drawing of him as a wolf. "I've never actually seen myself in wolf form before. Only reflections in windows or water."

I gape at him. "How is that possible?"

He shrugs, but his eyes remain locked on his profile. After a moment, he leans away and gives me a hesitant smile. "I came in here to tell you I'll be away for most of the day today."

I give him a blank look. He's never left me here alone before. "Uh...okay."

He sighs, his shoulders slumping, his head hanging. "I challenged Zac to be alpha."

I set my pencil down, giving him my full attention. "I overheard Foster asking you about a challenge on Thanksgiving, but I don't know what that means."

It can't mean anything good, though, if he's looking so forlorn about it.

He gives me a slow nod as he contemplates something, drumming his fingers along the table. "I'll have to fight Zac and either kill him or have him concede to me."

I blink. "Zac is Charlie's son. Alice's brother."

"I know." He meets my eyes, and I can see the conflict swirling in them.

"Why now? Why him?"

A muscle in his jaw twitches. "He almost *killed* you, Ellie. You were so close to dying."

"It wasn't him that hurt me, though. It was Marcus."

"I didn't know that at the time, and besides, he didn't stop it. He let Marcus almost kill you."

Seeing the fear and anguish in his eyes, I reach out to touch him. "But why today?"

"When he attacked you, I challenged him. The law of a challenge is stated that it has to occur within a month. Today is the last day. It has to happen today."

"What will happen if you don't?"

"There is magic tied to the challenge. It will kill me, or I'd have to concede and change packs."

"What? Die?" Panic rises in my chest. "I...no, that can't happen." If he doesn't fight—he'll die. But if he does, he might? How does that make sense? How is that fair? My heart aches at the thought of him dying. I can't lose him. "Will Zac concede to you?"

"No, he won't, he's too proud. He will try to win."

"You can just change packs, then."

"Changing packs isn't that simple. I'd have to find an alpha that would take me on before the challenge starts."

"Well, then just get an alpha to agree."

"That's just it, Ellie," he says, his eyes earnest. "No one wants a pureblood who just challenged an alpha. They're worried that I'll challenge them once I join their pack."

"You won't know unless you try."

He grimaces. "I did."

"What? When?"

"Whenever I needed to work, on the side of trying to find Marcus, I also contacted alphas around the states."

"Why didn't you tell me?"

"I didn't want to give you false hope in case I didn't find a way out."

"This is stupid. Why do you have to change packs, can't you just not be in a pack? Why are the only viable other options dying or killing? Why can't you just forfeit and stay in the same pack?"

"Forfeiting or conceding without a pack would make me a lone wolf and vulnerable. It's not something any lycan wants. Essence requires lycans to have a tie to others. As a pureblood, I'd slowly go insane and revert to my wolf form. If I didn't have a lot of essence, then the magic would simply fade over time, but that isn't the case. So, there's no way for either of us to be in the same pack."

"Why?" I want to growl, instead I bang on the table. This is so unfair. "Wait—essence?" I remember him mentioning it once.

"Uh, yes, sorry. I've been trying to keep it simple by calling everything magic. But essence is what we call magic in our blood." Ash rests his hand on top of my closed fist. "I know this is a lot to take in. But it's just the way the magic works. There are rules."

I look down at his hand on mine then at the drawing of him as a wolf. Both are him. I never thought much about it, but it makes sense that it's only possible through magic. "Were you created from magic?"

"In a way. But I was also born like you." He sighs and squeezes my fist. "I'm sorry. I wish I could explain more, but I don't have a lot of time."

My eyes snap to his, determination flowing through me. "You do, because I'm coming with you."

His face goes stone cold. "No, Ellie."

"Do you really think I wouldn't come after you told me? Of course I'm coming. I care about you."

"And I care about you, which is why I don't want you to come. I don't want you getting hurt."

"That's what you're worried about?" I scoff. "Me getting hurt? You're the one who is fighting."

"He could play dirty."

"More reason for me to come."

"No." His face is hard and fierce, but I'm not going to back out.

"Yes."

"Ellie," he growls.

"You could die, Ash." I unclench my hand to tightly grip his. The pain of losing my parents and then watching Will die flares to life. How much worse would it be if Ash were to die?

"I need to be there. I need to see you to make sure you stay alive. I can't have you die on me. I need you." Something breaks inside me at my words. I scoot to the edge of my chair to be closer to him and grab his other hand.

He softens and pulls me onto his lap, embracing me. "If you stay here, I'll know you'll be okay," he says into my hair as I rest my head on his shoulder.

"Ash." I hate to beg, but if it's the only way to change his mind, I will.

"It will be difficult to defeat Zac. I know he'll play dirty and try to go after you. I don't want to have to worry about your safety." He smooths the hair at the back of my head. "Have more faith in me," he says softly.

"I'm still coming." I lean away to glare at him.

He sighs and briefly brushes his knuckles across my cheek. "My resolve is weak when it comes to you. Just promise me you'll stay with Foster and Russell."

"I promise."

33

Ellie

The pack house is huge. Mansion huge. That could easily sleep a hundred people.

Ash opens my car door and helps me down. He interlocks our hands but pauses. Holding our joined hands up he asks, "Is this okay?"

I nod. I love the way my small hand feels in his large one. His hand is solid and warm, bringing much-needed comfort to my anxious heart.

Our feet crunch over the snow as he leads me around the pack house and onto a wide open field behind it. Already a group of people have gathered. Russell and Foster walk to us before we make it to the edge of the group.

As they get closer, I realize how tall they actually are. I like to consider myself average height, but with them near, I feel small. Ash is tall, but I had gotten used to only having him tower over me. With all three of them near, I feel like an ant.

Russell dips his chin in greeting.

"Long time no see, Ellie," Foster says with a smile, but today it doesn't reach his eyes. "How are you feeling?" he asks Ash.

Ash is stiff next to me, his hand tightly gripping mine. "Fine."

"Who are all these people?" I ask.

Foster glances over his shoulder. "People from the pack, supporters for Ash and Zac."

Looking up at Ash, I notice a tick in his jaw. He never really explained how he feels about this. Only that he's angry at Zac, but does he regret the challenge? He must, since he was looking for other packs to join.

Ash peers down at me. "You'll stay with them during the challenge. I trust them to keep you safe."

Foster strides closer and throws an arm over my shoulder as we walk the rest of the way to the group. I stuff my empty hand into my coat pocket to keep it warm.

I catch sight of Alice and Charlie.

Before I can comment on it, a commotion draws my eye to the other side of a ring that's beginning to form.

Dread sinks in as I recognize the dirty-blond hair. Breathing becomes difficult as memories flood back of him standing there as Marcus beats me. My mind goes blank and my body refuses to move as Zac walks onto the field flanked by two men and other supporters.

Foster leans down. "The redhead is Austin, and the female beside him is Eryn. They're his betas. She's nasty. Stay away from her." He nods to the remaining man. "The dark-haired brute on his other side is Rick, his delta."

My brows rise, but my eyes remain glued to Zac as the redhead, Austin, whispers to him. Zac's eyes move around until he catches sight of me. A frown appears on his face, his attention moves to Ash. "I see you decided to bring your lover. I didn't think you'd want her to see your death."

"Neither of us have to die if you concede," Ash says.

Zac laughs. "You really think I'd let you be alpha, brother?"

My jaw drops as Ash stiffens beside me.

Brother? Did I hear that right? Ash is Zac's brother? But...I thought Alice and Zac were siblings. I'm so confused.

Zac's eyes flash to mine then lands back on Ash. "What? Did you not tell her Ash? That you and I share the same mother?" Zac lets out a hollow laugh. "Wow, that's rich. I've been waiting so long for you to challenge me. To fight me back. To show everyone who the superior brother is. That I am the rightful alpha, not just a bastard. But you would never fight me until *she* came around." He looks me over with burning hatred and something else that I quite can't place. Regret?

They look nothing alike, except maybe for their blue eyes. But even then, I see more of Alice than Ash in him. I blink and jerk my gaze to Alice. She has tears streaming down her face as the man beside her looks stricken with grief, but at the same time fierce and strong.

"He *is* Alice's brother," Foster says. "They share the same father, Charlie, but have different mothers, while Ash and Zac share the same mother." His eyes are sad and locked on Alice's face. He looks down at me with a sorrowful, closed smile. "Small world, huh."

A small world that I know almost nothing about. I glance at Ash as a wave of betrayal hits me. Didn't he say no more secrets?

"Ash?" I whisper.

Ash flinches but releases my hand to step forward and in front of me, blocking my view. "My mother cheated on my father. My father only saw Zac as a reminder of her betrayal," Ash says without emotion. "My parents remained together, but she gave Charlie full custody of the child." Ash's gaze lifts to Charlie.

Charlie looks stricken with emotion now, but he's still standing tall with an arm around Alice.

Zac is tied to them all.

My stomach drops. Even more reason to stop this fight from happening.

"Isn't there anything we can do?" I ask Foster.

He looks down and shakes his head, his eyes full of pain. "This is the only way."

I look at Ash's back. Why didn't he tell me Zac is his brother? Is he ashamed? My heart is heavy, not for myself, but for Zac. What would it feel like to be rejected by your own mother? To not be able to get to know your only brother? I had two loving parents until they died, but I knew *both* of their love.

Zac snarls. "Don't pity me, Eleanor." My gaze snaps up and meets Zac's piercing gaze above Ash's shoulder.

He's right. I shouldn't since he still has a loving father and adoring sister. Maybe he had a step-mom that was good to him, but I can't help thinking how horrible it must have been for him to find out his mother didn't want him, that she wanted to stay with her other family.

"When I met you all those weeks ago," Zac says, "I had no idea what you meant to Ash. Just that he was keeping you a secret. In hindsight I shouldn't have…" He shakes his head. "Doesn't matter what I shouldn't have done. It's in the past now." His gaze jerks back to Ash. "Are we going to do this or not? I'm tired of waiting. It's time to prove I'm the rightful alpha."

"That's enough, Zac. Concede to Ash." Charlie's voice booms across the field.

Zac jerks back with shock, a flash of betrayal crosses his face. But his features harden just as fast. "I see. But you choosing sides won't change anything. I will *not* concede." He glances over Alice, a flicker of emotion in his eyes. He turns back to Ash. "Let's get this over with."

Ash grimaces, but recovers quickly, standing firm in front of me. "I didn't want to fight you, and you know that, but if you won't concede, I have no choice. You threatened my…" He turns his head slightly to me. "My chosen mate."

My jaw drops as a hush spreads across the field. I close my gaping mouth and look around—most seem surprised, even Foster and Russell.

A wave of utter surprise and dismay flashes across Zac's face, but it's so quick, I almost believe I imagined it.

Ash runs a hand through his hair. He sets his shoulders and takes a step forward. "Zachary Harris, I invoke the law of the challenge." His voice thunders through the field and bounces off the trees sending a chill down my spine. "I hereby keep my oath to fight for the position of alpha."

"I accept." Zac enters the ring in front of Ash. He doesn't appear as confident as before. He seems almost resigned.

My chest tightens. This is really happening. I lock my gaze to the back of Ash's head, only able to see part of his profile.

"Man or wolf?" Ash asks.

"Man, but partial-shift is allowed."

"Very well." Ash takes off his shirt and turns around.

My thoughts swirl, changing from shock to sadness to confusion, but the pain in my heart is constant.

What I'm most afraid of is not dying or my foster father finding me. It's Ash dying. I survived the death of my parents, survived the foster system, survived Marcus, survived running, but I won't survive the heartbreak that would come from Ash dying.

He's been there for me even when he didn't need to be. He kept me company, became a friend, saved my life, took care of me, taught me how to feel again. Ash cares for me even though he is under no obligation to do so. He found me squatting in his safe haven and didn't kick me out.

My eyes widen at the realization of how deep my feelings have become in such a short time. I knew I cared for him, but I may love him. If that's what I'm feeling.

But if he dies?

I shake my head.

That can't be a possibility. Him winning is the only option that's possible.

But how can I ask him to kill his brother? His only sibling?

Ash tips my chin up, his gaze full of concern. "I'll explain everything later, okay?"

My mouth opens and shuts a few times before I decide to just nod in response.

He caresses my bottom lip with the pad of his thumb. "If I..." His gaze lifts to mine. "If I don't make it, know that I love you." He places his shirt in my hands then turns back to Zac.

I can barely focus as they face each other and both partial-shift their hands.

Ash loves me.

I mean now that I really think about it, it was easy to see. He's practically said it without actually using those three little words, but this is the first time he's said it. I frown. Why now? Because he thinks he's going to die? Anger flares. First he announces that I'm his chosen mate, and now he tells me that he loves me right before he fights his brother.

With the first hiss of pain, my attention snaps back into the present.

It was Zac. He's holding his side where there's four slashes, but it's not deep.

He and Ash couldn't be more different in appearance and temperament. Zac with his blond hair and golden skin, Ash with his ebony hair and darker complexion. Zac has a temper, while Ash is calm. The only thing they have in common is their eyes. Both blue and vibrant, but different emotions swirl in each.

Foster wraps an arm around my tense shoulders. "He'll be okay, Ellie."

My hands wring together when Zac growls and jumps at Ash.

Ash easily side-steps Zac, but at the last second Zac stretches his arm out to swipe with his partial-shifted hand. Ash blocks it, but Zac's claws slash through the skin on his arm.

I fight back a cry at Ash's hiss of pain, even from here I can see the deep gashes on his forearm.

Zac doesn't let up for a single moment as he goes for another attack, but Ash is ready and ducks as Zac aims for his face.

The woman that was with Zac earlier, Eryn, yells from the other side of the ring, "If you want to catch his pretty face, you gotta do a surprise attack."

Zac doesn't pay her any heed as Ash tries to retaliate, going for Zac's injured side. He moves aside and punches Ash in the gut.

But Ash claws Zac's other side in the process.

Zac snarls in pain and anger, clenching his side.

In an instant, they both attack each other in a whirl of punches and claws that go back and forth. Blood flows from them both, but it's clear that Ash has the upper hand, landing more blows than Zac.

Zac advances, but it's slow compared to when they first began, while Ash seems to still have plenty of stamina. He's faster than Zac. This must be because of his special ability.

It seems like Zac has realized this too when he makes eye contact with one of his betas.

Tension stirs around us, and the air changes as Rick steps forward and into the ring.

Is that allowed?

"Bloody hell," Foster says, his arm stiffening over me.

Suddenly it's not just the beta, but everyone on Zac's side steps onto the field.

Rick is the first to shift, but soon others swiftly shift into wolves as well, all heading straight for Ash and us.

"Bastards." Russell growls on the other side of Foster. He shifts, shredding his clothes, and becomes a beautiful red-brown wolf. He leaps onto the field beside Ash.

Ash glances behind with wide eyes as his gaze lands on mine. He's terrified. Not for himself, but for me.

"Foster!" he shouts.

"Already on it, brother." Foster pulls me away from the fray.

But in the brief encounter with us, Ash is overcome by Zac, who has shifted into his wolf form completely.

Zac's teeth sink into Ash's shoulder.

Ash roars in pain, taking hold of the fur at the back of Zac's neck, digging his claws into the flesh and throws Zac off him.

But the bite was deep. Blood gushes from his wounds and flows down his body.

My hands fly up to my mouth as a sob escapes. I distracted him. His concern for me distracted him. I shouldn't have come.

"Ellie, we need to get you to safety." Foster urges me away. Even if I could fight back, I'm no match against a lycan.

Foster maneuvers us through the fray. Slashing at others and forcing me behind him when some get too close.

He stops us as we make it to the pack house. Looking back, we see Ash struggling against Zac and two other lycans in their wolf forms.

"Stay here," Foster says. He leaves me at the entrance of the pack house and races off to help Ash.

Looking around, I can't tell the difference between enemy and ally. Who's the enemy? Who isn't? How do *they* know? I thought they were all part of the same pack.

"Ah, there you are, little Eleanor," says a voice that cuts me deep inside, sending a chill through my body.

Slowly peering over to my right, Marcus stands tall and alone despite the fray around us. I turn to run, where I'm not sure, but I know I need to get away.

Sharp pain erupts from my scalp as I'm yanked back by my hair.

"Not so fast," Marcus whispers low in my ear.

Reaching up, I try to dig my blunt nails into his hands, but he simply laughs at my attempts.

"Ellie!"

I glance to my side, and search for the voice that called my name. Alice.

She's in mid-shift. But it's slow and appears painful if the grimace on her face indicates anything.

Marcus drags me back some more with a maniacal laugh. "What do you think you're going to do, little omega?"

A growl comes from Alice once she finishes her shift into a beautiful, white-gold wolf. She's so small compared to Ash.

Alice jumps and attaches herself, embedding her teeth into

Marcus' arm that has a hold of my hair. Marcus roars and releases his grip.

I scramble away from him, my entire body shaking. I don't even know if I can stand right now.

He looks at me, hate in his eyes. He snarls and pries Alice off.

Holding her up in the air by the back of her neck, he looks at her with disgust. "Omegas are weak. It was like a mosquito biting me—more of a pest than a problem."

Marcus throws her on the ground, and she lands with a yelp. He kicks her in the stomach. She coughs out blood and curls in on herself.

No. Not again.

Seeing blood coming out of someone I care about at the hands of someone I hate. Who's killed someone I cared about before.

Something snaps in me.

"Alice!" I scream and start to run when arms wrap around my middle, lifting my feet off the ground.

I squirm out, trying to break free and screaming bloody murder. "I have to save her."

"She'll be okay," someone says through clenched teeth. But I can't focus on who it is, or who has me, or even if they're the same person.

"Let me go," I scream, tears running down my face. I claw at the arms holding me. I can't lose another person I care about, I just can't.

My fight dies out as the hands around my waist refuse to loosen.

I look behind me to find Foster the one holding me, his jaw tight and his eyes hard. Noticing my gaze, he allows his hold to slack, but only slightly.

Snarling at him, I try to break free again. How could he stop me from trying to save one of his friends? What's wrong with him?

"Ellie," he says. "Look, she's okay."

I freeze in his arms and look where I last remember seeing her, and find that he's right.

Charlie is there, only partial-shifted as he fights Marcus, but he's holding his own.

Marcus has an ungodly amount of strength, but Charlie is more experienced. Charlie ducks and throws punches and slashes in sequence, like a dance.

He makes Marcus look sloppy.

Alice shifts back into her human form, holding her stomach with a grimace. She's covered in dirt and blood, only wearing a bra and underwear.

Foster twists us away and carries me out of the war zone, swiping his claws at anyone who comes near us.

A scream pierces through the air, stopping Foster mid-stride.

He slowly turns us, dread seeping in.

My body goes cold.

Ash

*M*y shoulder aches where Zac bit me, and I'm covered in my own blood. But I'm more pissed than hurt. I just want to end this and get Ellie to safety.

Zac advances in his wolf form with two other lycans at his side, one being Austin, the other Eryn. I'm not going to hold back this time.

I let my shift take over, my heightened emotions allowing me to shift faster.

The instant my paws touch the ground, I'm on Austin.

My jaw clamps down around his neck. I don't want to kill him, but they've given me no other choice. Once they entered into the fight and endangered Ellie, it was over for them.

Because I need to survive this. I need to be here to protect her.

White pain erupts on my right hind leg and my left side, but I refuse to release Austin from my grip, not until he stops moving. Then, and only then, will I drop him.

It's not long before Austin falls from my jaw.

I swiftly turn around and slash at Eryn, catching her on the face. Even in wolf form there are tears and fear lining her eyes. She whines, backing away from me while displaying her canines.

I nip at her in warning.

Her eyes dart to Austin laying behind me. Zac is huffing, struggling to stand, from the pack bond breaking from Austin's death.

I lower my head. *Go.* I growl at her, giving her one last warning.

She makes a break for the forest.

Zac grunts at her decision, his front legs giving out, as the pack bond they shared breaks from her abandonment.

Leaving the pack, breaking the tie, is as simple as making the decision to leave, to break that bond. The only other way is death.

And only an alpha can sense the pack bonds with each individual, and since the challenge technically isn't over, he's still the alpha.

Having already suffered from the first bond break and the wounds I inflicted earlier, Zac can no longer stand. Taking advantage of his position, I charge.

Noticing me coming, he struggles to stand, but it's too late. I'm already on him. I bite into his neck, piercing his tender flesh, but not deep enough to kill him.

Concede, I growl.

Never, he responds.

I should kill him right now. Should end this challenge and become alpha.

But when I try to end it, my jaw refuses to close. My entire body shakes as I struggle.

Why can't I do this? Is it because we share blood? We've never been close, but I always wanted a relationship with him.

Once I found out I was going to have a brother, I was so excited. I've always had a desire to be closer to Zac, to try and make a friendship. But it seemed it was never in our cards. Too many obstacles, my father being one of them. He ignored him, pretended Zac didn't even exist. But I always knew. Always wanted to get to know my brother. Can I not end it now because I did?

With a growl, I release him and move away.

Zac shifts back. With a hand to his neck he looks up at me with wide eyes.

"Why? Why didn't you end it?" he asks.

I shake my head then shift back as well. I glare down at him, angry at myself for our relationship turning out like this. I should've tried harder to be a better brother. To be a brother in general.

Before I can respond, a scream rents through the air, piercing me to my bones.

I whirl around and see Ellie screaming in Foster's arms. She doesn't appear hurt, but my eyes travel to where she's looking, and my entire body freezes.

Marcus is here.

Charlie is fighting him while Alice lays in wolf form on the ground.

I see red. My canines lengthen as I turn around to face Zac once more. "You brought him here."

He stumbles up into a standing position with a hand to his neck, his legs shaking underneath him. His other hand is up in the air, trying to ward me off as he walks backward.

"I-I...I can explain. I didn't have a choice."

"There's always a choice, Zac." Even to my own ears I hear the vile hate in my voice. "You just always decide to make the wrong one."

I stride toward him, intent to follow through this time when another scream echoes across the field.

It's Zac who freezes this time. His eyes full of shock and horror as he stares back at the scene.

I slowly turn around, and what I find sends ice up my spine as my heart sinks.

35

Ellie

The moment Foster and I had turned away, Charlie no longer had to fight just Marcus. A group of lycans attacked from all sides, overwhelming him. But that's not what seems to freeze time.

No. It's the arm protruding from Charlie's abdomen.

Marcus' arm.

Foster hands me off to another lycan I haven't met. "Stay here," he says, then races back to Charlie and Alice.

But it's too late.

Charlie is looking at Alice with love as his lips move, but I can't hear what he's saying from here. Alice shakes her head, tears streaming down her face.

Marcus removes his arm from Charlie's middle.

Charlie falls onto his knees, holding his gaping stomach. Marcus' eyes zero in on me. He strides toward me, blood cascading from his hand.

Foster blocks his path while Russell fights the other lycans that surround Charlie and Alice.

There's a raging roar, and I realize it's Ash. He's charging his way to Marcus, tearing through lycans that dare to get in his way.

Marcus changes directions, no longer focusing on me, but on the trees that surround us.

And just like that, the tension snaps; fear, confusion, and sorrow spread through the fray as some lycans follow suit, racing after Marcus into the forest.

Zac remains standing not far away from it all, but he's frozen in place. His face is stricken with grief.

"I...I concede," he says quietly, but his words slice through the now-quiet field. With just those words and the heartache on his face, he shifts into his wolf form and limps away—in the opposite direction of the others.

My head snaps back at the sound of heart-wrenching sobs.

Alice.

I glance at the man next to me. He looks just as confused, but he's also not paying attention to me anymore, so I dash to Alice.

"Hey," the man yells behind me, but I don't look back or stop. I don't slow down until I'm a yard away from Alice.

Walking the remaining distance, my heart breaks as she weeps over her father, his head resting on her lap.

Kneeling down beside Alice, I place a hand on her back. I know what it feels like to lose a parent. I understand the kind of pain she's feeling. The loss of my own parents flare up as I watch her anguish. I would never wish this kind of pain on anyone.

I brave a look at Charlie. His eyes are cloudy and glazed over. No life left in them. His chest doesn't rise or fall. Yet when I reach out and touch him, his skin is warm.

Weren't lycans supposed to be harder to kill? Shouldn't he be able to heal from this? How is this fair?

I only met him once, but in that short time, I saw the love he had for Alice and the others. The guidance and love he offered. And I saw the others show him love and respect.

Fighting back tears, my vision blurs. I don't feel worthy enough to cry, only having known him a short amount of time. Not when he has a daughter that needs him.

Foster kneels down on the other side of Alice and closes Charlie's lifeless eyes. He pulls Alice into his arms, removing Charlie's head from her hold. He tucks her against his chest and nods to me in gratitude.

"Ellie."

I lift my eyes to find Ash kneeling on the other side of Charlie, wearing only boxers. He must've shifted sometime during all of this.

I meet his concerned, sorrowful eyes. "Are you okay?" he asks.

Am I okay?

I glance over at Alice who's sniffling against Foster's chest. He's stricken with grief as well. They've probably known Charlie longer than I've been alive.

Ash shouldn't be asking if I'm okay. I should be asking if Ash is okay.

"Are you?" The question comes out as a whisper.

His eyes shutter as he looks at Alice and Foster then Charlie. "Seeing death never gets easier," he says and stands. He gives orders to those around him.

I'm taken aback at the swift change.

He takes control so easily. Commanding the pack, reorganizing them, and delegating tasks. Leaving himself no time to mourn with his friends. Does this mean he's the new alpha? What will happen now? A few lycans cover Charlie's body with a sheet.

"Ellie darling."

I blink, realizing Ash is now next to me, holding out his hand. How much time has passed since I first sat here? He helps me up and wraps me in a hug. He's shaking.

"Ash?"

He holds me tighter. "When I saw Marcus kill Charlie then focus on you...I was terrified. I...I couldn't make it to you. I'm sorry."

I wrap my arms around him, but I feel something wet. "Ash! You're bleeding."

"It's just a scratch, let me hold you for a little longer."

"We need to take care of you."

He leans down and nuzzles my neck, breathing in. "Just holding you is enough right now."

THE PACK HOUSE has a small medical room, which is where Ash and I find ourselves after he dealt with the rest of the pack.

His pack.

He took charge, helping others and directing orders, before he allowed himself to be taken care of. Ten lycans died in total, including Charlie, and one of Zac's betas, before Marcus ran. We don't know where he or Zac went. We're not even sure if they're still together.

Ash walks us to the back of the room where there's a bit more privacy. He stops us near a window, next to a row of cabinets and counters. He pulls open a drawer, grabs a cloth, and wets it in the sink.

Dr. Kathy, who splits her time between here and the hospital, and the other healers are busy with other injured lycans, so I offer to help Ash clean his wounds.

Ash sits down on top of the counter next to the sink and hands me the wet cloth. I examine him, looking for any injuries. There are more wounds than smooth skin. He has cuts and gashes all over his body, from his shoulders to his bare feet.

"Go ahead and ask me your questions," Ash says as I decide to work on the shoulder wound he received from Zac's bite. Zac didn't just penetrate Ash's skin, he created large gashes with his teeth when Ash pulled him off.

I wipe the blood off around it first then focus on the gashes. They aren't clean. They're deep and still ooze blood whenever Ash moves.

Refusing to meet his gaze, I take a step back to rinse out the blood in the sink beside us.

There's so much going on in my head, I don't even know where to start. He told me he loved me. That I'm his chosen mate.

He also kept a huge secret from me that Zac is his half-brother.

And there's the fact he's alpha now and that I'm not sure where that leaves me.

He also lost Charlie.

Everyone lost Charlie.

"Why didn't you tell me about Zac?" I ask.

"I...I don't know." I glance at him while wringing the cloth out, but his head is turned away, staring blindly at the rest of the room.

"You told me you wouldn't keep things from me anymore," I say, moving closer again and dabbing more blood away.

"I know. I'm not even sure why I did. Maybe because I'm ashamed."

My hand pauses on his skin. "Of him?"

He glances at me. "No. Of myself. I should've been a better brother. Should've been there for him."

I frown. "Why weren't you?"

Ash shrugs, and I glare at him when blood seeps from the gashes. His lips twitch, holding back a smile. He's not even sorry.

"Ash."

He lets out a sigh. "By the time I realized I wanted a relationship, he already hated me," he says. "But I made a promise to myself that I'd never hurt him. Physically, at least."

"Why would that be a problem?" I ask, putting pressure on his wound.

"He constantly tried to get me to challenge him."

I lift my gaze to focus on his face when a question pops in my head. "Is he the one that hurt you when I first met you?"

He shakes his head. "No. He started it, but his betas and delta finished it."

"The three that were beside him outside."

"Correct."

"Huh." I continue to clean the blood on his shoulder. "I thought your parents were mates."

"They were. Chosen mates."

"Because it's hard to find your destined mate," I say while exchanging my cloth with disinfectant liquid. I bite my lip and pour a bit of antiseptic on his open wounds.

"Yes," he says, without even flinching. "They chose each other because they loved one another."

"Then what happened?" I dry his wound, then spread ointment over it.

"I was really young when we moved here. Twelve, I believe. They had already been mates for over a decade, but this was the first time they were the alpha couple. With having a kid to take care of on top of that, I think they forgot to put each other first. So when my mom met Charlie, her destined mate, she fell hard. She loved and craved the spark and attention."

"And Charlie, didn't he know she was already married and had a kid?"

"No, Charlie didn't know. He wasn't in the same pack as her at the time so he had no idea she was already mated and had a kid."

Right. Mated. I gnaw on my lip and place a bandage over the gashes. "Is there anything else you need to tell me?"

"No, I swear that's it. And I always meant to tell you, but…"

"You've said that before."

He runs a hand through his hair, pulling at the strands. "I know. I just wanted you to look at me in the best light. And how I'm with Zac, how our relationship is, is something I'm not proud of." He looks down. "I know that's no excuse." He runs a hand down his face. "I'm sorry."

I avert my gaze. I know that feeling all too well. It took me a long time to tell him about Marcus and parts of my past. Really, I'm just as guilty as him—the only difference is that I found out before he could tell me. And he's been injured because of my omission. I should've told him sooner so he would've known what a mess my life was before falling for me. But he also should've told me.

"I'm going to need time to trust you again," I finally say. His face falls and I try not to feel guilty. "The things you omitted are huge things about yourself. How do I know you're not lying about the little things, too?"

His knuckles go white as he grips the edge of the counter.

"Not only that," I say, poking him in the chest as my anger swells. "You decided to tell me that you love me and that I'm your chosen mate right before you fight your brother in front of everyone." I notice blood on his chest, and pick up the cloth once more and scrub at it. "How could you do that? You didn't even give me the chance to respond."

"What would you have said?" he asks quietly.

I move in between his legs as I work my way down his chest and to his abs, following the trail of dried blood. "That I think I may be falling in love with you, too. That I want to stay here with you. But no, you just had to go off and fight your brother that I didn't even *know* about. Then all hell broke loose"—my chin wobbles—"and I wasn't sure if you would die or I would." My hand stalls when I reach the light trail of dark hair that leads to his pants. My gaze lifts to his, finding his pupils blown and his nostrils flared as he stares at my lips.

"Ellie," is the only warning I get before he takes my face and crashes his lips against mine. Claiming me. His kiss is demanding, but his touch is light. I know I could break the kiss right now if I wanted to, his grip on my face isn't immobilizing. But I don't. I *want* this. All the emotions he's been hiding, I can sense them. All the desires and thoughts he has kept locked up, pour out into the kiss, like he's been starving for this. For me.

I feel like I'm stumbling through the kiss. My hands press against his bare chest. His muscles firm under my touch. His scent overpowers the smell of antibiotics. I don't know what to do, and I can barely think with his lips against mine. All I know is how warm his lips are and how I'm pretty sure my heart has stopped beating.

He groans against my mouth and slows the kiss down, but thankfully continues to take the lead, coercing my mouth to move against his. The softness of his lips, the light scratch of his scruff, and his warm breath between kisses all overwhelm my senses. I can't get enough of him. I drop the cloth and grab onto his forearms, not to push him away, but to ground myself as I get lost in his kiss. Our lips locking and moving against each other. It feels right. *He* feels right.

He never takes it further, but it's perfect. I never allowed myself to imagine what my first kiss would be like, but this....this is more than I could've hoped for.

I'm not sure how long it's been, but I'm out of breath and my heart is racing when we stop. Ash still cradles my face as he gazes into my eyes. He's panting just as hard as me.

"I love you, Ellie. I'm going to try to do better, to do right by you." He takes a deep breath. "And I'm sorry I didn't ask permission before kissing you."

A small laugh escapes me as we touch foreheads. Even though I believe him, he'll still have to prove his words. But how can I be upset with him right now when my first kiss felt like that? How can I even think after a kiss like that?

36

Ellie

*M*y hands shake as I tug on my black dress. The last funeral I went to was for my parents. I look in the mirror and examine my messy curls. I look so much like my mother, at least from what I can remember of her. At eleven, I didn't think to grab a picture of her and my dad before I was placed into foster care. What even happened to all their things? Would I have gotten them after I got out of the system? What would they think if they saw me now? Would they be proud? Or horrified by what I've become? Someone that runs away from her problems instead of facing them head on.

Ash lightly raps on my open door. My eyes flicker to him as he steps in. His light-blue button up and tan slacks make his eyes and dark skin stand out even more than usual. My gaze lands on his lips next. It was three days ago, but I can still feel the press of them as if it were moments ago.

He's been trying to be more forthcoming with me. Sharing more about his rocky relationship with Zac and keeping me in the loop with everything else that's been going on. He lost about one hundred lycans after the challenge. But even with the loss of lycans he still has over five hundred lycans under him, and as alpha, he needs two betas and a delta. Before deciding he discussed with me who he was thinking of picking. I wasn't surprised that he wants to pick Foster and Russell to be his betas, but he wants to pick a girl named Sophie for his delta. Not knowing much about her or the position, I trust his judgment, but it also puts me a bit on edge that he's picking a girl that I don't know. Apparently, I'll meet her soon since she's out of the country right now, but I can't help the little jealousy I feel.

Ash's gaze trails my dress. "Hold on for a sec," he says, turning around and walking out.

Uh. Okay?

He comes back a moment later holding the green dress Emma gave me.

"Where did you get that?" I ask.

"Emma gave it to me, and I kept forgetting to give it to you." He hands it to me.

I look at his clothing then at the dress I'm wearing. "Is black not a normal color to wear to a funeral?"

He caresses my bare arm, his eyes tracking the movement. "For humans, maybe. But lycans do things differently." His gaze lifts to mine. "We try to focus on the brightness of their life and not the sorrow their death brings. Today will be about their bravery, their desire to protect and defend their pack, their strength, and their love. Even if they weren't fighting for us, they were still part of this pack." Ash kisses my temple. "I'll be just outside your door while you change. Come out whenever you're ready. But there's no rush, my love. Take your time."

I flush at his new pet name he's taken on since admitting his love for me. He lightly pecks the corner of my mouth before leaving and closing the door behind him.

I WIPE my hands on my dress and bite my lip while sitting in Ash's truck. I look different. Last time I wore this it practically hung off me. Now it fits like a glove. Has it really already been two months since I wore this last? So much has happened, but at the same time it feels like barely any time has passed.

Ash opens my door and helps me out of the truck, and my boots sink into the snow. It snowed all last night and the chill in the air seeps through my coat, but you wouldn't be able to tell just by looking at Ash since he's not even wearing a suit coat. The only thing that's weather appropriate are his black snow boots.

I look up at the pack house. Snow covers the wide roof, and icicles dangle from the edges. Just going to a funeral is bringing up painful, lonely memories. I was old enough to know what was going on, but too young to understand what came after. Heck, I still don't.

Ash grabs my hand, intertwining our fingers as we walk toward the house. I didn't realize how much I needed his touch until now.

"How are you doing?" he asks.

I give him a faint smile. "I'm okay."

His brows draw together and he stops. He turns to me, concern written across his face. "You don't have to do this. We can get right back in the car."

Before he finishes, I'm already shaking my head. "No, this is important to you and your new pack. And it's important to me. I didn't know Charlie well, but I want to be here." I may not know Alice well, but she lost her father. She needs all of us at her side right now.

"How are *you* doing?" I ask. He also lost someone in the battle. Not only that, he saw his parents right after they died. Is this bringing up painful memories for him?

Ash steps closer, placing a kiss on my forehead. "I'm doing okay." He squeezes my hand. "You ready?"

I nod and he leads us up the steps.

A wave of heat hits us as we walk through the door. The place is packed. I cling onto Ash's arm as we make our way toward the back of the cabin. Ash nods to others as we pass by, and like Ash said, no one is wearing black. Everywhere I look I see a kaleidoscope of colors. You wouldn't have guessed this was a wake if it weren't for the solemn faces.

When we reach the back of the pack house, it opens into a large room with tall ceilings and a rustic chandelier hanging above. Giant windows take up the entire back wall. There's an empty beige wrap-around sectional in the center of the room with a fireplace in front of it, and giant windows casting the light from the rising sun into the room.

Noticing my gaze, Ash leans in and murmurs, "My parents designed this place."

Everyone else is either talking to one another in hushed tones or giving their condolences to those near the unlit fireplace. My steps falter when I see Alice standing, clasping an urn in her hands. My heart aches at the sight.

Ash walks us straight to her.

"Alice." He clenches his jaw, his hand gripping mine tighter. "I'm so sorry. I have failed you and the rest of the pack."

My chest tightens at the pain in his voice. Does he blame himself for what happened? If anyone should be blamed, it should be me. For moving here and starting this whole mess. I squeeze his hand.

Alice's lip quivers as she shakes her head. "Please don't blame yourself," she says quietly. "He always knew you would take the place of alpha one day. I know he would be proud of you." A tear escapes and rolls down her cheek as she keeps her gaze downcast. "I'm sorry about Zac..." Alice clings more tightly onto the urn, clenching it to her chest as her eyes glisten from unshed tears.

"Nothing to apologize for," Ash says roughly. "We're always here for you, Alice. You're not alone."

A few more tears spill over. "Is it time yet?"

He briefly closes his eyes before nodding.

Not long after, he leads everyone outside. Alice trails behind us with Foster and Russell at her side. Behind them in sections are the other nine urns.

We cross the open field that lays behind the pack house and enter the forest beyond. We walk for fifteen minutes until we reach an area dotted with hundreds of different types of trees, all at different stages of growth. We walk through them until we reach an area where the snow has been shoveled aside. There are ten small trees—unplanted—next to ten holes.

Ash stands next to one of the saplings, keeping me at his side, and waits until everyone has settled. Each person holding an urn stands beside a tree. Ash gestures for Alice to join us. She takes her place on the other side of the tree. Foster stays beside her with a hand resting on her lower back.

It's a bit strange being the only human here and standing next to their alpha as an equal, but no one gives me odd looks or comments on it. Does the pack already trust him? What do they think of me?

Ash looks to Alice, who nods, and clears his throat. "Thank you, everyone, for gathering today to celebrate the lives that were lost to us earlier this week. I would first like to begin with our head warrior, Charles Harris." He takes a deep breath.

"When my parents died, Charlie went out of his way to be there for me despite the rocky relationship he had with them. He always put everyone else first and encouraged us to be our best selves. But he also never judged. When I did nothing to help this pack after my parents died, he never judged me—even though he probably should have." He pauses, breathing deeply through his nose. "Charlie was a safe place for not only me, but for a lot of us. If I could've picked an alpha to lead you today, it would've been him. He was one in every sense but name. I will try to do my best to make him proud and to lead you all well."

I wipe away a few stray tears once he's finished.

Being a leader comes naturally to Ash as he proceeds to talk about each lost lycan on a personal level, and how much they'll be missed. He already knows all of these people in his pack, and I didn't even have a clue. Despite what he said, he's meant for this position.

Once he finishes speaking, he turns to the sapling next to him and lightly grazes over its small leaves. "As we place their ashes with their saplings, let us remember their courage, strength, and love. For each of us packs are what we live and breathe by, and now they will forever continue to give air to the pack."

Ash gestures to Alice. She takes a shaky breath and nods to Foster.

Foster takes the lid off the urn for her. She reaches her hand in, grabbing a small handful of Charlie's ashes. Her hand hovers over the tree sapling as she slowly releases his ashes from her palm.

When done, she grips the urn with both hands and tips it over the hole, slightly shaking it as the ashes pour out and into the soil. Foster picks up the sapling and places it in the hole and covers it with more soil. Alice recloses the urn and places it beside the tree.

I realize the others have done the same with their own sapling and ashes. Everyone takes turns caressing the leaves of the plants before making their way back to the house. I stand by Ash until no one is left.

ASH SLUMPS ONTO HIS COUCH, and I sit down beside him. He looks exhausted, eyes downcast and his skin paler than normal. He leans against me, resting his forehead on my shoulder. I lift a hand and tangle my fingers in his already mussed hair, massaging his scalp like he's done for me countless of times. A small noise escapes him as his shoulders shake.

"Ash?" I turn to him, his head never lifting as it shifts to my chest. I touch his cheek and find it wet with tears.

My heart shatters. I wrap my arms around him, clenching him closer to me as he sobs. My chest aches, tightening with grief for him.

37

Ellie

*M*y throat feels like sandpaper and my body hot like a furnace. To make matters worse, my headache is on full blast. I roll over to look at the clock; it's two in the morning. We just barely got into bed an hour ago, after Ash and I had a much-needed cry fest. I glance back to find Ash passed out on his stomach, a hand under my pillow. I can tell he's in a deep sleep just by how he breathes now.

I throw off the covers and get out of bed. My legs give out underneath me, and I fumble to find the nightstand. The world is spinning. Forcing my eyes shut, I take deep breaths to ground myself.

"Ellie?" Ash asks in a sleepy voice. "You okay?"

Chancing a glance back, I find him rubbing his eyes, but the movement sends a wave of nausea through me.

I turn away, squeezing my eyes shut. "Yeah...sorry for waking you. I...I just need some water."

The sheets ruffle behind me. "Here, let me get it for you."

I swallow down the bile that rises when I look back at him. He already has half of the covers off of him. "No, I got it. I'm already up."

He pauses and squints his eyes at me. "You sure?"

"Yes, now go back to sleep."

He sighs, laying back down. "Alright."

Ash's eyes close before he finishes talking, and a moment later his breathing regulates. He's abnormally pale, making the dark circles under his eyes more prominent. Ash became alpha at the same time ten other lycans were killed, including someone he cared deeply for, making his first event as alpha a funeral. It has taken a toll on him. I want him to be able to get as much sleep as possible. I'm sure I'm fine, and it's just my concussion acting up again.

Moving slowly, I cross the room and enter the hallway. It's covered in darkness.

I place a hand on the wall and follow it down, making my way into the kitchen. Moonlight shines across the counters as I stumble against them. My arms shake as I lean against them, trying to give my wobbly legs a break.

Forcing the dizziness away, I stumble to the wall and fumble for the light switch. I groan against the brightness, the light temporarily blinding. The ache in my head intensifies and spreads through the rest of my body. I collapse against the wall and follow it down to the ground as pain overwhelms me.

Pulling my legs in, I cradle my head between my knees with a groan. My entire body burns. What's wrong with me? Did I get the flu?

"Ellie?" Ash's voice sounds down the hall. "Ellie." There's a light touch on my arm as he crouches down beside me. "What's wrong?"

I keep my head down. "I don't know. I think I'm sick."

Ash moves my hair aside and places a cool hand on the side of my face, his touch slightly easing the pain. "You're burning up," he says. He gets up and I hear him open a cabinet and shuffle through it. He comes back a moment later, crouching back down. I look up, curious. He holds a glass of water and hands me some pills.

"Here, this should help bring the fever and the pain down."

I reach for the glass but lose my balance and tumble into him. I moan against his chest at the impact. It feels like my skin is trying to peel off my face.

He wraps an arm around me to hold me steady.

"I'm sorry," I whisper.

"You don't need to—" He goes still.

After a moment of neither of us moving, I peer up at him. His pupils are blown as his eyes meet mine.

"Ash?"

"This can't be possible," he says under his breath, his brows drawn together.

"What?"

"Who were your parents?"

I blink. "Why?" I'm not really in the mood to discuss them right now.

He sets the water down on the ground and pulls me closer, lightly gripping my arms. His eyes swirl brighter with each passing moment. "Ellie, who were your parents?" he asks, enunciating each word.

"Addison and Gabriel Hollenberg."

"Hollenberg, Hollenberg..." he mutters, then his eyes light up. "That's a..." His gaze snaps back to mine. "What about your mother's maiden name?"

"Thornton."

A smile spreads across his face. Now I'm not just utterly confused, but also starting to get pissed. Why is he grinning while I'm in pain?

Ash tracks my movements as I reach up to rub my temple, my head continuing to throb. "Can I have water now?" I ask.

"How long have you had these headaches?" he asks instead of answering.

I sigh. "I don't know, since the hospital?"

"Anything else? Any symptoms you've been struggling with?"

"Maybe?" It's too painful to think right now.

"Try to remember, Ellie. I know you're in a lot of pain right now, but I need to know."

I rest my head against him, my head tucked under his chin. "I've been feeling warmer lately."

"Anything strange? Like maybe enhanced eyesight or hearing?"

"No. I—" The memory of hearing him and Dr. Kathy in the hall comes to mind. "Actually, yes," I say, then tell him about it.

He shakes his head. "How did I not see this?"

"What?" I peer up at him.

"You're not sick. I should've seen the signs: the larger appetite, the sparks I feel whenever we touch, how fast you healed in the hospital. The headaches, why you smell different...it all pointed to this. I was just too blind to see it."

"I don't understand."

His glacier-blue eyes pierce mine. "You're shifting."

"W-what does that mean?" It can't possibly mean what I think it means.

Ignoring me, he says, "But not only are you shifting, but you're a freakin' pureblood."

I shake my head and quickly regret it. I force out, "No, I'm not." Then another wave of pain rips through my body, forcing my back to bow out.

Ash stands up, pulling me with him. "I don't have much time to explain, but I need to get you to the basement before you shift." He holds me to him as he makes his way to the door that leads to the basement.

Visions of my past resurface, and I fight Ash's hold. *Please don't make me,* I silently beg him as darkness ebbs its way inside. I can't go back to that cold, dark place. I can't. "N-no. Please, don't." I half-heartedly push against his chest, trying to escape his arms. "Don't. Please. I can't."

"Shit," he says while I push against him. "I'm so sorry, Ellie. Stop fighting me, I won't take you down there."

Ash's pleading voice breaks through the fog of fear in my mind. I relax against him as a cry bursts from my lips. He holds me as my body shakes in his arms.

He brushes the hair out of my face. "Please, forgive me, Ellie. I wasn't thinking."

I nod, crying against him. There's too much going on inside me right now. Not only does my body hurt, but so does my mind as it rages with fear.

Ash lifts me and cradles me in his arms. "I'm going to take you outside. It's the next best thing."

I bury my face in the crook of his neck. His scent brings me comfort, even if it's brief, as he carries me outside. Even the chill of the air barely makes a difference to my fevered skin.

"What's happening to me?" I whisper against his skin. His normally warm skin feels cooler than mine for once.

Ash continues to carry me deeper into the trees when he answers, "I'm sorry I didn't realize it sooner, but you're a lycan, Ellie."

"How is that possible?" I can't shift into a wolf.

He stops and sets me down, but continues to hold me up. "Both of your parents are purebloods. I'm ashamed that I didn't recognize the name Hollenberg the first time you mentioned it. A lesser known name, but I recognize your mother's. She's of a powerful line."

My mind swirls with this new information. How did I never know this? How do lycans even exist? "You never explained how lycans came to be."

He grimaces. "I know, but after this I promise I will, okay?" I nod. "Now, I'm going to let you go and talk you through this. I'll shift with you. Do you think you can stand on your own?"

"I...I think so."

He takes a shaky breath and slowly releases me.

The throbbing intensifies as I use my own muscles to hold my weight, but I'm able to keep upright.

Ash removes his shirt, and I squeak as he begins to remove his pants. "W-what are you doing?"

Pausing with his hands on his waistband, he looks up. "If you don't want to ruin those cute pajamas, you're going to have to remove your clothes, too."

My eyes widen. "I'm not getting naked."

"They'll shred during the shift. I'll turn around." He does, and I quickly avert my gaze when his sweats continue to lower.

I frown down at my polka dot pajamas. I really would hate to ruin them, even if they're hot and confining right now. I fumble through the buttons before pulling off my shirt and pants. For once I'm grateful for all the times I had to squat because it forced me to get used to wearing a bra at night. Since living with Emma, I stopped that habit, but tonight I was too tired to take it off.

Despite keeping my underwear and bra on, my face flames from my near nakedness. Thank goodness it's dark. Wait. Can lycans see in the dark? My vision seems perfectly fine right now.

"Are you done?" Ash asks.

"Yes, you can turn back around."

He does, but keeps his eyes leveled with mine. I can't say the same for myself as my gaze rakes across his body—to his toned abs, the coveted V and lush skin tone, to his blue boxers. I bite my lip. I kind of wish they weren't the magic-infused ones.

Ash tucks his thumbs inside the seam with a smirk. "Would you like me to remove them as well?"

Yes. No! I fumble with my words, my face heating even more.

His smile widens. "I was jo—"

A shout passes my lips. His face falls. A sharp, stabbing pain travels down my spine, reminding me of the reason we undressed in the first place. He was a nice distraction for a while.

"Ash," I say through clenched teeth.

Hovering beside me, he rakes a hand through his hair and mutters curses under his breath.

"Ash."

"I know. I'm sorry, I've never done this before. It'll be less painful if you're able to relax."

"Kind of hard to do right now," I grind out.

"Right. I'm sorry." He rubs the back of his neck. "It's been a long time since my first shift. I'm trying to remember how my parents helped me."

I sigh and try to do as he says, but like I expected, I can't. If anything, taking deeper breaths makes the dizziness worse.

Sharp daggers shoot through my hands and travel through my body. I cry out when my gums start to burn. Tears stream down as I reach up and feel two of my teeth elongating.

"Breathe through the pain."

Glaring at him through my tears, my gaze quickly softens when I notice how distraught he looks. Before I can say anything, my joints shift inward, and I scream. It's as if my bones have shattered and are now stabbing every inch of my insides. Collapsing onto my hands and knees, I begin to sob.

Watching with wide eyes and a clenched jaw, light-gray fur with a hint of brown appears and disappears across my hands and arms. After everything I've had to endure, why do I have to go through more agony? Why couldn't I just live happily as a human with Ash? Why do I need to be a lycan as well?

I barely register as Ash kneels in front of me. "I wish I could take this pain from you, Ellie." His voice is thick with emotion. "If I could, I would go through this for you, but I can't. I can't stop this shift from happening. There are so many things I wish I could do for you right now, and I'm so mad at myself for being so blind. But I'm here for you. What can I do to help you through this? I don't know how to lighten this load. Please, my Ellie darling," he says, tears streaming down his own face.

"I can't do this," I sob.

He caresses my cheeks, wiping my tears away rather than his own. "You can do this. I know you can. You're so strong." He bites his lip as his voice quivers. "You amaze me with everything you've survived. You're the strongest person I know. You've endured so much, and revenge hasn't even crossed your mind. You're one of the toughest survivors out there. For once, don't fight the pain."

My head drops as tears fall to the ground. He believes in me.

But I can't.

Fighting the pain is all I've ever done. "I can't help it." How can I not? It's how I survived. How I survived my parents' deaths, the brutal years in foster care, the constant beatings from Marcus, and the life I had on the run.

"Look at me, Ellie." Ash nudges my chin up. "You're going to be okay. The pain is only temporary. Being a wolf is amazing, and I'm going to show you all the good that comes with it." I look down as another wave rolls through me. "But, Ellie?" I meet his eyes once more, his glowing, glacier-blue orbs. "You don't have to do this alone anymore. I'm here with you—always."

I cry harder at his words. That's all I've ever really wanted. And whenever I needed someone recently, Ash has been there. Either in wolf or human form. I know I can count on him.

"I still don't know how to *not* fight the pain, Ash. I don't know if I can relax through this."

His eyes are full of agony as he pulls on the strands of his hair. His eyes widen as they flash to mine. "I have an idea."

I huff. "Well, don't just sit there."

Suddenly, his lips are on mine. At first I'm tense against his tentative caress, but I quickly relax into it, and he grows bolder.

His tongue brushes against my lips, encouraging them to open farther. A shiver rolls through me as his warm tongue touches mine in greeting. I whimper as my skin blazes with fire. It hurts.

But just as quickly as the pain came, it's overpowered by Ash. His tongue moves against mine, demanding my attention, encouraging me to dance with him as he proves his passion and love for me. Whenever the pain flares, it's almost snuffed out in the next instant by Ash's relentlessness. The caress of his tongue and the soft but firm press of his lips are the only things touching me, yet it feels as if he's everywhere.

I cry out against his mouth as my bones crack. Ash lightly nips my bottom lip to distract me, but it only helps for a moment. My skin stretches so much that I'm worried it'll tear apart. Ash's lips are no longer on mine as my body feels heavier, but lighter at the same time. The agony that has been a constant companion is gone. All that is left is warmth and the buzz from Ash's kiss.

I open my eyes, not realizing I had closed them, to find Ash standing. My head is at his waist.

His eyes are bright as he gazes at me in wonder. "You're beautiful, Ellie." He reaches a hand to stroke my fur, sending a thrill through my system.

I nuzzle against his hand.

He smiles. "I'm going to shift now," he says.

I watch in fascination at how quick his shift is. His beautiful ebony wolf takes over his human form so quickly, I'd miss it if I blinked.

Ash is slightly bigger than me as a wolf, and more muscular. His eyes glow faintly. My head tilts to the side. Did they always glow? *Do* they always glow? Sometimes they appeared to glow, but I thought it was the trick of the light. Maybe they actually do at times, and it just wasn't something I noticed until now.

Ash nudges me with his head and the small pull I feel for him intensifies. I suddenly want to dig my nose in his fur and inhale while rubbing my scent all over him. I want to dig my teeth in his shoulder and shower him with love and affection.

Jerking away from him, I shake my head. Where are these feelings coming from? Yes, I'm falling in love with him—may have already fallen—but biting and rubbing my scent? Those are strange things to desire, right?

Breathing in, I'm surprised when my senses go into overdrive. I'm bombarded—I can smell and hear everything. The crunching snow under our paws, the squirrel running through the trees, the fresh air, the way Ash smells. Pine and snow mixed with musk. It's so much stronger now. And way too enticing.

Ash nudges me again, then strides in front of me. He glances at me and takes off. An urge to run, to follow him, rushes through me. I catch up to him, and we run side by side through the trees. He gives me a wolfy grin and I grin back. Ecstasy bubbles up as the wind rushes through my fur. The urge to howl overwhelms me and I give in. I howl at the moon. Ash follows suit, howling with me. Our howls combine and it's music to my wolf ears.

By the time we stop running and make it back to where our clothes are, my body is sore and waves of exhaustion hit me, reminding me what my body went through to get into this form. The rush of being a wolf has faded. Ash shifts back first.

"Shifting back won't be nearly as painful, but it will still hurt. Just keep your mind clear and let the pain flow through you as you focus on your human form."

Shifting into a wolf was a lot easier when it came to Ash's distraction, but shifting back isn't as hard as I was expecting. There's a slight pinching and bone cracking, but eventually I'm able to get back into my human form.

I wobble, and he grabs my arms to support me. I squeal, realizing I'm once again naked in his presence, and quickly step away. But just like before, he's only looking at my face.

"I'll order you some magic-infused underwear," he says as we both get into our discarded clothes.

I'm too tired to respond, and after a few steps toward the house —or where I think the house is—I stumble, and he lifts me into his arms.

Before leaving the cover of the trees, I'm fast asleep in his arms.

Ellie

I wake up to ringing in my ears. My head aches from all the sounds that bombard me. There's Ash's soft breathing as he sleeps beside me, the air conditioner, the normal things, but it all seems louder than usual. On top of that, past the closed window, I can hear the crunch of the snow as a woodland creature tracks through the brush and the rustle of birds as they ruffle their feathers.

How am I able to hear all of this?

Opening my eyes, I take in my surroundings. Everything is crisp and clear, even in the dark. I can zoom my vision in, focusing on a single speck of dust on a picture frame across the room.

My head snaps to Ash as he wakes. Even with this crazy sight, he's beautiful. He rubs his eyes, then jerks up as he sees me.

"What's wrong, Ellie?"

"Everything is…" How do I explain that my brain feels like it's about to explode from being overloaded?

Taking a deep breath to settle myself, I realize it's just not my sight or vision, but also my sense of smell.

Moaning at how wonderful Ash smells, I lean in closer. His pine, fresh snow, and musky scent is even better now.

"Ah, I see." He chuckles lightly as he lets me climb onto him. I settle on his lap, nuzzling my nose in the crook of his neck. He smells divine...and delicious. But not in a food way. Although, I do have an urge to bite him. Just thinking of marking him gives me immense joy. Now that I think about it, why haven't I bitten him yet? He's mine.

"Ash."

I purr and open my mouth, my teeth lightly grazing his skin. My tongue slips out next, giving myself a little taste.

A string of curses slips past his lips as a shiver runs through him. "Okay, no biting yet." He grabs my arms and lightly pushes me away. "Close your eyes, darling. I'll help you get your senses under control. There's a way to switch it on and off."

I blink a few times then close my eyes, but I can't help leaning toward him. I want him.

"Alright, try to focus, Ellie. I want you to think of each sense individually, then imagine it shutting off. One by one." His voice is soft and gentle. He's almost whispering, but I can hear him as clear as if he were speaking loudly. "I want you to do sound first. Focus only on the sounds of my voice and remember how it used to sound."

I do what he asks as he continues to speak. Thinking of how soft his voice is and how much quieter it usually is. It takes a bit, but then it clicks, almost like a switch, and his voice is in a normal soft whisper once more.

"I got it." I open my eyes to shut them swiftly again as I'm threatened with a wave of dizziness. Everything is still too clear.

"Good, now let's focus on your vision."

247

I SAVOR the last bite of my waffle. Taste was one thing I kept enhanced. The sweetness of the maple syrup and the crisp, crunchy waffle...I've never tasted anything so good. Except for maybe Ash.

Ash places his empty plate on his nightstand. After the long night we had and the funeral yesterday, Ash made us breakfast in bed.

"There's something I need to tell you."

Pausing mid-swallow isn't the smartest thing I've ever done. I start coughing. I reach for my milk.

"What's wrong?" I ask, still gasping once the lump has made its way down. My eyes narrow at his amused grin. "Well?" I playfully nudge his arm.

His smile wavers as he nervously tugs a hand through his hair. "I figured something out last night."

My head tilts. "Didn't we both?"

Chuckling, albeit tensely, he nods. "Yes, but you being a lycan isn't what I'm talking about."

"Okay..."

He runs a hand down his face then eyes me. "We're mates."

Frowning, I nod slowly. "Yes, you mentioned I was your chosen mate. In front of the entire pack, right before a battle, might I add."

He cringes. "Yes, but that's not what I meant." He turns to fully face me in the bed, taking my hands in his. "Do you feel that?"

My eyes widen. "You...you can feel that too?" The tingles I've grown accustomed to seem stronger than normal, but since I've always felt them with him, I've thought nothing of it. Just thought something was wrong with my nerves after all the abuse.

"I can."

"What does it mean?" I ask.

He grips my hands tighter. "It means...we're destined mates."

My mouth gaps open as a weight I didn't know I was carrying lifts off my shoulders. I didn't realize how much that was looming over me, that I was afraid of his destined mate coming along and taking him from me like what happened to his parents.

But I don't have to worry about it anymore.

Because *I* am his destined mate.

Breathing easier now, I ask, "So the tingles"—the corners of his mouth twitch—"are how you can tell we're mates?"

No longer able to fight it, a smile spreads across his lips. "One of them. Another"—he pulls me closer as he leans in and runs his nose along my throat—"is your scent. Now I understand why it always drives me crazy," he whispers that last part against my skin, sending shivers up and down my spine. "Also, the need to claim you has intensified." He begins placing kisses up and down my neck.

I bite my lip, fighting a giggle as his scruff tickles the sensitive area. "That...that makes a lot of sense."

He chuckles and leans back. "How so?"

"When I was a wolf, I had this intense desire to smell and bite you. I had it again this morning."

"Ah, yeah." He grins. "I may have enjoyed this morning a little too much."

I nudge him, but then grow serious as more thoughts tumble in. "Does this change anything between us?"

"Nope." He leans in and nips my neck, causing goosebumps to erupt. "I want you just as much as I did before I knew you were a lycan. This is just a plus. I don't have to worry about declining a future mate."

My heart skips a beat. "You mean, you were willing to be with me even if your destined mate came along?"

Abruptly leaning away, Ash captures me with his glacier-blue eyes. "Of course. I choose you as my mate, Ellie. I meant it when I said I wanted to be with you. I want a life with you."

"That's more than just a relationship."

"Yes, it is. I want to share our lives together. I want something permanent with you. Relationships can end, but mates? Those are forever. I want forever with you."

I blink rapidly as tears form from his admission. "How? Why?"

His brows dip. "I'm not sure what you're asking."

Trying to ignore the tightness in my chest, I swallow the lump in my throat. "How do you already know that it's me you want to spend your life with? I have nothing to offer you. Marcus...Marcus ruined me to be able to have any normal kind of relationship. I don't understand why you would choose me."

His jaw clenches. "You're not ruined. I hate that you think of yourself that way. You have everything to offer, but just spending time with you is everything to me. Hearing you laugh, talk. Sharing a bed and kisses. All I want to do is love you, Ellie." His eyes are earnest as he continues, "I wish I could show you what you look like to me. You're kind, strong, beautiful—inside and out.

"I know it was wrong when I told you I wanted you as a mate not even a week ago—at the worst time possible—and again right now. But I want to be transparent with you. I want to spend this life with you and be mates—if you'll have me. I know you said you may be falling in love with me, but I don't want to pressure you. I'm willing to wait for an answer, even if it's no. Although, I hope with every fiber of my being that it's not. And even if it's a no, I'll still be here for you. I'll still protect you and make sure you stay safe."

My thoughts swirl, as they tend to do whenever I'm front and center to Ash's attention and emotions. He's always taking care of me. With him I don't need to worry about a place to stay or when my next meal will be. But that's not why I've stayed.

I've stayed because I can't imagine not seeing him again. He's almost too good to be true, and I wanted to hold on to this strange thing we have as long as possible. Because once he realizes I'm not worth the trouble, he'll leave. At least that's what I've been thinking. But he's been saying the opposite this entire time and proving it through his actions. He's seen me at my worst. He was there when my past found me and has been trying to help me pick up the pieces. To figure out what's going on.

I know I already decided to stay and I've admitted to myself that I'm falling in love with him, but that didn't necessarily mean I was ready for more. I also hadn't really realized how serious he was—is—about me.

"If I were to accept being mates with you...what would that mean exactly? With you being an alpha and all that."

His eyes widen and his lips part. "It would mean we would run this pack together as the alpha couple."

I figured that would be his answer. Am I ready to be an alpha? Being with Ash doesn't scare me. I'm more worried he'll get tired of me and the problems that follow. But to be an alpha when I didn't know I was a lycan just yesterday?

"I'm not sure I'm ready for that," I say. His face falls and I quickly add, "But that doesn't mean I'm rejecting you...I just need time."

He sits up straighter. "You mean, you might want to be mates? With me?"

I bite my lip, my nerves going haywire as I contemplate confessing my thoughts and desires. "I do...I really like you, Ash, but I'm just not ready for such a huge commitment. I'm not ready to be an alpha, nor have I ever been in a relationship. I mean, there was Will...but it wasn't really a relationship."

He nods slowly as a small smile forms on his lips. "I'm okay with that. We can take it slow. We have time, especially now that we know you're a lycan."

It's so strange thinking I'm no longer human, that I'm actually a lycan. That I can now live hundreds—maybe even thousands—of years. I'm not even sure how changing into a wolf works. How did lycans even exist? How does any of this hidden side of the world work? He's explained packs before, but I never thought I'd be in one.

Wait.

"Ash, what pack am I in right now?"

Blinking at my sudden turn of topic, he refocuses. "That's actually another thing I wanted to discuss with you. You aren't in a pack right now."

"Is that a bad thing?"

Tilting his head back and forth, he says, "It can be. It depends on how much essence is in your blood."

"I don't understand. You've mentioned essence and magic before, but why would it matter?"

"Do you remember how I explained purebloods and omegas?" he asks.

I nod. "Yes, purebloods are from other purebloods." Which I am, apparently. "They don't have any human ancestors, while omegas have a lot."

"Correct. Essence is magic in your blood. This can get complicated, but the more essence you have, the harder it can be to control on your own. That's why we live in packs, and why stryxes and witches live in covens. I'm not sure why, but if you aren't linked to others, the essence inside of you goes haywire. You can turn into a wolf and be stuck in that form. And the opposite is true —those that don't have much essence will lose their ability to use it. Lycans and stryxes would no longer be able to shift or have their enhanced abilities, witches would no longer be able to use magic."

My voice is shaky as I ask, "I could shift and not be able to turn back?" Just the thought is terrifying. Being stuck in that form. I can't even imagine. "How do I join a pack? Can I be in yours?" I grab and clench his shirt to keep my hands from shaking. "You're an alpha now, that means something, right?"

Ash places his hands over mine. "Of course, Ellie. I won't let your essence take control. I would love nothing more than for you to be in mine."

"If I join, I won't be an alpha, though, right?"

He shakes his head as he lifts his hand to cup my face. "No, that's not until we perform the mate bond."

"What will I be then?" I ask.

"Anything you want to be. I never liked the forced placements."

"Okay." Tomorrow I can worry about my placement. Today I need to get into a pack. I take a deep breath, calming myself. "How do I join?"

His gaze drops to my lips as he clears his throat. "I will need to bite you."

My brows dip down. That seems a bit strange. I lean away and let go of his shirt. "I guess that's fine," I say, holding up my forearm.

A smile plays across his lips as he glances at my arm. "I have to bite you in a certain spot."

"Oh." I slowly put my arm down. "Then where?"

He moves a hand to my waist, his thumb beginning to rub against my shirt, causing my breath to hitch. "Your ribs."

I swallow. "Why?"

The warmth of his hand seeps through the fabric the longer it stays there. "The lungs and ribs symbolize you and your pack. The pack is the air you breathe and protect, but they are also the ones who will protect you and give you air."

The words he spoke at the funeral make more sense now. "That's why you bury lycans with trees."

Ash's brows rise. "Yes. Even in death we believe they are there to provide air to the pack and watch over us."

I smile. "I love that." I take a shaky breath and straighten my spine. "Will it hurt?"

His eyes lift from his hand still on my waist to my face. "It might. I've never seen it done. It's rare for people to change packs, and when they do, they complete the pack bond in private."

Well, even if it does hurt, I need to join a pack. "Okay, let's do this."

"Do you want to do it here or in another room?"

Why would we move? "Here is fine."

Ash takes a deep breath, then nods. His voice grows husky as he says, "Alright. Lay down for me."

Scooting down, I rest my head against the pillow.

My eyes widen when he swings a leg over me, his knees on each side of my body, trapping me underneath him. He moves until he's lightly sitting on my legs.

His large, warm body over mine sends strange things through my body.

Inhaling through his nose, Ash's hands hover over the edge of my pajama shirt. His gaze moves from my stomach to my eyes. "May I?"

Clenching the sheets next to me, I swallow and give him a nod.

His pupils dilate as he lightly grips the bottom of my shirt. I can't seem to catch my breath. Fingers graze over my skin while pulling my shirt up and stop right before my breasts. Fingertips lightly brush my ribs, causing goosebumps to erupt across my body. He leans down, his mouth a breath away from my skin. His warm breath dances across my rib cage. Hovering over me, his eyes ablaze as he meets my gaze.

"Still okay?" His voice is deep. His breath caresses my skin, sending shivers through my body.

Clenching my jaw, I give a short nod. I don't think I could form words even if I tried. This is a lot more intimate than I was expecting. Maybe we should've done this on the couch.

"Close your eyes, Ellie," he says softly, and I oblige.

I inhale sharply when I feel his parted lips against my skin in an open mouth kiss. The wetness from his mouth and the slight pressure from his tongue and teeth causes me to tremble under his touch. With my eyes closed, his touch is more vivid and intense.

His teeth graze my ribs, my skin the only barrier. I try to take a calming breath, but it catches when his canines lengthen and pierce my skin. My eyes open and a scream leaves my mouth. Liquid pain burns throughout my entire body.

"Ash!" I cry out, my hands go to his hair, gripping the strands tightly, forcing myself not to pull.

Ash presses his body into mine more, his hands moving to my arms to keep me still, but he doesn't remove my hold on his hair.

I swear his teeth hit bone once they lengthen completely. After a moment, my body slowly relaxes as well as my grip. Warmth soothes the pain, starting from his teeth. Almost like it's coming from them and spreading through my bloodstream.

My hands tangle in his hair as his thumbs caress the inner parts of my forearms, but he doesn't let go until my entire body is tingling. His canines retreat and he removes his mouth from me. I look down just as his pink tongue slips out of his mouth. His hooded eyes meet mine as his tongue touches my skin, licking the puncture wounds left behind. My toes curl as desire rushes through me.

I watch his throat bob as he swallows. He kisses each mark then pulls my shirt back down.

My lips part as he leans away. I say, "Why did you...?"

Moving off of me, he quirks a brow. "Lick you?"

"Yeah." My voice comes out more airy than I intended.

"Our saliva helps clot the blood."

Lifting my shirt once more, I peer at the marks to find them already gone. But I can still feel where he bit me. "What was I feeling?" I ask, fixing my shirt once more.

He leans against his pillow, his eyes tracking me as I move. "I was linking my essence to yours. You're now officially a part of my pack." He grows serious. "I'm sorry that it hurt."

Warmth spreads in my cheeks, and I avert my gaze, allowing strands of hair to fall to hide behind. "It only hurt for a moment."

Ash leans closer, tucking my hair behind my ear then nudges my chin to him. His eyes shift back and forth between mine. "You sure?"

"Yes." A smile grows on my face. "You're my alpha now."

His pupils blow out, the thin blue surrounding them glows. A small growl starts in the back of his throat. "Call me that again."

"What? My alpha?"

He hums as he leans in close. "I like that too much. May I kiss you, Ellie?"

"You don't have to ask," I say softly.

He quirks a brow, hovering his mouth above mine. "Oh, yeah?" Parts of his lips caress mine when he speaks.

I swallow. "Yeah," I whisper, clenching the sheets tightly, my entire body jittery with anticipation.

A corner of his mouth tips up into a smile before he erases the space between us, pressing his lips to mine.

Butterflies erupt at their soft touch and tingles start from our combined lips. His tongue presses against the seam of my lips, urging them to part, and tangles with mine. Sweet from the syrup and a taste that only could be described as Ash. I pant between kisses.

One of his arms snakes around me, pulling me firmly against him. Our limbs tangle, and I can't think of anything else. Nothing penetrates my mind when we're like this. His mouth and tongue demand my attention. It's only him. The way he feels, smells, tastes.

With a groan he pulls away, removing his mouth from mine, but doesn't release me from his hold. "I could do this all day, but there's one more thing I wanted to talk to you about."

Panting, I nod for him to continue.

A small smile curves his lips as he watches me try to regain focus. "I'd like you to start training next week, and to practice shifting. I don't plan on leaving you anytime soon, but just in case, I want you prepared."

I grow serious. I want to be able to defend myself, too. "I'd like that."

"Great. Now I'm going to kiss you some more before drawing you a bath."

He moves close and recaptures my lips, doing exactly what he said he would.

39

Ellie

The bath was just what I needed to feel refreshed. I stayed in for almost an hour. Each minute I soaked with a bath bomb and bubbles melted the aches away. I didn't realize how sore I still was from the shift.

Not knowing what else to do, I go searching for Ash.

Light spills out from the ajar door to his study. I lightly knock on his door to gain his attention.

He looks up from his computer and smiles. "Hey, come in. I just need to finish some paperwork."

I take a seat in one of the wingback armchairs in front of his desk rather than the loveseat this time.

Since moving in, I've realized just how clean Ash is. There isn't dust on any surface. His bed is always made. His toothbrush and toothpaste are never left on the counter. Clothes are never left on the floor. I can say the same for his study. There still isn't any dust, no clutter on his desk, just his laptop, a leather pen stand—because he's classy like that—and a lamp.

The snap of Ash's laptop closing gains my attention. He stands and walks over to me, offering his hand. "I want today to be a relaxing day, and I thought a movie would be a good idea. What do you say?"

"I say, 'yes'."

He grins as I place my hand in his. He interlocks our fingers then leads me out of the room and back downstairs. He takes me down the hall toward our room, but instead of entering one of those, he turns right into the laundry room.

"Uh, should I change?" I tend to wear one of the silky or cotton pajamas he bought me whenever we stay here. Which to be honest is all the time. But if we're going to leave, I'd like to change.

Pausing with his hand on the doorknob to the garage, he glances at me. My skin heats as his eyes trail over me.

"Nope, you're good. You look beautiful."

My mouth gapes at how easy it was for him to compliment me while my hair is still wet and I'm not dressed up. But before I can respond, he opens the door and I realize why I'm fine in only pajamas. Instead of a garage like I expected, it's a theater room. In his house.

I completely thought this was the garage, and the room is a lot bigger than I expected. There's a giant screen covering almost the entire wall to our right. But on the left, past multiple reclining loveseats, is a pool table in front of a garage door, yet there's no car in here.

"Did you have this added onto the house when you inherited it?" I ask as he leads me to one leather reclining loveseats.

"No, I designed this. I don't use it for any cars—as you can see." I sit down and watch as he walks over to a cabinet under the screen, squatting down in front of it. "I like to open the garage door during the summer when I'm with the guys. The house I grew up in burned down." I can't see his face as he continues, but his head hangs. "It burned down with them."

If I didn't have my new lycan hearing, I'd probably have missed that last part.

And I know who he means without him having to say.

"I thought you said that you found them drained of blood?"

"I did." He stands with a movie in his hands. He messes with a device on top of the cabinet.

"But..." I trail off, confused. I look down and fidget with the strings of my pants.

"I let it burn down."

My gaze flashes to him. "You burned it down?"

He sighs, running a hand through his hair. He turns toward me. "I might as well have. The fireplace had already caught the rug on fire when I got there, but it was small enough that I could have put it out."

"So, why didn't you?" I ask softly.

A glazed look comes over his face. "I smelled smoke when I came home from a run. I called out to my parents when I followed it to their room. But neither of them answered. Something...something felt wrong..." He moves a shaky hand down his face.

"Ash," I say, standing. I walk over to him and lightly touch his arm. "You don't need to tell me."

He grabs my hand and gently squeezes. "I-I want to." He takes a deep breath. "I found them lying on the ground... But it was too late. Their bodies were completely drained of blood." A shiver ripples through him, so I step closer to him. I wrap my arms around his midsection and find him shaking. His hands grip the back of my shirt. "Their lifeless faces... No matter how hard I try to forget..." He takes a shaky breath as he looks down at me with pale skin and tears in his eyes. He lifts a hand to the back of my head, smoothing down my hair in a soothing gesture. But I can still feel the tremble in his touch.

"That's why I let the house burn. I would never be able to live there without that scene haunting me. In hindsight, it was stupid. I would've been able to gather clues on who killed them, but I wasn't thinking straight. All I remember is the smell of rotten flesh. It's all I have now to go on to find my parents' killer. To make up for my stupid mistake, I planted two trees for them there. It felt fitting since they loved that place."

"I'm sorry." I wipe at the tears that stream down my face. "How long ago was this?"

"About twenty-five years ago," he says, nudging my hands away to wipe my tears himself rather than his own. "I've never told that to anyone before. Only Charlie knew what happened because he was the one who pulled me away from the burning house."

I cry harder. They died and the only other person who was there with him died, too.

My heart breaks for Ash and what he's had to go through to come out stronger. I can't even imagine how hard it must have been for him to see their bodies like that. I never saw what became of my parents' bodies. I only knew that they died in a car accident. All I could do was imagine, but I'm sure whatever I came up with wasn't as bad. Seeing it myself would've been much worse.

Ash pulls me into his arms. "Shh. It's okay. I'm okay."

"I'm so sorry. You shouldn't be the one comforting me."

He caresses the length of my back. "Your empathy and compassion...it's one of the many reasons I love you."

I hold him tighter. "I love you, too," I whisper against his chest, staining his shirt with my tears.

His entire body stiffens, his hand stalling. "Say that again," he says, leaning away, looking at me with burning adoration.

I discreetly try to wipe my nose. I can't believe it just slipped out, but now that I've said it, I can't deny my feelings for him any longer. "I love you, Ash. So much."

His eyes are wide. "Not just falling anymore?"

"No." I shake my head. "To be honest, I'm pretty sure I've been in love with you for a while."

A few more tears escape and roll down his face as he pulls me to him, wrapping his arms tightly around me. He leans down to nuzzle against my neck. "I'm so freakin' happy right now, Ellie. You have no idea. I love you so much."

My chest is tight as we breathe each other in.

When Ash pulls away, his eyes drop to my mouth before he leans down and brushes his lips against mine. It's brief and leaves me wanting more.

I try to follow his lips by going onto my tiptoes.

He groans and offers me another peck. "I'm trying really hard not to kiss you right now."

A watery laugh bursts from me as I smile. "I mean, I wouldn't stop you."

He growls, nipping my bottom lip. "Don't tempt me, if I start I won't stop. And I'm determined to watch a movie together. Or talk through a movie together. Either way, I'm not going to make out with you until after our date."

My eyes widen. "This is a date?" I squeak, glancing down at my outfit in horror. "I need to change." I turn to leave, but Ash grabs my wrist, stopping me.

"You look beautiful, Ellie. I already told you I don't want you to change." He turns slightly to press a button on the device he was messing with earlier. "Besides, it's not like it's our first."

"I always thought the guy was supposed to ask the girl on a date first."

He pauses. "I thought I did. Haven't we been dating?"

I blink. "Is that what we've been doing? You didn't tell me it was a date, though." I look at him earnestly.

I don't know why this is such a big deal, and maybe I'm stupid for not realizing it, but I've never dated before. Never been on a date. Well, I guess I have now. But I wished I had known. What would've been considered our first date? When I fell asleep on him that first night at Emma's? Oh gosh, I was a lousy date if so.

He chuckles. "Yes, that's what we've been doing." Keeping hold of my wrist, he leads me to the couch. Once taking a seat, he pulls me onto his lap. "But I guess you're right. I never specifically said any of them were dates. How about this will be an unofficial date, and I'll take you on an official one later. And I'll make sure you know it's a date. How does that sound?"

I grin. "Sounds good to me."

"It's a deal then." He nudges me to lay against him. "There's also something I wanted to mention." He pauses. "While you were taking a bath, I asked Foster to look into your parents. I hope that's okay."

I blink. "Yes, that's fine." With everything happening so fast, I surprisingly haven't thought about them. A wave of guilt and grief hits me. How could I have forgotten them for even a moment?

But now that Ash mentions them, I realize they hid that I was a lycan. That *they* were lycans. Were they an alpha couple? Is the pack where they went to whenever they had meetings? They would go to one at least once a month, but never actually explained what the meeting was about. "I'm actually glad you did. I want to know more about them and why they hid being lycans." I peer at him. "How did you know I was a pureblood just by their names, anyway?"

Resting his head on my shoulder, he points the remote at the screen, turning it on. "Everyone learns the last names of purebloods. Especially if you're a pureblood." He sneers. "The whole not wanting us to taint our bloodline thing."

"Were your parents hoping for you to mate with a pureblood?"

Delaying pressing play on the movie, he peers at me. "No, they wouldn't have cared. My grandparents might've, but not them."

"Are they still around?" I ask.

"They aren't. They'd like you simply because you're a pureblood." He sighs. "Makes it worse that they were Originals," he grumbles.

"Originals?" I turn in his lap to face him better. "As in the *Original lycans*?"

He grimaces. "Uh, no. I guess I haven't explained much, huh?"

I give him a pointed look and he chuckles.

"Alright, alright. I'm sorry." He shifts under me and sets the remote down beside us, keeping an arm around my waist. "Have you ever heard of the Fountain of Youth?"

"Of course." Only in fiction, I neglect to add.

He nods, resting a hand on my thigh. "Parents tell this as a bedtime story, but I'm sure it's in one of our history books as well. But a long time ago—"

"In a far away land."

He laughs. "Well, technically, yes. Two mercenaries went searching for the Fountain of Youth with their slaves."

I blink. "This really is a true story based a long time ago."

A corner of his mouth tips into a half-smile. "Yes."

I straighten. "Okay, proceed."

Chuckling, he tugs a lock of my hair. "Thank you for your permission."

"You're welcome."

My face splits into a grin as he roars with laughter.

"As I was saying," he says with a shake of his head and a smile. "They went searching for the Fountain. And they actually found it. But instead of a fountain, there was only a small trickle of it left. And no, I don't know why." He gives me a pointed look and I laugh. "Anyway, both mercenaries decided that they would each take a taste but bottle up the rest. After the first one took a drink, not only did his youth return, but he was changed."

"Changed?"

"Yes, he became the first stryx."

My eyes grow wide. "So this is not just a story about lycans."

"Correct. The water was pure essence. Not only did it rewind age, it made them powerful. Prettier, stronger, faster, etcetera. As the first mercenary transformed into his beast form—"

"Wait. Beast form?" I ask.

"Stryxes look human, albeit beautiful and perfect humans, but human nonetheless. When they change into their beast form, their eyes shift to blood red while their nails lengthen into points and fangs form. It's also harder to penetrate their skin in that form."

"So not into a wolf like us or any other creature." *Like us.* Still feels so strange to think of myself as a lycan.

"Nope. We just call it beast form." He kisses the side of my neck. "So as he turned, the other mercenary drank his share. That's when they learned that drinking the essence affects each person differently. Instead of turning into a stryx, he changed into a lycan. A large wolf that could change his form at will. He gained the same enhanced abilities as the stryx and retained his youth, but he was not as strong. They found that out as they fought over who would get the rest. Greedy. They wanted to test to see if it would make them into even more powerful beings. Right then and there.

"But as they fought, one of their female slaves, seeing what it had done to them, swooped in and drank the last of the essence."

I grin. "Good for her."

He smiles. "That's how she was able to free herself from them. Although, after she drank, her form didn't change. Instead, swirls of wispy colors surrounded her. She became the first witch, able to perform all kinds of magic, including blood magic."

"Okay, I thought magic and essence were the same thing."

He tilts his head back and forth. "It kind of is. Essence is in our blood and what links us to each other. It's what's inside of us, but witches are able to control that in an outward power, which we call magic. Also, anything spoken that enacts power we call magic: challenges, blood magic, potion makers, protective magic, weavers—who makes the clothes that don't tear during our shifts—that sort of thing. I'm sure there's more, but I haven't really researched witches. They tend to keep to themselves for the most part, not interacting with lycans or stryxes."

That's...that's a lot of different types of magic. Maybe someday Ash and I can learn about the witches together. "And are there a lot of witches and stryxes around today?"

"Witches, yes. Stryxes, no."

"Why is that?"

He adjusts underneath me. "I guess I'm giving you the full history of our past today."

"Yep. We may be here for a while." I go to move off him to allow him to get more comfortable, but he grabs my hips, keeping in place.

"Where do you think you're going?"

"I thought we'd get more comfortable."

"Are you uncomfortable?" Ash asks.

"No."

"Neither am I, so stay. Please."

Well, when he says it like that. I relax against him once more, his arms wrapping around me.

Ash begins pressing buttons to recline us back, simultaneously raising the legs, for us to lay down before continuing, "About a thousand years ago there was a war—"

War?

"Wait, when did the three Originals first drink from the Fountain of Youth?" I ask.

"We actually call the first three 'the Elites'. And they found it around the time Rome was founded, about three thousands years ago."

"And where do Originals tie in with all of this?"

"Originals are the ones changed by the Elites by the sharing of their blood."

"So normal humans drink the blood of an Elite and become like them."

"Not as powerful, but yes, that's correct."

When I'm silent, he kisses my temple. "Is this getting to be too much? I can wait to explain more."

I sigh, letting my head drop back against him. "I've been in the dark for so long." My whole life to be exact. "I want to know all of this. This is *our* history. But I think I'm getting overwhelmed with just how much I don't know."

"That was a lot just now. I have lycan history books lying around the house. Maybe instead of discussing more right now, we give your mind a chance to soak this in, then tomorrow or sometime this week we can go through them together?"

I did just learn a lot. Learning more about the death of Ash's parents, the Fountain of Youth, the Elites, and Originals. "That may be a good idea. I am a bit overwhelmed. But I still have one more question."

"Shoot."

I bite my lip, tapping my fingers along his chest. "Now that you're alpha, you could change things with your pack, right?"

His brows rise. "Yes, I suppose so. I'd love your help, though."

My eyes widen. "Mine?"

"Of course. Even though you aren't an alpha, you're still my equal."

My heart swells. I didn't think I could love him more. "Well, I already have lots of ideas." Like getting rid of how omegas are treated.

He smiles. "I'm glad. And I'd love to hear them all."

"Once I understand everything a bit better and understand how the pack runs, I'll make a list of suggestions."

He tugs me closer. "Sounds perfect. I'll bounce my ideas off you, too."

I beam at him. "Yeah? I'm excited now. I want this to be a pack safe for everyone."

He wraps his other arm around me to squeeze me to him. "I love you so much. You have no idea how happy hearing that makes me. We're going to run and change this pack together, making it better for everyone."

His eyes glisten with unshed tears as his arm tightens around me. "Thank you for listening and caring." He places another kiss on my forehead before starting the movie.

40

Ellie

*H*alfway through the movie, when I thought the soreness of my shift had passed, it came back with a vengeance and a little friend.

I'd forgotten what it felt like to have a period. I think the last time I had one was right before I left Jane. The cramping, the aches...

It sucks.

Why do I need to be punished for not being pregnant?

My shoulders slump in relief.

But at the same time, I'm glad I'm having one. It's not normal to go without one for years on end.

There's a light rap on the door. "Ellie?" A pause. "Are you okay? I smell blood."

I cringe—of course he does. "Yes, I...I just got my period."

"Ah, okay."

I sigh when I sense him retreat, giving me privacy.

Leaning over, I open the cabinet under the sink. I'm at an awkward angle, but I can just barely reach a tampon. The first week I was here, Ash showed me two locations, this half bathroom and the hallway closet upstairs, where he placed a basket full of maxi pads, tampons, heat pads, and pain meds. He even loaded a basket with different types of snacks in the closet. Being typical Ash, he overstocked in both places.

I didn't have the heart to tell him I rarely got a period.

I wonder why it showed up today, though, after not having it for so long.

Finishing up, I wash my hands and open the door to the hallway. My cheeks heat when I see Ash leaning against the wall a couple feet away.

He straightens. "Ellie, is there anything you need?"

"I think I need to lay down," I say. If I remember right, these cramps I'm feeling will only get worse before they get better.

He nods, my request not even phasing him, as he offers his hand. "Have you taken any pain meds yet?"

I shake my head, placing my hand in his. "I'm also craving chocolate."

One corner of his mouth tugs up into a small smile as he leads me to his room. "I'll get you some."

He lets go of my hand to pull back the sheets and helps me in. This is the first time I've ever been in his bed. We usually share mine. It's odd and exciting all at the same time.

"I was wondering when you would get one." When my head tilts in confusion, he continues with an explanation. "I know humans get periods usually once a month." He palms the back of his neck in embarrassment. "So I checked last week if I needed to restock anything and found it untouched."

Ah. So he knows I haven't had one here. "I don't get them often. Is that not normal for lycans either?"

He pulls the covers over me and sits beside me. He tucks some hair behind my ear. "When was the last time you had one?" he asks.

"Before I first left Jane."

His brows draw together. "About three years then, correct?" At my nod, he continues, "And the time before that?"

"The time before that was when I got it for the first time. It was right before I went to live with Marcus."

His eyes widen, slightly leaning back in shock. "This is only the third time you've had a period?"

I nod hesitantly.

One of his hands moves to scratch his scruff in thought. "I know for lycans, missing months is normal. I don't think I've heard of others missing them for longer than a year." His eyes move back to mine. "But considering what you went through for years on end, I shouldn't be surprised."

Ash stands suddenly and moves to his bookshelves. "I only know about periods from my mother." His hands move from title to title as he tries to find what he's looking for. "She had really bad cramps whenever she got one, which was about every three months. That's actually considered often for a lycan. Ah—" He removes one book and walks back over to the bed and sits again, but this time resting his back on the headrest. "This talks about periods in lycans. Let's see..." His finger moves down the index before flipping to a page. "I know in humans, as well as in lycans, that stress can delay a period. But considering how seldom female lycans can get pregnant, their periods don't come around monthly like they do in most humans."

Alice comes to mind. "What about the lycans that have less magic, I mean essence, in their blood? Alice's mother was a human."

He nods as his eyes scan the words on the page. How is he able to read and talk to me? "I'm not positive how often she gets one. But I'm sure it's more often than a pureblood." He taps the start of one paragraph and places the book on my lap "Here it is. How about you read it while I get some things?"

"Okay." I grip the edges of the book in my hands.

Once he leaves the room, I find the paragraph he marked with his finger and begin to read.

Periods in lycans are tied with the essence in their blood. Lycan periods are also tied to their bodies. The more stressed a lycan is, the less likely they are to have a period.

THE SAME GOES FOR SHIFTING. *While high emotions trigger shifts, when the body is under high physical stress, shifts don't occur and neither do periods. Shifting can only happen when the body can handle it, or else the lycan may die.*

I stop reading and take in what I just learned. Because of how stressful my life turned once my parents died, and probably also from malnutrition, I never shifted or had a regular period. But now that I've been eating larger portions, gaining some much-needed weight, I have a roof over my head, food on the table, friends supporting me, and someone that loves me...my life is significantly less stressful than it was on the run.

Ash walks in carrying the snack basket with pain meds stuffed in with them, more tampons and pads, a water bottle, and a heating pad. My heart warms at the sight.

"Okay, I think this is everything, but if not, just say the word and I'll get it." He places the basket on the nightstand along with the water bottle.

I close the book and place it beside the basket on the nightstand so he can hand me the heating pad. He then heads to his en suite bathroom to put away the pads and tampons.

"This is more than enough, Ash, thank you," I say after him.

He comes back smiling, walking over to his side of the bed. But before getting in, he opens the drawer to his nightstand and pulls out a remote. He aims it at the wall across the room and presses a few buttons.

There's beeping and mechanical sounds, then the wall above his desk moves.

My mouth gapes open as it reveals a television. Ash had a hidden panel in his room. I eye him suspiciously.

He glances over at me with a smirk that quickly turns into a frown. "What?" he asks.

I narrow my eyes. "What else do you have hiding?"

He laughs. "There's a safe in my office that's hidden, but other than that, nothing. Isn't this cool, though?" His face lighting up as he sits on the bed next to me. He shows me the remote and what each button does that mostly goes over my head.

I smile and shake my head. "I didn't even know you could do this...whatever this is."

He chuckles. "I don't know how Russell did it, but he's a genius when it comes to these kinds of things."

"Right, Russell owns a construction company." I remember Ash had mentioned it once.

Ash focuses on the television screen. It has apps and movies already on it, unlike the screen in the renovated garage. "Yes, he's also a welder, leatherworker, and chef—although he doesn't work as one anymore."

My eyes widen. "Wow, a man of many talents."

He freezes then turns his head to me, his eyes narrowed. "You're not starting to gain feelings for him, are you?"

"Well..." A growl leaves him and I can't keep a straight face any longer. I laugh. "No, only you."

A slow grin takes over his face. "Good."

He turns back to the screen and finds the movie while I settle in for a relaxing evening.

41

Ellie

Over the next week, I consume book after book about lycans. Each book briefly mentions witches and stryxes, but nothing about a war. It's honestly driving me crazy. Ash could've sworn it's in one of his books, but he hasn't been able to find it either. He offered to tell me everything he learned, but now I just really want to read about it in detail.

There was a war between stryxes and lycans that humans knew nothing about.

I walk into the kitchen and have a bit of a déjà vu moment when I find Ash already there waiting for me. He isn't cooking or in his pajamas this time. He's looking out the window above the sink, and it reminds me of my first morning here when he made me a stack of pancakes. I didn't think it was possible, but he's gotten more attractive since then.

Sensing me, he turns with a smile. "Ready?"

I nod and we head outside together in the snow. Ash has training equipment, but since it's all downstairs—in the basement—he thought the next best place was the great outdoors. Luckily, even in leggings and a tank top, I barely sense the cold, only a slight nip from the breeze. Perks of being a lycan now. Or I guess I've always been one...but I learned that lots of abilities don't show up until after your first shift.

My eyes travel the length of Ash as he removes his shirt. I try not to drool at the sight of his bare skin and muscles. I couldn't be more grateful that he runs hotter than I do. He only wears a coat to fend off questions from humans. At least that's what he told me.

Ash turns to face me in nothing but a pair of work out sweats and shoes. "I want you to come at me with everything you got, then we'll go from there."

"Uh, I got nothing." I may have had to defend myself a few times while moving around and squatting, mostly from thieves wanting my bag of supplies, but usually once I cut them with a knife they'd back off. I don't actually know how to fight.

"I'll decide that. Just come and attack me."

I sigh. "Okay."

Putting my fists out in front of me, I jump from foot to foot. Once I finish shaking off the jitters I rush at him. Before I can land a blow, he grabs my fist in mid-swing.

"First"—he pulls me closer—"we need to fix this." Catching me as I teeter off balance, he wraps a warm arm around my waist. He opens my fist. "You'll break your thumb with it tucked inside." He repositions my thumb. "This is the best spot for it."

I bite my lip as he steps away. "Try again," he says as he creates more distance between us.

Not wasting a moment, I run at him again, but he easily maneuvers away. I huff and try again, this time taking a swing at him. He easily blocks with his forearm. "Remember, you're faster and stronger now. Use that to your advantage. You could've put a lot more strength into that punch."

"But what if I hurt you?"

He chuckles. "I promise you won't."

Taking a deep breath, I nod. "Okay. Do you think I have a special ability?" I ask, remembering how fast he is.

"I'm sure you do, but it can take years to figure it out or for it to show up." He beckons me forward and I try a few more maneuvers against him, but nothing is landing and a growl forms in the back of my throat.

"Come on, little wolf, I know you can do better than that," he says with a stupid, cute smile.

I try another swing with my fist. I land it, but only on his forearm once again. Another small growl passes my lips, and I aim for his stomach. But he side-steps away from my fist, grabs my wrist, and holds it captive. He moves behind me when I try to kick him, twisting my arm behind my back. Not hard enough to hurt, but also not comfortable. I throw my elbow back, jamming it into his stomach, but I'm pretty sure his abs are made out of steel. With a throbbing elbow I try to twist from his grip, but he simply grabs my other wrist and holds it together with my already captured arm.

He clicks his tongue. "Be careful, little wolf. I wouldn't want you to injure yourself."

Letting out a noise of frustration, I throw my head back, aiming to headbutt him, but it turns out—I'm short. I end up just hitting his chest.

A rumble rolls through his chest as he laughs. "Did you forget our height difference?"

"No," I grumble, wishing I could fold my arms and pout.

He steps forwards, pressing his body against mine, my arms the only barrier between us. His mouth to my ear, his breath tickles my skin. "Don't lie to me, Ellie darling."

Turning my head, I bite his jaw.

In shock, he releases his hold on my wrists. I quickly dash away and resume my position with my arms in front of me.

But he doesn't move. His face is in a state of shock with a hand pressed against his jaw where I bit him.

Then he starts laughing.

"I did not expect that," he says with a grin and a shake of his head. "Maybe I should've said biting isn't allowed."

Frowning, I say, "You told me to come at you with everything I had."

"I didn't think you would bite me." He chuckles. "No one bites in training."

"Why?" I huff, dropping my arms and trying not to pout. Don't people bite when they fight? I don't think what I did was that ridiculous.

"Remember the mate bond I mentioned and the pack bond I gave you yesterday?"

"Yes." I cross my arms as my body flushes at the memory, desire rushing through me. Even though there aren't any physical signs left, I can still feel where he marked me.

Ash draws closer, stopping only a breath away. His hand brushes my ribs then rises to my shoulder, caressing my skin as he follows the curve to my neck.

His voice drops low when he leans in, placing his kiss to the crook of my neck. "This is where I'd bite you if I were to claim you as mine." I swallow as his lips brush against my skin. "Biting is reserved for mates or in battle. For intimate moments or to cause harm." He straightens, looking into my eyes. "And I have a feeling you weren't trying to harm me just then."

I shake my head.

"The only other time that it isn't either of those is when an alpha forms a pack bond."

My brows rise. "Pretty sure yesterday would've fallen under intimate."

He gives me a cheeky grin. "That was on purpose. If it was anyone else, I would've done it differently."

"Alright." I give a curt nod and swallow. "Then I won't bite you again."

"Oh, no. Please do. Just not anyone else." He winks and takes a step back.

For the next hour we spar, and he teaches me new moves, but

mostly he overpowers me. "I'd like to teach you to partial-shift now. Think you're up for it?"

I wipe the sweat off my brow. "Yeah, I want to learn."

He moves closer, taking my hand in his. "It'll be difficult at first to isolate the essence that links to parts of your wolf rather than a full shift. But once you do, it'll come easily." He lets go of my hand. "We'll start with your canines first. Close your eyes for me." He waits for me to oblige. "Now, open your mouth."

I do and wait for more instructions, but he's silent. Peeking an eye open, I find him staring at my mouth. My eyes pop open, and I quickly shut my mouth, becoming self-conscious.

"Is something wrong?" I ask tentatively after I swipe my tongue around my mouth—nothing seeming amiss. I even made sure to brush my teeth before coming out here.

His eyes move away from my lips, his heated gaze meeting mine. He blinks then clears his throat. "Nope."

My heart rate spikes as a blush flames across my cheeks. I wipe my sweaty hands on my leggings.

"Sorry." He smiles. "Let's try this again. I promise I'll try not to get distracted."

I hesitate, but when he arches a brow I quickly close my eyes. I inhale deeply and exhale slowly through my nose. I open my mouth again.

"Perfect," he says. "Now, my little wolf." I shiver at the nickname. "Think of how your canines first formed before you completely shifted. How did that feel?" He pauses. "Try envisioning it again."

I concentrate for a few moments, but nothing happens.

"Ash—"

"Uh-uh," he says, "keep that mouth open and those eyes closed."

I grumble, but oblige.

He seems closer than he was before when he hums. "Just relax."

I jerk a bit when his hands touch my arms. He moves them up and down in a soothing motion.

Relaxing my shoulders, I try to calm my emotions and imagine how my teeth felt when I shifted. It burned. That I can remember well. But what else did it feel like? It felt heavier, and they cut into my bottom lip when they lengthened.

"It's not working, Ash," I say. It shouldn't be so hard to just lengthen my teeth.

Never thought I'd ever think that.

Ash is silent for a moment, but his hands continue their movement up and down my arms. "Think of how it felt *internally*."

My brows scrunch together. How it felt inside?

It's hard to remember anything but the pain. And Ash's searing kisses.

Digging a little deeper, I think of the pack bond and the warmth I felt. Ash had linked with my essence. That must be what essence feels like inside. A gasp passes my lips. With just the thought, the warmth explodes. I focus on the warmth in my teeth and try to will it to form into my wolf canines. I think of the process and picture my teeth changing into wolf canines. The burning happens almost instantaneously. My eyes pop open to see pride in Ash's gaze.

"Good job, Ellie darling."

I beam at his praise.

"Let's try your hands next. I want you to do what you just did, but instead of your pretty little mouth, focus on your hand. This may be a bit more difficult because you don't want to completely shift your hand into a paw. You still want the function of a hand, but a hand that you can also use as a weapon."

Taking a deep breath, I nod once and close my eyes. I try to calm my emotions again, getting rid of the anxiety that bubbles up from thinking about the impending pain. I just need to focus on what happened within myself.

After concentrating—for who knows how long—my bones shift. I cry out and sense Ash's presence move. He's behind me and wraps his arms around my waist to keep me up.

"You've got this," he murmurs in my ear.

Opening my eyes and focusing on Ash's warmth at my back, I

try to push through the pain. It's strange watching my bones move underneath my skin just to reform the same as before.

My gaze doesn't waver as my nails elongate and fur erupts on my hand and up my forearm. When the partial-shift finishes, I move my fingers and flip my hand back and forth in fascination. My teeth went back to normal during the shift. The transformation was painful, but not nearly as much as the first time.

"I did it...I did it!" I spin around and jump into Ash's arms, my arms around his neck, my legs around his waist.

He grins as he catches me. "You did, my little wolf. I'm so proud of you." His gaze burns into mine. "Ellie." His voice has grown husky. "I'm going to kiss you now." He leans in, capturing my lips with his. He nips at my lip then takes the kiss deeper, his tongue dancing with mine as we taste one another. Our bodies pressing together sends a buzz through me.

Ash breaks off with a growl. My breath catches as he slowly lets me down, sliding me down his body. He pulls his phone out. Foster's name flashes across the screen.

Oh, so the buzzing wasn't from our touch.

"Yes?" he answers, his gaze lingering on my lips. His free hand moves to the back of my neck, his thumb on my jaw, pushing my face up to him.

His brows scrunch together. "That's unfortunate. I'll talk to Ellie about it." He hums a few more times before a frown forms. "Yes, you can bring her over. We'll see you in a few."

Ash sighs once he hangs up, but he keeps my head in place, tilting up toward him. Bringing his other hand up, he brushes the side of my cheek, stopping just as his fingertips tangle in my hair. Nudging me closer, he leans down and brushes his lips against mine.

"Ash," I say against his lips.

Instead of answering, he slides his tongue across my bottom lip before diving between them and inside, forcing a moan out of me.

Although I hate to stop this, I place a hand on his chest and push. "Ash, what did Foster want?"

He groans before leaning away. Rubbing my bottom lip with the pad of his thumb, he says, "He was updating me on the search for Marcus and Zac. Marcus seems to have disappeared into thin air. The bastard. There's more signs of Zac, but he's been moving around a lot. We don't think they're together."

I nod. "And the thing you need to talk to me about?"

He bites his lip. I shouldn't find that so attractive, but desire rises as I watch him. "I also got word about your parents' old pack. Turns out their pack—your old pack technically—dissolved after their death and joined into another pack. They refuse to give us anything over the internet. They're a bit old-fashioned and have everything in files, nothing digital."

"Okay. So what does that mean for us?"

"I was thinking of traveling there myself for a few days. Ask around about your parents and get your files."

My heart sinks. "Without me?"

"I want to bring you, but Foster is bringing someone over soon because he needs to go somewhere to deal with some family issues."

"Who is he bringing over?"

"Alice."

JUST A FEW HOURS LATER, Foster arrives with Alice. I understand now why someone needs to stay with Alice. She has lost what little weight she had. Her cheekbones are sharp against her hollowed-out face. Her skin is a sickly white with dark circles prominent under her blue eyes, and her blonde hair is greasy and unkept.

Foster looks miserable. Not in the same way Alice does, but in the disheveled, helpless kind of way.

Ash and I share a look, both full of concern. This is worse than we thought.

She's given up.

Ash ushers us all to the family room. I sit beside Alice.

"Alice." I take her hand, but she flinches, and I jerk my hand away. "Sorry."

I'm more shocked that I initiated the touch than I am at her refusal. Am I getting better? I know I've hugged Jane and Emma before, and Ash has always been the exception, but that ended my short list of those I was comfortable with. It seems my list may be growing.

She looks at me, then blinks and looks around slowly. As if just noticing where she is for the first time. She's been on auto-pilot. I know that feeling all too well.

Her gaze lands on Foster, who immediately goes into defense mode. "I'm not leaving you alone," he says, glaring at her.

Alice sighs and turns away. She grabs the remote and turns on the TV. Ash frowns, then tilts his head to the kitchen before standing.

Foster and I stand and follow him to the island counter. "How long has she been like this?" I ask Foster.

"Since the funeral," he says. "She stopped eating the day he died. After the funeral, she refused to take care of herself, refused to even do the bare minimum. She showers, but I'm not even sure she washes herself." He looks over at her, and I can tell he isn't disgusted by what he says, but rather states the facts and is deeply concerned. "I've been staying with her because I'm afraid...I'm afraid she'll take her own life. I'd rather not leave, but I have to go deal with some family drama. But I can't leave her alone."

Briefly closing my eyes, I nod before following his gaze to Alice. We watch as Alice mindlessly flips through the channels. She's had a lot thrown at her in a short amount of time. I don't know exactly what passed between her and her brother, but he seemed to have deeply hurt her.

Then her father was killed.

"Does she have any family?" I ask, but I pretty much already know the answer.

When neither respond, I look up to see Ash shake his head.

"So she's all alone," I say, my heart aching. I know what that feels like.

Foster bangs his fist on the table. "She's not alone." He growls low, his forest-green eyes blazing. "She has me, and the rest of us."

I blink. He's so different from the laughing, happy-go-lucky guy he was at Thanksgiving.

"It's not the same as having family. Her father and brother were there since the beginning, and now both are gone. Family is someone who's supposed to be there for the long haul and always love you."

"Key words: 'supposed to'. Not all families do. Family doesn't always have to be blood. She could choose us as her family."

I never thought of it like that. I glance over at Ash to find his eyes already locked on me. He wraps an arm around me and places a kiss on my forehead.

"You're my family," he murmurs in my ear.

I lean in to him. "You're my family, too."

"I'm family, too," Foster adds gruffly.

42

Ellie

*a*sh looks down at me with concern, his hands on my hips as we stand in the foyer. "I can delay my trip."

I shake my head. "You're only going to be gone for a few days. I'll be okay. Maybe the different scenery and having another girl around will help her." I shrug because I really have no idea. I was only able to cope in the past because I had my drawings. But to be honest, I don't really think I coped well. I was kind of just thrust into the foster care system and had to mourn in private, and I always made sure to put on a brave face for whichever family I was with. I wanted to be wanted, not a burden.

"If you're sure…"

Reaching up on my tiptoes, I plant a kiss on his lips. "I'm sure. I want to know about my parents. I'll be fine here. Besides, you're giving us guards."

"I've always had guards," he says.

"Well, you gave us an extra one. And this mysterious Sophie is coming to train me as well. Just be warned, I'm gonna be hard to defeat when you get back. So go, before I really do change my mind."

His lips curl into a half-smile as he leans down for another peck. Instead, he tilts my head up, deepening the kiss with the thrust of his tongue, leaving me breathless and wanting.

He pulls away, grinning in pure male satisfaction and plants another kiss. "Remember if you want to leave, just let Russell or someone else on duty know. Oh—" He pulls out his wallet and flips it open before pulling out a card. "This is for you." He hands it to me and I find my name on it.

"What is it?"

"It's a debit card."

I blink then hold it in the air, slightly shaking it at him. "I know that, but why are you giving me this? And why does it have my name on it?"

He shrugs. "It's yours. I had you added to my accounts. Feel free to purchase anything online or in person. Just sign the back."

"I can't take this. You already got me a new phone." This is too much. I didn't even want to accept the cell. I try to hand the card back, but he steps back, raising his arms in mock surrender.

"Ash."

"Just keep it. You don't have to use it if you don't want to. But it's there if you need it."

I sigh. "Fine."

He smiles. "I'll see you in a few days." He places a kiss on my lips one more time before leaving.

After watching him leave in his truck, my eyes travel to the stairs. Alice hasn't left her room since she was shown to it yesterday. Not to eat, not to pee, nothing. I mean, maybe she peed in the middle of the night, but since I've been awake she hasn't. Perks of super hearing.

I walk to the kitchen to make some toast and grab a bottle of water. With both in hand, I head up the stairs. If she hasn't eaten anything since her father's death then she needs to start small. How long can lycans survive without food?

Holding the bottle in the crook of my arm and the plate in my hand, I knock on her door while eyeing the food we left her on the ground last night—untouched.

"I'm not hungry," she says with a muffled voice, sounding like she's still in bed.

"Alice, you need to eat."

"I'm fine."

"No, you're not. Please, just open the door. At least take the water."

She's silent for a moment. "Alright. But not until you're back downstairs."

I frown, then let out a sigh. Gotta choose my battles. "Okay." I set the plate and water on the ground and grab the old dishes.

I take one last look at her door before going back downstairs to clean the dishes. Ash has a dishwasher, but I've always enjoyed taking the time to hand wash them. Oddly, it brings me satisfaction to scrub off food until it's shining and bright.

The doorbell rings, and I wipe my hands on a hand towel before heading to the door. I peer in the peephole, seeing a female on the other side. It must be Sophie.

I open the door, meeting emerald eyes that seem oddly familiar. Her dark-brown hair is pulled into a long, sleek ponytail.

"You're her spitting image," she says.

I blink. "Excuse me?"

She gives me a sad smile. "Sorry, I'm Sophie." She sticks her hand out and I take it. "Your mum was my cousin."

My mouth gapes open then closed a few times as she shakes my hand. When I'm finally able to speak, I say, "I thought I didn't have any family left alive."

"We weren't close." Her hands go back to her side. "And I didn't

SAVING ELLIE

know she had a daughter until Foster told me last week. I've been...away."

"Oh." I try not to sound disappointed as I let her in, but she must see it written across my face.

"I knew her enough to be sad when I heard of her passing." Her eyes fill with sorrow. "I regret not keeping in touch. Maybe then I would've known she had a daughter. I'm sorry I didn't come try to find you. I didn't even know she died until a few years ago."

I shake my head. "It's fine. Like you said, you didn't know I existed." What would my life be life if she had?

She arches a brow—seeing through me—as she passes and heads out of the foyer. "Everyone knows when a girl says 'fine' that she doesn't actually mean it."

I nod slowly, following her. My mind *is* reeling, not really comprehending that Sophie is family. My mom's cousin. What would my life be like if she knew about me? Where would I be today? Would I have ever been in foster care? Would I have ever met Jane?

"I guess you're right," I say. "It's a lot to take in. But we can't change the past."

"True, but I'm here now, if you ever need me."

My heart warms at her words. "Thank you." I glance up at the stairs as we pass by, hoping Alice is eating the toast. I should bring some more food up for her after Sophie leaves.

Sophie pauses and follows my gaze. She tilts her head as she sniffs the air. "Alice up there?" She can tell just by scent?

I nod. "Yeah, she got here yesterday."

"Well, what are you waiting for? Let's go get her."

"What?" I blanch, but she's already making her way up the stairs.

I quickly rush up the stairs as she bangs on Alice's door.

"Open up, Alice, I know you're in there. I won't stop until you open the door." Sophie keeps her word and continues to knock. I survey the ground and find the plate of toast and water bottle no

285

longer on the ground. A small smile forms on my face. Alice kept her word.

Alice throws open the door, only wearing a towel, but her hair is still dry. My guess is we stopped her from taking a shower.

"Why are you here?" she asks.

Sophie places her hands on her hips. "To train, of course."

Alice's shoulders slump, the fight already leaving her. "Ash made you the new lead warrior, huh?"

Sophie's face wavers. "Only temporarily. I'm the new delta," she says softly.

"I don't want to train." Alice goes to close the door, but Sophie sneaks her foot in.

"Uh-uh-uh," she tsks. "You're coming. It's not an option."

"Sophie." She sighs. "I was going to shower."

"I'm not saying you can't. But you can shower after. You need to get out of this room."

"I haven't even been here a full day," Alice says.

"Fine. In general, you need to get out."

Alice rolls her eyes. "Fine. Give me a sec to change." She gestures to Sophie's foot.

Sophie gives her a smug grin as she removes her boot. "If you don't come out in two minutes, I'm busting the door down."

Alice glares then shutting the door. It isn't long before she comes out again in a change of clothes and her hair in a pony.

"Much better." Sophie turns to me. "Ready?"

I nod and give Alice a hesitant look.

"Why are you doing this, Soph?" Alice asks, following behind us as we head down the stairs.

"Ash asked me to train Ellie, and if Foster knew I didn't try to get you out of bed, he'd give me hell for sure." Sophie must sense my questioning gaze because she glances at me as we make it to the ground floor. "Foster and I are cousins."

What? My mind is swirling. "But you said my mom was."

"Foster is from my dad's side. You and Addison are on my mum's side."

"Huh." The lycan world seems to be shrinking.

"Foster and I are closer in age. He's probably the only extended family I see nowadays. My mum is sisters with your gran."

I didn't notice before, but Sophie has a slight British accent when she pronounces certain words like 'gran' and 'mum'.

Sophie opens the back door and we follow her to the spot where Ash and I trained just yesterday. "Now, let's get started."

She stops and points to the tree line in the distance that has to be at least 200 feet away. "I want you two to run there and back five times. Stamina is important in a fight. If you're the first one to run out of steam then you're a goner. Won't matter if you know how to beat someone up if you can't lift an arm to throw a punch." She claps her hands. "Now go."

Not having ran in ages, I start off in a jog, alongside Alice. When I get to lap two, Alice passes me. I'm already feeling the burn in my legs and lungs. I'm so out of shape. Doesn't help that I'm still sore from my training session with Ash yesterday, and I'm practically trudging through the snow.

It makes me wish I could stomach going to the basement to Ash's workout area.

Alice seems to be fine on stamina and finishes before me, even with her jacket still in place.

I'm huffing and puffing with my hands on my knees when I finally make it. My head is pounding in sync with my heartbeat. I feel like I'm going to pass out with how lightheaded and weak I am.

"Well...that wasn't too great," Sophie says.

I let out a short, tired laugh. "Yeah."

"That's okay. That's just something we'll have to work on. Now we'll do some stretches to get your heartrate back to normal, but then I'm going to grab some of Ash's weights to do some weight lifting."

When she has us touch our toes, my fingers brush the snow around my boots. The chill is refreshing on my fevered skin.

"How long have you been here in Alaska, Ellie?" Sophie asks when we go into the next stretch.

Thinking back to when I first got here seems like forever ago. I arrived the last week of September and it's already mid-December. "About three months."

"So you got here just after I left," she says. "Okay, we're going to do some arm stretches now."

Alice and I follow her lead.

"Where did you go?" I ask.

Sophie sighs with one arm across her chest in a stretch. "My family doesn't like that I'm over here and no longer a part of their pack, so every fall to appease them and make sure I'm not suddenly betrothed to anyone, I visit them for a few months."

"Betrothed?" I ask, my heart rate finally settling down.

"Old way to say engaged," Alice says.

My eyes widen. "Why would they engage you to someone without you knowing?"

Sophie sneers. "They want me to mate a pureblood." She switches arms and we follow suit.

"Because you're a pureblood?"

"Yes, and so is Foster."

"And Russell?" I ask, and Sophie's face drops.

Alice is the one to respond. "He's not."

I look between the two of them. "Is that a bad thing?"

"No," Sophie says curtly. Spots color her cheeks as her features tighten. "It's not a bad thing. At least not to me." She drops her arms. "Okay, let's move on."

My brows rise at her abrupt change. I meet Alice's gaze, and she shakes her head.

"Your heart rate seems to be better now. Let's go inside and do some push-ups and sit-ups," Sophie says.

My arms go limp. Great.

"YOU DID A GOOD JOB TODAY, ELLIE," Sophie says when she finally lets us take a break.

I did not do well at all. Alice did better than me, but it seems we both lack combat skills.

I was worried I wouldn't like Sophie in the beginning. She's blunt, but not to the point where it's hurtful. She's honest, but doesn't shame us for being worthless. Because we are. Worthless in a fight, I mean.

"Once you're done, I want us to practice shifting."

I inwardly groan. I was hoping we would be done.

"I'm ready to be done," Alice says as she slumps down on one of the couches. "I just want to take a shower. Besides I already know how to shift just fine, thank you very much. I don't need any help from you."

I don't miss the snarky tone, and neither does Sophie. I watch Sophie's lips tighten.

"Well, I guess you can be done then." Sophie meets my gaze. "Once you're ready, just meet me outside."

"Okay," I say.

She goes through the back door, closing it behind her.

I walk over to the couch that Alice is on and hand her a water bottle and take a sip of mine.

"Do you not like Sophie?" I ask, sitting down beside her.

Alice gives me a confused look. "I like her fine, why?"

"You've barely said anything to her the entire time we trained. I know you're hurting, but this doesn't seem like you. I've never seen you act like this before."

She straightens, banging the bottle on the coffee table, water jumping out of the opening. "Why don't you tell me who I am then, Ellie? Because I sure don't know. I don't know where I'm going in life, and I sure don't want to be an omega. I have nothing going for me. I just didn't have to face the facts until I didn't have anyone left to share my life with."

"Alice, you aren't—"

"I am. Everyone already has lives that don't involve me. I know, I know. Foster has been there for me recently. But Foster isn't usually around this much. He's been traveling for years and I know he'll start up again once everything is dealt with." She slumps back down and grabs a pillow. Her arms shake as she holds it against her chest. "I'm alone, Ellie, and it terrifies me." She looks up at me with tears in her big blue eyes.

"I can't...I can't live like this. I know I shouldn't blame Sophie for her taking my father's position, but no one can replace him. He was the best lead warrior. I know her position is temporary until she picks someone else." She lays her head on the pillow, turning her face away, but I can still hear her as she whispers, "I just don't know how I can live without him." She sniffles. "I don't want to. I don't want to be alone." She looks up at me with tears rolling down her face. "I don't want to live like this anymore."

My eyes widen as my heart drops to my stomach. Foster couldn't have been right, right? "Alice, you can't mean..."

She averts her gaze. "I would be lying if I said I haven't thought about it," she says softly. "It's why freakin' Foster wouldn't leave me alone." She sighs. "But no, I'm not. Not anymore at least. I realized I wouldn't have any more chances to live if I did. And even though everything seems pointless and hopeless, I do still want to live. Foster was very adamant that I needed to remember that bad times pass and whatnot."

"So, you're okay now?" I regret it once it comes out. Of course she's not okay. Who is after someone dies?

"No, but I'm getting there. It's hard. All I want to do is sleep and cry and sleep some more."

I look out of the sliding glass door and see Sophie sitting down on one of the porch steps. "I think that's why Sophie is forcing you to be active."

Alice groans. "I know, but it sucks. I don't want to. I don't have a desire to do anything right now. It's draining to even get up to pee."

"I'm so sorry, Alice." My chest tightens. I wish there was something I could do.

She shakes her head. "Not your fault." She stands up and fixes her shirt. "Let's go shift."

I stand with her. "I thought you were done."

She smiles, but it doesn't quite reach her eyes. "Thank you."

"I didn't really do anything."

"Sometimes just having someone that's willing to listen helps." Alice gives me a small, sad smile before heading back outside.

43

Ellie

I let out a groan as I collapse on the bed. Shifting was torture. It was just as painful as the first time. Except it didn't happen. I didn't shift. And I don't have a clue why. Sophie and Alice said it must be a mental block because nothing seemed to be wrong when I partial-shifted. I wish Ash was with me. He'd know how to help me.

My new smartphone buzzes, and I roll over to grab it. I jolt up into a sitting position when I see a text from Ash.

Just call me when you get the chance. Miss and love you.

I scroll and see I've already missed a few calls from him. I tap his name and hit call. My heart pounds as I listen to it ring.

"Ellie darling," he says.

"Hey, sorry, I was with Sophie and Alice."

"Your tone doesn't sound like today went well."

I lay back down with an exhale. "Alice is struggling," I say.

"Sophie was able to get her out of her room, by force I might add, but I'm worried, Ash." I roll over onto my side and cuddle a pillow, looking at the bookshelf, but not really seeing it. "I'm not sure what to do about Alice."

He's silent for a moment. "I think just being there for her is a good start. She could use a friend."

I nod even though I know he can't see me. "I think so, too," I mumble on a yawn.

"Sounds like you had a long day, but before I let you go, how did training go?"

"Fine, but I think I liked the teacher that I had yesterday more."

He chuckles. "Glad I'm missed."

I smile into the phone.

"Were you able to practice shifting?" he asks. "I figured Sophie would try it with you."

Another groan slips past my lips as I'm reminded of all my failed attempts. "I wasn't able to shift."

"What do you mean?" I catch the worry in his voice.

"Just that. I wasn't able to shift. I felt it—I felt the pain—but I never was able to become a wolf."

He's silent for a moment. I can just picture him biting his lip as he ponders, or maybe he's scratching his scruff. "I think you might be thinking about it in the wrong way." I frown as he continues, "Your wolf is a part of you. *It is you.* Don't think of it as a separate being inside of you, because it isn't. It's just you in wolf form. I don't know if that makes sense, but try not thinking so hard about it. Think about how I taught you to partial-shift but on a grander scale, just let it flow through you. Focus on the essence in your body."

Rolling over onto my back, I stare at the ceiling. That makes sense. I was picturing my wolf as something foreign inside of me. But really, it's just another part of me. "Like my heart or lungs," I say.

"Exactly. But more like your arm or leg because it's an extension of yourself. You can control it—mostly. And you don't need it to survive. Also, the more you use your abilities and shift, the easier and more natural it'll become. Like walking."

"Okay, that makes sense. I'll try that next time." I twirl a piece of hair around my finger. "I've been thinking."

"About what, darling?"

"Since my parents were purebloods, wouldn't they have had special abilities, too? I'm curious to know what theirs were."

"They usually document them in pack files." He pauses. "I just remembered you telling me they had closed caskets for their funeral."

"Yeah. I never saw their bodies. They were too mangled up."

It's silent on his end and I sit up, concerned. "What's wrong?" I ask.

"Remember the funeral we had for Charlie?" I mutter a "yeah" before he continues, "All funerals for lycans are universal. Since they were lycans, they shouldn't have had caskets."

A chill runs down my spine. I wish I could see his face right now and feel his arms around me. "What do you think happened?"

"I'm not sure. It could just mean that because of their accident, humans took over the service. But even then that's a far-fetched idea. Next of kin is usually in charge of something like that. Their betas if they didn't have any family alive or close by, or the alpha or alpha couples if your parents weren't the alphas."

"I just found out Sophie was my mom's cousin, so they did...I did have family," I say.

"Huh. I forgot that Thorntons share a line with the Knights."

"Knights? As in knights in shining armor?"

He chuckles. "No, as in a last name. Sophie's mom was a Knight, and if I remember correctly, one of your grandparents on your mother's side was a Knight as well."

"I don't know much about my family lines. I never met any." Which now that I'm thinking about it, it is strange. Wouldn't my grandparents be involved in my life? "Wait, are they even alive?"

"I'm sorry, Ellie, I don't believe so. I think the only ones alive on that side would be Sophie's parents."

"Oh."

He continues, "But it's odd that Sophie and her mother weren't notified about you. At least not at the time. That worries me, but it makes sense why what happened, happened. You never should've been put into foster care."

What would my life have turned out to be like if I never had to jump from home to home? Never had to meet Marcus or suffer through the years of pain he inflicted? What would it have been like to be with family that I didn't even know existed? To learn that I was a lycan before I was twenty? "Sophie told me that Foster was the one to tell her about me. She didn't know about me before."

"That's...troubling to hear."

I grab a pillow to clench. "What do you think it means?"

"I'm not sure, but I'll find out tomorrow when I get the files."

"Is there anything I can do?" I ask. "I feel like there's so much you're doing for me, and I'm just a sitting duck."

"Oh, Ellie darling, you just being safe is plenty. Although it does give me peace of mind to know you're training."

I let out a sigh. "Me too. But I feel like I need to be doing more."

"You don't. But if you really want more, you also have Alice to focus on. Maybe think of something to do to cheer her up. Maybe some tough love like I gave you when you were in the hospital."

I hum, glancing over to where the copy of *Princess Bride* rests on the nightstand. "Tough love, huh? That's what you call giving me a book to get me to eat?"

He chuckles. "Well, maybe that was more of a bribe."

I smile into the phone. "Yeah, I think so." A yawn splits across my face.

"Alright, my love, I'll let you go now."

"Sorry," I say through another yawn.

"Don't be, you had a long day. Goodnight, Ellie. I love you."

My breath leaves me. I don't think I'll ever get used to hearing him say that. "I love you too, Ash. Goodnight."

The lack of his presence is felt once I hang up the phone. Loneliness rears its ugly head once more as I stare at the ceiling. I didn't realize how *not* alone I felt when Ash was with me. Even in my sleep I must have known I would always be safe with him because my nightmares would always disappear. I wish I would've listened to how my mind and body acted before. I wish it didn't take me so long to realize that I could lean on him and trust him to protect me. He's someone I can rely on. I don't need to do everything myself, at least that's what I'm starting to realize.

My eyes drift closed. It's hard to forget that the other side of the bed is empty, but after such a long day of training, sleep claims me.

Ellie

I follow Sophie and Alice inside after another rigorous training session. We didn't try to shift today, though.

"How do you still look so good?" Alice complains, wiping moisture off her forehead with a towel. I peer over at Sophie, who looks just as perfect as she did when she first came over. Not a lick of sweat on her. I'm only a *tad* jealous.

Sophie's green eyes twinkle with mischief as she gives Alice a wry smile. "It's because I'm immune to sweat."

I chuckle as Alice rolls her eyes. "No one is immune to sweat."

"Except for me." Sophie grins.

A corner of Alice's mouth tugs up into a smile as she shakes her head.

Training seemed to help Alice today. She's still acting differently than before her father's death, but I'm not sure if that's a bad thing. She isn't as timid anymore and speaks her mind, but she's sadder.

My phone buzzes on the kitchen counter where I left it to charge.

"Must be Ash. She has that stupid grin on her face," Sophie says.

"Ha, ha, ha." My lips twitch, fighting a smile as I try to send a glare her way. She simply winks with a smirk as she and Alice sit on the couch. "I'll be right back, I'm going to take this."

"Oh, hey. I'll get that watch for you tomorrow, okay?" Sophie calls after me as I walk down the hall.

We talked about Christmas gifts during training, and I was at a loss on what I should get Ash. Alice said that her dad saved a few of Ash's parents' belongings after he got Ash out of the fire, and his father's watch was one of them. Ash hasn't asked after them. Alice doesn't think he knows Charlie had them in a safe for him. But she doesn't want to go back to her house right now, so Sophie volunteered to get it for me.

"Okay," I say before answering Ash's call, afraid that I might miss it. "Hey."

"Hello, my love, how was it today?" The way he sounds never ceases to affect me. I love his voice.

"Good, Alice joined again. It's been nice hanging out with them."

He chuckles. "Training has become girl time, huh?"

I smile, closing the door to my room. I haven't been able to sleep in his room without him. "In a way. But you know Soph, she's hardcore—makes sure we never get too off track."

"Sounds like Soph," he says in amusement. "How is Alice doing?"

A sigh slips past my lips as I slump against the door. "I think training has helped her a bit. It's like an outlet for her anger and sadness. At least that's what I'm hoping. She's eating a bit more and is talking to us, so that's a start. Not the same as before though."

He hums. "Yes, death can change a person. Especially when you think you'd have more time with them."

"It's good that she's more outspoken though. I feel like it fits her more. She's even looking us in the eye."

"I guess I'll have to agree, even though I haven't seen it yet."

I bite my lip. Not sure if I want to ask my question yet.

"What's wrong?"

I chuckle. "Nothing gets past you even when you're thousands of miles away."

"I've been around you along enough to tell just by your breathing."

A smile forms across my lips. "Like that's not creepy."

He laughs. "Maybe just a tad."

I tilt my head back, resting it against the door. "Any word on Zac?" Can Alice hear me from over there? Maybe I shouldn't have asked.

"Not much. I believe he became a lone wolf rather than stay with Marcus."

Does that mean his essence could go out of control? But rather than voice that question, I ask a different one. "Do you think he regrets what he did?"

He's silent for a moment before he sighs and says, "I don't know."

I look back down at my feet. "And Marcus?"

"It seems he's in Europe right now."

My brows scrunch together. "How do you know he's there?"

"Foster has connections everywhere, including at the airports. They forwarded a security photo to us. Apparently he's been using a private jet."

"And why there?"

"There are two packs there, so maybe he's involved with one of them. We have an idea on which one, but it's not concrete." He sighs again. "It's frustrating how little we know. We can't simply follow him and attack until we figure out the why and where. I thought maybe he'd go back to his place, but he hasn't been back since he first found you."

"So it's been a wild goose chase."

"More like wild wolf chase," he grumbles, and I don't know why, but I find that funny and laugh.

He chuckles lightly through the phone. "I'm glad you found that amusing."

"So…"

I jolt as a knock sounds on the door I'm leaning on.

"Ellie?" Alice's voice filters through the door.

I tilt the phone away from my mouth. "Yes?"

"Sophie left, and I'm going to head to the shower. Just thought I'd let you know."

"Thanks."

The light brightens under my door once more as her shadow moves away.

"Sorry," I say, making my way to my bed. I sit down and lean against the headboard. "How's it going over there? Find anything out?"

"I did. Do you want me to tell you over the phone or wait until I get back?" he asks.

"When do you think you'll make it back home?"

When he doesn't answer I look down at my phone to see if we're still connected, and find we are.

"Ash?"

"I…" He clears his throat. "Sorry. You caught me off guard… Do you really consider it your home?"

I blink, shocked. I didn't even realize I had called it home, but now that I think about it—I do. But not because it's the house I've been staying at, or else I would've considered Emma's house my home as well. But no, it's because it's *his* home. Where he lives is home to me, too. Wherever he is, is home. "My home is with you."

He groans. "Ellie…you can't say those things when I'm not there to kiss you."

"Sorry." I grin. "So, when will you be home?

"I should be back by tonight."

"I thought you weren't coming back until tomorrow."

"Yes, but I thought I should tell you in person what I found."

My throat constricts and my hands shake. I grab a pillow to place on my lap. "Just tell me, Ash."

"I got your parents' file, but that's not what's concerning."

He's silent as he waits for me to respond, but I'm not sure what he's looking for in a reaction from me. "Okay?"

"Ellie...all I found was a birth and death certificate in your file."

My lips part on a gasp. "What? How? I...I don't understand. Did the pack think I died along with my parents?"

"No, it's dated just a few days after your birth."

"But I'm not dead."

"No, you're not."

"Then why?"

"I don't know, it's obviously fake. But it makes sense why no one knew about you and why you weren't taken in by family or the pack."

"It's why Marcus didn't know I was a lycan," I mumble in thought.

"I have some connections that I asked to look into it for me. They did some digging and found that the state has a different last name on your birth certificate than the one in the pack files."

"What? What is it?"

"Your real name is Eleanor Hollenberg, like you already know. The birth certificate wasn't fake, but the state and foster care system have you listed as Eleanor MacCallum."

I blink. "Is that name supposed to mean something to me?"

"No. It's literally a random last name."

I rub at my temple. "Okay, so people thought I was human because of that last name and weren't able to connect me to my parents. What else did you find out?"

He's silent on the line for a moment.

"What is it?" I ask.

"This is harder than I thought it would be to tell you."

"Just tell me, I need to know."

"The bodies of your parents were found completely drained of blood." A chill runs down my spine. Drained of blood? Like Ash's? *Does that mean...*

"And your mother was unrecognizable," he says. "They only

assumed it was her because your father was a few feet away. Her...
her entire head was smashed in and her fingers were burned to the
point where they couldn't get a fingerprint." I cover my mouth just as
a cry breaks out, trying to muffle it. "The authorities assumed it was
from the accident and the car blowing up. It's also assumed that they
didn't have seatbelts on, since they were both found outside the car."

I squeeze my eyes shut. I've never heard the details before. "I-I
don't understand..." I curl around my pillow. It makes sense they
were badly injured in the accident. So why is he so concerned?

"They were purebloods, Ellie. Let alone that the blood loss is
identical to my parents' case, but a simple car crash shouldn't have
killed them or done that much damage. I don't know anything for
sure, but it doesn't add up.

"I also found out that they were the alpha couple and that the
pack disbanded after they found out they died and their bodies were
in human custody."

My stomach clenches. I feel like I'm going to puke. He's right. It
doesn't add up. Maybe if they were normal humans like I always
assumed they were, they could've died like that, but they weren't.

My hand shakes, clutching the phone. "You mean...you think
they were killed on purpose? That...that it wasn't just an accident?"

"I—yes. This is why I wanted to tell you in person." There's
regret in his voice.

Even though it feels like my world has been thrown off center,
I'm glad he told me now. Although I wish he could hold me, I also
don't want him to see me falling apart.

"I'm getting on a plane right now. We can talk more about it
when I get home. Or not. If you're not ready. Whatever you want."

What I want is to scream. Scream so loud that I can't even hear
my own thoughts or feel any emotions.

And cry.

Cry so long and hard that maybe it would be enough to bring
them back. Not just to tell me why they hid things or to explain
what happened to them. But to hold me like they used to—to feel
their love again. I miss them. I miss them so much.

"Ellie? Are you there? Are you okay?" Ash asks on the other end of the line.

No, no, I'm not okay. All these years and I never knew my parents were murdered. It's as if they just died all over again. I'd hoped knowing more about the car accident would help, but instead, it just added more questions. I'm even further from knowing the truth.

My wolf claws burst out and I yelp, almost clawing my face. I didn't even realize it, but my shift is close to the surface and there's no pain this time. At least not physical pain.

I want to shift. I want to tear through the forest, free my inner turmoil. A growl rumbles in my throat. It's almost painful to hold my shift back. I watch as ripples of fur appear and disappear on my arm.

The shift is close, and this time I'm going to welcome it, pain and all.

45

Ash

*I*t's silent on the other end of the line. I stride up the steps onto my jet with a duffle bag slung over my shoulder.

"Ellie darling, please say something," I say into the phone.

"I need to go."

"Wait, Ell—" I hear the end click of the phone call as she hangs up on me.

I curse under my breath and try to call her back. A growl tears from my throat as it goes straight to voicemail. I knew I should've waited to tell her in person.

I dial Russell as I take my seat, throwing my bag in the next one over.

He answers, but I don't wait for him to speak. "Do you have eyes on Ellie?"

Russell pauses. "No, I went to get food. But Sam is there. I'll give him a call."

"Why isn't there another?" I ask. It was fine only having one lycan watching the property and house while I was there, but I wanted two to three while I was gone.

"Sophie was there before I left."

I close my eyes, trying to calm down. Of course, Sophie is talented in fighting. It would make sense why he thought he could run to grab food. But I have a feeling that isn't the only reason why he left. "Sophie left while I was on the phone with Ellie."

"I'll call Sam and head back over." He hangs up and I try not to break my phone while I wait. The stewards and pilots prepare for takeoff.

"Alpha Sylvester, would you like anything before takeoff?" one flight attendant asks.

"No, thank you," I snap, instantly regretting it. "Sorry."

She nods then scurries off. I run a hand down my face and pull at the strands of my hair. This is a different kind of torture.

It feels like ages when he finally calls back.

"She's pacing the kitchen while talking to Alice. I asked Sam to move in closer to hear what she's saying. She's telling Alice she needs to shift."

My shoulders relax, but I'm still on edge. I just dropped a bomb on her, of course her emotions are high. Her shift would be close to the surface. She'd want to run off all her emotions. I just wish I was there to help her through it.

"She turned off her phone," I say.

"She probably did it to think."

I can't really blame her. I let out a heavy sigh. "Alright. Thanks, Russ."

"No problem. Any trouble?"

I laugh without humor. "It seems likely that her parents were murdered."

"Shit."

"Yeah. I'm about to be up in the air for seven hours with no reception. I just needed to know she's not in danger before liftoff."

"I'll be back there in twenty minutes to keep a close eye on her."

I close my eyes and lean my head back on the headrest. "Thanks."

MY BODY IS ENCOMPASSED in a wave of ice and a sharp pain surges, hitting me square in the chest. Air leaves my lungs as I hunch over.

"Alpha Sylvester? Are you alright?" One of the stewardesses comes over with concern.

I can't answer her as I'm consumed by the pain. It's my new alpha link. It feels as if a part of it has been ripped out from me. I go through my pack bonds and pause when I find Sam no longer there.

He either left the pack, or he died. Since he was loyal, I'm guessing the latter.

Bile burns the back of my throat. My hands shakingly pull out my phone, but as I expect there's no reception.

I fight through the rest of the flight with a phantom pain in my chest. I can't help thinking that Ellie is in trouble. Her link to me is still there, but I can't sense anything this far away. A growl escapes in frustration. If she was my mate, it would be in an entirely different situation.

I'd not only be able to sense her and her emotions this far away, but I'd be able to speak to her without being a wolf.

When the plane starts to descend, I don't wait for us to land. I quickly turn my phone off airplane mode and curse under my breath as it reads no service. I wait impatiently as the minutes tick by until I see a single bar pop up, and my phone starts buzzing with incoming text messages and missed calls.

Only one from Russell, updating me that Ellie has shifted and wants to run, and that he'll be following her in wolf form.

The rest are from Alice. What sends dread through me the most is the last message I received from her with the time stamp just an hour ago.

They found

They. Her message is incomplete, and I can only assume she means Marcus and the lycans under him.

It can't be Zac, right?

Another growl leaves me, more animalistic this time. I'm going to be a wolf by the time we land if I don't get myself under control.

I listen to Alice's voicemails:

Ash, Jane just arrived. I didn't know she knew your address, but since I can't get in contact with Russell while he's with Ellie, I wanted to make sure you knew she was here. She said she hadn't heard from Ellie in a while and wanted to stop by before her flight in a few days. I said that was fine.

I go to the next one.

Ash. I can't find Sam. Wasn't he supposed to stay once Russell got here? Or maybe I heard him wrong.

Next one.

Ash, Alice sobs into the phone. He's gone. I-I...I found him. Jane is still in the house. I'm going to have us hide in the basement. I can't hear anyone, but I'll defend her. I've been training. I can do this. This can't end like it did with my father.

That was her last voice message before her text.

The plane lands and I grab my bag and rush to my waiting car. I've got a few hours drive until I'm back.

Once I get in and get onto the road, I dial Ellie. The line goes straight to voicemail, so does Alice's when I try.

I call Russell next, but he doesn't answer.

My mind is racing, and I'm trying to not think of the worst-case scenario. Everyone's bonds are still in place except for Sam's, so I can only hope that they're okay—at least for now. I dial Sophie.

"Alpha," she says. "To what do I owe the honor?"

"Sophie, I need you to gather a group of warriors then head to my house." I pause. "Actually bring warriors, healers, and hunters. They were attacked. Sam's gone. I'm not sure about anything else."

She's silent.

"Sophie," I say, my nerves shot and my patience gone.

"Sorry." She comes to. "I'm on it. Is...is Russell okay?"

I grind my teeth. There's so much unknown to me right now, my wolf form is at the forefront, claws already out and digging into the leather of the wheel.

"I don't know," I say through my teeth. "He isn't dead. His bond is still there. Call me if you make it before me."

I hang up and keep an eye on all their bonds. The bonds seem to come alive the closer I get.

Ellie's link is chaotic, with underlining emptiness and pain. And fear. So much fear I almost choke on it. I forget to breathe as I focus on her link growing faint. The icy emptiness I felt in the plane begins again.

A horn honks, snapping me out of my downward spiral. I swivel back into my lane. I speed down the road as fast as I dare with the snow.

Checking Alice's next, I find her link silent, almost as if she's sleeping, but it feels different. I try not to think that I may lose them tonight if I'm not fast enough.

My chest is tight as I search for Russell's and a wave of relief hits me when his emotions—anger, frustration, and pain—come through.

At least he's conscious.

My phone rings and Foster's name appears.

"Foster," I answer.

"I'm on the way to your house."

"How—do you know what happened?"

"Your place was attacked while Ellie went on a run as a wolf." I force myself to loosen my grip at the sound of my phone cracking. I knew they got attacked—I felt it. But it makes it more real hearing about it. "Russell followed Ellie and left Sam with Alice. Jane showed up worried about Ellie because she hadn't heard from her. But Ellie and Russ were gone for hours, mate. Alice called me frantically when she couldn't get a hold of them or you, and I took my family's jet that second. Now I can't even get a hold of her. I don't know anything else, but I'm almost there. I landed an hour ago."

"Sam is gone," I say, my mind going a million miles a minute.

I'm frantic and hate being stuck in a car, not able to do anything. Completely useless until I get there.

"And Alice?" Foster asks, his voice shaky.

"She's still alive from what I can tell. Only Sam so far."

His relief flares through our pack bond.

"I'll meet you there soon." When I reach the part of the freeway that's been cleared, I hang up and press down on the gas, watching my speedometer crawl up.

46

Ash

*W*hen I get to my cabin, I park next to Foster's car. Getting out, I sniff the air. I scent him, Alice, Jane, and a few other foreign lycans, but their scent is old by a few hours.

Please. I can't be too late to save them.

Walking past the busted front door, I pause at the threshold. Everything outside looked untouched. Inside is a different story. There are claw marks on the walls and blood everywhere. "Foster, where are you?" I say, knowing if he's near he'll be able to hear.

He rushes down the stairs a moment later.

"Ash," he greets, "there's no sign of the other lycans. I've only been able to check upstairs."

I nod as we walk further into my home, but freeze when we enter the kitchen—it's in complete disarray.

Our growls bounce off the walls, our wolves coming to the

surface. The foreign lycans' and Alice's scent are strong here. Foster's eyes begin to glow; he's close to shifting.

"Get your emotions in check. You won't be able to help in wolf form."

He blinks, his eyes returning to normal, and nods.

Despite his eyes reverting, blood drips from his palms from his shifted nails digging into his skin. He's growing frantic, just barely able to contain his shift. We need to find Alice. I've never seen him so unhinged, but then again, so am I.

I need to find Ellie. I won't be able to stay calm until she's safe in my arms.

"Let's check the basement," I say, heading to the basement door, Foster close behind. I open the door and am hit with the smell of blood.

Foster snarls, more wolf than human, and barrels past me and down the stairs. I rush after him and hear his wolf whine from below.

When I reach the landing, I find Alice there, lying on the floor with Foster standing, hovering over her. His arms are completely covered in fur. Alice's arm and a leg are at odd angles, blood slowly seeping out of a head wound. I close my eyes as another wave of anguish washes over me. I could've prevented this. I should've had more than just Sam and Russell, but there are so many people I don't trust right now.

I take a deep breath. We can't have anyone else die tonight. "We need to save her."

"We will," Foster says, his voice sharp and menacing. My gaze snaps to his face and there's a dark look in his green glowing eyes, his canines already out with fur along his cheek bones. "We'll save her and kill that bastard," he growls. Foster kneels next to her and looks over her head wound, carefully brushing strands of hair out of her face with his claws. He leans over, placing his forehead against hers. He closes his eyes and inhales her scent.

One hand shakes as it cradles her face while the other is locked in a fist, knuckles white as he presses it into the ground, blood seeping from his palm.

Looking around, dread seeps in. The basement is trashed, my equipment is destroyed, the weights scattered, the machines broken, but that's not what makes my chest tight. No, it's Jane. Not just Jane though, but another lycan lays under heavy machinery not far from her. A foreign one. At first glance, they both look dead. I walk over and place two fingers on Jane's neck. It's faint, so very faint, but it's there—barely.

"No internal bleeding," Foster says, still next to Alice. "She has a severe concussion, but the gash on her head isn't as bad as it looks. Her right wrist is shattered, right arm and leg broken, and some cuts and bruises."

That's good news. "Come over here, Foster. Jane needs you."

He strides over, his shift slowly receding back, and presses his forehead to Jane's while I walk over to the other lycan. I search for a heartbeat, but he's dead. His neck is broken and a metal bar is through his stomach.

I hold my breath as Foster mutters his findings. "Internal bleeding, concussion, a few broken ribs that caused the bleeding."

He sits up and looks at me. "I need to stay with them and encourage their healing."

I nod. I'm extra grateful he came back when he did. His special ability might keep them alive until Kathy or another healer can get here. "Call Kathy."

I grunt and take out my phone and dial Sophie.

"Are you close?" I ask once she answers.

"Ten minutes."

I growl. I can't wait ten minutes to go find Ellie. "I'm leaving the house now. Find me in the woods in the back. Follow Ellie's scent."

"Ash, you can't—"

I hang up, refusing to hear the rest. Heading up the stairs, I pause on a step. "Stay here and wait for Kathy or any healers that come with Sophie before following."

He pins me with a look. "Follow your own advice and wait for back up before you go off and try to be a hero. You'll end up dead."

I growl. I know he's right, but I can't wait. "I'm going."

"You're losing control."

My nostrils flare and I close my eyes. But even I can tell taking a deep breath won't push my shift down.

"I can't wait anymore." I bound up the rest of the steps, not willing to hear a reply.

Once outside, I let my shift take over and run hard, following Russell's and Ellie's trail. Going as fast as I dare while being aware of my surroundings. Pines zip by me, my feet barely touching the ground.

Hearing a voice, I stop in my tracks. "You're making my life extremely difficult." My blood boils as I recognize it as Marcus'.

I slowly tread through the trees before crouching down in the bushes. Marcus glares down at Ellie, snarling with tight fists. Ellie is lying in the dirt and snow. Blood and dirt cover her naked body, and seeps into the snow underneath her.

It takes everything in me not to go to her.

"Like...I...care," Ellie gasps out, her stubbornness to fight shining through. It's one of the things I love about her. She always amazes me with how much she's been able to handle.

Dread seeps inside as her heart rate slows down more.

Where the heck is Russell? I look for his pack bond and find that it's close, but not close enough to see him.

I sniff the air, searching for others beside Marcus. I find them, but the smells are old, it seems like Marcus is the last.

Ellie is the first to spot me. Her eyes widen. There's a layer of panic in them. Although, what I'm most concerned about is the way the color of her skin and the glow in her eyes are fading.

She's going to die.

I can't let that happen. I won't be able to live without her.

Ash, Foster's voice enters my head—must mean he shifted. I'm on my way with Sophie and a few other warriors and hunters.

It's only Marcus, I respond. I'm going to lead him away from Ellie. Get her to Kathy. She's dying. Send the hunters to find Russell. Send Sophie and the other warriors to me.

On it. She'll be okay.

I finally pry my eyes away from Ellie. Marcus is standing beside her, leaning over to pick her back up. I can't let that happen. I can't let him take her from me.

A growl leaves my throat as I rush out of the brush and leap over Ellie. I collide into Marcus, biting his already damaged shoulder. But too soon, he pries me off and swiftly shifts into his wolf. His wolf is dark brown and huge, bigger than mine, bigger than the last time I saw him. I don't know how that's possible since he isn't a pureblood.

Marcus crouches down. Quickly turning, I run through the trees, hoping he'll take the chase. He does, and I lead him away from Ellie and Russell.

It's not long when Foster's voice is in my mind again. *I got her.*

A wave of relief rolls through me, but I'm not done here yet.

Sensing Sophie near, I give her quick instructions as a plan forms.

When we're far enough away and nearing the river, I come to a halt and face him. Instead of stopping, Marcus lunges for me.

I'm expecting it, though. I dodge and nip his side. He yelps out but lands on his paws.

Spitting out the chunk of his fur and flesh, I stalk toward him.

With a snarl, he backs away. He turns but stops short when he sees Sophie and three other wolves blocking his exit. We corral him, filling the spaces around him.

We each take turns swiping as we shrink the circle around him, but he retaliates. All of us are marked with scratches.

But Marcus isn't as fast as he was last time. I grin, realizing he's grown tired.

He must have been out here for a while, and my mood suddenly grows solemn at the thought. How much did they have to endure before we got here?

Marcus shifts back into his human form. I let out a growl in warning, but don't attack.

He laughs. "You got it all wrong."

My steps falter, and I shift back into human form. "Explain." I don't see how I could have possibly gotten it wrong.

"The real enemy you need to be worried about isn't me."

I take a deep breath to calm myself. "You killed my parents."

Marcus' eyes widen and a laugh bursts from him in disbelief. "You think I was able to kill Buwan and Isla?" He spits some blood onto the ground. "Trust me—it wasn't me. But I wish it was."

Red fills my vision as I let my shift take over, but he's running and shifting simultaneously. I'm picking up speed as I chase him, but just before I'm able to snatch him with my teeth he jumps into the freezing water. I halt just barely in time before plunging in after him.

Scanning the rushing river, I try to catch a glimpse of him under its depths. No one dares to rush in. We may be strong, but water this cold and fast can still drown a lycan.

Ash, Foster's voice enters my mind.

What's wrong?

It's Ellie...we're losing her.

My knees weaken as ice-cold dread hits me square in the chest. As if I took that dive into the river's icy depths.

Ellie can't die.

I need her. I need her smile, her laugh, her kindness, and her warm snuggles in the middle of the night. I haven't had time to show her what she truly means to me. She needs to know she's cherished. That she's loved and will always have me. I can't lose her. I can't think of what would happen if I do.

Ellie

I relish the feel of my paws crunching in the snow, picking up speed until it feels like I'm flying. I sense someone following me, but know it's only Russell as a red-brown wolf. He's close enough that he's within reach if I need him, but far enough away to give me a sense of privacy. I'd rather be alone, but I know he's here for my protection.

Getting lost in my thoughts, I continue running, maneuvering through the snow-covered trees.

I lose track of time as I ponder, but Russell never complains. He just silently follows me from a distance, giving me space.

My parents were murdered.

Someway, somehow. I sense the truth in it. I never thought hard about how they died, and how little I knew, because I didn't want to think about. But now that I know more about their deaths, I can't *not* think about it. They were purebloods, some of the most powerful lycans in the world, and they just died in a car accident? Yeah, that doesn't seem likely. Nor do their injuries match up.

All those years under Marcus' rule, and he could've very well been the one that murdered them. But how would he not know about me if he did? I was their only child.

Then there's the whole funeral and my death certificate.

Were my parents hiding me to keep me safe from the very people who killed them?

Nothing is adding up, and I'm even more confused than I was before. Before it was only Marcus, staying away from him and surviving.

Why *does* he want me so badly? Why won't he give up? Why does he want my blood?

The answer is just in the back of my mind when Russell's voice in my head jars me out of my thoughts. I forgot we could talk to each other in this form.

Hold up, Ellie.

I stop in my tracks at the unspoken warning in his voice. *What's wrong?*

Do you hear that?

Looking around, I realize how late it's gotten. It's not sunny for long during this time of year, but the sun was up when we left. Now it's practically night, and I hadn't even noticed. I quirk an ear to listen to our surroundings.

I don't hear anything.

Exactly, he responds and I realize what he means. It may be winter, but we should at least hear small animals scurrying around or birds flapping their wings. But there's nothing. Instead, an eerie quiet has settled across the land.

Russell looks around, his eyes scanning the surrounding landscape.

Let's head back, he says. He nods toward the path and turns.

But that's when others move in. We're surrounded. I didn't even hear the crunch of snow. How did they get so close without us detecting them?

Get back-to-back with me.

I do as he says and turn around until our backs are to each other. Russell growls at them as they move closer. I try not to whimper.

Do you recognize these wolves? I ask Russell.

No. They are not of this pack.

Well, I figured that.

He shoots me a side-eye glare. *Then why did you ask?*

I thought you might know lycans outside of your pack. If I could roll my wolf eyes at him right now, I would.

I'm going to draw them away. I need you to run as fast as you can back to the house. Sam and Alice are there, have them call for help.

I'm not leaving you here by yourself, I respond. We're unlikely to win two on six, but you're even less likely one on six.

Ellie, this isn't up for discussion.

You're right. I'm not leaving. End of discussion.

He huffs.

The wolves come in waves, each nipping our sides so fast we can't keep up. At least I can't keep up. Russell seems to be doing fine with barely a scratch on him. I never trained in my wolf form. This is only the second time I've been a wolf.

Ellie, I'll make a gap in their circle. I want you to run.

I already said—

I'll be fine, they are untrained. Go and I'll be right behind you. We'll run together, but you first.

Great, these wolves are untrained, and I'm faring poorly against them. I look around after dodging a set of teeth. The only chance we have is running. *Alright, just tell me when.*

Russell goes on full-offense mode, surprising them as he snarls, bites, and claws his way through. He jumps on one, catching it off-guard, and latches onto its neck and tears its throat out.

Now.

He growls. I leap out of the circle through the gap he created and run. I race through the trees until I realize Russell isn't behind me. I turn around, panting, finding nothing but pines, snow, and dirt.

Liar, I yell at him in a panic.

I'm...sorry...I...had...to.

His words come out in bursts. I can tell he's still fighting, but that he's struggling without having the other three focusing on me.

"Hello, Eleanor."

Just two words and fear ebbs its way deep into my soul. I've heard that voice so many times in my life, and way too much recently. All it ever does is bring me pain. I slowly turn around, dreading what I already know, and come face-to-face with Marcus.

His foreboding figure towers over me even as a man. His rotten scent burns my nostrils making me gag.

He *tsks* and steps closer.

A growl vibrates inside of me as I step back.

He grins. "It's been a while since we've actually been alone, hasn't it? Are you ready to come with me now? I'll call off the other lycans. We've only killed one so far. But I think there's still two others we could kill, and that's not including Jane."

My eyes narrow on him. One dead? It couldn't be Alice, right? And what does Jane have to do with this?

Please tell me she's safe and not here.

"Oh, you didn't know?" he says, reading the confusion on my face. "She came by just at the right time."

A whimper slips past my lips.

Marcus moves beside me in a blink of an eye and grabs a chunk of my fur. I snap at him. He quickly lets go, but not before I get a chunk out of his arm.

He roars and shifts. My knees shake at his size. My body freezes up, as if I shrunk two sizes with his wolf hovering over me.

How is he so large? I thought he was terrifying as a man, but he's petrifying as a wolf.

Marcus lunges at me and I skid away, but not fast enough as he snips my rear. I yelp and hunch low. Now would be a really good time for my special ability to emerge.

Come now, Eleanor. You don't want your friends to die now, do you? Marcus' voice enters my mind.

I stumble back, shaking my head to try to get him out. How is this possible? How did he get in my head? We aren't members of the same pack.

I growl at him as he grows closer.

Don't act like that. Just come with me and everyone else survives.

I retreat backward until my hind hits a tree. Quickly jumping aside, I move around it and rush away. Tears are leaking from my eyes as I run. But I'm not fast enough. I can hear him closing in.

I'm yanked back from my tail, and my yelp of pain is cut short when I receive a blow to my side. Crumbling to the ground, I try to catch my breath when he latches his teeth in my stomach.

His eyes flare with hatred. I told you that you couldn't get away from me.

I paw at him, making sure my claws catch onto him and dig deep. He snarls but doesn't remove his teeth from me.

Let go! I scream at him.

My energy wanes, and I shift back, not of my own accord. My mind warns me that shifting was a bad idea while I'm hurt. But I couldn't stop it, I couldn't keep the form. Why did I shift back?

I slip from his jaw and scream from the pain of his bite. I clutch at my stomach, finding it wet with blood and ripped in shreds. My brain goes blank as pain flares all over my body. I scream, curling into myself.

Marcus shifts back and I try to scramble away. But it's no use. I can't move.

He lets out a huge sigh. "Now that wasn't too hard, was it? Let's go."

I struggle to stand. I'm not going down without a fight.

He throws his head back and laughs without humor. "Seriously? I was hoping this backbone was just a phase."

"I will never go willingly with you. I refuse to give up."

His canines grow as his brown eyes blaze with fury.

Terror freezes me. Marcus moves so fast that after a single blink he's in front of me, sticking his partial-shifted claws into my right arm.

I jab my left elbow into his stomach. He slightly loosens his grip and I rip my arm away, stumbling backward.

Stretching my uninjured arm out, I grip onto a nearby tree and hunch over, trying to remain standing.

"Foolish girl, you're going to bleed out."

"Thanks to you," I growl back.

My eyes catch a movement behind him, but before I can register what, Marcus is jumped from behind by a wolf.

It's Russell.

With him distracted, I partial-shift my uninjured hand and slash it across Marcus' face.

He roars and shifts back into a wolf, dislodging Russell and throwing him against a nearby tree.

"Russell!" I scream and rush toward him, but Marcus snatches me up.

"No, you don't. I have other plans for you." His sick breath slides across my face as he whispers in my ear. He takes off in a run with me in his grasp. I watch in horror as his wounds stitch back together.

How am I supposed to win this? He's healing faster than Ash can.

Not willing to give up, I allow my canines to lengthen and bury them into the closest thing I can reach—his shoulder. I clamp down hard and put as much hate and anger into it as I take a chunk out of him.

Marcus roars, dropping me onto the ground. He lays into me with his fists. It's not long before he switches to his claws.

I phase in and out from the intensity of the pain, but each time I can focus, I make sure to take a shot at him. His arms have blood flowing down them from my efforts.

But I know my efforts are pointless. He still has so much energy left, but I take pleasure from seeing that his shoulder wound is still visible. It's taking longer to heal than the little marks I'm giving him now. I'm slowly losing the strength to keep going. I wish I was stronger. I thought being a lycan and a pureblood would give me a better chance at beating Marcus.

In one last ditch effort, I get my feet underneath him and use all my strength to kick him off, but he won't budge.

My attempts are pathetic. I'm pathetic.

I'm not sure how much time passes when he finally stops, panting over me, sweat dripping down his face with my blood coating his hands. I can barely move.

He looks down at me with disgust. "You're making my life extremely difficult."

"Like...I...care," I say between gasps.

My head is about the only thing I *can* move.

"What am I supposed to do with you now?" he says, then growls.

I ignore him as he mutters about how his head alpha will be pissed if I die. Why does he even care? What's been the purpose of any of this?

Instead of dwelling on my questions, I look up at the night sky. There's a chill in the air as I lay on a patch of dirt and snow, yet I don't actually feel the cold. Instead, I feel...almost peaceful.

And tired. So very tired.

There isn't a moon tonight, but the stars shine brighter than I've ever seen them before. I wish I could be looking at them in a different scenario with Ash by my side. I can just picture him holding me close as we point out the different constellations. Not that I know any, but I bet he does.

I picture his beautiful face, his eyes that remind me of glaciers, but there's still so much warmth in them when he looks at me. Taking a deep breath through my nose, I can almost smell him. The smell of pines and fresh snow combined with his unique musky scent. It's probably just the pine trees around me, but I pretend it's him. My eyes grow heavy as exhaustion overtakes me, my head lulling to the side.

Glowing glacier-blue eyes meet mine through the bush.

Suddenly alert, fear gives me an adrenaline rush.

Ash.

He shouldn't be here. He *can't* be here. Marcus will kill him. He's more powerful than I realized. He was holding out on his full strength when he thought I was just a human.

I try to shake my head, to tell him to leave, but my head barely moves. I grind my teeth in frustration, tears building up.

Marcus hovers over me, reaching to pick me up when Ash jumps out of the bushes. He collides with Marcus and latches onto his injured shoulder.

I watch in horror as Marcus pries Ash off and shifts. Ash regains his footing quickly and turns, disappearing as Marcus bounds into the forest after him. I try to get up, but pain sends a wave of dizziness, and I collapse in a heap on the ground.

48

Ellie

*M*y eyes track Marcus' movements in horror as he slides a finger against the whip that's now coated with my blood and licks his fingers clean.

He's never done that before.

His eyes widen with surprise as his gaze lands on me.

"Well, what do you know? I'm one lucky bastard, finding you." His smile turns menacing. *"We're going to have fun with you."*

We? A shiver runs down my spine.

Marcus drops the whip and pulls out his phone. Grinning, he holds it up to his ear. "Head alpha, I found one." He pauses as he listens. "Yes, don't worry, she won't be going anywhere. It's one of the foster kids." He frowns. "She doesn't smell like one," he says. "But her blood...well, let's just say it's obvious how potent it is with just a drop." He chuckles.

I tighten my arms around my legs and bury my face in between my knees, ignoring the pain from my back. Dealing with this for four years has numbed the pain. My hope of making it out of here alive is slowly dimming. By this rate, I'll die before I make it to eighteen.

"Yes, she'll be ready to leave by the time you get here."

My head snaps up, a sense of dread overwhelms me. He rarely ever lets me leave the basement, he keeps it locked most of the time, trapping me here. But now he's planning on taking me somewhere? I can't let that happen. Something inside tells me that whatever he's planning is going to be far worse than this. I need to leave.

"Yes, see you soon." He ends the call and walks over to the mini fridge that's down here. Not full of food or drink for me, but full of beers for him.

"Well, Eleanor, it looks like it's time for a celebration." His grin makes me sick. He pops the lid with his bare hands and takes a swig. "That's some good stuff." He chugs the rest down and reaches for a second. He pouts, looking back at me. "Sadly, I probably shouldn't harm you anymore, but the wait will be worth it," he says more to himself than to me.

He downs the second, grabs a few more, then heads up the stairs. "Goodnight, Eleanor. Dream of me tonight." He chuckles as he closes the basement door behind him, but in his excitement, he forgets to lock the door.

BITS AND PIECES of conversations filter through my mind as I fade in and out of consciousness, in and out of forgotten memories. Hours could've passed and I wouldn't have known. The only thing I can feel is the soft fabric of a blanket that's covering me.

The skin on my hand lights up with tingles and warmth. I know what that feeling means. "Ash," I say, my voice barely a breath out of my slightly parted lips. I'm not sure if he heard me. I can't even hear myself.

His skin grows warmer and warmer against mine until it feels like it's burning. I weakly try to pull away, but my limbs won't listen to me. I try to open my eyes, but everything is blurry. Disorientation and dizziness surface, so I quickly shut them again.

Ash tightens his grip on mine. "She's so cold. Why isn't she healing?"

"She's too far gone to be able to heal herself. This was only her second time shifted, yes? It takes a toll on your body. She doesn't have enough strength or energy," a woman's voice answers. It sounds like Dr. Kathy.

"Isn't there something you can do?"

It's silent for a while, or maybe I passed out again.

Ash still has a hold of my hand.

"You should say goodbye," she says.

"No." His voice is strained. "There has to be something else we can do. I can't just watch her die. Have you tried everything?"

I already had a feeling it was too late for me. I was resigned to the fact in the woods, but hearing Ash reminds me how much I don't want to die. My mouth refuses to move as I try to speak. To tell Ash I don't want to die and not to give up on me. Instead, I end up screaming inside with frustration.

"We tried everything that we could but..."

"But what?"

"Well, there is one thing we haven't tried."

Ash growls. "Why haven't you?"

"Well..."

"Kathy," he growls.

"It's not something I can do. You would need to claim her."

"I can't do that to her. She'll never be able to look at me the same again. I can't take away her choice."

"She'll be dead if you don't. You're giving her a chance to live, and she'll still have the choice to claim you or not."

There's a deafening silence before Ash speaks again, his voice hard and quiet. "I'll do it. But I want everyone out."

There's a patter of footsteps and fabric ruffling as people shuffle out. A door clicks shut, then silence.

A moment later his fingers caress my face, the same burning sensation follows. Ash lifts my head to sweep my hair to the side, his touch sparking more heat. His fingers follow my jawline down to my neck and stop at the junction of my shoulder. He pulls the blanket slightly down. A cool breeze hits my exposed flesh.

Ash places a kiss on my cheek, a drop of something wet lands on my skin and slides down to my ear. "I'm so sorry, Ellie. I want to make you mine, but not like this." His voice cracks. "Never like this."

The air stills around me. There's a light touch of his scruff against my skin as he places a gentle kiss. Then his canines pierce my skin in the soft area between my shoulder and neck.

Too soon it burns, as if he's slowly pouring boiling water inside of me. It starts in my shoulder and neck, then spreads like a wildfire, completely engulfing my body. I scream inside, my body and voice still refusing to work.

As suddenly as it started, the pain stops. A warmth seeps in—similar to when he marked me with the pack bond—and takes over, but it's so much more intense. An ecstasy joins it, intertwining with the warmth, making my insides tingle and burst at the same time. My body is completely weightless as swirls of color dance underneath my eyelids.

My heart pumps faster. My nerve endings come alive.

My body is slow to respond, but I can wiggle my toes and move my fingers.

Gasping, my eyes flash open. My insides seem to expand.

"Ash," I whisper.

His teeth return to normal after detaching himself from me. His tongue sneaks out, licking the small wounds. I shiver at the touch.

"You're okay," I say, my voice raspy.

His eyes are rimmed red as he grips my face, gazing at me lovingly. "You're okay." His voice cracks. "Will you ever be able to forgive me? I...I wasn't here to protect you like I promised, and I forced the..." His voice cracks, his eyes squeeze shut.

I reach a hand up, caressing his face. "There's nothing to forgive. I'm alive because of you."

His eyes open wide. "Y-You heard us?"

"I heard everything."

Tears well up in his eyes and slide down his cheeks. "I'm so sorry, Ellie. I wanted to give you the chance to accept me."

"I know, but I was always planning to accept you."

Grabbing my hand that was on his face, he places it against his chest. He leans over me to place his head on my shoulder as a sob racks through his body.

My heart breaks. "I love you, Ash," I say, choking on all the emotion between us.

He lifts his head, tears streaming down his face. "And I love you, Ellie." He leans over and kisses me oh-so-gently. "I'm so glad you're alive," Ash says against my lips, his warm breath sending butterflies into my heart and stomach.

I grip his shirt where my hand lays above his heart. His hand comes up and covers it. "Thank you, Ash."

He leans away, his brows scrunched together, cheeks wet from his tears. "You're not angry with me?"

"How could I be? You saved my life."

He squeezes my hand. "But I left you. I wasn't here to protect you."

I shake my head. "You tried to protect me even far away. How were you to know what was going to happen?"

His eyes flash, glowing brightly before going back to normal. "Can I join you? I need to be closer to you."

I start to nod but realize I'm naked. "Actually, could I have some clothes first?" I look around, realizing I'm in his bedroom—in his bed.

His brows rise and a small smile curves his lips, humor just barely touching his forlorn face. "I mean, I wouldn't mind how you are now."

"Ash."

He snickers and gives me a brief kiss. "I'll go get you something comfortable to wear."

Once Ash leaves, I lift the blanket to peer down at myself. My stomach is covered in bandages, but I don't sense any pain.

Peeling back one, I find my skin completely unharmed. And now that I think of it, I feel fine. Actually, better than fine. More like amazing, except for some soreness.

I quickly cover myself back up when Ash enters, carrying a

bundle of my clothes. He grins when my cheeks flush from the sight of my undies in his hands.

"Am I healed now?" I ask as I quickly take them from him.

"You are," he says as he turns around giving me privacy. "The mate bond healed you."

"It can do that?" I test my weight on one foot before standing.

I remove the bandages that I find not just on my stomach, but also my legs and arms.

"Only during the initial marking," he says.

"So, if you marked me again, it wouldn't work?" I ask, tying the strings of my pajamas.

"Is that an invitation?"

"No." I grin, sliding back into bed. "I'm done now."

He turns around and climbs in the bed with me.

"Would it, though?" I ask.

"No," he says, pulling me against him, and snuggling close. "But I can give you strength and help you heal faster through the bond." He moves my hair to trace where he marked me. It's already healed, but both of us know exactly where he bit.

"Can I do that for you?"

"Not yet." His fingers brush against my skin in strokes, sending shivers up and down my spine.

"Why not?"

Lifting his gaze, his eyes find mine. "Because you haven't marked me."

I swallow. "So, if I were to...mark you, I would be able to heal you? If you were injured, I mean."

"The initial bite, yes."

"And after."

"The same as me." Leaning close, he kisses the spot. *I can also speak to you in your mind.*

I feel his grin rather than see it when I gasp.

"I thought you could only do that in wolf form."

"Now that I've claimed you, I can speak to you in any form. You'll be able to do the same once—if you claim me."

"I have a question."

Amusement dances in his eyes when he pulls away. "I may have an answer."

"Why didn't you know I was your mate when we first met?" I ask.

His gaze shifts between my eyes. I try to fight the desire to hide from the intensity of them. "Do you think I hid the fact?" he asks. "That I knew before the shift?"

"No." I lift one shoulder in a shrug. "It just doesn't make sense."

He nods as his eyes travel back to my shoulder. He can't seem to leave it alone. "Everyone has a mate link, but no one can actually sense it. Not until you touch your mate, and it flares to life."

"Still doesn't explain how you didn't know."

A corner of his mouth quirks up. "I'm getting to it."

"Proceed."

He laughs. "Thank you for your permission." He reaches up and tucks a strand of hair behind my ear. "I did feel something, but I thought you were human."

"Because humans don't have the mate link."

"Exactly, the mate link and bond is from the essence in our blood, just like the alpha and pack bonds. My best guess is because you hadn't shifted yet. Maybe that dulled the link, made it harder to detect until you shifted. Now that I think back on it, the signs were there, but I was oblivious."

I brush over where he bit. "I felt something when I first shifted. This insane desire to mark you. But so much has happened that I didn't connect the dots."

He covers my hand with his and squeezes.

"Is there a difference between links and bonds?" I ask.

"Link is before the bond is in place. So, for example, the link was solidified and became a bond for me when I marked you, but yours is still a link."

I'm a bit hesitant to ask the next question in case he gets the wrong idea. "And what happens if you refuse the link?"

"The link breaks...snaps in half. I've heard it's extremely painful."

My heart pings. "Y-you were willing to feel that pain if I declined you?"

He sighs, his thumb brushing back and forth over my skin. "Yes, but I didn't want you to know."

"Why not?"

"I didn't want to sway you. You would never purposely inflict pain on me, let alone anyone."

My chest tightens. "I love you."

Resting back on the bed, he pulls me to him. "I love you too, my mate."

Gripping my hair, he gently pulls it, forcing my head to move until my neck is bared to him. "Do you know what else the mark means?" he asks as his fingers caress the invisible mark. My breath hitches, his touch more intense than usual.

I hold my breath as his fingers dance up my neck. "Well?" he says, his breath caressing and tickling my skin.

"Not exactly," I say, breathless. "Just that it means you claimed me as your mate."

"Yes, but there's more." He nips my ear. "Not only is it a claim, but also a promise. A promise to always love you, cherish you, protect you, and care for you." He cups the back of my head, pulling me forward until we're once more face-to-face. "You are my number one, above everyone else, even before the pack. I will never want another, only you. Forever you, Ellie darling." His eyes mist over with unshed tears as he gazes into mine. The warmth in them is stronger than I have ever seen before. "I was afraid I would lose you. I love you, my mate, my love."

Tears burn my eyes as I choke out, "I love you too. I love you with all my heart, Ash—I don't know your middle name —Sylvester."

He breaks out in a laugh with a watery smile. "It's Buwan. It was my father's name, and his father's before him." He leans in and kisses me briefly. "And I love you with all my heart and soul, Eleanor Rose Hollenberg."

"How did you know mine?"

He grins. "Birth certificate."

I chuckle. "Figures."

49

Ellie

I wake up to the mattress moving and watch Ash climb out of bed and stretch, revealing a sliver of his smooth light-brown skin. He sighs then turns around, catching me ogling him. A blush heats my face as he sends me a smile.

"I'll be right back," he says and enters his adjoined bathroom.

Turning onto my side, I listen to the water running. It's still too early to get up, and I don't want to. After everything that happened yesterday, I just want to spend all day in bed.

My heartbeat spikes.

"Am I an alpha now?" I whisper into the dark. Ash and I are now the alpha couple because he claimed me, right? I look over to the bathroom. The only thing left to do is for me to mark him. And I plan on it, but not until everything has calmed down and we can make it special. Not sure how to do that quite yet.

His phone buzzes, making me jolt. A moment later, Ash comes out and picks it up, scowling down at it.

"Any news?" I ask, not being able to hide my curiosity.

He sighs, places the phone back down, and rejoins me in bed, snuggling close. "Russell suspects witches are involved. They snuck up on us too easily."

I jerk up into a sitting position. "So Russell is okay?" Does it make me an awful person that I forgot about him for a moment?

Ash pulls me back down to him. "Yes, he has some deep gashes and a few broken ribs that need some extra care, but he'll be fine." He chuckles lightly. "To his horror, he'll have to take it easy for a while."

I relax into Ash's embrace. "Oh good. He'll be okay." I sigh and then jerk back up. "Wait. Jane!"

He pulls me back down again. "She's in bad shape but Kathy is personally watching over her. She is optimistic that Jane will have a full recovery."

I place a hand over my heart as it aches. So Jane really was there. Marcus wasn't lying about it. Ash wipes a few of my tears that escape.

"And Alice?" I whisper.

"She was hurt badly, but will also make a full recovery."

I did this. Marcus was after me. If I wasn't there, no one else would've gotten hurt.

"Ellie, stop it." Ash props up over me, gazing into my eyes. "I know what you're thinking. It's not your fault. It's Marcus'."

I blink rapidly. "But—"

"No. Marcus is the one who attacked. Don't blame yourself."

"How did he get to be so powerful?" I ask, terror eating at me. "Is it because of witches? Did they use magic?"

"It appears that way. They could've been hired, or the lycans could've bought potions to dim our senses or to camouflage themselves. Hard to say which it is."

"Would a witch need to be present to use magic?"

"Not if it was a potion."

I nod and think back on the attack before Marcus. "Well, I didn't notice any non-lycans. But I guess they could've camouflaged themselves."

"Russell said the same thing." He lets out a pent-up breath. "Also, Sophie and her team couldn't find Marcus."

"Why am I not surprised?" I say, bitterly. "How?"

"He got away by jumping in the freezing river. There are no tracks leading out of the water anywhere, but also no body." The picture of the river enters my mind as I remember running by it yesterday. It was half frozen with chunks of ice floating down it.

"Do you think he could survive that?"

"Even a pureblood would struggle healing if exposed to that water for long."

"I feel a 'but' coming."

He gives me a solemn look. "But he's larger than even a pureblood, stronger and faster too, and his scent is wrong."

"What's wrong with it?"

"He smells rotten."

I try to remember his scent. He did smell rotten to me, but I'm not used to using my enhanced abilities yet. Sophie said you have to think about it in human form to use them, like I have to do when I partial-shift, but in wolf form it comes naturally.

"So you think he survived?"

"Considering our recent experiences with him? Yes."

I knew it would be too good to hope for this to be all over. "Our luck has been pretty bad."

It's strange to think about everything that happened yesterday, everything I found out. I don't even know where to start. I guess looking at my parents' files might help. Maybe it'll tell me something that will help because I want to get this behind us. To move on. But that can't happen until Marcus is no longer an issue and the mysteries behind our parents' deaths are solved. Maybe then we can all focus on healing and moving on with our lives, including making this a pack to be proud of because...because now that I'm Ash's mate.

"Not all the time." Ash nuzzles closer and mutters into my neck. "If we didn't have some luck, I wouldn't have found you, nor would you have survived last night."

I turn into him more and cuddle back. We stay like this for a while, both of us lost in our own thoughts. It's been too long since we've been able to just relax and think with one another. It's nice, just listening to his even breaths and heartbeat. Although, his breath on my neck is a bit distracting.

A caress on my cheek jars me from my thoughts. I turn my face into Ash's light touch.

"What are you thinking?" he murmurs.

"If I wasn't a lycan, would you still have wanted me?"

His brows scrunch together as he turns to face me. "Of course. I didn't know you were a lycan until you shifted, and I wanted you before that. Remember? I've told you multiple times."

"I know, but I would've died before you if I was human. I would get old while you would still"—I gesture to him, and he grabs my hand and kisses the tips of my fingers—"look like this."

"I wouldn't care."

"How do you know?" I ask.

"Because I've seen it with others. Charlie was married to a human and loved her. He even had a child with her—Alice. She didn't die when she was old, but he mourned her for years and years after."

"But if she were a lycan, maybe she would've lived longer and—"

"If she were a lycan, we wouldn't know the Alice we know today, and with a fifty-fifty success rate of the bite working—"

"Bite?"

"Right, I forgot we haven't talked about that yet. There are two ways to change a lycan, either to receive the blood of an Elite and become an Original, or be bitten."

"Is that how there became so many?" I ask.

"Yes. For example, the witch Elite freed a lot of her fellow slaves by sharing her blood and making them Originals. Then there are the bitten. They are the ones that were changed from being bitten by either an Elite or Original. And the bitten aren't as strong."

"Okay, I think I get it. So, if the bite didn't work on Alice's mom, nothing would change, right? Alice would still be half human, half lycan."

"No...if it didn't work. There would be no Alice, because her mother, Lily, would've died. Those who don't change into lycans are killed by the bite."

My eyes widen. "That's horrible."

He nods. "But people were willing to chance it."

I can't fathom why. "Why?"

"Because of love or power. Only the Elites can change others with their blood. So, if an Original wants to change someone they have to bite them."

"Could you or I change someone with a bite?"

"Yes, but the chances of survival decreases with the essence in our blood. The less we have, the less likely they'll change."

"Does this still happen today?" I ask.

"No," he answers, lowering his hand to my waist, the heat of his touch sparking something inside, "at least it's not supposed to. It was banned after the war by a vote of the Originals and alphas. There aren't many rules that we all follow, usually each alpha decides for his pack, but that's one of them. The others are no killing in cold blood, no slaves...those kinds of things. But how each pack is run is up to the alphas."

Letting out a long exhale, I rest my head on his chest. There's still so much to learn, yet I can't keep everything in line in my mind. "I may be a bit overwhelmed again with everything."

"I may have a solution to distract you."

Peering up at him, I notice his roguish grin. I prop myself up on my elbows. "What are you thinking?"

He leans forward and captures my lips in a searing kiss. "I'm thinking of doing a lot of that."

He works his way over, placing kisses in a trail along my jaw then down my neck. My heart races and my skin warms as he adjusts the collar of my shirt until my shoulder is revealed. His hot mouth lands on his mark, sending a jolt of desire through me. He grins against me.

"Ash, I—"

"Shh," he whispers and captures my mouth once more. "Let me show you how much you mean to me."

"You already do, all the time," I say between kisses.

He takes advantage, swiping his tongue across my bottom lip and inside my part lips, brushing my tongue with his. "No more talking."

I hum in response and let him take the kiss deeper, focusing just on him and his touches. His hands tangle in my hair.

Wet drops land on my face. I open my eyes to see tears fall from Ash's closed ones.

My chest tightens. He's been putting on such a brave act for me. I've put him through so much in such a short amount of time.

Reclosing my eyes, I grab his face in between my shaky hands, feeling the soft scruff along his jaw and cheeks, and tentatively take charge of the kiss. I've never initiated like this before. But I want to. And I want more this time.

I push against him until it's me who's on top, straddling his waist. I try to show him just how much I love and care for him with this kiss. How lucky I am to have him. I hope he can feel what he means to me. He's been here for me every step of this process. But I'm not just wanting this because I want to prove my love, no, I want this simple because I *want* to. I want the intimacy it brings. Why should I have a reason to want more than that? Shouldn't loving him, him loving me, and having a mutual desire for this be all we need?

I elicit a moan from him when I suck on his tongue. One of his hands strays away from my hair to move down my back until it reaches a sliver of exposed skin.

Ash's breath hitches when I tug on his shirt, wanting to feel more of his skin on mine.

His hand stalls as he breaks away, breathing heavily. "Ellie, I…"

I sit back on my heels and look down at him. "I want this, Ash. I want you."

He swallows. "But yesterday…"

"Just showed me how much you mean to me, and how much I want this. Us. Please, I want more."

His gaze burns into mine. "We would be us, even without this."

I smile. He always says the perfect things.

"I know. But I want more. Do you?"

He bites his lip and nods. "But if you aren't sure…"

I brush a lock of his ebony hair off his forehead. "I am sure."

His throat bobs. "Any time you want to stop, just say the word and I will."

"Okay."

Ash takes a shaky breath. His body trembles under me as he gently tugs me back down to him. "I love you, Ellie," he says against my lips before taking them with his own.

"I love you too," I say back and tug at his shirt again.

He chuckles, and I lean back when he moves to sit up.

With one hand, he takes off his shirt, while his other hand rests heavy on my hip.

I swallow. His abs and chest are on full display now. Heat radiates from his body as I brush my fingers over the dust of soft hairs on his chest.

"Ellie," he mutters with a groan, then retakes my lips. One hand slips under my shirt and crawls up my side while the other curves over my butt. His fingers dig in as he pulls me flush against him. I thrust my hands in his hair and grip the ends when I feel his hard length underneath me. My body acts on its own as I move my hips, grinding my need against his.

He breaks away, panting, his breath featherlight on my lips. "I want to see you," he says a bit breathless, his lips brushing mine. His pupils are blown, and his eyes are glowing a soft blue as he plays with the edge of my shirt. "May I?"

I nod, almost frantically. I lift my arms up as he pulls my shirt off and over my head.

My hair falls around my bare shoulders and my heart pounds in my chest when he pauses and stares.

His eyes flash to mine, silently asking permission, and I nod.

Almost reverently, he palms my breast with his hand and a giggle threatens to escape me, but I give him a wide grin instead. "You're acting like you've never seen one before."

He squeezes and lightly flicks my nipple, eliciting a moan from me. "I haven't seen yours before."

Looking into his eyes, I see the heat and love in them, and it ignites me, heating me from the inside out, and a knot forms in my throat as a wave of emotion hits.

How did I get so lucky? I grab his face and kiss him hard.

He pulls me flush against him, pressing our chests together skin to skin. He lies down, bringing me with him, and our lips continue their tug and pull war.

I gasp when I feel his thumbs hook under the waistband of my pajamas. As he tugs them down, he tries to keep our lips locked, unsuccessfully. A small laugh bubbles out of me as he finally gets them off and chucks them across the room, but it's cut off when he goes for his pants next.

My breath grows shallow. "Let me."

He freezes and I sit up, hovering over him. I meet his eyes, silently asking permission, like he did. He gives me a short nod, his eyes tracking my every movement.

Grabbing the waistband of his pants, I begin slowly pulling them down. When I get to his butt, he has to lift his hips for me to go past. His black boxer briefs are revealed along with his large bulge. My breath hitches when I see the outline of his desire. So much larger than what I was expecting, even covered with fabric.

"Ellie." He groans, his length twitching. "You can't look at me like that."

I blink owlish eyes up at him.

He growls through clenched teeth. "My pants. Take them off." His throat bobs. "Please."

My head snaps down to my hands, and with his large bulge in view once more, I almost get distracted again.

Determined, I quickly finish getting the rest of his pants off and go for his boxers. There's this *need* inside of me that has to see all of him completely bare. But just before I touch the fabric of his boxers, I hesitate and glance up at him.

Ash clenches the covers on either side of him, his nostrils flared, as he stares at me. "You're so freaking beautiful." His voice is husky and strained.

My heart swells and I lean down to kiss the skin above his boxers. Grabbing the waistband, I pull them down until his length bobs free, and I almost forget to breathe.

"Please." One of his hands comes up and cups my face, gently urging me to look up. "I need you." His eyes are glowing brighter now and his canines have lengthened.

I finish pulling them the rest of the way down, loving the view of his muscular legs bare and on display, but when I reach to tug the remaining piece of clothing off of me, his hands cover mine.

"Allow me," he says, and I'm not sure how much more my heart can take.

He runs a finger under the waistband of my underwear, caressing the skin underneath. Goosebumps erupt across my skin, and his touch sends tingles straight to my core. My hips jerk forward and a growl rumbles in Ash's chest.

He grips my underwear and tugs them down, his eyes glued to my center.

I wobble with my legs still parted and my underwear stretching above my knees. He chuckles when I can't keep my balance, but it quickly turns into a groan when my front presses against his and I wiggle around to get my underwear completely off.

His hands caress up and down my back and over my butt, gripping it and pulling me closer.

My breath picks up as he starts to grind slowly against me.

"Ash," I whisper.

He rolls us onto our sides and slides a hand between us. A shiver runs through me as he places kisses along my neck. My heart races as his hand brushes the skin on my stomach and continues lower until he touches me between the apex of my thighs for the first time. Tingles erupt throughout my body and I gasp as his canines scrape against his mark.

His lips meet mine again, but instead of the frantic need he was showing before, it's gentle and slow.

"I'm ready," I say in between kisses.

He pauses, panting, then rolls us until I'm back on top of him.

I give him a questioning look.

He pecks me on my lips. "I want you to take it as slow as you want."

Biting my lip, I sit back, straddling him. "I..."

"I know." His hands follow me on my hips. "If it's too painful, we can stop. You're in control."

My throat grows tight. Just another reason why I love him. I need this control right now, and he knew.

I touch his hard length for the first time and take a moment to admire him until a low rumble rolls through him and a small laugh bursts from me. "Sorry."

A slow smile grows on his face. "Don't be."

I smile shyly and rise on my knees.

"Wait." He twists slightly, reaching over to his nightstand and pulls out a square foil packet.

"When did you get those?" I ask.

His cheeks darken as he tears it open. "Around the time you told me you loved me back. I'd never want to assume anything or for you to feel pressured, though."

My smile grows. "You're so sweet."

He shakes his head and pulls out the condom. "I wouldn't consider buying condoms to be sweet."

"That's not—can I help?" I ask as he positions it over himself.

He pauses. "Of course. Since I already have it placed, all that's left is to unroll it."

I swallow and slowly roll it down his shaft.

His hand covers mine once I finish. He's breathing heavily again. Rising again, I position myself over him.

"Ready?" I ask softly.

A strained chuckle leaves him. "Shouldn't I be the one asking that?"

I grin and move down. He helps guide me with one hand while his other rests on my hip. I slowly sit on him, there's a lot of pressure and a pinch.

His fingers flex on my hips. "Wait, my love, let yourself adjust."

Swallowing, I nod, give myself some time, then sink down a couple inches more, and repeat the process until I'm fully seated.

My eyes flash to his, his chest rising and falling fast. My breaths are coming out just as fast.

"You okay?" he says with a strained voice.

I nod. "What now?"

"We move." He gently thrusts up, forcing a moan from me.

I lie back down over him and kiss him as we move.

A pressure builds up and tingles start in my toes and fingers. "I love you," I say with a gasp.

He cups my face, keeping his other on my hip. "I love you too, my Ellie darling."

Our lips connect again, and he hits just the right place over and over until the pressure builds and floods over. My brain short circuits as a wave of emotions roll through me.

His thrusts grow more frantic before his entire body tenses and a growl leaves him, vibrating as his own release hits.

Wrapping his arms around me, he holds me close as he rolls us onto our sides again.

Cuddling skin to skin brings a different kind of intimacy. His scent is stronger and his skin is warm against mine and there's a sense of complete trust and love that builds the longer we lie in each other's arms. I spread my fingers out on his chest and listen to his pounding heart. It's beating just as hard as mine.

Even though he said we didn't need this next step if I didn't want it, I'm glad we did. I feel closer and more attached. Like my soul has connected with his on a deeper level. It's hard to describe it with words, but I feel more attuned to him. To his feelings, thoughts, desires, and his love for me.

His love is *so* strong.

I can almost feel it physically wrap around me in a warm hug.

Tears burn the back of my eyes as I squeeze him to me and nuzzle against his chest. I couldn't be more grateful that my first time was with him. Someone I can trust my heart and body with.

His hands gently caress up and down my back. "I wasn't too rough, was I?"

My heart pings. "No." I shake my head against his chest and cuddle closer. "You were perfect."

A deep rumble starts in his chest, his happy hum, as he holds me closer and kisses the top of my head. "I love you."

I cling onto him tighter, my heart full. "I love you too."

50

Ellie

$\mathcal{A}$sh places a cardboard box of my parents' things on the kitchen table for me. "I'm sorry it's not more. This is all they gave me."

"It's more than I had before." I grab the files that lay on top. "Did you look through these already?" I ask.

"Only briefly. Do you want me to go through it with you?"

I glance up at him. "You don't have to. I know you have some work and searching you want to do before Christmas." Christmas is only two days away and the surprise attack was three days ago. We want to be prepared, but we decided that on Christmas we would take a break and relax.

He bites his lip, looking at the box then to the files in my hands. "I think I'll grab my laptop and bring it in here in case you have any questions."

I smile. "Sounds good," I say, sitting down at the table. He leaves the room while I open my dad's file first. His birth certificate sits on top.

My eyes bug out when I see his birth date is in the sixteen hundreds. He was at least four hundred years old. My heart pings—that was around the same age as Charlie.

Alice is still staying with us, but right now Dr. Kathy—I mean Kathy as she requested I call her—wants to keep a close eye on her, so she's been in the hospital since the attack. Along with Jane and Russell. Jane is in a forced coma like I was, but it's likely she'll be under longer.

I open my mom's file beside my dad's and find she's younger than him by a hundred years. A smile forms on my face. Kind of like Ash and I.

Removing the rest of my dad's files, I spread them out in front of me and place my mom's to the side for the time being.

There's a small family tree with him and his parents, their birth dates and deaths. I'm surprised to find out that my grandparents were both Originals, making it a short line of lycans, but there's also humans listed before my grandparents were turned, such as great-grandparents, great aunts and uncles, but it doesn't mention anyone past my grandparents. No cousins of my dad. Does that mean he doesn't have any, or that they just didn't want to do the genealogy for humans?

I let out a sigh and focus on another paper. His name, *Gabriel Hollenberg*, is written on top and below it lists his rank as *Pureblood, Hunter, Alpha, Alpha Couple*. Underneath that is *Enhanced Hearing*.

Does that mean his special ability is enhanced hearing?

I reach for my mom's folder once more and go through the pages until I come across one similar.

Addison Thornton
Royal, Pureblood, Healer, Alpha, Alpha Couple
Enhanced Healing

Royal?

Ash walks back into the room with his laptop in hand.

He pauses mid-step. "What's wrong?"

I glance down at the page then back at Ash. "Are there royal lycans?"

He walks over and sits beside me, placing his laptop on the table. He leans over and examines the paper. After a moment, his eyes bug out as his mouth slightly parts in surprise.

"What? What is it?"

He blinks then meets my gaze. "Uh...wow." His eyes shift between mine in awe.

"What?"

"You're a direct descendant of the lycan Elite."

My brain short circuits. "I don't understand."

"There's no hierarchy now, not since the war, but before that there were royals for stryxes and lycans. And witches have a council."

I take a deep breath and let it out slowly as I put the paper down. "Okay, back up." I still know nothing about the war.

"Right, okay." He stands. "I actually found a history book about the war while I was in Philadelphia. I'll be right back." And then he's gone again.

My hands shake. This is crazy. I'm a direct descendant of the Elite? How? I don't even feel like a pureblood, how am I supposed to be royalty?

I shake my head, Ash even said they don't have a hierarchy now, so I guess it doesn't actually matter.

Ash comes back in with an old, worn leather book. He waits for me to clean up my papers before placing it in front of me and sitting beside me.

My hands hover over the cover, but before I open it, I remember why I opened my mom's file. I pick it back up and find the page again. *Enhanced Healing.*

"I was wondering...on these papers where it says *enhanced*, does it mean those are their special abilities?"

He takes the paper I offer, his eyes scan the page then hands it back. "Yes, those are them. Usually special abilities are just an enhancement of what we already have, like me with my speed, and your parents, but for some it's extra special."

My head tilts. "What do you mean?"

His fingers tap against the wood of the table. "For example, with Foster, he can tell what exactly is wrong within someone's body by placing his forehead to theirs, it links him to their essence. And he's able to encourage their natural ability to heal faster."

My eyes widen. "That's really cool."

He nods. "Helps when a healer isn't close by."

"Do healers have a special ability to heal?" I ask.

"Not exactly. Those that work at the hospital or medical field are knowledgeable, but they also seem to have a natural ability to know what's wrong and how to help."

"Huh, okay." I put the paper away, then go back to the book as Ash opens his laptop.

I open the leather binding and stop. "I can't read this."

Ash leans over and peers at the pages. "Ah, it's in Latin."

My eyes narrow. "Ash."

He chuckles. "Sorry, I'll read it to you."

I gently move the book in front of him. "It's okay, just tell me what you learn while I go through my parents' things."

Standing, I tug the box closer and pull the top folds apart to open it.

Lifting on my toes, I peer inside and reach in. The first thing I pull out is a photo album. My hands itch to go through it, to see their faces again, instead I set it aside for later. Next is a jewelry box.

The lid squeaks slightly as I peek inside, finding some of my mom's favorite jewelry, just not my mom's wedding ring. Was she buried with it? Ash said her fingers were burned, did her ring make it? My chest tightens. I hope it did. I remember gazing at it all the time when I was younger.

Reaching in, I pull out a leather-bound journal. I sit down to unravel the leather ties and open it.

A sigh escapes me. It appears to be the same language as the history book. Looks like I need to learn Latin.

I look over at Ash to find his brows creating a crease as he reads. "Ash?"

"Huh?" He marks the page with his finger and meets my gaze.

"Could you read this after for me as well?" I ask.

His eyes drop to the journal before gesturing for me to give it to him.

"You don't have to do it now."

He gives me a smile. "It's fine."

I hand him the journal and he places it on top of the history book.

His brows rise as he scans the page. "It's the journal of the mate of the Elite."

"W-what?" If it's in my parents' things, does that mean she's no longer alive? I haven't looked at my mom's family tree yet. I grab her file, but when I find her family tree it stops with her dad, my grandpa, on the Thornton line, neither are marked as Originals. How far does it go back?

There's a knock at the door that jars me from my thoughts.

Ash glances up. His head tilts to the side, his eyes unfocused. "It's Foster and Soph, do you mind letting them in?"

"Nope." I stand then leave the kitchen.

Foster has a huge grin when I open the front door. "Ellie, how are you?" He strides in and lays an arm around my shoulders, giving me a little squeeze before moving to the kitchen without waiting for a response.

"Uh..." I glance back at Sophie, who's laughing lightly. She shakes her head as she enters. Her dark-brown hair is down for once.

"Hey, Ellie," she says.

I smile. "Hey, what are you doing here?" I ask, closing the door. "Not that I mind the company."

"We just went to the hospital and thought we'd give you two an update," she says as we walk to the kitchen.

"And a phone call wouldn't suffice?" Ash says, as he peers up with a quirk of his brow.

"Nope," Foster says, rummaging in the fridge.

"Alright, so how are they?" Ash asks.

"Same as they were this morning." Foster scowls at the inside of the fridge. "Russell's grumpy, Alice is back to not talking, and Jane will be woken up the day after Christmas."

"So, tell me again why that required an in-home visit?"

"We were bored." Foster looks up. "And your place is closer than mine."

"What does that have to do with anything?" Ash asks while I retake my seat beside him.

"Sophie was driving."

"My driving is fine." Sophie glares at Foster as she takes the seat to my right, at the head of the table.

Ash chuckles and leans back, his hands behind his head. "Well, you can read this history book for us while you're here."

Foster pauses, his open mouth hovering over the apple. His forest-green eyes narrow on Ash. "You seem too happy about that."

Ash's smile grows. "It's in Latin."

Foster groans. "Bloody hell, you know I hate reading Latin." He bites into the apple and strides over to us.

"What is all of this stuff?" Sophie asks, touching my mom's wooden jewelry box.

"My parents' things."

Her eyes widen on the box before flickering to me. "Is this...is this Addison's?"

I nod.

"Do you mind if I look?"

"Not at all."

Sophie slowly opens the lid. She wipes her hands on her black jeans then reaches in. She pulls out one of my mother's necklaces with a gold chain and a small green emerald, almost the same shade as Sophie's eyes.

"She kept it," Sophie says, her voice wavering.

"It was one of her favorite necklaces. She would switch between that one and a pearl necklace my dad gifted her."

Sophie blinks rapidly before meeting my gaze, her eyes seem brighter as they glisten with unshed tears. "We have the same color eyes, only ones in the family with this bright of a green. I gave her this one on the eve of her mating ceremony with Gabriel."

My chin wobbles, my heart aching. There's so many stories that I don't know about my parents.

She gives me a watery smile. "Could I give you a hug?"

I nod. She reaches over the corner of the table and wraps me in her arms. It's at an awkward angle, but it's one of the best hugs I've ever received.

After a moment, she releases me.

"I want you to keep it," I say.

"What?" She gasps. "No, this is yours now. I couldn't possibly take it."

"It means more to you than to me. I'm sure she would want you to have it."

She clenches her jaw when her bottom lip quivers. She gives me a short nod and with shaky hands tries to put it on.

"I'll help you, cuz," Foster says softly, and makes his way to stand behind her chair. He moves her long brown hair aside and places the necklace around her neck and clasps the back.

"Thank you," she whispers, keeping her eyes downcast to the emerald. She grasps it tightly in her hand as she meets my eyes. "Truly, thank you. Since I learned she died, I regretted not keeping in touch."

It's my turn to give her a watery smile. "I'm happy we found each other."

Her face lights up. "Me too," she says, and looks back down at the necklace.

Ash wraps an arm around my waist and pulls me closer. He places a kiss at my temple. "I love you," he says with adoration in his eyes.

"Thank you for getting these things for me."

"Anything for you, Ellie darling."

51

Ellie

t isn't until after dinner that I get to hear more about the journal and history book.

"So, who's going to go first?" Foster asks, sitting on the ground with his legs stretched out in front of him. He's leaning against the couch with the history book on his lap.

Sophie sits crisscross on the rocking chair.

"You can," Ash says, sitting beside me on the couch. I clench the journal to my chest. Ash didn't read it all, but he said he was able to skim a good amount.

"Do you know anything about the war, Ellie?" Foster asks.

I shake my head. "Not much."

"About a thousand years ago, there was a war between lycans and stryxes. They found that drinking our blood allowed them to be more powerful and that we aren't as fragile as humans. So they enslaved us, used us as blood pets, or would kill us if we were deemed problematic."

I swallow. "But that isn't the case anymore, right?"

"Correct. Although, no one really knows how we won the war except for the remaining eight Originals, and maybe some of the bitten, but no one talks about that time."

"Wait, there's only eight remaining Originals?" I ask.

Foster eyes narrow on Ash. "Have you taught her nothing?"

Ash growls. "I have, just not everything. Our history is a lot to take in all at once."

Foster sighs. "Yes, but—"

"I asked him to stop whenever I got overwhelmed," I say.

He blinks. "Alright, well, you just let me know as well then, yeah?"

"Okay."

Foster taps his fingers on the book. "So, yes, there are only eight remaining Originals. Three of them being my grandparents, Sophie sharing one with me."

I perk up. "Does that mean I have one alive?"

"I'm sorry, Ellie," Sophie says. "It's on my dad's side, a Wagner. The only Knight still alive is my mum, but she's not an Original."

"And my mum is a Wagner," Foster adds. "My mum and Sophie's dad are siblings, and it's their dad, Arlo Wagner, who is alive. The other would be my dad's parents."

I slump down. I guess that means I have an aunt alive still. And maybe an uncle, if Sophie's dad is still alive...I should just be happy that I have family alive.

"Okay, proceed."

Foster arches a brow and Ash laughs. "She does the same to me."

I shrug while Ash puts an arm around my shoulders.

"Anyway," Foster says, still chuckling, and opens the book. "I learned how we won."

"What?" both Sophie and Ash say in unison.

Foster looks smug as he flips to a certain page. "That's right. I learned how we won the war. There were two hybrids that sided with the lycan royal family that somehow changed the game."

"Somehow?" Sophie asks, unfolding her legs and leaning forward. Her eyes narrowed on him.

Foster shrugs. "It doesn't give details, and the final battle isn't described. Just that hybrids joined, turning the tides."

"Hybrids?" I ask.

"Half-lycan, half-stryx," Ash says. "Except, they were always assumed to be a myth."

"Doesn't appear that way anymore," Foster adds.

"No...the journal actually mentions it as well," Ash continues. "She doesn't mention her name, just that she's the mate to the Elite. But she had a grandchild who disappeared with a stryx and came back years later, bearing a child with lycan and stryx traits."

"What else does she say?" I ask, staring at the journal.

"Just day-to-day things, mostly. Nothing really important. It ended with her grandson coming back with his child, so there's probably another journal that comes after."

I nod. And I'm sure if my parents had the journal, it's long gone with the rest of their stuff.

52

Ellie

veryone arrives together on Christmas. Sophie and Foster carry in a tree together with Alice and Russell following behind, Russell holding a box of decorations. They were just discharged today, so Sophie and Foster picked them up early this morning to make it here by lunch.

Alice has her right arm in a cast and a boot on her right leg that forces her to limp. I know Russell had a few broken ribs, but if he's still injured, I can't tell.

"Happy Christmas!" Foster smiles at me as he passes us by.

Ash chuckles. "*Merry* Christmas, Foster."

We follow them into the family room. Russell places the box on the coffee table, volunteers to make everyone hot chocolate, and moves to the kitchen. Ash turns on the television and plays Christmas music as Alice opens the box with one hand. We each grab lights and ribbons to decorate the tree. It's real and fresh and smells amazing.

"Do you guys cut this down yourself?" I ask, reaching around the tree to hand my section of ribbon to Foster to get his side of the tree. Sophie and Ash are trying to untangle the lights and Alice comes over to stand beside me and help.

"No, we bought it from someone in the pack. They raise Christmas pines and sell them," Foster says from the other side of the tree.

Finishing the ribbon and then lights, I grab an ornament from the box but pause when I see it's a picture of a blonde-haired toddler with pigtails in the lap of a younger Charlie. "Is this you, Alice?"

Alice peers around me and a smile grows on her face. "Yeah. I was three, I think."

Foster's head pops around and he snatches the picture frame ornament from me. His eyes light up as he stares at the picture. "You were such a cute kid. You have Charlie's smile."

Alice's eyes mist, but a smile stays on her face. "You think?"

His gaze lifts to her. "Yeah." He looks back at the photo. "You're going to have cute kids someday, if they look like you."

"I hope so," she says softly watching him place it on the tree.

Foster straightens and peers down at her, and I know that look. It's the look Ash gives me. I turn away, feeling like I'm intruding on something.

"Movie?" Sophie asks when she walks into the room holding two mugs up.

"Give those to Foster and Alice," Ash says as he grabs me and leads me to the couch where we sit side by side.

He turns off the music and changes the television to a Christmas movie.

It's only ten minutes in when Ash grabs me and sets me down on his lap.

"Ash." A small giggle passes my lips. "I'm trying to watch the movie," I whisper.

He nuzzles my neck from behind. "You can still watch it." His breath tickles my neck.

"You've been extra needy recently," I say.

He always likes being near me, but since he came back from Philly, he's always wanting to touch or hold me. I'm not sure if it's because I almost died, the mate bond, our intimate moment, or my acceptance of everything. Either way, I don't actually mind.

He kisses my neck, making me squirm. "All of it."

"What?"

"All four are the reasons."

I gasp and look over my shoulder at him. "Did you just read my mind?"

He gives me a cheeky grin. "You're projecting."

"Huh?"

He chuckles. "You have such a cute confused face."

"Ash," I whine.

"Alright, alright. If you think your thoughts loudly, I can pick them up through the mate bond."

"Think my thoughts loudly…" I don't remember screaming my thoughts.

He chuckles again, a rumble that rolls through him. "You didn't." When he doesn't continue, I send him a glare and he grins. "It's easier to pick them up when we're close. Once you mark me you'll be able to do the same." Hm, I would like to know what goes on inside that beautiful head of his. "I can teach you sometime how to block your thoughts from me if you want."

Even though he brought it up, it doesn't look like he actually wants to teach me. It makes my answer even easier. I shake my head. "No, it's okay. I don't mind you hearing them. But only you."

Ash places a kiss on my forehead. "Of course, no one else will be able to."

Russell walks into the room, and I slip off of Ash so Russell can hand both me and Ash a mug. Russell bends down and whispers something into Ash's ear. Ash's gaze collides with mine as I take a tentative sip of the hot chocolate.

"What is it?" I whisper.

Ash sets his cup on the coffee table. "They found Marcus."

My eyes narrow on him. "I thought we were taking a break?"

"We were—are. They weren't."

I give Russell a pointed look and ask, "Where is he?"

"Italy," Russell answers.

"What is he doing there?" In all the years I lived with Marcus, he never traveled outside the country. He rarely traveled inside the country until I escaped.

"There's a pack there that's run by an Original."

From what I learned about Originals and purebloods, he would have had to take the blood of one of the Elites. "Do you think the Original knows what Marcus has been up to?"

"I'm sure Morbal orchestrated it," Ash says this time with a scowl. "I had a feeling it was him behind it, but we still don't know anything for sure. Just that Marcus is secretly a part of his pack."

"It's no wonder he's been able to get away with this for so long," Foster says on the other couch, sitting beside Alice, his arm outstretched behind her.

My memories are hazy, but after that dream I had... "What are Original lycans called when they are alpha?" I ask.

"Head alpha," Ash answers. "Why?"

The blood drains from my face as I place my mug next to Ash's. *It couldn't be, right?* It's too much of a coincidence. Could Marcus really be acting under an Original? What are we really up against? Marcus isn't a pureblood and yet we've had a difficult time with him. How are we supposed to defeat an Original that's also an alpha?

"Ellie?" Ash shifts closer, concern in his eyes as he takes my hands.

"If we're up against an Original, what do we do?" I ask.

"We'll probably have a battle on our hands if we go there," Russell says.

"But we are going there, right?"

Ash's gaze doesn't leave mine. "We are. We're pretty sure he's been the one killing purebloods and draining them of their blood."

"Don't forget the disappearances of lycans, witches, and stryxes as well," Sophie says, taking a wide berth from Russell as she walks into the room and sits on the other side of our couch.

"Wait, how long has this been going on?" I ask. "And why has no one done anything about it?"

"Because no one had the right leads," Ash says. "No one still does, except for us. If Marcus wasn't so hung up on you, and if we never met, you would still be on the run and my parents' murder case would still be cold."

"But what about Morbal's other lackeys?" I ask. "I'm sure Marcus isn't the only one."

"I'm sure you're right, but there's no way to know who they are unless we go to the source, and even then it's not likely," Foster says, and Alice beside him fidgets with the blanket that's wrapped around her. "It's better to take out the main guy and slowly find the others. If we can't, we'll just wait until they resurface. Those with dodgy intentions just can't help themselves. And when they make a mistake, we'll be there to nick them."

I blink. Sometimes his phrases take a moment for me to understand. "But you all knew about the disappearances and the murders?"

"Yes, but we haven't been able to connect them to one person," Ash says, looking around the room before meeting my gaze again.

"We did know of some strange disappearances going on and that it was likely they were connected with the killings," Sophie says.

"We aren't sure they're connected," Russell says, giving Sophie a sharp look, which she ignores.

Everything they say just convinces me more that Marcus isn't at the head, but maybe Morbal... "I think they're connected. Marcus and Morbal. Before I ran away—at least I think it could be Morbal who Marcus was talking to—they talked about bringing me somewhere. I think that's why he's still after me...for my blood."

"Why wouldn't they just drain you like everyone else?" Foster asks.

"No idea." I bite my lip. "It could be someone else, too, I just know Marcus was talking to someone on the phone after tasting my blood, and called them head alpha. And the person wanted to come get me."

Ash scowls. "I don't like the sound of that. But it confirms our suspicions. Marcus isn't working alone and is under an Original's control. If you think it was Morbal and they were the ones that killed our parents *and* wanted to kidnap you…it ties the murders and kidnappings together. It seems like our next step is to start a war. If there are others still alive, we need to save them."

"And stop the killings," Foster adds, and Ash nods.

I swallow. This is getting real. Are there even enough of us to start a war and win? And how many does Morbal have under his belt? "Morbal is an Original lycan and still alive. Are there other Original lycans willing to help us? Or could they be involved with him as well?"

"The ones who got along with Morbal have passed, from what I've heard," Ash says. "The ones that might help us are Arlo Wagner, Sophie and Foster's grandfather, and Layland Lancaster and Harriette Fletcher, Foster's other grandparents." Ash's gaze moves to Foster, then Sophie. "Any ideas if either of your grandparents would help us?"

Foster and Sophie share a look before Sophie answers. "They both probably would. Arlo is a bit old school, so he'll probably want to be more involved than the others. I'm also pretty sure him and Morbal have had disputes in the past. Foster and I will contact them this coming week."

"Why hasn't Arlo taken action, then?" Russell asks, still standing with his arms folded in front of him.

Sophie turns her head away from him, refusing to speak. I look between them. Have I missed something?

Foster rolls his eyes at them with an exasperated sigh. "Probably for the same reason we haven't. One pack alone won't be able to defeat him, and no one has had proof. We wouldn't have been able to do anything either if Ash wasn't the alpha."

"When do we plan on going then?" I ask.

Ash frowns. "I rather you not go, but I know you won't be okay with that. I was thinking in February. Gives us enough time to train you some more and to ask others for help, but not too long for Morbal to get suspicious."

"You'll also need to choose a new lead warrior," Sophie says. "I'll need to be fully invested in my role as delta."

Ash nods. "Of course. After the funeral we can all talk about who should be the new leads."

My stomach drops. I forgot about the funeral. Sam and another wolf I didn't know were killed. We'll be burying the other lycans that died as well, but in a different location.

Ash and I decided it would be best to wait until after Christmas, give everyone a time to enjoy the holiday and get things prepared. And now that I'm probably a part of the alpha couple with Ash, I should learn the names of the pack members. Not sure how I'm going to memorize five hundred members, though.

"I'm going," Alice speaks up, drawing everyone's attention. She's been silent this entire time until now.

Foster turns a sharp glare on her. "No, you're not. You're still healing, Alice."

She scowls. "I'm going. I've learned to fight and have gotten pretty good at it. I held my own against three lycans just two days ago."

"Yes, and look how close to death that put you."

"That's only because I was alone." She pouts and his eyes soften.

"But you're still injured, Alice." He turns more toward her. "And I can't handle finding you like that again. You could've died."

"I know, but I don't even have to fight. I can be in the back helping those that get injured." Alice looks over to Ash and me. "I just want to go."

Ash and I lock gazes. "I think it would be wrong to try to keep her away. She deserves to go wherever she wants," I say.

Ash nods in agreement and looks at Alice and Foster. "It's ultimately her decision, Foster. But I think being with the healers is the
best choice if you do decide to go, Alice. Along with Ellie."

"No."

Ash peers back at me, squeezing my hands. "I can't lose you," he
says softly. "I almost did. You need more training, especially in wolf
form, before you can go into battle."

I close my eyes. I *know* he's right. Having almost died a week
ago, it would be stupid to not listen. But there's this need inside of
me that has to be there to make sure Marcus meets his end.
Reopening my eyes, I stare at him in determination. "If I train this
next month, will you let me be more involved?"

His eyes peer into mine, shifting between them. He relaxes
against the couch with a sigh. "Fine."

I arch a brow. "You didn't put up much of a fight."

A corner of his mouth tugs up slightly. "I didn't expect to win in
the first place."

WE STOP TALKING about Marcus and Morbal for the rest of the
movie—Sophie chided us for discussing it on Christmas.

She moves to the other couch with Alice and Foster while Russell
sits in the recliner. I spread out, and Ash takes my feet, placing them
on his lap. He gives them and my calves a much-needed massage.

After the movie ends, Ash waits until everyone leaves before
speaking. "I have something to give you." He looks nervous, but a
wave of jitters hit me as well. Sophie wasn't able to get me the watch
—it needs to be fixed first. Besides, no one brought gifts today, so I
thought maybe I would be okay.

"I don't have anything for you," I say, wringing my hands.

Ash stands. "I wasn't expecting anything," he says as he helps
me up. "I also have somewhere I'd like to show you."

"We're going somewhere?"

He nods. "I haven't been able to keep my word and take you out on an official date. So, Ellie"—he faces me, taking both of my hands in his—"will you go on a date with me?"

My mouth slightly parts. Who knew such a simple question would get my heart racing? I swallow and nod. "I'd love to."

A grin appears on his face, reaching his eyes. "I have two gifts for you." He keeps one of my hands and leads me to his room where I find two wrapped presents waiting. "You can open them."

Grabbing one, I eye Ash while peeling the paper off. Underneath the wrapping is a white paper box. I lift the lid to find multiple sets of underwear—bra and panties. At least five of each in different colors. I blink then look up at Ash, seeing an underlining red tint under his light-brown skin.

"Uh, thank you?" I say, my own cheeks heating up.

He briefly averts his gaze with a hand palming the back of his neck. "They are the magic-infused ones I promised you. They won't shred when you shift."

"Oh." My eyes widen. I had forgotten about them. I set the box on the ground and shrink the distance between us and hug him. "Thank you so much."

He clears his throat and wraps his arms around me, holding me tight. "You're welcome."

Removing myself from him, I grab the other present and find another white paper box underneath. I silently hope it's not more underwear—I might die from embarrassment.

Instead, I find a cute high-waisted pink and green two-piece swimsuit. Why would I need a swimsuit in the middle of winter?

"Why don't you try it on? I'm going to head to the bathroom and grab my suit while you do."

And just like that, he's in the bathroom.

I stare at the swimsuit. I guess this place he's taking me to includes water.

There's no door, but since he's already seen me naked, I try to ignore my nerves and take my clothes off and put on the swimsuit. I'm not really sure where we'd go swimming during this time of year. Must be somewhere indoors. Peering over my shoulders, I let out a sigh when I see some of my scars peeking out between the fabrics. Thankfully most of it is covered. If this was a bikini it would be a different story. I put my clothes back over my suit.

"All done?" Ash asks, still inside the bathroom just as I finish pulling down my shirt.

A smile forms on my face. He's still showing me respect by giving me privacy. It's only been that one time we've been intimate, but he must sense I'm still insecure about my body. Even though he made me feel so loved and special that night.

"Yes, I'm done."

Ash comes out in black and blue swim trunks and a white t-shirt with a bag over one shoulder. "Ready?" he asks as he holds out a hand.

I nod and take his hand. He gives me just enough time to stick my feet in a pair of boots and grab a coat before leading me outside and into his truck. The inside is already warm. Did he have someone come start it for us?

He leans over the middle console and places the bag in the back on the floor before driving away from his house. The drive isn't too long, only about ten minutes. We do most of it off-roading on a dirt path. When he stops, we're in a small field, no buildings in sight.

After we get out, Ash takes me by hand and leads me away from the field and through the trees. Different thoughts on what it could be filter through my mind.

And although I shouldn't be surprised that one of my guesses was right—I am. But it's so much more than what I was expecting.

"Is this on your land?" I gasp out, my eyes wide.

The hot spring has large rocks and boulders almost completely enclosing it, giving a sense of privacy. Only one spot is clear of them, just wide enough for us to enter.

The rocks and pine trees that surround us are covered in snow, but someone has already shoveled the snow away from the entrance to the spring to create a path that leads to a small circular wooden pavilion off to the side, with a few tables underneath.

"It is." Ash takes me straight to the hot spring, dropping the bag next to one of the rocks. He drops my hand and grabs the back of his shirt. I hold my breath as he takes it off and I can't stop staring. His beautiful skin and hair contrast with the snow. His muscles bunch and move as he folds and places his shirt in the bag. He's all muscle. He turns and grins when he sees me. His eyes travel the length of my body. "Are you going to take those clothes off?"

My cheeks heat and fidget with my coat. How am I supposed to undress—even with a swimsuit underneath—while he stares at me?

"Turn around," I say. He arches a brow. "Please?"

He chuckles. "I could help you. It's not like I haven't before."

I send him a glare. "Ash."

He smiles but turns around.

With shaky hands, I remove my clothes and shoes, and clench them to my chest.

"Okay," I say.

He turns around and eyes my bundle of clothes. "Here, let me take that from you." I let him take them and watch as he puts it into his backpack.

I clasp my hands in front of me as nerves get the best of me and look out on the water, watching the steam rise into the cool air.

Soon, Ash's body heat draws closer, and my cheeks grow warmer. He stops right beside me. I inhale sharply, his fingers lightly grazing up my arms and across my shoulder.

Ellie. Butterflies flutter inside as I hear his voice in my mind.

My breath hitches when his lips brush where he marked, sending goosebumps across my skin. He groans and lifts his head. Placing his hands under my jaw, he nudges my face to him. *You look beautiful.*

His features turn golden in the setting sun. Looking into my eyes, I'm mesmerized at all the love and adoration in his gaze. I'm overcome with emotions. How did I get to be so lucky to have someone look at me like this?

"I love you," spills from my lips.

His eyes light up. "I love you too, Ellie," he says and touches his lips to mine, stealing the air from my lungs. Sparks fly across our lips and warmth spreads from the top of my head to the tips to my toes. Too soon he leans away, and I take a shaky breath.

"Let's get in," he says softly.

I let him lead me into the water. Although, I no longer need its warmth. The water laps at our feet as we walk in together. As I sink in, I let my body relax and close my eyes. The water is almost too hot, even with my new tolerance to the cold and heat.

"Ellie," Ash says, his voice husky. I open my eyes to find him standing tall in the water, steam rising off his skin. He clears his throat. "Turn around, please."

My brows scrunch together, but I stand and turn around. He pulls me against him and lowers us both back into the water.

His hands trail over my shoulders and across my scars. "You're so beautiful, Ellie darling. Every single part of you. I want to dote on you. To make you feel loved and cherished," he says, starting to gently massage my sore muscles. He begins at my shoulders and makes his way down my back. Taking his time, he makes sure he hits every spot. When he gets to my lower back, my chest tightens as a sudden wave of tears threaten to spill. He always makes me feel so loved. No one has ever shown this level of devotion to me before.

Ash's hands still. "Is this not okay? You're tensing up."

I give him a quick shake of the head. "Thank you," I say softly.

"For what?"

"For loving me."

He gently turns me around. Keeping one hand on my hip, the other comes up and caresses my face. "You don't need to thank me, Ellie. It's easy to love you, and I always will. I plan on showing you just how much for the rest of our long lives. This is just the beginning."

"So...does that mean I'm an alpha now? That we're...the alpha couple?"

He hesitates, searching my eyes with a furrow of his brows. "Is that not what you want?"

"No. That's not why I'm asking." I bite my lip and think for a moment, trying to figure out a better way to explain my thoughts.

His gaze flickers to my lips.

I try to ignore the flutters his heated gaze sends.

"What I mean is...I don't know how this all works. Do I need to bite you before I become an alpha and we become the alpha couple, or are we already now that you claimed me and you're an alpha?" As I ramble his smile grows larger and larger. "What?" I ask at the end.

He gives me a quick peck. "You can be whatever you want, Ellie. Even before I claimed you, you were by my side. I never planned on making decisions without you. If you want the title, you have it, Ellie. You always have."

"I...really?" My voice cracks. It hadn't really dawned on me that all those times he asked for my opinions were because he thought they were important. That I was already on equal ground with him. I didn't need to be an alpha to gain that respect.

My opinions have always been important to him. Before he became alpha, he cared what I thought, even when he didn't agree he made sure I had a voice. "I love you, Ash."

"And I love you." He leans down, claiming my lips for his own.

53

Ellie

Sophie was right when she said Arlo didn't get along with Morbal. He jumped at the chance to help us and wants to be involved with every single detail. Including being the one to end Morbal.

Because that's apparently what lycans do. No, they don't throw them in jail—they kill them. But considering we think Morbal killed and kidnapped a bunch of supernaturals, I guess it's fitting.

Foster's other grandparents, on the other hand, didn't want to get involved, but his parents thankfully offered some hunters and warriors that wanted to join in our efforts. There's also a few members from other packs that Foster has traveled to over the years that want to join. A lot more have been affected from the killings and kidnappings than we had realized.

Hopefully word hasn't spread to Morbal though.

"Are you ready?" Ash asks me with a smirk. I think he enjoys these training sessions a little too much.

For the past month and a half, he, Sophie, Foster, and Russell have been taking turns in training me. Today, though, we are all together, in my ultimate test to see if I'm ready to go or not tomorrow.

"Bring it on, old man," I say.

He quirks a brow. "If I'm an old man, then you've had—"

"Nope!" I yell, and rush at him.

He laughs and maneuvers away, but deflecting is his signature move that I was prepared for.

I psych him out and change directions, putting me right where he is and allowing me to sweep a leg underneath him.

He stumbles with wide eyes before a grin takes over his face as he easily regains his footing. "Ah, little wolf, you have learned something."

"Kick his arse, Ellie," Sophie yells from the side.

"You're going to distract her, Soph," Foster says.

"Distraction will happen in a real fight," Russell says. "It'll be good for Ellie to learn how to multitask."

I jerk my head to the left at the crunch of the snow.

Ash is a foot away.

I fling myself forward into a roll to avoid Ash, but he catches my ankle and tugs me up in the air upside down.

A growl leaves me, and I aim a punch to his stomach, but he swings me out, making my punch come short.

I use my free foot to kick at the hand that still has me.

He curses, his grip loosening as he also tries to keep me away from his body.

"Arms out, tuck," Russell yells just as I'm released from Ash's grip.

My gaze snaps down, I keep my arms bent as I hit the ground and roll away from Ash.

Ash growls. "No helping."

I'm yanked back by my shirt. I kick a leg out behind me, eliciting an *oof* from Ash.

I spin around, finding him slightly hunched with an arm around his stomach.

Taking the opportunity I'm given with him closer to my height, I punch him in the face. I freeze when it actually connects.

"Oh my gosh." My hands go to my mouth. "Ash, I'm so sorry." Shaking my head, I take a wobbly step forward.

He works his jaw with a hand on his face as he laughs. "Don't be sorry, Ellie darling, that was good." He drops his hand. "You've definitely improved from when we first started. Got a nice right hook now, too."

I grin. "Yeah?"

He smiles. "Yeah." Then his smile turns devious. "Let's try two-on-one now."

Ash walks over to the side as Foster steps forward while Russell starts stripping to shift into his wolf. My brows rise as I catch Sophie ogling him.

Foster saps his fingers, gaining my attention. "Ready, Ellie?" Foster grins, coming to stand in front of me. "Remember what we taught you about fighting in wolf form."

My body is coiled tightly as I nod.

"Ready, Russ?" Foster asks. Russell's in his dark red-brown wolf. He dips his chin.

Foster's smile grows. "Alright, let's go." Both he and Russell prowl forward.

These boys take way too much pleasure in this.

I tap into my essence and let my shift take over before they get too close.

I'm almost done with my change when Foster reaches for me. I duck and dodge his grabby hands, but I land right in front of Russell.

He growls in warning before he lunges, which he never actually does in a fight. He's a silent predator. But he's always the one to go soft on me during training.

"Russell," Ash chides.

I maneuver away, but I end up running into Foster.

Foster chuckles, but I keep my momentum and plow through him. His hands brace me as his heels dig into the ground.

"Bloody hell," he mutters.

There's a small nip on my tail. I kick my hind legs out, catching Russell just briefly in his chest.

Remember to keep your surroundings in mind, Russell says.

He's reminding me of two different things: Foster isn't my only opponent, and that I can use my surroundings to my advantage at times.

"Russell," Ash says with a growl. "What is the point of this test if you keep helping her?"

Being connected to my mind, he probably caught that Russell talked to me.

Ignoring him for now, I focus on things around me. There are trees everywhere, but they're too far away, but there's a dip in the ground not far from Foster. I push harder, forcing him to take steps back. When we reach it, he stumbles back and falls. I jump on him to keep him down, and an *oof* comes from him.

I look up to see Russell hovering close. I push off of Foster, eliciting a grunt, and aim for Russell.

Russell easily moves away and paws my side. If he'd use his claws, I know I'd have a deep gash there.

I press down onto my front legs and kick my hide legs out, catching him in the face.

Quickly turning around, I see him shaking his wolf head and Foster standing back up. Crouching back, I pounce and jump onto Russell. I hover over his neck with my teeth. Russell submits, and Foster laughs in the background.

I release Russell and glance at Foster, who's shaking his head with a giant grin.

Ash sighs, coming toward us. He pets my head. "Good job, Ellie darling. Although that would've been a longer fight if Russell didn't go so easy on you."

Russell lowers his head sheepishly, while I give Ash a wolfy grin, my tail wagging.

I only had to win against one of them in this fight.

Meaning, I get to go.

I BUCKLE my seatbelt as everyone takes their seats aboard the plane. Russell and Foster take the seats behind Ash and me, while Alice and Sophie sit across the aisle. I didn't realize that Ash had a private plane, let alone three of them. We'll only be taking two of them, full of healers, warriors, and hunters. Ash and I left behind any that wanted to remain here and help take care of kids and anyone else that may need help.

We also decided that we'd let anyone come if they wanted to. But we weren't surprised that most omegas decided to stay back. A few are coming, but will help the healers. Hunters and warriors will be in battle, and no matter how much I wish for complete equality, the omegas just aren't trained enough to help this time—if they even wanted to.

Someone who shocked us by staying behind was Kathy, the head healer. She didn't give us a reason, just that we'd be okay without her with almost all the other healers coming. Jane is still under her care and also awake now. We told her about lycans, and like with everything, she took it in stride.

Glancing behind me, I notice Russell's disheveled look. He releases his unruly russet hair out of its bun and drags his fingers through it before pulling it back up. All the while bouncing his leg. The plane jerks forward and Russell's hands go straight to the arm rests gripping them tightly.

Foster glances at his white knuckles then focuses on his face. "It'll be alright, mate." Foster pats him on the shoulder. "Just close your eyes and take deep breaths."

"Is he okay?" I whisper to Ash.

Ash glances behind us. "Flying makes him anxious."

"I'm sorry, you must remain in your seat, we're getting ready to take off soon," a flight attendant says, and I look over to find Sophie getting up and moving toward Russell.

"Foster, trade me seats," Sophie demands, ignoring the attendant.

Russell's eyes shoot open, giving her a bewildered look.

Foster unbuckles without a fight and moves out into the aisle, taking Sophie's seat. Russell tracks Sophie's every move. Once she's buckled, her hand hovers over his briefly before she places it on his and gives it a squeeze.

Even though I'm curious, I turn away, feeling like I'm intruding. I wish I could ask Ash right now about them, but they'd be able to hear me.

Ash gives me a soft smile and grabs my hand, placing a kiss on the knuckles. "How are you holding up?"

"I'm excited." When his brows rise in surprise, I quickly explain. "I've only been on a plane once, but nothing this fancy."

"Yeah, a little too fancy for my taste, but comes with the status." He squeezes my hand.

My eyes widen. "You get all these planes for being an alpha?"

He nods. "It's smart to have a quick getaway for everyone."

"Why would everyone need to leave?" And where would we even go?

He shrugs. "Under attack from another pack, or the government finds out and wants to experiment."

"What? Has that happened before?"

His smile dims. "It's just one of the guesses as to why there are so many supernatural disappearances."

The plane jerks forward. I lean over Ash to get a look outside.

He chuckles. "You should've taken the window seat."

"But I'm going to have to get up and pee a lot throughout the flight." This extremely long flight that will take all day and part of the night.

"Well, if you ever want to switch, I'd be happy to. We'll also need to get up and do stretches throughout."

I smile and smooth out the crease between his brows. "Stop worrying. I'll be okay. Now let's watch us take off."

He matches my smile and squeezes my hand. "Okay."

54

Ellie

I'm completely haggard when we finally land in Naples, Italy a day later. Ash and Arlo rented an entire villa for our packs outside of the city, closer to Rome, and I can't wait to collapse into a bed.

When we step out of the plane, a lean man with golden hair and crow's feet around his eyes waves us over in front of a caravan of vans. He's flanked by two others and a few more staggered around him.

If recruiting people didn't look suspicious, this certainly will. How are we supposed to keep this a secret from a powerful Original lycan?

"Won't Morbal notice a large amount of lycans suddenly coming into his territory?" I ask as we approach the group of people.

"Probably, but even if he does, he won't have time to ask for help from other packs. Arlo, Sophie and Foster's grandfather, is the closest alpha."

I hum in thought as we stop in front of the group.

Ash holds out his hand. "Hello, head alpha Wagner, thank you for arranging to meet us and coming to our aid."

The golden-haired man takes his hand. "No need for formalities, Ash, I'm happy to help you and my grandchildren. Morbal has been a thorn in my side for ages. I'm happy to rid the world of his existence."

Well, that escalated quickly.

Ash gives me a side-eye, humor in his gaze. I bite my lip. He must have picked up on that thought.

We don't discuss much more, wanting to keep it for when we're not out in public, before heading into the vans. We leave in increments and Ash plans for our van to leave in the middle, giving us the most protection.

As we finally begin driving, I take a moment to look out the window as Ash speaks to the driver in what I can only assume is Italian. *How many languages does he know?*

It's hard to describe Naples. I'm overcome with conflicting emotions. Beautiful but chaotic. Lively but stressful. The historic buildings are covered in graffiti, but I kind of love it. The old and new colliding.

I'm surprised at how skilled our driver is as he moves the large van quickly into the river of cars, and proceeds to maneuver between them. Soon I find out that driving here is a lot different than America. Scooters weave in and out of cars, no one stays in their lanes, some not even on their side of the road. People walk right in front of traffic, forcing everyone to slam on their brakes. I'm trying not to pull my hair out from the stress. There's no structure to this madness. I grab Ash's hand. I know I should be more worried about our upcoming battle, but right now I feel like we won't even make it past this street.

Ash pauses mid-sentence, his mouth slightly parted. I rarely take initiative when it comes to touching, so I must have shocked him. But when he looks at me, there's a twinkle in his eye as his lips roll inward. He squeezes my hand.

"You aren't going to die," he says as a grin spreads across his face, no longer being able to hold it back.

"Stop reading my mind," I grumble.

He laughs.

Hearing Ash, our driver, Francesco says, "*En Italia...*" I'm lost as he continues speaking rapid Italian. He points to his eyes, the side of his head, then the back of his head as he keeps glancing at us in the rearview mirror.

Ash replies and smiles. He turns back to me. "He says in Italy everyone has to have three sets of eyes when driving. Eyes in front of their head, a set on the sides, and a set behind."

Foster, who is sitting up front, begins speaking in Italian. Francesco perks up and rapidly speaks back.

Glancing back, I find Sophie passed out, her head against the window. Alice gives me a small smile in between Sophie and Russell, who's staring out the window. Alice's boot and cast are finally gone. Since she's an omega it took almost as long as it would a human.

I look out my window once more at the cars, vans, scooters, and buses surrounding us. Everyone is honking their horns, but I realize that there actually is a method to this madness. Everyone somehow proceeds around each other in the direction they're aiming for. I take a deep breath and squeeze Ash's hand. I'm going to try to enjoy the beauty of Italy while I can.

AFTER AN HOUR OF DRIVING, we arrive at the villa Ash rented. Although it's huge, there's already a group of lycans building tents around the property.

"They're used to this," Ash says, following my gaze. "But I don't plan on everyone being here for longer than a week."

"They'll be okay?" I ask.

"Yes, we can shift into wolves after all." He gets out and offers a hand as he continues, "Most have slept in wolf form on the ground at least once. Don't you remember when you found out about lycans? " He winks once I'm down beside him.

Alice, Sophie, Russell, and Foster follow us out. Alice fidgets, as she has been since the plane.

"Are you okay?" I ask her.

She gives me a tight smile and nods, but doesn't answer as Arlo and one of his betas greet us. We follow Arlo into the estate and he shows everyone to their rooms. Sophie and Alice will share a room while Russell and Foster share another. Ash and I will also be sharing a room together, but unlike the others, there's only one bed.

"I figured we'd discuss more about our plans after supper?" Arlo asks as he drops us off last. "After resting, of course."

"Yes, we'll go over everything tonight," Ash says and Arlo leaves us.

I lay out on the bed, happy to finally be able to stretch out. Ash sets our bag on the ground before joining me.

"Do you think our plan will work?" I ask.

Frowning, he turns his head to look at me. "I personally hate our plan."

I sigh. "I already know that. But I want to know if you think it'll work."

When he doesn't respond I turn my head to peer at him. He's staring at the ceiling. "I would rather find another way."

"Ash—"

"*But*"—he glances at me—"I do believe that it could work. Although I think we could figure something else out."

"Everyone agreed this would be the best way to draw them out, though."

He props himself on his elbows. "Having you be the *bait* is never the best way," he growls.

I peer up at him. He's been against the plan ever since the beginning. But I can't really blame him since if it were reversed, I would hate it, too. "I'll be okay. You, Foster, Russell, and some of Arlo's will all be there watching over me in the shadows. No one can get to me without passing one of you."

He collapses back on the bed, a furrow between his brows. "I still don't like it. I have a bad feeling about it."

I shift onto my side. "What's bothering you exactly?"

His face relaxes with a sigh as he turns his head to me. "There's so much that can go wrong. We don't actually know what kind of manpower Morbal has. Something just feels off about it all."

Pondering, I ask, "Not just because I'm going to be bait?"

"I *hate* that you're going to be bait, but no, not just because of that."

I hum. "Well, if you really don't feel good about it, we can try to figure out something else."

He chuckles without humor and looks back at the ceiling. "In two days? No"—he shakes his head—"I'm sure it's just the mate bond hating that I'm putting you in danger."

His worries are understandable. I've been training an insane amount of time over the past month, but I can't help having doubts. I know my weaknesses show up more when there's more than one on me. My lycan abilities have grown and become stronger, but my special ability still hasn't made an appearance. Will I be able to hold my own against an Original?

"Do you think I'm ready?" I can't help asking.

"I think we prepared you as much as we could without waiting too long to act."

"That's not really an answer."

Ash rolls onto his side to face me, and caresses my arm. "I wish you had more training—years, in fact—but that's not realistic. I think you made a lot of progress from when we first began. Does that mean I think you're ready for a battle? Honestly, I don't know. I hope so. But I don't think I can ever be okay with you going into a fight. I think the question you should be asking is, do *you* think you're ready?"

I bite my lip. That's the question I have been asking myself. I'm ready for this to be over. I'm ready to move on from Marcus. But we have to defeat him first to do that. If that means I need to be ready now, then I will be.

55

Ellie

he twisted faces of the gargoyles looming before us send chills down my spine as if I had never left the frosty hills of Alaska. Morbal's gothic mansion is in the distance, past the statues and iron gates. There's a foreboding darkness that exudes from it, just waiting to consume us if we dare to take a step forward. It must have been built in the sixteenth century. It stands out of place with the surrounding green hills and vineyards.

I thought gargoyles were supposed to ward off evil?

Ellie? Ash's voice sounds in my head. Ash, Foster, Russell, a few other lycans, and I are in our wolf forms. Everyone else is outside Morbal's territory. Ash will signal to Sophie—who's also in wolf form—if we need backup. We aren't sure if Morbal is able to sense lycans like other Originals, such as Arlo, but this plan bets that he can.

I move on from the entrance. I trot in the middle of the group, into the trees surrounding Morbal's estate. We each keep our eyes open. My senses on high alert. I've practiced more on being able to control them in and out of wolf form.

After a few minutes, Russell says, *This should be good.*

I stop, and everyone spreads out from there.

Everyone is on edge as we wait.

The hope is that he'll sense us and send someone out that we can capture and question. We don't want a full-on battle yet. But we're prepared if it turns out differently.

How long do you think it'll take for him to sense us? I ask, sending my thoughts to Ash.

But it's Foster who answers. *Oops,* still not good at projecting correctly.

He should already know, we've been in his territory for fifteen minutes.

My hackles rise. Well, that would've been nice to know earlier.

I scan through the trees around me. Everyone is hidden from my sight except for Ash. Ash paid a small fortune for the potions that dull the supernatural senses, as well as enchanted necklaces enabling us to communicate with Arlo's pack in this form. It's only me and Ash who didn't take a potion with the hope that our presence will draw someone out and not an army.

There's a shift in the air to my right, but when I look there doesn't seem to be anything awry.

Lowering my head, I slowly crouch to inspect the area better.

Ellie? What is it? Ash asks, noticing my movement.

I'm not sure. It's probably nothing.

I sniff the air and catch whiffs of lavender. My head tilts. I don't remember noticing any lavender plants on the way here. Examining the ground, I don't find any here either. Lifting my head and narrowing my eyes, I search the area, but nothing else seems off.

I'm overreacting, nothing seems amiss. I turn back around to go back to my spot.

My hair stands erect as the air shifts again, lavender and blood blooming in the air.

Just as I'm about to turn back around, hands grab me from behind and in the next instance my vision goes blurry.

Ellie, run. Ash's panicked voice fills my mind before I'm engulfed in darkness.

56

Ash

*T*his is supposed to be a quick in-and-out. Snatch one of Morbal's lackeys, get answers and plan from there. But I can't help thinking that something is off. We should've already been stopped this close to Morbal's estate.

My eyes follow Ellie as she turns away from the spot she was examining. I'm not sure what she sensed, but I trust her to be cautious.

A breeze picks up just as there's a shimmer in the air behind Ellie. A young woman appears in a ragged gown and grabs her. She has blood markings on her face and exposed arms, with metal bands on her wrist.

Ellie, run. I warn, as I rush toward her, panic filling me. But before I make it, another shimmer appears around them and they're gone.

Just poofed into thin air, leaving only the smell of lavender, roses, and blood behind.

My legs shake as I search the area. Russell and Foster not far behind me.

How could this have happened? How did Morbal get a blood witch? Blood magic is illegal and a magic almost no one practices anymore.

I turn around and race toward Morbal's estate. I need to save Ellie. I need to find my mate.

Someone barrels into my side, knocking me useless as their weight crushes me onto the ground.

Rage fills me. A snarl rips from my throat as I try to escape.

Ash. A growl enters my mind. It's Foster's. Looking up, I find him as a gray wolf hunched down in front of my face. Which means it can only be Russell who's on top of me.

Get off me, I snarl.

Foster's head tilts to the side. Are you going to go get yourself killed?

I growl.

Foster shifts back to a man, crouched down in front of me with a sigh on his lips. "Thought so." His gaze shifts to Russell, still pressing his weight into me. "Contact Sophie."

The four other lycans with us are standing around us, keeping an eye on our surroundings.

Foster runs a hand down his face and cusses up a storm. "What the bloody hell are we going to do?" he asks under his breath.

A whine escapes before I can stop it. His glowing green eyes meet mine.

"I care about her too, Ash," he says. "We'll figure something out, but I have to make sure we don't also lose our alpha in the process."

I can't focus on anything right now, except the need to save Ellie. But I know he's right. I need to get it together if we have any chance of getting her back.

"They won't kill her," Foster continues. "At least they gave us no indication they were going to. But you would sense it if she were killed."

My body freezes as I search for my bond with her.

He's right.

She's still there. Unconscious, but okay.

At least for now.

Russell gets off as I shift back. My eyes blaze as I stare at them both. "Let's start planning," I say, my voice more animalistic than human. "I need my mate back."

57

Ellie

he smell of mildew is what I wake up to on a cold cobblestone ground—no longer a wolf. I'm in a thin, white gown over my underwear. Someone must have put it on me while I was unconscious.

My body screams at me as I roll onto my side and find a woman lying on the ground beside me, her chest heaving up and down. Long, tangled, ink-colored hair covers most of her face, but between the strands I can see that she's unconscious with blood markings on her forehead and a horizontal line of blood across her nose and cheeks.

I'm sure her gown used to be white like the one I'm wearing, but now it's covered in a layer of grime with blood splatters, and the ends are frayed and torn.

Groaning, I try to sit up, but my arms give out under me. A scream forces its way out, my wrists flaring with pain. I collapse onto my back and hold my shaky arms up to find metal bands around my wrists.

With trembling fingers, I tentatively touch one of the bands to jerk it back as sharp daggers stab inside my wrist. It's embedded deep into my skin. Tears stream down my face as I fight back another scream.

"Ellie?" a voice whispers, making me freeze.

I tilt my head up, peering around the room upside down. I'm in a cell near the bars and entrance. There's a woman sitting in the back, chained to the cobblestone wall, her head hanging and her wrists bear the same bands as mine. Grimy strings of blonde hair cover her face. Her thin frame is covered in a similar filthy dress as the woman beside me. My head turns to the side to find bands on the black-haired woman as well.

Peering back up, I ask, "How—" I clear my throat when it comes out scratchy and try again. "H-How do you know my name?"

The woman struggles to lift her head, but when she does her emerald eyes clash with mine.

My heart stops.

My entire body frozen as I try to make sense of what I'm seeing.

This...this can't be possible.

I'm imagining things.

She...she died.

"Mom?" I gasp out on a sob, my throat tight.

Her chin wobbles. "Oh, my Ellie." Her voice is scratchy and frail.

Without using my arms, I roll onto my stomach, my entire body protesting. I try to get my feet under me, but my body is weak. My legs can't hold me right now.

What happened when I was out?

I grit my teeth, holding back a scream, as I drag myself to her using my forearms and elbows.

I'm just barely able to prop myself on the wall beside her in a sitting position.

Breathing heavily, and with a trembling arm, I reach out, wanting to touch her. To make sure she's actually real. My eyes meet hers before I make contact.

She gives me a wobbly smile and nods.

The skin of her arm is cold under my touch, but it's solid. It's *real*.

Mom. I want to hold her, to hug her, but with her chained and so frail, I'm more afraid of breaking her. Of losing her again after I just got her back.

"How is this possible?" I whisper, my mind swirling. I can't seem to comprehend that she's alive. "How...how are you alive? Is...is dad?"

She audibly swallows and gives me a small shake of her head.

Tears start anew. It's like hearing he died for the first time all over again, but worse. It's permanent.

"Ellie, baby," she says, choking on a sob.

"W-what happened?" I ask, letting the tears flow as I stare at her, memorizing her features. Despite the layer of grime, and thin frame, it's obvious it's her. Her hair has always been more blonde than mine, and her eyes a bright green. She looks sickly now. Her cheeks are sunken in, and everywhere I look there's nothing but skin and bones.

"Your father and I...on our way home, we stopped at a gas station." A cough racks through her body, and my heart aches at how painful it sounds. Has she been here since her supposed death? "Your father heard their plans while he was filling up the car, but it was still too late. He got back in and tried to lose them, but they crashed into us." She wheezes as another cough comes as she struggles to retell the memory. "There were too many of them, and they had help from stryxes. But when they realized the bite couldn't paralyze me, they figured out what line I came from and decided to keep me as a prisoner."

"But I don't understand...the bite? The body?" Is being a descendant of the Elite really that important?

"I'm sorry I never got to explain before what you are, but it seems you already know the truth." Her eyes beg me to understand, to forgive.

I give her a nod. "Yes, I know I'm a lycan now."

She sighs, her shoulders visibly relaxing. "The Thornton line is immune to a stryx's nerve toxins, and our blood is more potent because of ancestry."

"The Elite," I say, and she nods. I remember Ash mentioning stryxes had the ability to paralyze others, but it feels like it was ages ago.

Ash. Is he okay? What happened after I was taken? Are they safe or in the dungeon somewhere?

I shake my head. I can only focus on one thing right now. I'm...I'm sure he's fine.

I swallow. "I'm still confused. They found your body."

"Yes," she says, her head straining to stay up. "They killed one of the lycans that attacked us, crushed her face and burned her fingers to make her unrecognizable." She scowls. "It was easier for them to kill one of their own than it should've been."

"And me?" I know now is probably not the time to get answers to all my burning questions, but I can't help asking. It's been so long.

"What do you mean?"

"Ash found my fake death certificate."

"We knew about the disappearances and the killings, so we decided to take precautions." A small smile forms on her mouth. "Ash?"

I clear my throat. "He's my mate."

Her eyes light up. "I'm so glad you found love."

My chin wobbles. "Me too," I whisper.

"Come here, honey." I scoot until I can give her a makeshift hug, making sure I don't hurt her or bump my wrists.

A moan from the other side of the room has me jerking away from my mom and sitting in front of her.

It's the other woman. Was she the one that took me?

She sits up and looks around, her silver eyes glazed and full of panic.

"Wylla," my mom says.

The woman, Wylla, blinks a few times until her gaze focuses on us. "Addison."

"Yes, you're okay. It's only me and Ellie, my daughter."

Wylla's eyes zero in on me before guilt fills them. "I'm sorry."

I'm not really sure what to make of Wylla. "You were the one who took me?" I ask, my eyes narrowing.

"She was forced to by Morbal," my mom says and another coughing fit hits her.

Wylla stands and rushes over to her, holding the end of her dress up. Now the blood splatter makes sense.

"What's wrong with her?" I ask Wylla, my chest tight with anxiety.

She glances at me as she kneels and wipes my mom's mouth. "She's dying. Even lycans need food and water after a while."

A chill runs down my spine.

"Wylla," my mom says. "People usually have some tact when they say things like that."

Wylla frowns. "Right, sorry."

My hands shake. "W-We have to get her out of here."

"We can't."

I clench my jaw, glaring at her.

My mom sighs. "Forgive Wylla, she wasn't always like this. What she means is that we can't leave, not with these bands on."

Lifting my arms up to examine them again, pain shoots through my wrist. A hiss passes my lips when I wiggle a finger. "What are they?"

"Wylla, please?" my mom asks, her voice strained as she lets her head hang once more.

"Of course." Wylla sits beside me and shows her bands, black veiny marks spread out from them, reaching the blood marking on her forearms. "They are embedded into our skin to touch the essence in our blood. Morbal controls our shifts, essence, magic...everything that makes us lycans and witches."

My gaze moves to hers. "So, you are a witch."

She nods and lowers her arms. "I have barrier magic. I can also make potions."

I blink. "How did you grab me and bring me here?"

"Blood magic," she says, gesturing to the markings on her face and arms.

"So you also have blood magic?" I ask, trying to piece everything together.

"No, I can do blood magic. No one can have it, but anyone can perform it if taught."

"Okay. So what is barrier magic?"

"It's—"

"Someone's coming," my mom whispers, and we go silent. I tune into my hearing. There are footsteps in the distance. Apparently the bands can't control everything.

After a few minutes, when the footsteps subside, my mom sighs. "Just patrol, but I don't think we have much longer."

"We need to figure out a way to escape," I whisper to them. There's no way I'm staying in this dungeon. I've had enough of being trapped for one lifetime. "We need to think of a way to get these bands off of us."

We sit in silence, each lost in our own thoughts, trying to figure out a way to get out of this, when Wylla says, "I may have a plan."

When she doesn't continue, I ask, "What is it?"

"Just follow my lead when they come and get us."

Ash

"Sophie and Foster, you're with me. Russell, you'll stay with Arlo. I want you and Foster in your wolf forms to communicate just in case the necklaces stop working." I scan the faces around me: my betas, delta, and leads—minus Kathy—along with Alice and those in leader positions in Arlo's pack, including his son, Logan.

We're surrounded by greenery off Morbal's territory, but night has already fallen. All of us are relying only on our night vision to see. I look to Arlo on my left. "Would you like to add anything?"

"No, you summed it up nicely. You may be a new alpha, but you're a natural at this." He grips my shoulder and gives it a squeeze. "Glad I could be here to offer support. We'll get your mate back."

"Thank you." I straighten. "Well, if there's nothing else, we're moving out."

The circle disperses, each going to spread the plan. Alice leaves with Kathy's second.

Sophie readjusts the gun on her belt as she makes her way to me. Lycans don't normally carry weapons since they're useless when we shift, but she'll be one of the ones remaining human. Russell and Foster start stripping, leaving only their boxers and shift. Russell will be on standby with the rest of the pack and Arlo's.

Foster, Sophie, and I—along with two other lycans—start to jog. Logan volunteered to join along with Maria, a hunter, for this retrieval. We're forced to keep it small because of the limited number of potions I have that dull our presence. Arlo showed us a map on his phone where he believes the entrance to the underground tunnels are.

Most Roman aqueducts were built high up in bridge-type structures, but Morbal built an underground tunnel system for his waterways. If it weren't for Arlo, we'd never know these existed. The problem now is to find the right path that will lead us to Ellie.

When we get to the area, we spread out and search. I rummage through bushes, lift fallen tree limbs, but don't find anything. Foster barks to my right. My head jerks up. He's a few yards away and pawing at the ground.

Using my speed, I reach him first and kneel. He steps away, revealing a square drain grate. I swipe the leaves and twigs away from it. Its bars are rusted and thick with grime and algae. The spaces between the bars are small, and my fingers slide against the filth as I grip it. I pull up, using my legs for leverage, but it doesn't budge an inch.

I mutter a curse. "You're gonna have to shift back to help me," I say to Foster before calling the others over.

Foster, Logan, and I grunt as we lift the grate together. It thumps when we toss it aside onto the ground.

"Let me go first and scout," Sophie says, and when I give the okay, she jumps down. A splash is the only indication that she reached the bottom.

"Clear," Sophie calls up quietly, just loud enough for our ears to pick up.

I nod at Logan to go down next, and I scan the area.

Once Foster and Maria have jumped down, I reach for the grate, but my hand clamps up, another tremor moving through my body.

Ellie's in pain.

It's been happening on and off since she's been taken. I can sense her in the mansion but can't pinpoint her location. Instead, I've been trying to send her strength through the bond, but something's blocking my connection to her.

When it passes, I grab onto the grate and strain against its weight as I drag it partly over the opening.

My hope is that it covers the hole enough for it not to be so noticeable if Morbal has patrols that come out here.

Before joining them, I bite my pinky and mark it with my blood.

My boots make a small splash when I hit the bottom. Examining above us, it appears we just came through one of the tunnel's shafts. The tunnel itself is made completely out of stone and concrete. It's dark and damp, but the square-like shape allows more space for us to stand side by side.

In hushed tones, I give directions. "Sophie, I want you to lead. Foster, I'd like you to shift and stay by her side." I turn to the other two. "Is either of you willing to shift and take up the rear?"

Logan offers, but doesn't bother removing his clothes before shifting. The rest of us take our positions and move.

Sophie, with Foster by her side, leads us slowly through the tunnel. Our footsteps make ripples in the water, but the only noise is the draft through overhead shafts and drops of water. Air currents change, bringing different scents with each whiff.

It's not long before we come upon our first intersection that breaks off into three different paths.

Everyone stops when Sophie holds up her hand. She sniffs the air and tilts her head. Sophie is one of the best hunters in the pack. I wouldn't trust anyone else to find Ellie. It also helps that her special ability is enhanced smell.

After a few moments, she drops her hand and chooses the far-right tunnel.

We proceed in this manner, stopping and turning when she indicates, until the air grows cold.

Sophie pauses and looks back at me. I step closer. "What's wrong?" I ask.

"It's strange. I'm following where her scent is strongest but when we move on to the next tunnel or the air changes, it's coming from the complete opposite direction."

Dread sinks in. How is that possible? Is it because of how elaborate the tunnel system is? We haven't come across any signs that we're near the mansion yet.

I curse myself. I shouldn't have allowed us to enter blind. Since Ellie's been taken, I haven't been able to think straight, but I'll find another way. We don't have time to wander the tunnels for hours.

"Are you able to lead us back?" I ask.

She closes her eyes and sniffs the air, her face scrunching up in concentration.

"Maybe," she finally answers after a while, reopening her eyes. "I think I need a refresher."

I nod and bite my pinky again. I hold it up to her as she leans forward and smells my blood before the cut closes again.

"The scent is faint, but I think I got it," she says and straightens. She strides past me, back the way we came.

"Foster, let Russell know we're heading back."

He nods.

After a few turns, Sophie hesitates. We've reached a section that's split off into two different directions. She looks right to left and back.

"What is it, Sophie?" I ask.

"Your scent is coming from both directions."

My brows scrunch together. That can't be right. I examine the area. Nothing looks familiar. *Something's wrong.* If we were heading back in the right direction, the tunnels would become more familiar, not less. Guilt eats at me.

"Is there a direction it's stronger?" I ask.

Sophie sniffs the air again. "It smells stronger to our left."

I nod. "Then let's try that path." I pray it's the correct one.

After ten minutes, a breeze sweeps over us, bringing a chill that seeps deep into my bones. My vision darkens even with my ability to see in the dark. The only sound is our feet shuffling through the thin layer of water.

"We're almost there," Sophie whispers.

The tunnel suddenly opens up, the chill stronger. We freeze in our steps as sets of glowing red eyes start popping into existence.

There's a hissing that grows the longer we stand here. My heart is in my throat as I inch our group back, trying to keep our movements as small as possible.

Slowly peeking behind us, I stop as more glowing eyes find their way around us.

Flames burst from torches behind the glowing eyes, lighting up those surrounding us.

It seems we've accidentally found our way to an underground coven.

A stryx coven.

The grate with my blood on it is in the grasp of a stryx.

Each and every one of them has their fangs out, hissing and growling at us. Their eyes glow red, and their nails elongate into black sharp points. They're in beast form.

Skulls and bones cover the walls. Multiple archways are spread out around the room, leading to other areas full of skeletons.

We're in a catacomb.

The underground home of the dead. Fitting for the vampires in stories, but not so much for the living. Why are they down here? Are they involved with Morbal?

Growls erupt from my group as the stryxes close in, our backs to each other. My claws and canines are out, preparing for an attack.

Suddenly the hissing stops and the stryxes' aggressive stances begin to straighten. They move, parting like the Red Sea for a single person.

A woman.

Her black dress flows around her as she steps toward us. Her long dark-brown hair folded into a braid and over her shoulder.

I'm on high alert. Who is she, and why is every single stryx listening to her?

Sophie aims her gun on the woman. But we both know it's pointless against stryxes in their beast forms.

On edge, I step forward in front of my group, blocking the woman from them. I hold back a growl but show my canines.

She stops at the edge of her group of stryxes. She looks me dead in the eye as a grin forms on her face with fangs peeking out.

"It appears we have guests."

Ash

"Well, who should we taste first?" the woman asks as she glides around us.

A few of the stryxes snicker and one responds, "The women are always the tastiest."

The woman sneers, her blood-red eyes snapping to the male stryx. "I already know your opinion, Gaius."

She turns back to the group, near the end, close enough that when she reaches out, she brushes her hand against the fur of Logan's golden tail.

A smile appears on her face when he tucks his tail in and growls.

"Come out and play, little wolf. I promise I won't bite." Her fangs stick out when she grins. "At least not too hard."

"Come on, Octavia, let us play too," a female stryx whines.

Logan's head pops up.

The woman, Octavia, whirls around on the female stryx. "What did you just say?" The stryx hunches her shoulders as Octavia strides to her.

"I'm sorry, I won't do it again," she says in a small voice.

"How many chances have I given you already?"

"Three," she mutters.

"Three too many. You'll be someone's snack tonight." She hums, tapping her cheek with a surprisingly blunt nail. "I'm thinking Gaius." Gaius grins as the girl's eyes widen in horror. "Of course, he's not allowed to drain you, but..."

"It'll be painful!"

Octavia lifts a shoulder in a shrug. "Maybe it'll teach you to not be so impatient." She spins around and eyes us.

"Octavia"—a male stryx steps forward—"give Zoe another chance."

Her eyes flare with anger and she whirls around, her dress fanning around her. "It seems everyone needs a lesson today. These lycans are *mine* now."

Hissing and yelling erupts.

"Silence," she yells, a wave of power echoing it, and the room goes quiet. With the amount of magic flowing through her demand, she's either high up or has a large amount of essence in her blood. "You know my conditions. They may be food, but they are still outsiders. Two of them are wolves and could easily relay anything they wish right now. I'm not sure *why* I'm needing to explain that." She glares at everyone before turning to a group in the corner. "Take them to my room."

Four stryxes step forward. Two males and two females.

"You're going to let the half-blood have a taste?" Zoe says, curling her lip in disgust. One of the girls in the group with short, light-brown hair flinches.

Octavia stiffens, her gaze firmly remaining on the group. "Gaius. Drain her. Now," she commands, her voice quiet but deadly.

Gaius perks up and eagerly strides toward Zoe.

A deathly silence takes over the room. Zoe spins around to run, but other stryxes block her from escaping. The man who tried to help her earlier is now averting his gaze to the side. Zoe cries out when Gaius reaches her. He opens his mouth, his fangs on full display, and roughly bites into her. She claws at him as he keeps his teeth embedded into her, drinking her blood.

A growl starts in the back of my throat. What is this? Even Zac wasn't this bad. Is this how stryx covens are run? Disobey and you'll be drained?

"Get them out of here," Octavia yells at the group.

They step into action and stride over to us. The burly man grabs Sophie.

"We'll go willingly," I say with a snarl.

He raises his hands in surrender, then gestures for us to move forward.

I scan the room full of stryxes, their beast forms are on full display despite their non-aggressive stances. My eyes land on Foster beside me in his wolf form as we share a look. We have no chance against this horde.

We walk across the room through the stryxes. We're led out of the large room and down multiple hallways. The intricate layout is just like the tunnel system, but the stryxes appear to know where they're going.

They take us into a room full of an assortment of old furniture: chairs, armoires, bookshelves, and couches.

Two of the stryxes, the burly one and the one Zoe called half-blood, stay and lock the doors while the other two stand just outside the room.

We each stand on high alert. I survey Sophie and Foster, both sending daggers with their eyes at the guards. Logan in wolf form examines the furniture, intrigued. And Maria surveys the room. None of us dare talk with stryxes near. Even if none were in the room, they'd still be able to hear us.

I'm not sure what they have planned for us. I'm supposed to be the alpha, yet I haven't a clue what to do to get us out of this situation.

I screwed up.

After a moment, there's a knock on the door. Burly unlocks and opens it. Octavia strides in as the doors close behind her. She passes us, making her way to a throne-like chair.

Before sitting, she whirls around and holds up a finger. "I want to make one thing clear. Just because they listen to me does not mean they won't betray me."

I blink. What is the point in telling me that? I'm not surprised after the show she just put on.

With a sigh, she collapses on one of the larger throne-like chairs. "Now that that's out of the way. Explain who you are and why I should keep you alive before one of the little bastards tells Morbal. And be truthful, I can tell when you're lying."

She quirks a brow when my entire body goes rigid.

"Well? What were you doing in the tunnels? Actually—" Her eyes turn to Foster and Logan. "They need to shift back, or I'll have you all drained."

I meet the gazes of both Foster and Logan and nod. They both shift back in nothing but their boxers.

"Tav—Octavia." The half-blood with short, light-brown hair steps forward. She glances at us as she passes, her eyes catching on Logan. She leans down, whispering in Octavia's ear.

Using my senses, I hear her say to Octavia, "They're looking for the alpha's mate."

A growl leaves before I can stop it.

"Thank you, Ariya." Octavia's eyes land on me. "I assume you're the alpha."

I glance at the two not in my pack, then nod.

"And where is your mate?"

Deciding there's no point in lying, I say, "Morbal took her."

She gives me a slow nod. "It seems we have a common enemy then. I've always liked the saying, 'the enemy of my enemy is my friend'." She waves her hand in the air, the band on her wrist catching the light of the fire. "Is that what you're doing in the tunnels? Trying to get into his self-proclaimed castle to find your mate?"

"Yes."

Logan steps forward. "Why is a daughter of the Elite under Morbal's *self-proclaimed* castle?"

My head snaps to Logan, Octavia's blood-red eyes on him. "What gave it away?"

"The eyes, then your name confirmed it," Logan says. I did find it was strange that her red eyes weren't glowing. Does that mean that's her natural eye color?

"And have you told anyone, wolf?"

He stands up taller. "What if I did?"

"Who did you tell?"

"Head alpha Wagner."

She curses.

Ariya looks at Octavia in horror. "Tav."

"I know," she grinds out and stands. "And is he on his way?" Power lines her voice.

Logan eyes them both with confusion. "Your powers don't work on me."

She steps forward, her hands in fists. "Just answer the question."

"Are you in danger?" Sophie speaks up.

"My—Arlo wouldn't harm them," Logan says.

"I know," Sophie says, turning briefly to Logan, "but there must be a different reason."

But when we turn our attention back to them, they're frozen in place.

"What's his name?" Octavia asks.

Sophie hesitates, looking at each of us before answering, "Arlo Wagner."

"Not Linus Wagner."

"No, that was my great-grandfather. He passed away years ago."

Octavia shares a look with Ariya. "Are you sure?"

Sophie straightens her shoulders. "Yes."

This is getting ridiculous and annoying. I *don't* have time for this. I need to find Ellie. A growl leaves me. "Explain." Power laces at my command.

Octavia's sharp red gaze turns onto me. *"You're not in control here, alpha."* Her powers radiate out of her.

Ariya touches Octavia's arm. "I don't think they're our enemies."

Octavia is wound tight as she scans us and lets out a sigh and nods. "I suppose you're right." She slumps back in her chair. "Fine. I'll help you with finding your mate, if you help me."

60

Ellie

Marcus is here, just like we expected. But seeing him makes it real. And so much worse. It means we were right that he and Morbal are working together. There's no doubt about it now.

He stops in front of the cell with two bulky men. Guards, maybe?

One of the guards unlocks the cell before they enter. A malicious grin grows on Marcus' face when he spots me. "Long time no see, huh, Eleanor?"

I press myself against the back wall as they enter. One comes to me and roughly grabs my arms. I cry out when he takes me by the wrists and puts shackles on them just below the bands.

The other guard focuses on Wylla while Marcus strides to me. My guard keeps a hold of me as Marcus kneels in front of me. He lifts a clammy hand and cups my face. I try to turn away, but he grips my face with both hands, forcing me to meet his eager eyes.

I cringe away as he leans in close, his rotten scent worse when he talks. "We're going to have so much fun with you, my little Eleanor."

A tremor rolls through my body. I try to focus on my essence, but it's silent inside. There's no warmth left. Just a chilly, dead emptiness. I fight back tears at how helpless I am.

This must be what Wylla meant by controlling us.

"What do you want with me?" I say, sounding stronger than I feel.

He releases me and stands, towering over me. "Your blood, of course. You're a descendant of the Elite. Isn't that right, Addison?" He grins, turning his head over to her, still chained to the wall.

My gaze moves to my mom. She sends daggers with her eyes to Marcus.

"What? Aren't you happy to finally be reunited?" He bends down to get in her face. "It took longer than it should have. After all, you did try to hide her from us."

"Go to hell," she says, her voice raspy.

He chuckles, then straightens and turns back to me. "You'll be taking her place, Eleanor. We'll be using your new, young blood for our potions. Which is where we're heading now." He grabs the chain between my wrists and pulls up. A scream bursts from my throat, my wrists burning from the movement.

Wylla starts laughing, throwing her head back as if seeing me in pain is the funniest thing she's ever seen.

Marcus pauses, my arms stretched above me. "What's wrong with you, witch?"

"I just think it's hilarious that you need to restrain her. You're probably worried she'll get away from you again, aren't you? After all, you don't want your big brother to get mad at you again."

Big brother?

"Shut up, witch. You don't know what you're talking about," he says and spits at her, tugging my wrists harder, forcing a whimper from me.

She grows serious. "What? I'm just pointing out your own insecurities. Can you not handle a little lycan without chains and bands? She doesn't have powers like I do."

He glares at her but doesn't say anything.

"Thought so." She shrugs one shoulder.

He growls and releases the chain, dropping me to the ground and giving my wrists a much-needed respite.

"I can handle her," he says with a growl and gestures to one of the guards. "Release her."

My eyes widen as the guard grabs one of my arms and unbinds me from the shackles.

I stare at Wylla. What's her plan? Even if I'm free, what am I going to do? I don't know the layout of this place to get out. And I can't take everyone on by myself.

"Those too." Marcus gestures to my bands.

If looks could kill, Wylla would be dead. Instead, she appears bored.

The guard hesitates and meets the other guard's gaze.

"Do it," Marcus yells.

"We don't have the device, sir."

He growls. "Watch them," he says and storms off. He comes back, gripping the handle of a circular device. He pushes the guard out of the way.

A whimper escapes me as Marcus yanks my wrist to him. He sticks my wrist in it as if he were putting a bracelet on me. I watch in amazement as it shrinks down, completely enclosing the band. *A magical device?*

It clicks into places with a buzz, then a pop of release before the device slowly expands back out with the band. There's a suction sound and pain flares in my wrist.

I can't hold back a scream as the band pries off, inch by inch. My nerves are on fire, my wrist dead. I can't hold it up or let it hang. Anything I do sends a shockwave through my system. Marcus pulls the device with my band off. He presses a button, and it releases the band, letting it clank onto the ground. Staring through blurry tears, I find bloody circular wounds dotted along my entire wrist.

Marcus inserts my other wrist, and the process starts all over again. A scream leaves me as my overly sensitive nerves take another hit.

When he removes the device from me again, I stare at the gruesome wounds. The bands have nubs along them that were embedded into my skin. The pain dulls as I'm flooded with warmth. My strength returns and overflows through me. I watch in awe as layer by layer my skin reattaches and heals.

He grins. "This is an unexpected surprise. You heal faster than I expected."

I don't think I did it on my own.

Ash

$\mathcal{H}$elping Octavia ends up being an easier decision than I expected since our goals align. She wants freedom, which means ending Morbal. Something we were already planning on doing.

After Octavia explained the bands on her wrists, I ask, "And all the other stryxes?"

"Some want to be here, some don't. Look for their bands. If they have one, they are on our side."

"But..." Logan eyes Ariya and her bare wrists. Her eyes are golden now that she's no longer shifted. The other two remain outside as we discuss, but both Ariya and the burly stryx, Ethan, have switched out of their beast forms.

"Except Ariya," she says.

Ethan lays a hand on Octavia's shoulder. He doesn't say a word, but she gives him a subtle nod.

"You're not a child of the Elite," Logan says, eyeing Ariya.

She eyes him right back. "I'm not."

"Then how are you tied to Linus?"

"I don't think now is the time to discuss that. It isn't important."

He tilts his head. "You don't have bands, why stay here?"

"Because of Tav," she says, as if it's obvious.

When she doesn't elaborate, he opens his mouth to ask more questions, but Foster interrupts him. "I'd give it up, mate. She's not going to answer your questions."

Sophie lets out a sigh and asks, "And how is Linus tied to you?"

"I think I know," Logan says.

I tilt my head. Wasn't he just questioning Ariya how she was?

Octavia arches a brow and gestures for him to continue. "Be my guest."

Logan leans against the wall. "I was told this story a few times growing up... Linus and Arlo, father and son respectively, were both turned by the lycan Elite, making them both head alphas—Originals. But the lycan Elite refused to turn my grandmother. My grandfather, Linus, wanting to live a long time with his wife, went to the stryx Elite instead.

"The stryx Elite promised Linus that if he were allowed to feed off of Linus and Arlo, he'd turn his wife. Linus of course agreed, but my father, Arlo, refused. Arlo believed they were trying to trick Linus. Going back to the stryx Elite, Linus offered himself, but couldn't offer Arlo. The stryx Elite, displeased, killed my grandmother in front of Linus. Linus sought revenge and promised to come back and kill the stryx Elite and everyone in his family."

Octavia sneers. "My father was a vile man. He wanted nothing but power."

"And you don't? I saw the power you held back there."

"She was faking it," Ariya says.

Logan straightens, his brows high under his shaggy blond hair.

"Ariya," Octavia warns, moving forward, but Ethan holds her back.

"What? Why wouldn't we tell them the whole truth?"

Octavia sighs. "Fine."

Ariya turns back to us and sets her shoulders. "The display you saw when you first met us was fake. That's not how she really is. She hates acting that way. It's a scare tactic to be able to stay in control, even if half of them pretend to follow her, it's better they fake it than not listen at all."

"Because some follow Morbal," Maria says.

"Exactly." Ariya tucks a strand of her short hair behind her ear, revealing their slightly pointed tip. Is that another stryx trait I didn't know about? "They want the power he can give them."

"Which is?" Foster asks.

"He makes a witch create a potion—"

A grunt leaves me as a burning ache erupts around my wrists. I look down, but there's nothing wrong. Is something happening to Ellie again? I hate how silent the bond has been since she's been taken. I hate that I'm only able to feel her when she's in tremendous pain.

"Ash, you alright?" Foster asks.

I look up just as a wave of agony courses through me, dulling my senses. My legs give out under me. Sharp stabs start in my wrists and spread through my entire body. *Ellie.* I can feel her pain. The *full range* of her pain. The emotional trauma she's suffering along with the physical. My eyes tear up. What have you been going through, my little wolf?

Focusing just enough, I send strength through our bond, hoping that it'll reach her this time. That it'll help her be strong through whatever's causing her so much pain and to help her hold on.

When I come to, Foster and Logan are holding me up. "What happened?" Foster asks.

"It's Ellie, I can feel her again."

"The bands must be off," Octavia said. "Can you pinpoint her location?"

I shake my head, leaning against Foster. "We haven't completed the bond."

Her eyes narrow. "I'm not one to judge"—Ariya snorts and Octavia briefly turns her glare on her—"but that's stupid."

I let out a growl in warning.

"But," she interrupts my growling and smiles, "I may still have a way to find her. If you give me some of your blood."

62

Ellie

I don't understand how Wylla did it. My wrists are free. I'm unbound. I won't do anything to compromise it.

Marcus and the guards usher me out of the cell, dragging Wylla and my mom in chains behind us. My mom struggles. Her breathing is heavy when coughs aren't racking through her body. I grind my teeth whenever the guards yank her chain.

As we walk through the dungeon, there's cell upon cell full of people, either in chains or with bands like I had.

What is this place?

One thing that's clear is that Morbal and Marcus were kidnapping people.

It makes me sick to my stomach.

Before we reach the end of the dungeon, Marcus stops us by the back door and walks into a nearby room with the device. He comes back out after a moment with blindfolds.

"If you give me a hard time, the bindings are going back on. Actually, I think we should put the shackles back on." He tips his chin to one of the guards.

The guard rushes back to the cell as Marcus and the other guard begin wrapping the blindfolds around our eyes.

It's like a switch flips inside. Panic rises as my vision darkens. Even with my enhanced eyesight, everything is black, reminding me of the basement. Marcus' putrid scent, the cold, dry air, the darkness.

Always the darkness.

I'm being swallowed by it. I start to hyperventilate. I'm surrounded by the hollowness of it. It consumes me.

The cold bite of the metal shackles as they're wrapped around my wrists sends visions of the basement to the surface, and I'm that little girl once again, trying to fight off demons that I'm too weak against.

There's no use fighting when the outcome will always be the same. I'm pathetic. There's no point in living like this. But I can't show weakness. Not in front of him.

I clench my hands in fists to keep them from shaking.

No, don't think like that.

I'm not weak anymore. I never was.

Focusing on the one sense that will help me, I tap into my hearing because smell will send me back in time. Back to a place I don't want to be.

Instead, I focus on the sounds around me that aren't quite the same as the basement. Coughing, sniffling, and shuffling bounces off the walls behind and around me.

The door creaks open in front of us and Marcus pulls the chains between my wrists, and I'm dragged out of the dungeons.

I stumble on steps as I'm tugged up the stairs. He leads us up and down stairs, around multiple corners and halls.

I'm not sure how much time has passed when I hear the scuff of latches on a heavy door.

Marcus forces me inside whatever room he brought us to. Then there's the thundering sounds of the door closing behind us.

The blindfold is ripped off, making my vision go white. My enhanced eyesight hurts against the brightness of the chandelier above. Once I get my eyesight back to normal, I find we're in a throne room. At the top of a set of steps sits an empty black throne with spikes along the back, and in the middle of the room is a short black marble pillar.

A door on the side of the room catches my eye as it opens. A man comes out wearing a long dark trench coat as if it isn't the twenty-first century. His dark hair lies on his shoulders, his matching dark eyes twinkle as they land on me, and I'm hit with a sense of familiarity. He looks oddly similar to Marcus. My gaze flashes to Marcus, then to the man.

Is this the brother? My stomach churns. Is this *Morbal?*

Marcus bows his head and pushes mine down, as he says, "Head alpha, I have brought them as you requested."

Head alpha? This *must* be Morbal. But why does Marcus call him by his title and not by his name if they're brothers?

I watch through my lashes as Morbal takes his throne and gestures for someone on my left to come closer.

The sounds of chains and shackles moving draw my attention. Wylla moves into my line of sight as she walks forward.

Marcus releases my head when Morbal gestures to the open door he came out of. A woman walks out holding a metallic black bowl, her wrists free from the bands. I glance at the guards and find their arms bare as well.

Does that mean they're here willingly? How twisted can someone be to kidnap and kill people? For what purpose? For a potion?

Once the woman places the bowl on top of the pillar, she bows and moves to stand off to the side.

The scuff of the doors opening behind me draws my attention as more guards come in. They drag in a struggling, hissing man with glowing red eyes, fangs, and bands on his wrist. His nails are black and long and pointed. Is this a stryx?

Morbal frowns. "I didn't want him. I wanted Octavia. I want this to be the most powerful potion yet."

The guards share a look over the struggling stryx. "We couldn't find her, head alpha."

He sneers and lounges back, tapping his foot. "She's always in the catacombs."

"That's where we looked, head alpha."

"Well, look again," he yells, pounding a fist on the armrest.

"Yes, sire." They bow their heads. "What should we do with this one?"

Morbal's eyes narrow on the stryx as he brings a hand to his smooth face. He appears young, in his twenties, not over a thousand years old. "Wylla, restrain him for now while they go searching for Octavia."

"Yes, Morbal."

His head snaps to her. "What did I tell you about calling me that? It's *Master* to you."

Wylla bows her head and apologizes. She turns toward the stryx straining against the guards.

Taking a deep breath, she holds out a hand, the band still encasing her wrist. Her eyes change from silver to a glowing lilac. Her long inky hair lifts and floats around her, her gown softly flapping around her.

Thin, luminous, lilac wisps of what I could only explain to be strands of magic leave her hand and combine into one thick strand and stretches throughout the room. Wylla almost appears unearthly, and I'm struck with a combination of fear and awe. Her magic wraps around the stryx like a tentacle, confining him in its grasp. She drops her hand once he's trapped, but her eyes continue to glow.

I thought she had barrier magic—what the heck is this?

Morbal sighs as he waves the guards away. "Now with that taken care of..." His eyes lock back on mine and a slow smile appears on his face. "Eleanor, isn't it? Marcus, why don't you bring her over, and we can begin."

Marcus pushes me forward, and I stumble to catch myself from falling.

I glare at them. "What do you want with me?"

Morbal's brow rises, moving his gaze to Marcus. "I thought you would've told her. You do love to brag to our prey about what you're going to do to them before killing them."

A chill runs down my spine.

"We're not killing her this time," Marcus says simply as he grabs my chains and pulls me forward.

I glance back at my mom still by the door, then at the bowl. Is this where they're going to make the potion? What kind of potion needs blood?

The bowl gives off a dark and ominous omen the closer we get.

Marcus stops in front of the pillar and grabs my arm. He forces my wrist above the bowl, moves my shackle higher, biting into my skin. The sinister warning grows stronger. I try to yank my arm away, but his grip is painful. If he tightens it even a fraction more, my bones will break. He partial-shifts a single finger while I try to pry him off me. He slices my wrist with a shifted nail and lets the blood flow into the bowl while I struggle to get away.

Morbal laughs. "It's futile, girl." He stands and walks down the steps to stand in front of the pillow. He reaches into his trench coat pocket and pulls out three vials. One is brown, one green, and one clear.

Holding up the clear one and twirling the clear liquid, he says, "Ready, Wylla?"

Through tight lips, she responds, "Yes, *Master*."

Morbal's eyes narrow, but he doesn't say anything as Wylla steps forward to stand beside him.

He hands her the vial while blood continues to drip from my wrist.

I stare at Wylla. What's her plan? She said she had one. It couldn't have been just for the bands to be removed from me. I could shift right now, but what good would that do? While I take one out—*if* I can take one out—the other will be ready and on top of me in a second.

With the clear vial of liquid in her hands, her glowing eyes jump from Morbal to Marcus to behind me, then to me. She mouths, *wait*. And I'm hit with a sense of relief.

"Marcus, would you like the honors this time?" Morbal asks.

Marcus' eyes light up. "Truly, brother?"

Nausea rolls through me. I was right, they are brothers. Brothers that are sick in the head. And I lived with one. I was imprisoned by one...and now both. What's their goal?

Morbal sighs, exasperated. "Yes, *truly*." Morbal draws closer and grabs onto my arm to keep me in place while giving the remaining two vials, the green and brown ones, to Marcus.

Marcus uncaps the brown one and holds it upside down over the bowl. Pieces of dark brown soil fall from the vial and join with my blood.

"The soil from the dried-up Fountain of Youth," Morbal says, his eyes alight as he watches Marcus. "It was very hard to find."

Marcus tucks the empty vial in his pocket before opening the green one. When he turns it upside down, a fine green powder cascades out.

"The algae from the rocks of the stream bed," Morbal continues, his grip still tight on mine. He glances over his shoulder. "Wylla."

Wylla steps forward with her vial. This one has a clear liquid inside as she pours it into the bowl.

"Essence extracted from the blood of the witch Elite."

My gaze jerks up to Morbal. *How?* Did he kill her? Is she a prisoner in the dungeons?

Morbal looks to the large doors at my back. "Where the hell are they? How hard is it to find a witch?" His gaze shifts. "Bring over the sacrifice."

My eyes widen as the guards pull my mother over. *No.* I tug harder at my confined wrists. *Why?* Why after I just got her back.

One of the guards takes out a knife and holds it over my mother's heart, waiting for the signal from Morbal.

"Blood first, for the witch," Morbal says, trying to contain me, but I just struggle harder.

I cry out in horror as the guard creates a deep gash on my mom's arm with the knife.

"No!" I scream, tears rolling down my face. "Don't hurt her."

"Wylla," Morbal bellows, his face growing red, power flowing through the room.

Wylla grimaces, her face growing pale. Black veins creep up from around the metal bands, trailing up her arms and down her hands. More peek out of the top of her gown, spreading out like fingers.

My mom gives her a small smile. "It's okay, Wylla. You don't have a choice."

When Wylla takes a step toward my mom, the black recedes. A tic forms in her jaw as she dips her fingers in my mom's blood, then applies it to the spots along her face and arms where the dried blood resides.

My heart is racing as I fight Morbal's hold.

Guards burst in. "Head alpha! We're being attacked."

Morbal stiffens. "You're lying, I don't sense anyone." His grip tightens on me.

The guards fidget, unsure what to do. "Fine," Morbal says, jaw tight. "Get the stryxes to take care of them. Marcus. Take her." Morbal thrusts me into Marcus' arms.

Bile rises, sweat lining my upper lip as Marcus moves behind me. With the combination of his putrid scent and presence so close to mine, my body rebels even more.

My shift is close to the surface. If I tap into it, maybe I could save us. Or I'll just get us all killed faster. But it seems backup is close. Maybe I can hold on a little longer before acting.

Marcus keeps a hold of me, forcing my arm above the bowl.

"They're almost here, sire," one of the guards says.

Morbal places his hands on either side of the bowl and scowls down at it. "We can't wait any longer. Wylla, bring the stryx over," Morbal commands.

The stryx locked in Wylla's magic is lifted off the ground and floated forward.

When the stryx is near, he tries to bite Morbal.

Morbal snarls and partial-shifts his hand, slicing a nail across the stryx's throat. Blood sprays everywhere, landing all over the ground, bowl, and Morbal.

"Over the bowl," Morbal commands Wylla, and the dead stryx floats above the bowl, blood weeping out of the gash on his neck and into the bowl.

My stomach turns, and I turn my head as puke pushes out of my mouth to cover Marcus' shoes.

"Disgusting." Marcus curses and pushes on my head to keep it down.

"Wylla, start the spell. Guard, bring the sacrifice closer."

She hesitates, and another wave of power passes Morbal's lips. "*Now.*"

Wylla begins a chant.

Panic rises. *No.* I can't wait for Wylla or anyone else, not when my mom's life is in the balance.

Focusing on my essence, I partial-shift my hands. It comes so much faster than when I first started.

I dig the claws of my free hand into Marcus' exposed arms that grip my wrist.

Marcus hisses and grabs hold of my hair. He pulls back hard while tightening his grip on my wrist. The sound of my bone snapping is the first thing I register before sharp pain flares to life. A scream rips from my throat as I release him.

But then I start slashing at anything near me as everything goes hazy.

I'm overwhelmed with pain, but I continue to claw anything I touch. I hear broken pieces of their argument.

"Fool! Why did you take her bands off?"

"Can't we just have the witch confine her?"

The question sends an ice bucket of water through me. The next thing I know, wisps of magic are in my line of vision. Marcus and Morbal are in front of me, beside the bowl and pillar.

My head snaps to Wylla, who's just to the left of Morbal.

Wylla's wisps of magic waver as she points to her bands. My brows scrunch together as I hold my wrist to my stomach. Is she wanting me to remove them? I can't get them off. I don't have the device, and Marcus left it somewhere in the dungeon.

She mouths the word, *shift*.

It clicks.

I know what she wants me to do.

Tapping into my essences again, I let my shift sweep through me. The shackles bite into my skin as my arms morph. My wrist kills, but I force myself to ignore it. Focusing only on my body as I completely transform into a wolf.

"Witch," Morbal bellows as both he and Marcus jump away from me, almost knocking the bowl over. Marcus' body morphs as he shifts, but Morbal spins and grabs the bowl. He brings it to his mouth and chugs it down.

Unease settles in my gut, my stomach churns at the sight. But I ignore it and leap, passing them.

I jump on top of Wylla, knocking her over and clamping part of my mouth around one of her metal bands.

"Do it," she grits out through clenched teeth, her gaze is unwavering.

I slowly apply pressure and hear the band crack under my jaw. She screams and I yelp as an electrifying current shoots through me, leaving me numb.

I'm sluggish as I try to move, but Wylla replaces her wrist with the other one in my mouth.

"Last one, Ellie."

I whimper, but before I can apply pressure, I'm distracted by a commotion behind us.

"Ellie!" Ash's roar reverberates through the room.

Ash? He's here? Tears well up as joy bursts from me. It's quickly replaced with white-hot pain across my hide. Claws rake across my back and dig into my flesh, trying to pull me away from Wylla.

A growl vibrates deep in my throat.

"Focus, Ellie." My attention snaps back to Wylla, and she nods as we make eye contact. "That's it," she says, perspiration dotting her forehead. "Once I'm free, I'll make sure to get him off you—I swear it."

Trying to calm my racing heart, I focus on applying enough pressure to break her band, but not her wrist. I know it works when that same electrifying current shoots through us once more. My limbs go weak, and I'm just able to force myself away so as not to collapse completely on her.

I'm limp and numb, laying on the ground. My body vibrates and tingles, but not the kind I get when Ash and I touch. Growls, snarls, and grunts sound in the room. I blink until my vision comes back.

Wylla cries as she pries the bands off. She throws them aside as blood drips down from her fingers, staining her dress. She stumbles up and raises her arms, focusing on Morbal as wisps of her magic appear, wrapping around him and prying him off me. I hadn't even realized he shifted and was the one attacking me.

Morbal snarls at her like a rabid dog as she lifts him into the air.

Wylla screams, her face contorted in pain, as the bands tighten around him and her hair floats around her. I'm completely mesmerized.

My eyes wander until they connect with Ash.

My Ash.

63

Ash

*L*ight-purple magic wraps around Morbal, prying him off Ellie. Morbal roars when Logan bites into his leg.

Ellie lies limp on the floor, still in her wolf form. My soul aches to be near her, to hold her.

Her eyes lock onto mine. I hope she can see just how sorry I am that it took me so long to get here. Octavia was able to track Ellie by tasting my blood. Since I marked Ellie, some of her essence flows through me from the bond.

Teeth skim my side, reminding me that I can't be distracted right now.

Marcus, in wolf form, nips at my arms and legs, but it's easy to dodge him as a man with my speed. As long as I'm paying attention. For a bitten, he's abnormally strong and fast.

Marcus swipes at me, trying to catch me with his claws.

I snatch one of them and throw a punch into his snout. Pulling him closer, I knee him in the throat and push him away.

He pants and stumbles away as I stride toward him.

I hate him for what he's done to Ellie. The sick bastard took pleasure in harming and scarring her.

But no more.

There's a shift in the air, and my gaze is drawn back to the scene where Morbal is.

The magic around him shatters as the woman it came from collapses, but thankfully Logan is still there to attack him.

My head snaps back to Marcus as he tries to escape.

Just as I reach him, movement on my right diverts my attention. There's not enough time to react as Morbal barrels into my side and slams me against the wall, forcing the air out of my lungs.

The pressure is unbearable as I try to catch my breath. I attempt to pry him off, scratching him with my claws.

Glancing over his shoulder, I find Logan in his wolf form struggling to stand up, coughing up blood.

How is this possible?

On our way up we were battling with lycans and stryxes alike, but that shouldn't have inhibited Logan's ability to fight Morbal. And Logan trained with his father, an Original. He should be able to hold his own longer than a few minutes.

I dig my claws into Morbal's fur, deep into his side.

He jerks away, and I drop to the ground, clenching my ribs. My chest is tight from the hit, and there's a sharp throbbing in my side.

I probably gained a few broken ribs.

More lycans and stryxes pile in through the open door as I stand. But none from our side. I'm grateful for Octavia and her stryxes. She's taking down two at a time on the other side of the room.

Arlo and Russell should be moving in by now. We just need to be able to hold out long enough for them to make it.

My side aches when I shift into my wolf.

Russell, how far out? I ask through the pack bond.

Just breached the front door. Even while communicating with me,

Russell isn't distracted. I can sense his undeterred concentration on the fight at hand.

I focus on my own battle as Marcus and Morbal close in. I should be larger than Marcus, but both he and Morbal tower over me. They corner me, but there's not much I can do about it.

When I see an opening, I lower my head and nip at Marcus' front legs as he steps forward for the next onslaught.

I taste metal as his blood enters my mouth.

I rip a chunk out of his leg and spit it onto the ground then jump toward Morbal.

But Morbal is ready. He stands on his hind legs, making him as tall as a giant grizzly. His eyes glow brighter, and his body grows larger by the second. *How is that possible? How is he getting bigger?* He snarls as his teeth sharpen and elongate even farther.

But I don't back down.

I ram into his stomach. He drops his weight, crushing me.

He seems to get heavier as he presses his weight into me.

Pushing on the ground underneath me, I try to dislodge him, but he doesn't budge.

Is my mind playing tricks on me, or is Morbal getting stronger?

Morbal repositions, freeing my lower half.

Why did he move?

Morbal holds my front down as Marcus' claws slash across my hind legs. Agony shoots through me as Marcus carves a path down my side.

My desperation to get away increases, but my hind legs give out.

Morbal rises off me and stands while Marcus shifts back into human form. Marcus grins down at me.

"Ah, the mighty alpha, protector of Eleanor, the pureblood." Marcus laughs. "How does it feel to be defeated by me?"

He partial-shifts his hand and leans in close.

I snarl and gnash my teeth.

He jerks back and sneers. "Just give up. The end is near. It's obvious who will win this."

I glance to my side as snarls erupt near the entrance. Arlo and

Russell have made it in with our packs. And they're headed straight for Morbal.

Breathing deeply, I center myself and focus on my prey.

Marcus takes a step back but thinks better of it and shifts back into wolf form.

He lunges for my stomach.

And I allow it.

Adrenaline pumps through me. Once he connects, I lower my head and latch onto his neck.

His entire body freezes, his teeth still embedded in my side.

But I don't let him move or think about what's about to happen.

I dig my teeth in deeper and rip my head away, tearing his throat out.

I shove him away and watch him collapse as I spit his flesh onto the ground. A death rattle leaves his body, and his eyes grow dim.

Relief floods through me. I wish I felt more satisfaction from ending him, but all I can think about is Ellie and how she's safe from him now.

Turning away from Marcus' prone body, I find another battle behind me. Morbal is holding his own against Arlo and Russell, but they're at a stalemate. I know I'll need to join to turn the tides. But first, I look around for Ellie.

I see her not far from where she was last time. But she's no longer a wolf. She's helping a woman hold up the witch from earlier.

She's still okay. She's safe.

Seeing her, even for a brief moment, lifts a weight off my chest before I stride into another battle.

Foster is just finishing his own fight, so I call him over and together we corral Morbal from the back as he focuses on Arlo and Russell.

Foster bites down on one of Morbal's hind legs and pulls. And I do the same to the other.

Morbal snarls, his teeth on show as he fights us, trying to tug his legs free.

Stupid pup, Morbal's voice enters my mind.

My body tenses. How is he able to speak to me? He doesn't have an amulet. Is it because of the potion he took? I growl and sink my teeth deeper into his leg.

I should have killed your parents in front of you.

His words hit like a bucket of cold water.

Morbal turns his head toward me. *Ah. There's the despair I was hoping to see.* His laugh sounds in my mind as he slips loose. He kicks me with his now-free hind leg, and I fly backward.

I crash into the black pillar in the center of the room, my back cracks, and pain flares through my body. My legs shake as I stand back up.

Blind fury overrides the pain. He killed them.

I rush back to Morbal. Another lycan has taken my place. The other lycan and Foster pull together, force Morbal off balance, and yank him onto the ground.

Morbal claws the ground as they drag him back. I jump on top of him to help hold him down. I grind my teeth as I dig my claws into his side. He snarls and turns, snapping at me.

You'll regret this, Morbal says.

I drive my claws deeper. *I don't think I will.*

Russell jumps on Morbal's other side while Arlo clamps down on Morbal's neck. Arlo keeps his teeth firmly in Morbal's throat as Morbal squirms.

Morbal uses his front claws to try to pry Arlo off. I turn my head and bite down on one of his front legs to keep it away from Arlo while Russell takes the other. My teeth sink into his flesh, and he tries to twist out of our hold. Arlo's jaw tightens, remaining in place.

Morbal's movements slow, his efforts pointless as his strength wanes. But Arlo doesn't let go until Morbal's body is completely still and limp.

Morbal is dead.

I release Morbal's leg from my mouth and step away. I lift my head and search for Ellie as I shift.

Shifting probably isn't a good idea right now when I'm not sure what's damaged, but I want to hold Ellie in my arms. To feel her body against mine.

When my eyes finally lock onto her, ice-cold dread seizes me.

A stryx is latched onto her neck.

Ellie

a roar sounds behind me as the stryx detaches from my neck, grinning with a mouth full of blood and fangs.

My hand goes to my throat and comes back red and wet. With each heartbeat the wound throbs, but the pain is minimal compared to other injuries I've suffered.

His eyes widen as we stare at one another and nothing happens.

The stryx's top lip curls into a sneer. He changes his stance, and his black, elongated nails catch the light as he holds his hands up.

Before he can attack, Ash, now a man, is behind him.

Ash thrusts his partial-shifted hand into the stryx's back.

When Ash pulls his hand back out, it's grasping the stryx's heart. Life drains from the stryx's eyes, and he slumps to the ground.

Ash lets the heart fall from his hand with disgust and steps over the body.

He shakes the blood off his hand and reaches for me. "Can you move your arms and legs?" With his clean hand, he searches for any injuries. "Do you feel sick?"

I grab his hand to still his movements. "I'm okay."

Ash meets my gaze, his eyes full of surprise and wonder. "How is this possible?"

"What do you mean?" I glance over my body—nothing out of the normal cuts and scrapes.

He stills. "I think we found your special ability."

"What?"

A small smile forms on his face. "You're immune to stryx bites."

I blink, trying to comprehend what just happened.

"No paralyzing effects, and no signs of their poison spreading." He cups the side of my neck. "Even the bite is healing."

"Actually," I say, "it's because of my family line..." My eyes trail down his face and lock onto his abdomen.

Flashbacks to the barn where I first met him filter through my mind.

My hands shake as they lift to his wounds.

I'm seeing too much of his insides for him to be standing like this. "Ash," I say. My voice wavers as bile rises in my throat.

"What?" He looks down at himself and chuckles without humor. He meets my gaze again, blood draining from his face. "It seems adrenaline masked the wound." His knees buckle under him, and I jump to catch him.

Even with my newfound strength, he's too heavy, and I have to slowly lower us onto the ground.

Wounds cover his entire chest and abdomen, and they're deep. So deep.

How can someone be alive with these kinds of wounds? Why isn't he healing?

Tears wells up in my eyes as I search for anyone that can help. The room is in complete disarray but at least everyone has stopped fighting. Wylla is lying on the ground, my mom hovering over her. Foster, Russell, Logan, and Arlo are delegating and dealing with the aftermath of Morbal's and Marcus' deaths. Sophie is on the other side of the room, patching up a lycan. Healers should be contacted soon to help the others, but right now there are none.

My body grows colder the more frantically I look. "Someone, please? Anyone?" I whisper.

"Ellie darling." A cold, shaky thumb touches my cheek, wiping away a tear.

I look down at Ash, and to my horror, Ash's normally light-brown skin has paled completely.

"Did you know Marcus was a bitten?"

I blink. "What?" Why is he bringing this up now?

"Marcus was a bitten," he says, his voice softening with each breath. "His brother...Morbal...received the blood of the Elite, but he didn't. So Marcus took the chance with the bite and survived. But his brother was an Original, while he was a bitten."

I wipe away one of my tears that has fallen onto his cheek. "Ash..."

"And as sick as it may sound, they were brothers and loved each other even though their power levels were different. Do you...do you think Zac could've ever loved me?" His voice breaks. "Maybe if I had tried harder. Maybe if I had tried to make us seem not so different from each other... Do you think...I could've made him feel wanted? Loved?"

"Oh, Ash." My heart breaks, more tears flowing down my cheeks. He's talking as if he's dying and these are things he's worried about. Not himself. "Don't talk like that." Through blurry eyes, I smooth his ebony hair back, away from his dimming glacier-blue gaze. "Of course he could've, and of course you could've, but there's still time to fix that relationship."

"Ellie darling..." His hand falls from my face. "I don't think I have much longer."

My body trembles while I try to comprehend what I'm seeing, what he's saying. *No.* There's no way. He can't be dying, it's not possible. He's a pureblood, an alpha. My mate. He can't die from this. He's too strong.

Ash's eyes close as the place where he marked me begins to burn.

"N-no." I grip his face, but he doesn't let me see his beautiful eyes again. "Ash, come on, please, you gotta stay awake."

My gaze focuses back on his gaping gashes, and I move my hands. They shake as they hover over his seeping wounds before I lower them to stop the bleeding. Or try to.

Blood oozes through my fingers, and I hyperventilate. My heart races. He's going to bleed out.

"Ellie." My mom's voice breaks through my haze as she kneels beside me. Her worn body shakes from the strain of the chains still attached to her, but the bands are no longer there, only slowly healing wounds. "You need to bite him. You need to mark him."

My eyes widen. "Mom?"

"This is your mate, right?"

"Yes."

"And you haven't marked him?"

How did she know that? "No, but I—" I'm being stupid. I wanted to mark him after all of this, but if he dies here, there will be no *after*.

"Okay," I say. "I will." I'd do anything to save him.

My mom struggles to stand before she turns away and moves back to Wylla.

Taking a deep breath, I gently lift Ash's head off my lap and slip from underneath him.

My canines lengthen as I move over him, my bloody handprints cover the side of his head. I tilt his head to the side, exposing his neck better and lean down.

I hover my canines over his skin, just in between the shoulder and neck. My body on high alert, my heart racing.

"Please work," I whisper and plunge my canines into his flesh.

It feels wrong biting into him, but at the same time, it feels right. He jerks slightly underneath me. I press my body more fully against him to keep him still as I force my teeth deeper inside of him until they're fully sheathed.

Am I even doing this right? How does this work exactly?

All I know is the bite.

I squeeze my eyes shut as tears begin to burn. I refuse to cry more. He's not dead. I need to stay strong right now. But how do I know this is working? Nothing *feels* different.

Maybe the bite has to deal with intent. It probably has something to do with my essence as well.

I focus on the link I've felt since I met him. But I do more than that. I focus on my essence flowing from me to him. Making him whole and healthy. I picture him in my mind, the gorgeous smile he wears whenever he sees me. His beautiful skin and how it feels against mine, his glacier-blue eyes that take hold of my soul every time I gaze into them. How kind and thoughtful he is. The desire he has to make this world a better place with me at his side. His laugh. His love. I can feel the love he has for me, like it's a tangible thing. I grip him tighter as my body shakes from holding back sobs. I need him to live, to be whole and safe in my arms.

No! My canines shrink on their own accord, leaving his body.

My eyes pop open in a panic. He needs to wake up first. Why isn't he awake yet? The shaking gets worse as I cling onto him. He can't leave me like this. "Please don't leave me. Please, my mate. I can't live this long life without you."

My breath hitches when he stirs. "Ellie."

I lean back, just enough to get a look at his face. "You're not dead?"

He smiles. "I'm not dead."

"It...it worked?"

"It worked."

The dam breaks and tears flow freely down. "It worked." I sob as he sits up and pulls me into his arms, cradling me against his chest.

"It worked," he whispers as he cups my face.

He pulls away, just enough to take my lips with his own. One arm is wrapped around me while the other cups the back of my head. His mouth is just as desperate as mine. He deepens the kiss, claiming me as his and I claim him as mine. My salty tears combine with our mouths. I was so close to losing him. To never being able to do this again with him. Never able to feel his love or to show him just how much *I* love him.

His breathing is heavy when we finally separate. He cups my face. "Ellie darling, I love you so much." His thumb brushes back and forth against my cheek, wiping my tears away. His eyes are full of love and desire.

I sniffle and nuzzle against his chest, relishing being in his arms, taking in his scent. It feels like coming home.

"I'm so glad you're okay," I choke out.

He kisses the top of my head. "Thank you for saving me."

"No, thank *you*." I close my eyes, basking in everything that makes him *him*. "You saved me first."

Ellie

*M*y heart rate increases with each step we take down the steps to the dungeons. My chest is tight as tunnel vision forms from thoughts of the basement. All I can see is the dark bottom of the steps.

But I want to help. I want to free those people.

Ash stops just before we make it down the steps. My clammy hand clenches Ash's hand. But he doesn't seem to mind.

Lycans and stryxes alike, in raggy old gowns and long shirts, are being helped out of the dungeon and up the stairs, bypassing us. Some are being carried out in gurneys, in worse shape or similar to my mom.

It's only been a few hours, but my mom has seemed to be doing much better since the bands fell off. But it's the opposite for Wylla.

If the haunted look in her eyes is anything to go by, she has more to deal with than just healing physically. Wylla has been the only witch since she was captured. Making her the prime candidate to do Morbal's bidding. She won't go into details, but I wouldn't be surprised if she's been forced to hurt others. A lot of the prisoners are missing a lot of blood, which could only mean she's performed a lot of rituals and potions. Maybe even had to use their blood for her blood magic. None of them will talk about it, for obvious reasons.

Everyone that's been affected will receive treatment here and either go into a rehabilitation center or return to their homes. Ultimately, it's their choice. But Wylla chose neither and will be returning with us once we've done all we can here before giving the full reins to Arlo. We also will need to have another funeral for all the lycans that died during the battle. Each pack lost a lot.

"Are you *sure* you want to go in?" Ash asks.

"Yes." I meet his concerned gaze.

His eyes shift between mine before he gives in. "Alright, let's go. But if at any time you change your mind, I'll get you out."

I give him a small smile. "Deal."

We take the final steps down and the smell of decay and rot hits me first before we even make it to the door.

We wait for a group to come out before we enter. The air is dry and musty, and it's like a switch flips. I start to shake uncontrollably. My mind goes blank. Even though Marcus is dead, my mind and body can't seem to forget what it went through.

"Ellie, *please*, let me take you back," Ash pleads, cupping the side of my face with his free hand.

I keep my eyes downcast. "No, they suffered worse than me, I...I can do this. I want to help."

His frown deepens. "Don't compare what you went through to what they went through. They aren't comparable. They have scars, but so do you. They suffered, and it's horrible what they had to endure. But that doesn't mean what you went through wasn't horrible as well. They are survivors, but so are you. Don't diminish the hardship you went through."

I blink up at him, meeting his piercing gaze. *Don't diminish the hardship you went through.* "I'm a survivor, too."

He gives me a small, proud smile, his eyes rimming red. "You are."

I sniffle. "If you cry, I'll cry, and I don't want a cry fest in the dungeons."

A grin breaks out on his face as he chuckles. "Okay, I won't. I actually have somewhere I'd like to show you before we help, if you're up for it."

I nod, and he drops his hand from my face. He slowly leads me deeper into the dungeons. Cobblestone and metal bars are everywhere we turn.

We walk down a hallway lit with torches. More people pass us until we make it to an archway at the end of the hall, made out of concrete and brick cobblestone.

Ash grabs a torch before we enter.

The ground turns to dirt once we step through it, but the tunnel's walls and ceiling are made from the same material as the arch, but in a more angular formation. The tunnel slightly slants downward as we walk. The air gets cooler and sounds seem to fade as well.

"Ash." I cling onto his arm. "Where are we going?"

He gives me a small smile. "This is how I got into the mansion."

My eyes widen. "Through here?"

He nods. "A small group and I stumbled upon a catacomb, which is where we met Octavia and her group."

"Ah, right, the stryxes." He had introduced me to them once we found some clothes and cleaned up, right before coming down here.

He chuckles. "Yes, *the stryxes*." He briefly stops to set the torch down. "When we were on our way up, we took a shortcut through a side cave that I knew I had to show you before we left." The tunnels grow dark, so I switch over to my wolf eyes.

We take a smaller path off one hallway, and the concrete disappears with only dirt remaining around us. The air grows warmer the further we get, and the sound of dripping water grows louder.

The room opens up when we turn a corner, and I'm hit with warm, humid air. The damp walls glisten with the reflection of blue light. My gaze lifts to find hundreds of bioluminescent glowworms glittering up above like stars and constellations. A pool of water reflects the light, and it's like I've been swallowed into the night sky.

I hope she likes it.

"I love it," I whisper.

His breath hitches. "Ellie."

"Yes?" I glance over my shoulder.

"Did...did you hear my thoughts?"

I blink. "I...I guess I did." A smile grows on my face. "Perks of us being mates."

A grin takes over his face, and he picks me up in a hug. "We completed the mate bond," he says into my hair.

"We did." I nuzzle into him. "And I couldn't be happier. You mean everything to me, Ash. I'll never want anyone else but you. I'm yours and you're mine."

His arms tighten around me. "Forever you, Ellie darling."

I hold him back just as tight. "Forever us."

Epilogue

Ellie

Four months later

$\mathcal{W}$e spent almost two months in Italy helping Arlo. Since he killed Morbal, he gained his pack, which had a lot of members who had been imprisoned. There's also the concern of where he got all those magical artifacts that helped him control others because Wylla sure didn't make them. He either bought them from the dark market, which I just learned about, or had another witch in secret. But there's been no other signs of another witch except for those artifacts.

We'll still look into it, but now that Morbal and Marcus are gone, we are focused on other things. Like implementing changes to our pack.

Not only do Ash and I want omegas to choose their own paths, but I realized *most* lycans are placed in positions and can't move, whether they are warriors, healers, or hunters. So we're changing that as well. It's a slow process and people are scared of change, but we're determined. We'll never force someone to change if they like where they're at, but we're giving them options which is what counts. The next step is treating everyone equally, especially the omegas.

With the help from Foster, Russell, Sophie, Alice, and a few others, we're making progress. Alice seems lost, though. I keep telling her she doesn't need to decide anything right now, and even when she does, she can always change her mind.

I'm also adding more human careers to the town and pack. Humans don't always stick to one job, so why do lycans? Okay, that's a lie, humans usually stick to one career. But I want us to be able to explore different avenues. I don't want anyone to feel confined. Even if they pick a job right now, I want them to know they can always change and do something else later.

"You look beautiful, Ellie." My mom turns me around to face the full-length mirror we added to my room just for today. Even though Ash and I are already mated, I wanted a ring ceremony. I've always thought that that tradition was so beautiful and romantic. I know I would've regretted it if I never did it for myself.

"I really love the dress you chose," Jane says.

A smile forms on my face as Jane tugs my dress down a bit, smoothing out the wrinkles. Not only does she know about lycans now, but so do Tom and Emma, who are outside with the other guests.

Kathy grew attached to Jane when she was a patient of hers. But now it's grown into so much more for both her and Jane. Her and Jane's relationship is new, but it's like it was meant to be.

Finally, I lift my eyes to peer at myself through the mirror.

My dirty-blonde hair—which has lighter streaks in it from the time spent in the sun in Italy—is down in curls. My skin is tanner and the freckles are more prominent along my nose. The ivory, lacy dress reaches to my knee. It's not a wedding dress, because it felt strange to wear one when this is only a ring ceremony, but I love this dress. It makes me feel elegant and beautiful.

"I really like it, too," I say.

Jane tucks a piece of my hair behind my ear. "I'm so happy for you, Ellie."

A grin forms on my face. "Thank you. I'm happy for you, too."

Hearing my mom sniffle, I turn to her.

"I wish your dad was here," she says, her eyes glistening.

Tears well up in my eyes. "Me too."

She wraps her arms around me in an embrace. Even though it has been months since I found out, I still can't believe she's alive. That I'm able to hug her again.

"Don't you two dare cry," Sophie says. "I'll be pissed if you mess up your makeup." Her bottom lip juts out in a pout before grinning.

I laugh, letting go of my mom. "You're right. Thank you, for everything." I wrap her in my arms next, my anxiety with touch under the surface, but more manageable now with those I care about.

She returns my hug. "Thank you for letting me be a part of today." She squeezes me then lets me go.

Sophie turns her head and grabs Alice and Jane, bringing them into a group hug. A laugh bursts from me as she almost knocks us over.

Ellie darling, I don't think I can't wait much longer. Are you done yet?

I fight back a giggle.

I can detect his impatience through our bond, but I can also feel his love. It's been so interesting sensing everything Ash feels. Our relationship has deepened even more since I marked him.

I'll be out soon. You can wait a bit longer.

He huffs, and I have to bite back a laugh.

Sophie's eyes narrow. "You're getting that dreamy look on your face. Are you talking to Ash?"

I give her a sheepish smile.

She sighs. "Tell him it's time before he goes all alpha on us."

By "TIME", I thought Sophie meant time for our ring ceremony. Not for Ash to come here, to my room. But apparently, they had discussed this beforehand—all of them did. Sophie stuffs a small bag in the hidden pocket of my dress and sends me a wink before heading out. The rest follow close behind.

My mom is the last, but instead of leaving, she turns to me and takes my hands into hers. "You know, your father and I were destined mates."

My eyes tear up as I clench her hands. "Really?"

She nods. "Like every couple, we had our ups and downs, but we were lucky to have found each other. Over the past few months, I've gotten to know Ash, and from what I've seen, he seems like a good man who will always love and protect you. Always put you first. Just like your father did for me. I know he would approve of him—after giving him a hard time, of course."

I chuckle and hold back tears.

"I love you, Ellie. You are the daughter I always wanted. I'm so sorry I couldn't continue raising you and that you had to suffer at the hands of an awful man. We foolishly thought that making lycans unaware of you would protect you, but it seems to have backfired on us." Her chin wobbles, but she straightens. "Despite our mistakes, you turned out to be strong and beautiful, inside and out. I'm proud to call you mine."

"Oh, Mom." I give her a watery smile as I pull her into a hug. I close my eyes and soak in the peace and comfort I get from her embrace. I never thought I'd ever be able to hug her again, and after Marcus, I never thought I'd ever be able to hug again in general.

We break apart, but she takes hold of my hands one more time and looks over my shoulder. I follow her gaze to Ash leaning against the doorframe. Noticing my attention, he straightens. His ebony locks are slicked back, and his glacier-blue eyes pierce mine, sucking all the air out of my lungs. He's in a black, tailored suit that shows off his lean, muscular form.

He strides over to me but looks over my shoulder. "Thank you, Addison, for letting me take care of your daughter."

"Welcome to the family, Ash." She turns to me. "I'll be outside, waiting with everyone else. Take as long as you need." She kisses me on the cheek then walks out the door.

"What are you doing here?" I ask. I thought I'd be meeting him under the arch we have set up outside.

Instead of answering, he gives me a light peck. "You look beautiful, Ellie."

My cheeks heat. "Thank you, so do you."

He grins and takes one of my hands, and I let him lead me out of the room.

"Ash?" I ask as we begin going up the stairs.

He pauses on the steps and turns to me. "I thought we should have our own private ceremony away from everyone."

A knot forms in my throat.

He hesitates, conflict swirling in his gaze. "Or did I read you wrong? Would you rather—"

"No," I interrupt with a shake of my head. "I much rather do it in private. We can say something simple in front of them."

A grin grows on his face. "It's good to know that I know my mate."

Heat creeps across my face again as I nudge him forward.

Instead of moving up the stairs, he hums. "I actually have a better idea." He tugs me forward before sweeping an arm under my legs. He lifts me up, cradling me against his chest. "Much better. I prefer to have you in my arms," he says as he continues up the stairs, carrying me.

"Ash!"

"I always said I liked you better in my arms."

I shake my head, but there's a smile on my face.

We walk past his office and the guest bedrooms until we reach the far end of the hall. There's another set of stairs leading up.

"I didn't know you had a third floor."

He quirks a brow. "How long have you lived here? Haven't you explored?"

"I only like to explore outside."

"Huh," he says as he goes up the steps. "I guess your loss is my gain." He sets me down on the landing and opens the only door that's up here. "I had the house designed similarly to my parents' house and during construction, at the last minute, I added this space. If it seems random, it's because it was." He winks, grabs my hand, and turns the handle.

My heels click against the wood flooring as we enter the room, and I'm struck speechless. "What is this place?"

"It's yours. I thought you'd like a space to call your own."

I turn around in a circle, taking in all the details. The room is lit with candles. One of the walls is lined with floor-to-ceiling bookshelves. They're mostly empty except for a few shelves.

The opposite wall has a row of cabinets and counters with a sink, like what you would find in an art room. There's a round table with four chairs, followed by a couch that faces a large window where we can see the setting sun. There's an easel on each side of the window. "When did you get this done?"

"After we defeated Morbal and Marcus, I called in a favor. I debated whether I should fill the bookshelves or not, but I decided to add a few of my own collection that I thought you might like. I figured you'd want to do the rest to yourself. I know I enjoyed doing mine, in my office." I grin at his ramblings and turn to him. He has his hands in his pockets and is looking at me with a sheepish expression. "Do you like it?"

"I love it."

His smile grows. "Yeah?"

I nod and walk over to him with tears in my eyes. "I have a gift for you, too. Although, not as grand as this."

"You do?"

I laugh. "Don't look so surprised."

He schools his face and offers a smile. "Sorry."

I had a pocket sewn into the dress just for this. I had planned on giving it to him after our vows, but it feels more appropriate to do it now. Digging into that pocket, I thank Sophie for her meddling as I take out the slightly heavy bag.

A slow grin builds on his face. "Don't tell me you got me drugs."

I smack his arm as a laugh bubbles up and he joins in. "No, I didn't get you drugs. This bag isn't even that small," I say as I hand it to him, our fingers lingering.

I bite my lip, gripping my dress.

He glances at me as he undoes the string. "You didn't have to get me anything." He holds it upside down and it clanks as it lands in his palm. He flips the watch over, looking at the engravings. He opens his mouth, but no words come out.

"Maybe this was a bad idea—" I reach to snatch it back, but he holds his hand away.

"No." He looks up, his eyes rimmed red.

"Ash." I reach again, but he shakes his head and holds it up higher.

With his free arm, he snakes his hand around my waist and pulls me against him. "It's perfect," he says in my hair, wrapping both arms around me. "How did you get this?"

He rests his chin on my head as I relax against him. "Charlie went and grabbed it after saving you from the fire. I was going to give it to you for Christmas, but after everything happened, I wasn't able to get it in time."

"But he's…"

"Alice knew about it."

"And then you added to the engraving?"

I nod against his chest. "I hope that's okay." He leans away and looks at the engraving. Before it was only his parents' names, but it didn't feel complete giving him the watch with just their names, so I added an infinity sign and our names.

∞

Bowan & Isla
Ash & Ellie

"I love it." He puts it around his wrist and clasps it. "Fits perfect," he says.

He rubs his eyes with one hand, wiping the evidence of his tears. His intense gaze meets mine, eyes shining. "Thank you, Ellie."

I nod, suddenly self-conscious, when I notice the piece of paper on the table.

I peer over at it. "Y-you got a marriage certificate?"

His brows scrunch together as he touches the edge of the paper. "Should I not have? I thought that's why we were doing this."

Tears well in my eyes. "No, it is. It's just—" I sniffle, overcome with emotions. Who knew such a simple thing would set me off. "I didn't actually think about doing it legally yet. This is just so thoughtful and I—"

He wraps me in his arms, lifting me to tuck my head into the crook of his neck. Taking advantage, I breathe him in.

"Why wouldn't we do it legally? Being my wife is just as important as being my mate. I don't want you to ever have an excuse to leave me."

I push at him lightly. "I'm not going to leave you."

He smirks. "Not after you sign it."

I lean away, shooting him a glare. He chuckles and leans down, brushing his lips against mine. Slowly grazing my bottom lip with his tongue, he nudges my lips to part. I eagerly comply, needing to taste him. Together our tongues begin a slow dance.

We stand like that for several minutes before he stops and rests his forehead against mine.

He lets out a slow, minty breath and stands straight. He takes my hand and leads me until we're in front of the window. The sky is growing darker, and the stars are beginning to twinkle in. I can see everyone down below, mingling with each other as they wait for us. Candles are lit everywhere, courtesy of Wylla, and lights are strung above. "It's beautiful."

He hums, and I look at him, finding his heated gaze locked on me. I tuck a strand of hair behind my ear and give him a coy smile.

"I have something else for you." He reaches inside his jacket pocket and brings out a ring box. "I know, our mating was unconventional. Hell, our whole relationship has been unconventional." I chuckle. "But I wouldn't change it for anything because it led us here today, together. I want to be by your side for the rest of our long lives. I love you, Ellie Rose Hollenberg. I don't want anyone else, only you. And if I had to wait an eternity more for you, I would, because no one else could compare. I want to change the world with you."

He opens the box, and I gasp as it reveals my mother's ring—a rose-gold band with three diamonds, two small ones and a large one in the middle. I hadn't even noticed she wasn't wearing it. Ash places the box on the windowsill then steps closer and takes my left hand. "You're the best thing to ever happen to me, Ellie. You helped me change into the man that I always wanted to be, that I had aspired to be, but that I had lost my way to. You saved me, and"—he looks into my eyes as he slips the ring on my ring finger—"I promise to love and cherish you forever because I know how lucky I am to be able to have you as a mate and as a wife." A shiver runs through me as he lifts my hand and kisses my knuckles, keeping his piercing eyes locked on mine.

He starts to unclench my hand, but I won't let him let go.

I bite my lip. "I was stupid—"

"Ell—"

"No, let me finish." I take a deep breath. "I was stupid for not seeing how I felt about you sooner and not trusting you enough to want to stay. There's still a scared little girl hiding in the corner of a basement, afraid of letting anyone in. But you wormed your way in."

He grimaces. *Wormed?* he mouths.

A giggle escapes as I lightly slap his arm, and he smirks. "Okay, so, maybe but not the best wording, but you get the point. You're more of a romantic than I am. I have trouble expressing or saying how I feel, but you never judged me for it. You loved me anyway. There's no one else that could be better for me than you. You love all of me even though I'm a work in progress, but there's no one else I would rather spend forever with." I dig into my pocket once more.

"How many things do you have in this mysterious pocket?"

Smiling, I shoot him a playful glare as I pull out a ring that I had specially made for him out of a pine tree. "I had Wylla enchant it. When you shift into a wolf, it'll shift with you."

I slide the wooden ring onto his finger. "Ash, I promise to always love you. I promise to be your best friend, lover, and confidant. You mean more to me than anyone else. You saved me from a life on the run. You saved me from myself by loving me unconditionally. You saved me from a fate worse than death. *You saved me from death.* I hope I'll be able to show you for the rest of our long lives just how much you mean to me."

When I go to kiss his hand like he did to me, he tugs my arm and I stumble into him. My hands are trapped against his chest as his move to my waist. He slightly squeezes while he leans down and touches his lips to the shell of my ear. His warm breath causes goosebumps to erupt across my skin. "I want your lips on mine," he says softly and nips my ear.

"That can be arranged."

Leaning back, his smile turns into a smoldering grin. "I was hoping you'd say that."

Stretching, I reach up and press my mouth to his.

His lips are warm against mine. Our kiss is solid and passionate. He moves his lips expertly, and I arch into him at the first taste of his tongue. A hint of mint and the unique taste of him. I savor him, letting our tongues feel one another. Nothing else compares to the way he tastes and feels against me. I don't ever want to stop because it feels right.

Because he's right.

He's home.

AFTERWORD

IF YOU made it this far, thank you! Thank you so much for reading *Saving Ellie*. Ash and Ellie have a special place in my heart, and their book ended up being a lot bigger than I intended. I hope you enjoyed it!

Could I ask you to do me a favor and leave a review? It can be short and simple. And if you do, thank you for taking the time to write it.

WANT TO KEEP UP TO DATE? Sign up for my newsletter.

WWW.WHITNEYRBAUTHOR.COM/SUBSCRIBE

I'LL NEVER SPAM YOU, only keep you up to date on what I'm working on. The Witch Elite is currently available for pre-order set to release November 28, 2022

ACKNOWLEDGMENTS

Writing a book takes a lot of time. I couldn't have done it without my support system. First and foremost, I have to thank my husband for all his love and support. Every day he had off from work, he would watch our three young kids so I could write. Literally, this book would not exist without him.

Another big thank-you to my CP, Mak, who hypes me up whenever I'm feeling down in the dumps. Your comments and suggestions always make my day. You helped more than you know. Thanks for helping me make SE better.

Thank you to my developmental editor, Sydney, who told me to either get rid of Ash's POV or add more. Since I didn't have the heart to delete them, I added more. So if you loved his chapters (and the Thanksgiving chapter) you have her to thank.

I also want to thank my editor, Elle. She helped me make SE look professional! Her guidance and suggestions on fine-tuning this story were so helpful.

And thank you to my proofreaders, Elsie and C.M., who were flexible with their schedules for me and made sure they made time for me and my book. Couldn't have published without them!

Thank you to all my friends and family and the writing community that has supported me since the first edition of SE! I'm truly grateful.

Now, I want to thank my readers. Thank you, thank you, thank you. Readers are the lifeblood of a book. Without them, books would end up vanishing. So, thank you for taking a chance on Ash and

Ellie. I hope you love them as much as I do. Be sure to watch for the next one.

ABOUT THE AUTHOR

Whitney R.B. has a love for all things romance and fantasy. Her love for writing started in middle school and has blossomed since then. Now she lives in Texas with her soulmate and their three young kids, who take up most of her time. But in her rare free moments, she reads (a bit too much) and writes.

www.whitneyrbauthor.com

Instagram @whitneyrb.author

TikTok @whitneyrb.books

Facebook Readers group

www.ingramcontent.com/pod-product-compliance
Lightning Source LLC
Chambersburg PA
CBHW021119260626
47169CB00005B/1363